Desiring the Prince

Fancy looked into Stepan's dark eyes, anticipation flaring to life and flooding her body. Resisting his magnetic pull, she dropped her gaze to his lips. His hand on her shoulder began a slow caress, a delicious shiver tickling her spine.

She wanted to kiss his invitingly shaped lips.

She wanted to glide her fingertips across the warm flesh covering his hard muscles.

"Do not think," Stepan murmured. His handsome face inched closer, her nerves rioting in response.

Instinct surfaced, vanquishing her shyness and her resolve. She lifted her face, her lips meeting his, and pressed her body against him.

His arms surrounded her and pulled her tighter. Her arms glided up his chest to entwine around his neck.

Their kiss deepened. He flicked the tip of his tongue across the crease of her lips, coaxing them open, and slipped inside to taste her sweetness.

His lips were warm and firm, his tongue coaxing her surrender. His heat and his strength enveloped her, his gentle touch persuading her trust.

The world faded away and Fancy returned his kiss with equal ardor. They fell back on the sofa, his unyielding muscles covering her soft curves . . .

Books by Patricia Grasso

TO TAME A DUKE

TO TEMPT AN ANGEL

TO CHARM A PRINCE

TO CATCH A COUNTESS

TO LOVE A PRINCESS

SEDUCING THE PRINCE

PLEASURING THE PRINCE

Published by Zebra Books

PATRICIA GRASSO

Pleasuring
the Prince

ZEBRA BOOKS
Kensington Publishing Corp.
www.kensingtonbooks.com

ZEBRA BOOKS are published by

Kensington Publishing Corp.
850 Third Avenue
New York, NY 10022

All Kensington titles, imprints and distributed lines are available
at special quantity discounts for bulk purchases for sales promo-
tion, premiums, fund-raising, educational, or institutional use.

Special book excerpts or customized printings can also be created to fit specific needs. For details, write or phone the office
of the Kensington Special Sales Manager: Attn. Special Sales
Department. Kensington Publishing Corp., 850 Third Avenue,
New York, NY 10022. Phone: 1-800-221-2647.

Zebra and the Z logo Reg. U.S. Pat. & TM Off.

ISBN 0-8217-7711-4

First Printing: April 2006
10 9 8 7 6 5 4 3 2 1

Printed in the United States of America

Chapter 1

London, 1821

"Loves me, loves me not . . ."

A tall gentleman, dressed in formal evening attire, stood on the summit of Primrose Hill in the predawn gray of a mist-shrouded morning. Carried on the wind, the unmistakable smell of the Thames tainted the early spring air, and a raw clamminess permeated his exposed skin.

The man gazed almost lovingly at the woman, beautiful in death, giving proof to the peacefulness of her passing. He dug into his leather pouch, clutched a handful of rose petals, and sprinkled them one by one the length of her body from head to feet.

"A waste of true beauty," said a hoarse voice.

The gentleman looked at the short, plump woman standing beside him. "Return to the coach." Knowing she would obey without argument, he took another handful of rose petals from his pouch.

"Loves me, loves me not . . ."

* * *

Royal Opera House

I refuse to become my mother.

Fancy Flambeau sat on a stool in a pigeonhole dressing room and prepared for her operatic debut. Pots of theater cosmetics cluttered the tiny table in front of her, and a minuscule mirror hung on the wall over the table.

Noting the mirror's long diagonal crack, Fancy wondered if bad luck would mar her talent or test her determination. If bad luck walked through the door, she hoped it would not take the form of an aristocrat.

I refuse to become my mother, Fancy reminded her distorted image in the cracked mirror.

Beyond normal nervousness, her debut did not frighten her. Fancy had more important worries such as aristocratic males who preyed upon singers, dancers, and actresses. Long ago, she had resolved never to love an aristocrat or let herself become love's victim. Like her mother.

Keeping that resolve had been easy until today. Once she stepped on the stage, every wealthy gentleman in London would set his gaze on her for the first time and target her for his next conquest. Men of the aristocratic ilk considered women like her their quarry, toys to be used and discarded as they pleased.

Fancy had dressed for the role of the adolescent Cherubino in *The Marriage of Figaro*. Her costume consisted of black breeches, a white shirt, and a red jerkin.

After wiping her hands on a linen, Fancy peered in the mirror at her six sisters crowding the dressing room. She turned around and gave them her most confident smile. "By this time tomorrow, I will have become London's most famous prima donna."

Ranging in age from nineteen to sixteen with two sets of twins, her sisters laughed at her feigned bravado.

The only missing family members were Gabrielle Flambeau, her mother, and Nanny Smudge.

Fancy wished her mother and her nanny had lived to see this day. She sighed, thinking she had many unattainable wishes. More wishes than money.

"We should go to our seats." Nineteen-year-old Belle opened the door and gasped in surprise when something small and hairy ran past her into the room.

A monkey climbed onto Fancy's lap. With its hands the animal covered its ears, then its eyes, and finally its mouth.

"A capuchin monkey." Eighteen-year-old Blaze crouched beside her sister's stool. She imitated the monkey's actions and then lifted it into her arms, cradling it against her shoulder like a baby.

"Miss Giggles, there you are." With an apologetic smile, a stocky man stepped into the dressing room and carried the monkey away.

"Who is that?" asked Raven, the youngest.

"Sebastian Tanner is the prima donna's husband," Fancy answered, "and Miss Giggles is her pet."

"Giggles hates the Tanners," Blaze said. "I saw it in her eyes."

"The monkey has good taste," Fancy said, making them smile.

Her sisters filed out of the dressing room to find their seats in the audience. Only Belle and Raven lingered behind.

Fancy produced a white linen handkerchief, two of its corners embroidered with the initials MC. She passed the handkerchief to Raven.

"Is he in the audience?"

Raven closed her eyes. "I feel his presence nearby."

"Seeing his oldest bastard on stage should surprise him." Fancy plucked the handkerchief out of her sister's hand. "I hope he suffers agonizing pangs of conscience."

"Why do you nurse a grudge against the man who sired us?" Belle asked. "Bitterness hurts you more than him."

"His neglect put Mama in an early grave."

"Mama was responsible for her own fate," Raven said.

"He never loved us," Fancy continued, as if her sister had not spoken.

"You cannot know what dwells in another's heart," Belle said.

"His money has supported us through the years," Raven reminded her, "and he sent Nanny Smudge to care for us."

"Do not make excuses for a father you could not recognize if you passed him on the street." Fancy sighed, knowing but refusing to admit the rightness of what her sister said. "Losing Mama hurt, and now Nanny Smudge has joined her."

"Nanny Smudge has gone nowhere." Raven touched her hand. "You know she protects us still."

Hearing the orchestra begin the opera's overture, Fancy reached for her hairbrush. "We'll meet outside after the show."

After her sisters had gone, Fancy gazed into the mirror. She brushed her black hair away from her face and wove it into a knot at the nape of her neck.

Stage fright caught her without warning.

Fancy gagged drily over the small pot beside the table. She grabbed a cup off the table, swished water around her mouth, and spit it into the pot.

"Wish me luck, Nanny Smudge," she murmured.

The aroma of cinnamon scented the air inside the pigeonhole dressing room, giving her confidence. Her nanny's scent.

Fancy grabbed the costume's hat and, leaving the dressing room, hurried toward the stage to await her cue. In keeping with her role of Cherubino, she donned the boy's cap and smiled at Genevieve Stover, the woman playing the role of Barbarina. The two had become friends during rehearsals. Fancy was still surprised the other girl did not begrudge her the coveted role of Cherubino.

"Did you hear about the ballet dancer?" Genevieve whispered.

Fancy shook her head.

"The rose-petal murderer got her." Genevieve heard her cue and hurried onstage.

Fancy banished the murdered dancer from her mind. *Think adolescent boy,* she told herself. *Charming. Eager. Randy.*

Stepping onto the stage, Fancy focused on the music and lyrics. A petite woman with a big voice, Fancy attacked the song and immersed herself in it. Emotionally involved, she forced the audience to follow wherever she led them.

Her powerful voice could break their hearts. Or mend them.

During Cherubino's plea to the countess, Fancy turned toward the audience, downstage center, perilously close to the edge of the stage. Patrice Tanner, playing the countess, stuck her foot out.

Unable to stop her forward momentum, Fancy tumbled off the stage and flew into the orchestra pit. She heard the audience's collective gasp but kept singing. Several musicians caught her and lifted her onto the stage.

Fancy narrowed her gaze on the prima donna in an unspoken declaration of war. She threw her arms out in a sweeping gesture and struck the prima donna with a backhanded slap.

The audience loved it and roared with laughter.

Fancy glanced sidelong at the audience and gave them an exaggerated wink, making them laugh even more.

Both women exited the stage. Director Bishop waited in the wings, his expression long-suffering.

"The twit struck me," Patrice Tanner complained. "Get rid of her."

"Slapping you was an accident," the director said, "and Fancy is sorry. Aren't you?"

"I am *not* sorry."

Patrice Tanner gave her a murderous glare and stalked off. Loitering near them, her husband followed her.

"Prince Stepan Kazanov requests an introduction during intermission." Director Bishop smiled at her. "The prince wants to gain the advantage over the other young swains."

A passing stagehand gave Fancy a cup of water. She swished the liquid around in her mouth, turned her head, and spit it out. Several droplets of water splashed the director's shoes.

Fancy lifted her violet gaze to his. "Sorry."

"Why don't you drink it?"

"If I swallow the water," she answered, "my nerves will regurgitate it. Probably onstage."

"About the prince?"

"No."

"I cannot tell His Highness you refuse to meet him," the director said. "Prince Stepan is the opera's most generous patron."

"I am not for sale."

"Meeting our patrons is part of your job," he told her. "You do want to keep your job, don't you?"

"Very well, you may introduce Prince Stepan after the show," Fancy agreed, reluctance etched across her expression. "Tell him I refuse to become his mistress."

"Tell him yourself."

* * *

"There she is."

Sitting with his three brothers in an opera box, Prince Stepan Kazanov stretched his long legs out and relaxed in his chair. He fixed his dark gaze on the woman making her operatic debut, following her every movement.

Miss Fancy Flambeau stood a mere two inches over five feet, a slender woman with a full-bodied voice. Which had attracted his attention the afternoon he had stopped at the opera house to speak with the director. Stepan had listened to her singing and known he would claim her for himself.

"That is the object of your interest?" Prince Viktor asked.

"She dresses like a boy," Prince Mikhail remarked, casting his younger brother an amused glance.

"Is my baby brother hiding a shockingly sinful secret?" Prince Rudolf teased him.

"Miss Flambeau is playing Cherubino." Irritation raised Prince Stepan's voice. "Hence, the boy's attire."

"Shush."

The four Russian princes looked toward the opera box on their right. Lady Althorpe sat with the Duke and Duchess of Inverary. The older woman glared at the four brothers.

Sitting closest to the lady, Rudolf gave her his most charming smile. "We apologize for the unnecessary noise, Lady Althorpe."

Stepan returned his attention to the stage. In the middle of Cherubino's plea to the countess, Fancy Flambeau tripped over the prima donna's foot and tumbled off the stage.

The audience gasped and leaned forward in their seats. Fortunately, several musicians caught her and lifted her onto the stage. The singer missed no lyrics. She took revenge by stepping close to the prima donna at the moment of an arm-sweeping gesture and struck the other woman.

Stepan chuckled with amusement. When the opera singer winked at the audience, he roared with laughter, as did everyone else in the theater.

"I cannot believe those two did that on stage," Prince Viktor said.

"The reigning prima donna resents the rising star," Prince Mikhail said.

"Miss Flambeau seems strong-willed," Prince Rudolf said. "Her spirit will keep you in tow, baby brother."

"Shush."

Prince Rudolf glanced at Lady Althorpe. "Sorry for the interruption, but my baby brother is misbehaving."

"Take a paddle to his backside," the lady drawled.

The three oldest Kazanov princes burst into laughter.

"Shush."

Stepan ignored his brothers' gibes. Being the youngest in the family, he had learned to disregard their teasing criticisms. Which, as he saw it, was the only drawback of being the youngest. His older brothers would always accept responsibility for his livelihood, whether he worked in the family businesses or not. Life was one long country house party.

"Your Highness?"

Stepan looked over his shoulder at the opera director. "Yes?"

"Miss Flambeau begs your indulgence," the man whispered, "but prefers to meet you after the show."

"Thank you." Stepan almost rubbed his hands together in glee. How many evenings would making her his mistress take?

Intermission began, the time when society mingled. Usually, Stepan left the Kazanov opera box and circulated among his many friends, speaking with the males and flirting with the females.

Tonight was different, though. Stepan stood to stretch his legs and sat down again, surprising his brothers.

"If you do not visit the Clarke box," Viktor said, "you will disappoint Lady Cynthia and her mother."

"Mother and daughter are trying to trap me into marriage," Stepan said. "The thought of passing my life with Cynthia Clarke gives me the hives."

"What about the merry widow?" Mikhail asked.

"Lady Veronica would be happier with you," Stepan said, "and you do need a stepmother for your daughter."

Prince Mikhail raised his eyebrows. "Veronica Winthrop is decidedly unmotherly."

"If you direct your attention across the hall," Rudolf said, leaning close, "you will see Lady Drummond sending longing looks in your direction here."

"Elizabeth Drummond is married."

"If she is already married," Rudolf said, "then you need not worry about her trapping you into marriage."

Stepan glanced at his oldest brother. "I am meeting Miss Flambeau after the show."

"She looks awfully young," Viktor said, drawing his attention.

"Once taken, her innocence can never be returned," Mikhail reminded him.

"You assume I plan to make her my mistress," Stepan said. "Who knows? I may propose marriage."

"Give over, baby brother." Rudolf eyed him with amusement. "The prince and the opera singer?"

"I would never corrupt an innocent." Stepan winked at his oldest brother. "Unless, of course, the innocent wanted corruption."

* * *

Fancy felt exhilarated. She stood in the wings and waited her turn to cross the stage and take a bow.

The director had sent the male leads out first and then Patrice Tanner. And now her turn had arrived.

Fancy stepped into the audience's view. Thunderous applause erupted, the deafening sound music to her ears.

In keeping with her role of Cherubino, Fancy swaggered like an adolescent boy and, making a show of her bow, swept the hat off. Her heavy mane of ebony cascaded around her, almost to her waist.

Someone in the audience tossed a rose at her feet. Another followed that. And then another.

"Encore," someone shouted.

And the audience took up the chant. "Encore, encore, encore."

Fancy looked around in confusion. She saw the fury etched across the prima donna's face, and then the director walked onstage.

"Sing something else." When she nodded, he ushered the others offstage.

Fancy had never felt so alone. She stood in silence for a long moment, wondering what to sing, and the audience quieted.

Somewhere in this theater sat the aristocrat whose emotional neglect had killed her mother. Thrusting a symbolic dagger into his heart appealed to her, and she seized the chance to let him know the damage he had done.

"As a child, I always begged my father for a ride in his coach," Fancy told the silent audience. "Papa said we needed to wait for a sunny day. When I grew older, I realized my father visited on rainy days only." She heard the audience chuckling. "I never did get that coach ride, but I did write a ballad about a magical land beyond the horizon where raindrops were forbidden from dawn to dusk."

Without musical accompaniment, Fancy began singing about the land beyond the horizon. Her perfect voice and bittersweet words transported the audience through time and space to their own childhoods. Her lyrics recalled long-forgotten dreams and heart-tugging disappointments.

When the last word slipped from her lips, Fancy walked offstage and ignored the wild applause. Tears rolled down her cheeks, leaving her stage cosmetics streaked.

"How touching." The sneering voice belonged to Patrice Tanner. "Did you really believe an aristocrat would take his bastard into society?"

Fancy ignored the prima donna. She shut the dressing room door and leaned back against it, needing a few minutes of privacy after baring her soul to those strangers.

What had her father thought of her song? She hoped—

What did she hope? Her father would beg her forgiveness for his neglect? Would remorse return her mother to life? A man she hadn't seen in fifteen years would feel nothing for her or her sisters.

And that damn prince expected to meet her. Bed her, more likely. How much of a royal pain in the arse would His Highness become?

Fancy caught a lingering whiff of cinnamon. She thought of her beloved nanny and knew her advice.

Listen to your head, child, but follow your heart.

Her mother had followed her heart and paid the price. Seven daughters.

No husband. No love. No prospects.

From outside the dressing room door came the unmistakable sounds of relief. Performers and stagehands talked and laughed as they went about the business of closing shop for the night. On this side of the door, traces of cinnamon mingled with fragrant theater cosmetics and the musty wood smell from the floorboards.

Fancy knew only she could detect the cinnamon scent. Of all seven Flambeau sisters, she was the one physically sensitive to the unseen. She saw, heard, smelled, and sensed what others could not.

Fancy practiced caution, though. She had no wish to be locked in Bedlam.

Her sisters possessed their own special talents. Which she admired more than her own at times.

Fancy pushed away from the door. Moments were ticking by, and she did not want the prince to catch her undressed.

Growing anxiety urged her to hurry. She scrubbed her face, leaving her complexion flushed.

Fancy stripped the boy's clothing off and donned her simple gown, its violet shade matching her eyes. She grabbed her black shawl at the same moment someone tapped on the door.

Whirling around, Fancy stared at the door. She needed to reject the prince without insulting his pride or risk losing her job. How could she do the impossible?

Men were incredibly proud, stupid creatures. The fatter the purse, the bigger the pride, the emptier the head.

Another knock on the door.

Her heartbeat quickened. Her only experience with men was Alexander Blake. What the blue blazes could she say to a prince?

"Fancy?" the opera director called.

She took a fortifying breath. "You may enter now."

The door swung open. Director Bishop stepped aside.

Temptation walked into the dressing room in the shape of a Russian aristocrat.

Prince Stepan Kazanov stood a couple of inches over

six feet, his imposing presence filling the tiny dressing room. He possessed the dark good looks that women found intriguing. Broad shoulders, lean hips, and solid muscles showed to best advantage in his evening attire.

His good looks caught Fancy by surprise, igniting a flame in the pit of her stomach. Jet-black hair framed an angular, high-cheekboned face. A dark intensity burned in his black eyes, fringed with sinfully long lashes and straight brows. His nose was long and straight and his lips thin but perfectly shaped.

Unexpected humor gleamed at her from his black eyes. His lips quirked into a boyish smile that said he did not take himself too seriously.

Uh-oh. Fancy knew she was in trouble. She needed to reject this disturbingly attractive aristocrat. She wished the prince were a common laborer because she did not want to send him away.

Having seen her from a distance only, Stepan was no less surprised by Fancy. Violet eyes framed with long black lashes, generous lips, and a heart-shaped face lent her an air of sultry vulnerability.

Uh-oh. Stepan knew he was in trouble. Her innocent beauty screamed commitment. Every instinct shouted at him to bolt out the door, but a stronger force refused to let him turn away.

Stepan stepped further into the room. Fancy shrank back against the table.

"I do not bite, Miss Flambeau."

Fancy gave him a wobbly, embarrassed smile.

"Your Highness," Director Bishop said, "I present Fancy Flambeau."

The prince caught her hand and bowed over it in courtly manner, surprising her. "*Bonsoir*, Fancy. *Enchanté.*"

She snatched her hand back. "Speak English and call me Miss Flambeau."

Prince Stepan raised his brows at that. Director
Bishop coughed. Fancy shifted her gaze from the prince
to the director.

Stepan glanced over his shoulder. "You may leave,
Bishop. Miss Flambeau will not insult me into with-
drawing my financial support." He looked at her
again. "I find her prim formality refreshingly sweet."

"Leave the door open on your way out," Fancy ordered, making the prince smile. "I mean no insult,
Your Highness."

"Call me Stepan."

Fancy considered refusing the familiarity but then
inclined her head. "As you wish, Stepan."

"Your voice makes my heart ache with emotion." He
inched closer, staring at her upturned face. "Your eyes
are exquisite Persian violets, and your beauty steals my
breath."

"Steals your breath?" Fancy was not buying what this
aristocrat was selling. "Leave now, catch your breath,
and live."

Stepan gave her his boyish smile. "A sharp-witted
woman is a rose with layers of petals to peel away."

"You have too much leisure time," Fancy said. "Instead of wasting your days creating outrageous
compliments, try getting a job."

The prince grinned at her insult. He looked like a
boy caught in a prank.

Fancy felt her heart twist at the beauty of his smile.
Her peace of mind demanded she get rid of him, but
her lips refused to speak words of rejection. Had her
mother felt like this when faced with her father? Gawd,
she hoped not.

"Your biting wit will not insult me," Stepan told her.
"I have developed a thick skin from suffering years of
my brothers' teasing."

Fancy had never considered princes would tease

each other like commoners. She gave him an unconsciously flirtatious smile. "Oh, drat."

"You should use your lovely smile more often," the prince said, "and your eyes *do* remind me of Persian violets."

"Thank you."

"I would like to celebrate your success with supper," Stepan invited her.

"My sisters are waiting for me outside," Fancy said, refusing him.

"Do you have your own coach?"

"No, I have my own legs."

Surprise registered on his expression. "You and your sisters cannot walk home at this hour. We will escort your sisters home and then go to supper."

"I don't want to sup with you."

The prince looked perplexed. Apparently, he could not comprehend any woman refusing him.

"I met you in order to keep my job," Fancy told him. "Otherwise, I would not speak with you."

"Do you dislike foreigners?"

"My mother was French."

"Do you dislike Russians?"

"No."

"Do you dislike me?"

"I do not dislike you personally," Fancy tried to explain, "but you are an . . . *aristocrat.*"

"Your lips say *aristocrat*, but your tone says *leper.*" Stepan cocked a dark brow at her. "Before tonight, I had never felt inferior because of my wealth and title."

"I am honored to add to your life experience." Fancy wanted him to leave before she changed her mind.

He lowered his voice to a seductive tone. "I know more pleasant ways to increase my life experience."

His remark shocked her. Her back stiffened at the

insulting suggestion. He would never say that to a society lady.

"I should have expected no respect from an aristocrat."

"*Aristocrat* is not the name of a fatal disease."

Fancy lifted her chin a notch, her gaze cold on his. "I have experience with the aristocracy."

"You are referring to your father." Stepan inclined his head in understanding. "Like commoners, aristocrats are not all the same. Please consider my supper invitation for tomorrow evening. We may have more in common than you realize."

"I doubt that."

"Come." Prince Stepan held out his hand as if asking her to dance.

Fancy wanted to place her hand in his, but her distrust proved too strong. She would allow no man to do to her what her father had done to her mother.

"I will escort you and your sisters home." Stepan took her hand in his. "I will worry for your safety even though you dislike me."

His sentiment made her feel like the meanest creature in London. The prince seemed like a decent man, and she had hurt his feelings.

"I will sup with you tomorrow evening," Fancy relented, "but I refuse to become your mistress."

Amusement gleamed at her from the black depths of his eyes. "I did not ask you to become my mistress."

Fancy blushed, embarrassed by her presumption. She was the product of an illicit liaison between a duke and an opera singer. What other reason could he have for wanting her company?

"Trust me." Stepan lifted her hand to his lips. "I would never seduce a reluctant innocent." He gestured to the door. "Shall we?"

With her hand in his, Fancy walked in silence through the deserted theater to the lobby. She felt self-conscious,

her mind blanking at a topic for conversation. Gawd, tomorrow evening's supper promised a veritable dumb
show.

They stepped outside the theater onto Bow Street,
which should have been nearly deserted. Instead,
coaches lined both sides of the street.

Fancy looked at him in confusion and tightened her
grip on his hand. "What is happening?"

Chapter 2

"Your admirers are offering you the coach ride you never had."

Stepan gave her hand a gentle squeeze and smiled at the surprise on her upturned face. She was disarmingly lovely, her spirited innocence an irresistible siren's call.

"Why would they do that?" she asked.

"There are as many motivations as men," Stepan answered, "but the main reason, I suppose, would be stealing your virtue." Her expression became disgruntled. "You do possess attractive . . . *etcetera*."

Fancy blushed. "Thank you, I think."

"I will protect you from these would-be thieves of your innocence."

One ebony brow arched. "And who will protect me from you, Your Highness?"

Before he could reply, six young women surrounded them, budding beauties who resembled the opera singer. "Introduce me to your sisters."

"Introductions are unnecessary," Fancy said. "You will never see them again."

"I am Prince Stepan Kazanov," he introduced himself, his smile easy.

"I'm Belle," the nineteen-year-old said.

"You were aptly named for your beauty." Stepan bowed over her hand, making her blush and the other five sigh.

"Meet Blaze," Belle said, "and this—"

"What glorious hair," Stepan said to the only red-head in the group. "Gentlemen will be drawn to you like moths to a flame."

Eighteen-year-old Blaze gave him a dazed smile. She gestured to the dark-haired girl standing beside her. "Bliss is my twin, though you would never guess it from our different hair colors."

"What sweet bliss your beauty will bring to a lucky gentleman." Enjoying his own outrageous flattery, Stepan glanced at the opera singer and warned, "Be careful, Fancy, or that grimace will freeze and mar your lovely face." Giving her no chance to reply, he turned to the next sister. "And you are?"

"Serena, Your Highness."

"Serene and beautiful are a rare combination."

The seventeen-year-old blushed. "Are you a *real* prince?"

"You don't look like a prince," Blaze interjected.

Amusement gleamed from his dark eyes. "How does a real prince appear?"

"You should be wearing a crown."

"All princes do not wear crowns."

Bliss touched his forearm and then announced, "The gentleman is a true prince."

Stepan fixed his black gaze on her. "How do you know I am not an imposter?"

Bliss gave him an ambiguous smile. "I know things without being told." She gestured to the girl standing beside Serena. "Sophia and Serena are twins, too."

"Sophia means *wise*," Stepan said. "Are you wise as well as beautiful?"

"*Mon Dieu, la nausee,*" Fancy muttered.

Stepan slanted an amused glance at her. "Your nausea will improve once I find gainful employment and no longer waste my time creating outrageous compliments."

"My stomach and I await that day with eagerness." Fancy gestured to the last sister. "Meet Raven, Your Highness."

"I believe Raven is the cossetted baby of the family."

The sixteen-year-old inclined her head. "One baby recognizes another."

"How do you know I am the youngest?"

"I am the seventh daughter of a seventh daughter."

"I see." Stepan had no idea what that meant, but would never consider admitting he didn't know everything. He did know that, armed with these introductions, he would court the singer by winning the sisters' approval. Yes, it was a tad devious, but all was fair in love and—

"Miss Fancy Flambeau?" The voice belonged to a liveried coachman.

"I am she."

The man gestured to a nearby coach. "The Duchess of Inverary wishes to speak with you."

Stepan suppressed a smile. For a woman who disliked aristocrats, she had chosen a profession that would surround her with those she despised most. Poverty did not promote the arts. With the six sisters following behind, Stepan escorted the singer to the ducal coach.

"Your Graces, I present Miss Fancy Flambeau," he made the introduction. "The Duke and Duchess of Inverary are my brother's uncle- and aunt-in-law."

"You sing like an angel," the duchess said.

"Thank you, Your Grace." Fancy peeked at the duke and then told the duchess, "My mother sang in the opera."

"Though her career was short, I remember Gabrielle

Flambeau," the duchess said. "Stepan, you did not take long to stake your claim."

"This surpasses your own record time, Kazanov." The duke sounded gruff.

"The lady and her sisters are safe with me."

"We are in danger of nausea," Fancy qualified.

Stepan smiled at her wit. "A rose with petals and thorns."

The Duke of Inverary looked at Fancy. "You seem unhappy despite tonight's success."

"Since I have never met you before tonight," Fancy replied, "you cannot know if I seem happy or not."

"No offense to us," Stepan told the older man, "but Fancy dislikes aristocrats. If I ever chance to meet her father, I will call him out for giving her a bad opinion of men like us."

"Perhaps men like us have earned the bad opinion."

"Introduce us to your friends," the duchess said.

"These are Miss Flambeau's sisters," Stepan informed the duke and the duchess. "Belle, Blaze, Bliss, Serena, Sophia, and Raven."

"We would be honored to escort you and your sisters home," the Duke of Inverary invited them.

Fancy dropped her gaze. "Thank you for the offer, Your Grace, but—"

"The lady is riding with me," Stepan said. "Her sisters will ride with you, though." He looked at the sisters, who were bobbing their heads.

The coachman opened the door. Chatting with excitement, the sisters climbed inside the coach.

"You will be escorting Miss Flambeau directly home?" the duke asked.

Stepan gave the older man an unamused look. Rudolf had put the duke up to this in order to embarrass him.

"Well?"

"Yes, of course."

Without another word, Fancy turned away and heard Belle telling the duke, "We live in Soho Square." She watched the coach drive past her, waved to her sisters, and rounded on the prince. "I have decided to walk home."

"I will walk with you and my coach will follow."

His announcement surprised her. "Princes walk?"

"I learned walking early in life."

"I meant, you are a prince."

"Alas, even princes exercise to keep their etcetera in good shape." Stepan winked at her. "Where do you live, my lady?"

Fancy narrowed her gaze on him. "Are you insulting me?"

"I would never do that."

"You called me *my lady*."

"And so you are my lady." Stepan looped her hand through the crook of his arm and started walking down the street.

Fancy didn't know what to think. She was the bastard daughter of a French emigré, yet this prince had called her his lady. Was this a ploy to gain entrance to her bed?

She was stepping dangerously close to liking the royal rascal. He was charming and handsome, a deadly combination.

Excitement and attraction mingled with cautious anxiety to keep her nerves in riot. Should she believe his gallant words? After all, she would never have imagined a prince walking her home from her debut. Perhaps she wasn't so different from her mother. That fear sent her spirits crashing. Surely, one evening walk could not alter her life?

The journey from the opera house to Soho Square was twenty minutes as the crow flies, slightly longer otherwise.

At the end of Bow Street, Stepan and Fancy veered left and passed Covent Garden. Then they walked north on Charing Cross Road.

The crowds thinned gradually until the street was nearly deserted. Only the sounds of the prince's coach and horses broke the night's silence.

"I never realized the beautiful sights I missed by riding in a coach." Stepan looked at the night sky. "Like that crescent moon."

A smile touched her lips. "Miss Giggles's moon."

"I do not understand."

"Banana-shaped. Miss Giggles is the prima donna's capuchin monkey. Her sole trick is the hear, see, speak no evil gesture. She dislikes the Tanners."

Amusement gleamed in the prince's eyes. "Did Miss Giggles tell you that?"

Fancy shook her head. "She told Blaze."

Stepan laughed at that. "Tell me about your family. Do you live with your mother?"

"No."

"Just *no*?"

Fancy sighed, suspecting the prince would not allow her retreat until he heard her entire life story. "My mother died five years ago, and Nanny Smudge passed last winter."

"Who was Nanny Smudge?"

"My father . . . I mean, the man who sired me . . . sent Nanny Smudge to help my mother when she was carrying me," Fancy told him. "My mother's whole family died in the Terror."

"You and your sisters live alone?" He sounded surprised.

"We own a guard dog."

The prince slipped his arm around her shoulders, drawing her close against the side of his body, but kept walking. "Do you know your father's identity?"

Fancy gave him a sidelong smile. "Do you intend to call him out?"

Stepan answered her smile with his own. "I will if it pleases you."

"The others cannot remember him, and I will not reveal his identity. He stopped visiting after Raven was born. I wonder . . ." Fancy hesitated and then asked, "Do you think circumstances would have been different if we had been boys?"

"Producing males is the goal of most men, especially aristocrats," Stepan said, "but I would prefer a house filled with females to cosset. Little girls are more wondrous than unicorns."

His sentiment surprised her. She had assumed that all wealthy gentlemen wanted sons.

"I adore their tea parties."

Fancy shifted her gaze to his. "Tea parties?"

Stepan nodded once. "One day each week, I collect Mikhail's and Viktor's daughters and attend a tea party hosted by Rudolf's daughters. The under-ten gossip entertains me."

Fancy could not have been more surprised. "You attend a little girls' tea party every week?"

Stepan cocked a brow at her. "You are surprised?"

"You must admit that attending tea parties scarcely fits with your reputation."

"What do you know of my reputation?"

"Nothing."

"Would you like to know more about me?"

"No."

Stepan said nothing.

Guilt for her rudeness swelled, forcing her to stop walking and face him. "I am sorry," she told his chest, "and I do want to know more about you."

With one finger, Stepan lifted her chin. He leaned close and planted a chaste kiss on her lips. "I will en-

lighten you tomorrow night at supper." He gestured to their surroundings. "We have arrived in Soho Square."

The Flambeau residence was a three-storied, red brick structure with three steps leading to an arched doorcase. The north-facing front door had been painted a vibrant blue with white trim.

"Sophia painted the door," Fancy said. "Blue in the north brings the household good luck. Or so Nanny Smudge always said."

The prince appeared amused. "And doors facing south?"

"Red is the most auspicious color." Fancy hesitated for a millisecond, worried the prince would find her home deficient.

"Fancy!" A man jogged toward them. In his midtwenties, the man stood as tall as Stepan.

"Alex." Fancy laughed in delight when the newcomer hugged her.

Stepan felt the unfamiliar pangs of jealousy. He had no idea who this was, only that he disliked him.

"Your Highness, I present Alexander Blake," Fancy introduced them. "Alex, meet Prince Stepan Kazanov."

Stepan stared at the other man. Alexander returned his stare. Neither offered his hand.

Alexander Blake did not appear pleased. "Have you forgotten your vow after one night only? Do you want to end like your mother?"

Fancy stiffened at the rebuke. "I have forgotten nothing."

"I am thinking of your welfare."

"I appreciate that."

"What vow have you made?" Stepan asked.

"Fancy vowed never to associate with men like you," Alexander answered for her.

Stepan narrowed his black gaze on him. "You know nothing about me."

"We know your type."

"Enough." Fancy gestured toward the door. "Please, come inside for a glass of wine."

Alexander led the way, his familiarity with the house irritating Stepan. Inside the foyer, Stepan paused to close the door.

An enormous dog leaped at him, catching him off guard, pinning him against the door. Standing on its hind legs, the mastiff licked his face, making him laugh.

"Sit," Fancy ordered, her voice stern.

The brindled mastiff with its black-masked face obeyed in an instant. It grinned at Stepan while its long tail swished back and forth across the polished wood floor.

"You call this big baby a guard dog?" Stepan asked. "Does he kill intruders with kindness?"

"Puddles protects us when necessary."

"Apparently, Puddles approves of me. How did he get his name?"

Fancy gave him a pointed look.

Stepan grinned. "I will use my imagination."

"I didn't realize aristocrats had any imagination." Fancy gave him a sweet, thoroughly insincere smile.

Stepan followed her down the hallway in the direction of female voices. "What is your relationship with this Alexander Blake?"

Fancy stopped walking and rounded on him. "That is not your business."

"You consider him your friend," Stepan said, "but he considers you something more."

The kitchen was spacious and inviting. The freestanding cabinets and wall shelves were made in solid oak, and the floor was green terra-cotta tiles. The main focal point was a marble-topped table with enormous iron legs and lion's feet.

"What an unusual piece."

"My father bought my mother that table." Fancy led him into the dining room.

Stepan noted the expensive furniture. A fine linen cloth topped the table set with porcelain plates, cups, and saucers as well as crystal glasses. A French ormolu candelabra sat in the center of the table. One wall had a large mirror and another a sandstone mantel over the fireplace. A French armoire stood in a corner, and the sideboard was a paneled elm coffer.

The family parlor lay beyond the open French doors. Comfortable-looking sofas, a French chaise, and an Aubusson rug complemented the light blue walls and a white-painted mantel mirror.

The Flambeaus had not suffered by their absentee father, Stepan decided. The anonymous aristocrat had been generous, meeting his daughters' material needs.

"I can help you," Raven, the youngest sister, was saying.

Alexander Blake reached out to mess her hair. "Listen, brat. Good investigation solves murders, not hocus pocus."

Fancy handed Stepan a glass of wine. "Alexander works with Constable Amadeus Black. Have you heard of him?"

"All London knows the constable." Stepan looked at the other man. "Are you close to an arrest in the rose-petal murders?"

Alexander shook his head. "He preys upon singers, dancers, and actresses. Only the beautiful ones, of course."

"He could be a she," Raven suggested, making everyone smile. "She could be jealous of beauty denied her. Isn't that called motivation?"

"Women do not usually kill in cold blood," Alexander told her. "A good investigator eliminates the probable before turning his attention to the possible."

"How does he kill them?" Fancy asked.

"We have not determined that yet," Alexander answered, "but he slashes their faces after death."

"How do you know the slashing is done postmortem?" Stepan asked.

"Blood settles after a body expires," Alexander explained. "Their facial slashes are bloodless."

"Ladies, I urge you to extreme caution until this monster is apprehended." Stepan set his glass on the table and turned to Fancy. "I must leave you now." He looked at the other man. "And so must you, Blake."

Stepan nodded at the sisters and headed for the foyer, calling over his shoulder, "Come along, Blake."

Both men were passing through the foyer when the sound of crashing crystal reached them. Stepan paused and looked over his shoulder in the direction of the dining room.

"Oops," one of the sisters exclaimed.

"You must control your anger," the opera singer said. "We are running low on glasses."

The front door closed behind Stepan.

"Who appointed you their guardian?" Alexander challenged him. "Fancy won't give you what you want."

Stepan stared at his rival. "You do not know what I want."

"Are you planning to marry her?"

"My plans are none of your business."

"If you hurt her," Blake threatened, "I will tear you into pieces and feed your bones to Puddles."

"I intend to live to a ripe old age." Stepan turned to walk to his coach but paused to ask, "Do you need a lift somewhere?"

"No, thank you, Your Highness." Alexander gave him a smug smile. "I live next door."

Stepan swore in Russian and climbed into his coach.

* * *

"You won't hit me, will you?"

"No."

"Are you certain?"

"No."

Fancy and Belle stood in the small garden behind their Soho Square home late the following morning. The day was a spring rarity of clear sky, warm sunshine, and a gentle breeze, which enticed the winter-weary plants to grow. Cheerful yellow forsythia nodded gaily to their old friends, the purple and gold pansies, hiding in characteristic shyness beneath the shade of the oak tree.

"Hold the target out straight to the side of your body."

Belle gave Fancy a nervous look. Then she lifted the two-inch-square paper up and away from her body.

Standing ten feet from her sister, Fancy took a white marble pellet from one pocket and her slingshot from another. She held the forked wooden stick, placed the pellet on the flexible tubing, and aimed for her target.

Whoosh! Fancy let the pellet fly.

"You hit dead center." Belle laughed in relief.

"I'll back up another five paces and shoot from there."

Belle walked toward her. "I refuse to tempt fate by holding the target again."

Fancy feigned a hurt expression. "You don't trust me?"

"I came outside to work in the garden, not participate in your target practice. You should try gardening yourself, Sister, and learn to relax."

Fancy touched her sister's shoulder. "I need you to tell me how to get rid of the prince without insulting him."

Belle patted her hand. "Give the man a chance."

"A chance for what?" she countered. "You cannot believe his intentions are honorable and include an offer of marriage."

Her sister shrugged. "You never know what fate has planned."

"I know what fate does *not* have planned," Fancy said. "Real life will never mirror that old tale about the king and the beggar maid."

"Charles is taking me to meet his mother on Sunday," Belle told her. "If I can be accepted into society, then so can you."

"I know you love Baron Wingate but"—Fancy could not mask her troubled thoughts—"I don't trust him with your heart. Remember Mama, and let her pain—"

"Charles loves me," Belle insisted. "Introducing me to his mother is the first step toward marriage."

"If you say so."

"I do say so. Mama loved a man unavailable to marry her."

Fancy refused to argue the point. She sensed Charles Wingate was less than honest and hoped her sister would not be too hurt. Like their mother.

None of her sisters understood their mother's pain. Why should they? Nanny Smudge had virtually raised them, insulating them from their mother's anguish.

Fancy remembered what the others could not—joy and agony, happiness and grief. Emotional anguish, both hers and her mother's, haunted Fancy during the night's silent hours.

Many times the faint sound of her mother's weeping awakened her. On several occasions, she had risen and gone to her mother's bedchamber. When she opened the door, the weeping ceased, and the room was empty.

Gabrielle Flambeau did not rest in peace. Fancy did not want to suffer the same fate.

"Sisters, look at this."

Fancy and Belle turned around. Clutching a newspaper, Blaze hurried across the garden.

"The *Times* mentions you." Blaze passed her the newspaper.

LONDON'S FANCY announced the article in bold black letters. Beneath that, the reporter had written a whole article about her debut.

> *Miss Fancy Flambeau stole the show last night during her debut at the Royal Opera House, even outshining the current prima donna. Blessed with a full-bodied voice, the petite singer demonstrated incredible talent and versatility by effortlessly changing musical scales. Her perfect pitch and remarkable range stunned all, and her emotional intensity drained the audience, leaving nary a dry eye in the theater.*
>
> *The daughter of a French emigré and, rumor says, a well-known English nobleman, Miss Flambeau won the hearts of London's elite as evidenced by what transpired after the show. Gentlemen lined their coaches on both sides of Bow Street in hope of winning her favor and escorting her home. A certain Russian prince, one of society's most eligible, disappointed the competition when he exited the theater with the lovely singer clinging to his arm.*
>
> *This reporter will live on tenterhooks awaiting news of this liaison.*

Fancy stared at the article, startled by the reporter's arrogance. How dare this man write about her private life? She had expected a review of her performance but never this. Had the gossips written about her mother's and father's affair? How had her mother coped with the intrusive public? Was that the reason her mother had quit the opera? Was she destined to walk the same path?

Not all opera singers became mistresses, though. Patrice Tanner was a good example. The woman had been married four times and buried three husbands.

"You do not seem especially pleased," Belle remarked.

"Becoming fodder for the gossips is a less than appealing prospect."

"Fancy!"

What now? She looked toward the house, where her youngest sister stood.

Raven beckoned her. "The prince's courier is waiting for you."

Dressed in a footman's uniform, a middle-aged man stood in the foyer. He passed her a long, thin package. "A gift from His Highness, Prince Stepan Kazanov."

Fancy looked at the package and then at the man. "Thank you, Mister—?"

The footman appeared surprised by her question. "Milton."

"Aren't you going to open it?" Belle asked, once the man had gone.

Fancy unfastened the ribbon and opened the package. Inside lay a single white rose and a note. "Your beautiful eyes would have shamed my Persian violets," she read aloud.

All six of her sisters sighed. One said, "How romantic. Like a fairy tale."

"Fairy tales do not come true." Fancy rolled her eyes but, despite her skepticism, lifted the rose to inhale its sensual scent.

The Russian was a romantic. Or a rake experienced in persuading women into his bed. Only an aristocrat could afford to purchase a rose at this time of year.

Tha barest hint of a smile touched her lips. Romantic or rake? His behavior that evening would prove what he was.

Fancy focused on her sisters' smug smiles. She knew the best way to disperse them. "Which of you will hold my target?" The knocker banging on the door saved them from answering. "You need not look so relieved by the interruption."

Intending to send the uninvited intruder away, Fancy yanked the door open and gasped at the unexpected sight of the prince. Harsh daylight did not diminish his amazing good looks. If anything, daylight improved his perfection. She was definitely in trouble.

Prince Stepan smiled. "You seem surprised to see me."

Being caught off guard made Fancy feel like a henwit. She hid her insecurity behind sarcasm. "Shouldn't you be elsewhere creating all those outrageous compliments?"

"Your beauty has stolen my creative concentration." Stepan winked at her. "Will you invite me inside?"

Fancy hesitated, her mind and her heart at war. Invite the devil into her home? Or send him away? Her heart won the battle, and she stepped aside to allow him entrance.

"No, Puddles."

The mastiff leaped at the prince and pinned him against the door as it had done the previous evening. The dog bathed the royal cheeks in slobbering licks.

"Sit." Stepan looked at the singer. "You should emulate your pet's welcome."

Fancy blushed, at an unusual loss for words. Her sisters' giggles registered on her, making the blush deepen to a vibrant scarlet. She opened her mouth to send her sisters scurrying, but the prince was faster.

"I wish to invite all of you on a Sunday picnic," Stepan told them.

Fancy tried to refuse. "We couldn't poss—"

"A Sunday picnic sounds wonderful," Bliss exclaimed.

Fancy sent her sisters a quelling look which, to her dismay, went ignored.

"Is Puddles invited?" Blaze asked.

Stepan patted the dog's head. "Even Puddles will

join us, and I will provide the food and transportation."

"I doubt we'll fit in your coach," Raven said.

"A good point," Fancy agreed. "And that is the reason we cannot—"

"I own more than one coach." Stepan interrupted her refusal. "If we wish, each of us may ride in our own coach. Even Puddles."

"I do believe two coaches will be sufficient, Your Highness." Fancy felt trapped. Had her mother felt that way? At least, numbers provided safety, and the prince would play the gentleman with her sisters in attendance.

"Take His Highness into the parlor," Belle suggested.

Fancy watched her sisters drifting away in the direction of the kitchen. She forced herself to smile at the prince and gestured toward the parlor. *Mon Dieu,* but she felt gauche. Except for Alex, she'd never actually been required to converse with a man. If she used her conversational topics today, what would they discuss at supper?

"Please, be seated."

"Ladies first, mademoiselle."

Fancy sat on the sofa and realized her mistake when the prince sat beside her. She would remember that for future reference.

"Have you seen The *Times*?" Stepan asked.

Fancy nodded.

"Your success does not make you happy?"

"I would enjoy my success," she told him, "if that reporter would refrain from comments concerning my private life."

Stepan stretched his long legs out as if he owned the sofa. "Ah, the high price of fame."

Fancy lifted her gaze to his. "Are you laughing at me?"

"I would never do that."

Her gaze slid from his dark eyes to his chiseled lips. "You cannot possibly enjoy the newspaper's comments."

"I have learned to ignore such transgressions against my privacy." Stepan shrugged. "Besides, the reporter did me a favor by marking you as mine so no other gentleman will bother you."

"I belong to myself, not you." Fancy said. She was a woman, not a possession. "You must think highly of yourself if you believe no other gentleman will tempt me."

"The competition does not concern me." Stepan flashed her his boyish smile. "Why drink the water when you can savor the finest champagne?"

The prince was stuffed with conceit like a Christmas goose. Diverting attention away from more personal matters, Fancy said, "Thank you for the rose, Stepan."

"Its perfection reminded me of you."

"Where did you get a rose at this time of year?"

"Gardening relaxes me," Stepan answered, "so I built a hothouse on my country estate."

"You grew that rose?" Tea parties and gardening seemed at odds with a rake. "I suppose growing your own saves money, considering the number of women you gift with flowers."

"Precisely. Gardening also helps me focus on creating outrageous compliments."

Fancy lost her struggle against a smile. The rascal oozed charm and possessed a wry sense of humor. Her attraction to him made her nervous, and without thinking, she took the slingshot from her pocket and twiddled it in her hand.

"What is that?"

Fancy looked down at her lap. "This is called a slingshot."

"I meant, what are you doing with it?"

"I am practicing my revenge against Patrice Tanner," Fancy answered. "The prima donna will regret tripping me."

Stepan gave her a long look. "Violence solves nothing."

"When someone hits me," Fancy said, "I hit back."

"Thank you for the warning, *ma petite chou*," Stepan said, laughter lurking in his voice.

"Please refrain from referring to me as your little cabbage."

"*Excusez-moi.* You do look adorable contemplating your revenge."

Perhaps the prince could help her. Fancy gave him a flirtatious smile and rose from the sofa. "Would you consider helping me practice?"

The prince stood when she did. "I would love to assist in your practice."

Stepan followed her through the French doors into the dining room, where she grabbed an apple from the bowl on the table. He smiled at the sway of her hips as she led him outside.

Pausing a moment to scan the garden, Stepan noted the forsythia and pansies. Several shrubs and an oak tree also called the garden home.

A loving hand tended the flowers, plants, and tree. He would bet the Kazanov fortune that the object of his interest did not possess the patience for such a pastime. She seemed too passionate to appreciate the solitude of gardening.

"Hold this, Your Highness."

Stepan looked at the minuscule paper target. "You are joking?"

"Please?" Her voice became a silken whisper. "Do it for me?"

His lips twitched with the urge to laugh. The minx

was trying to seduce him into holding her target. Subtlety was not her forte.

Stepan inclined his head. "I would do anything for you, *ma petite.*"

Fancy blushed and passed him the target. "Lift your arm and hold it out to the side of your body."

After counting off ten paces, Fancy drew a white marble pellet from her pocket. She placed the pellet on the flexible tubing and aimed at the target. His smile made her hand tremble, and she closed her eyes to compose herself.

"You will not shoot with your eyes closed, will you?"

Fancy couldn't concentrate with him staring at her. "Please, Stepan, close your eyes."

"Why?"

"Your gaze is making me nervous, and my nerves are shaking my hand."

Stepan smiled, pleased with himself. Her nervousness meant she was attracted to him. Not that he had doubted the outcome of desire.

"Your Highness?"

Stepan closed his eyes.

Fancy placed the pellet on the flexible tubing, aimed, and . . . paused.

The prince seemed to have stepped out of every maiden's dream. Glossy black hair and an intriguing face conspired with his warrior's body to wreak havoc with her innards. Her pulses quickened, and a melting sensation flowed from her belly to other, private regions.

Stepan opened his eyes. "Why are you waiting?"

Fancy blushed a vibrant scarlet. Was her heat caused by her embarrassment or her admiration of his masculine beauty?

She lifted the slingshot again and aimed for her target. *Whoosh!* The pellet flew like a homing pigeon toward its target.

Feeling the strike, Stepan opened his eyes and laughed with relief. "You hit dead center. Where did you learn to shoot with such accuracy?"

"Alex taught me."

He was sorry he'd asked. Irritation replaced light-hearted humor. "I should have known," he muttered. "What else has this paragon taught you?"

Fancy walked toward him, pulling the apple from her pocket. "Balance this on top of your head."

"I beg your pardon?"

"I want to shoot the apple off your head."

"Like William Tell? I think not."

Fancy looked at him through enormous violet eyes, her expression guileless. "You don't trust me?"

Stepan grinned. "I trust you as much as you trust me."

"*Touché.*" Fancy rubbed the apple against the sleeve of her gown and then offered him the shining apple. "Take a bite."

"Ah, an English Eve offering forbidden fruit from her Garden of Eden."

"I did not pick this apple from the tree of knowledge, Adam." She gave him a long look. "Or are you the serpent?"

Fancy bit into the sweet, succulent apple. A dribble of juice dotted her stubborn chin.

Her generous lips and the enticing drop of juice conspired against Stepan. He felt his privates hardening and nearly groaned with frustration.

"I never thought to be jealous of an apple." His voice was husky. She blushed, but her expression told him she had no idea what he meant. "Where did you get an apple out of season?"

"My father sometimes sends us hard-to-find items."

"Perhaps this anonymous aristocrat cares for his daughters?"

"Do not confuse a guilty conscience with genuine love."

Stepan did not want himself associated with the much-despised parent and opted to change the subject. "I surrender to temptation." He lifted her hand to his lips and bit the apple. "I must leave you now but will see you after tonight's performance."

"Is this tea party day?"

"No, *ma petite*. I leave you in order to seek employment."

That made her laugh.

"I almost forgot." He reached into his pocket and produced a small, paper-wrapped package. "For you."

Fancy looked from his dark eyes to the package and then opened it. Her gaze snapped to his. "Cinnamon sticks?"

"I knew you adored cinnamon. Your dressing room reeked of it."

Fancy stared after him in surprise. The prince had scented Nanny Smudge? Even her sisters were unable to do that. No doubt, her beloved nanny was sending her a message. Listen to her head? Or follow her heart?

Chapter 3

Standing in the wings, Fancy listened to the main characters performing the opera's final song. With her stood Genevieve Stover, who played the role of Barbarina.

"You look pale."

"My brother has been escorting me home since the rose-petal murders began," Genevieve told her. "Tonight is impossible for him, and walking home alone frightens me."

"Is that all?" Fancy smiled at her. "Prince Stepan and I will gladly drive you home before going to supper."

The other girl's expression cleared. "I will meet you and the prince in front of the theater."

Fancy listened to the music and singing, her gaze following the stagehands communicating with hand signals. Satisfied that no one was watching, she slipped her slingshot from the waist of her costume's breeches and took a pellet from her pocket.

This is wrong, she thought, and then promptly ignored her conscience. The prima donna had tripped her, and she refused not to hit back. Turning the other cheek invited abuse.

"I would not do that if I were you."

Fancy shifted her gaze to her new friend. "Patrice Tanner cannot trip me and expect no retribution."

Lifting the slingshot, Fancy placed the white marble pellet on the flexible tubing and aimed for the prima donna. The pellet flew through the air and hit the woman's cheek, escalating the war between them.

Startled, Patrice Tanner lost focus and pitch. Her voice cracked, eliciting murmurs from the audience, but she regained her composure and kept singing.

Clearly displeased, Director Bishop hurried to the wings. Sebastian Tanner joined him a moment later.

Her face a mask of fury, Patrice Tanner marched off the stage. She halted in front of Fancy. "I'll get you." The prima donna glanced at Genevieve, adding, "And your friend, too."

Fancy gave the older woman an amused smirk. "You are the one who's bleeding."

Patrice Tanner lifted her hand to her cheek and then stared in horror at her bloody fingertips. She swooned dead away.

Sebastian Tanner knelt beside his wife. "Patrice cannot tolerate the sight of blood."

"Genevieve, you may leave," Director Bishop said, and then looked at Fancy. "Do not move from this spot." He helped the prima donna rise from the floor and return to her dressing room.

"Good luck." Genevieve sent Fancy a commiserating look and hurried away.

What did the director expect? Fancy thought. She could not let the prima donna's action pass without reaction. That would be committing professional suicide. She would have passed her operatic tenure flying into the orchestra pit.

Director Bishop reappeared a few minutes later and began his lecture. "If you ever pull another stunt like that, you will find yourself without employment. Which, I dare say, would suit the prince's purpose."

"Patrice started this war," Fancy defended herself.

"And I am finishing it." Director Bishop paused a moment, his cold stare making her uneasy. "A word of advice, Miss Flambeau. Do not believe everything you read about yourself in the newspaper. No one is indispensable."

"Thank you for the advice, sir." Fancy lifted her chin a notch, proud even in her defeat. "I will consider your words before taking further action."

"An apology to Patrice would be wise." Without another word, Director Bishop turned his back on her and walked away.

Her confidence waning, Fancy retreated to her dressing room. Director Bishop had taken the self-righteous sails out of her revenge voyage. He was correct, though. She had behaved badly. The opera was a business, not a game, and she needed to manuever around the prima donna until her own star shone more brightly than the other woman's.

Sabotaging her operatic career would ruin all her plans. Without income, she would be forced to marry, and a man could trap her into becoming love's victim. Like her mother.

A whiff of cinnamon scented the air, reminding her of Nanny Smudge. *Listen to your head, child, but follow your heart.*

Was avoiding marriage listening to her head? Or following her heart?

Leaving her dressing room to take her final bow, Fancy noted the prima donna's absence on stage. Guilt for what she'd done filled her, and she determined to apologize to the older woman before departing the theater that night. Perhaps they could begin their professional relationship again.

Fancy scrubbed the cosmetics from her face, leaving her complexion flushed. Her eyes sparkled with nervous anticipation as she dressed for her supper with the prince. She had chosen a forest green gown with gold embroidery, its neckline high, more modest than any sophisticated society lady would wear.

A tap on the door drew her attention. "Enter."

The prince stood in the doorway. Once again, his masculine beauty startled and delighted her. He smiled then, showing his straight white teeth, adding to his perfection.

Fancy decided he could charm the chastity out of a nun . . . but not out of her.

"I passed Director Bishop backstage," Stepan said, sauntering into the room. "He grimaced when I said your name."

"The director has given me a severe set-down and a warning."

"I advised you against rash action." Prince Stepan bowed over her hand, his warm lips touching her skin, sending a delicious shiver of excitement down her spine, weakening her resolve to abstain from men. "You are perfection, an English Aphrodite . . . the goddess Kalliope."

"I gather your job hunting was unsuccessful?"

"How did you guess?" Stepan winked at her. "Do you possess unworldly powers?"

"Something like that." Fancy slipped her hand through the loop of his arm, the action feeling as natural as breathing. "I would stop at Patrice Tanner's dressing room to apologize and ask that we give Genevieve Stover a ride home."

"Your wish is my command."

"Only if my wish does not include your leaving me alone."

Fancy tapped on the prima donna's dressing room door. No answer. She knocked louder. Still no answer.

Patrice and her husband had left the theater. Well, she would apologize the following evening.

Fancy saw her friend waiting for them. "Your Highness, I present Genevieve Stover."

Prince Stepan bowed over the girl's hand. "I recognize pretty Barbarina."

Genevieve gave him a shy smile. "I hope—"

"Escorting you home pleases me," Stepan interrupted. "I would worry for your safety otherwise."

"Fancy."

She turned around.

Alexander Blake stood there. "Your performance was outstanding."

Fancy smiled at her neighbor. "I am pleased you took a few hours off work." She looked at her new friend. "Genevieve, I present Alexander Blake, my oldest friend. Alex works with Constable Amadeus Black, who is trying to catch the rose-petal murderer."

Fancy saw Alex's interested gaze fix on the blue-eyed blonde. She recognized the blonde's answering look of interest.

"The rose-petal murders frighten me," Genevieve said. "My brother cannot escort me home tonight as he usually does. The prince—"

"I will escort you home," Alexander said, offering her his arm. "I will protect you with my life."

Genevieve looked from him to Fancy, who nodded. Then she slipped her hand through the loop of his arm and walked away with him.

Fancy smiled with satisfaction. She liked Alex, and she liked Genevieve. They appeared to like each other.

"Nicely done, mademoiselle." When she gave him a blank look, Stepan explained, "You got rid of Blake without insulting him."

Fancy gave the prince her sweetest smile. "If only I could work that same miracle with you."

The prince assumed a disappointed expression. "You do not mean that."

With the prince's assistance, Fancy climbed into his coach. He sat beside her and gave her a wolfish smile. Which told her that, from his point of view, things were progressing satisfactorily.

Fancy masked a disgruntled grimace by turning her head to look out the window. She slid the palm of her hand across the leather seat. Softer than a lady's lap. Royalty certainly enjoyed luxurious accommodation.

"Where are we supping?" If he answered *his house*, she would leap out the door now.

"*Belle Sauvage*."

"Beautiful Savage?"

"*Belle Sauvage* is a riverside establishment attached to a coaching inn," Stepan told her. "I thought a taste of your mother's native France would appeal to your appetite."

Fancy gave him a sidelong look. "What do Russians eat?"

"Opera singers."

She laughed at that. And wished the prince were not so charming.

Belle Sauvage perched on a beautiful stretch of the Thames, its three-storied terraces facing the wooded and secluded Eel Pie Island. A bay window beside the front door overlooked the street and added decoration to the structure's white-painted front.

Dark wood and shadowy nooks lent the interior a private atmosphere. Guests spoke in hushed tones while sitting at the candlelit tables squirreled into small alcoves.

Prince Stepan ordered *moules marinieres*, mussels cooked in wine and served in shells. Then he gave her his full attention. "Tell me what happened with Director Bishop and Patrice Tanner, my sweet Kalliope."

"Who is she?"

"Kalliope means 'she of the beautiful voice' and was a daughter of Zeus, one of the nine muses," Stepan explained.

Fancy smiled at his compliment. Flattering a person's accomplishments was acceptable.

"Director Bishop advised me that no one is indispensable."

"Are you planning to heed his advice?"

"Yes."

"A wise choice," Stepan said. "Tell me about yourself and your family."

"Gabrielle Flambeau was the youngest child and the seventh daughter of a French aristocrat," Fancy said. "She and her nanny arrived in London without funds, the only Flambeau survivors of the Terror."

"Nanny Smudge?"

Fancy shook her head. "Nanny Smudge came later. When her own nanny died, my mother auditioned for the opera. The promise in her voice would never be fulfilled because she met my father, who insisted she retire. Then she became pregnant."

Stepan lifted his goblet and sipped his wine. "And then Nanny Smudge arrived?"

"As the youngest Flambeau, my mother had become accustomed to having others care for her," Fancy said. "Nanny Smudge, her own nanny, my father."

"Nanny Smudge helped your mother raise you and your sisters."

"My mother helped Nanny Smudge raise me and my sisters," she corrected him.

Stepan raised his brows at that. "So, Nanny Smudge was like a mother to you."

"Quite so." Fancy lifted her wine goblet and, under the

guise of sipping her wine, gazed at his mouth. She wondered how his lips would feel pressed to her own. How would he taste? And how would those strong hands touch her body, his long fingers caressing her flesh?

"Fancy, where have you gone?"

She forced a smile, attempting to bury this unfamiliar yearning, and covered her discomfit with conversation. "Nanny Smudge was a Highlander from Scotland who had married and buried her husband.

"Nanny adored cinnamon." Fancy rolled her eyes, making him smile. "We ate cinnamon sticks, cinnamon cookies, cinnamon bread, cinnamon buns, cinnamon biscuits, cinnamon scones . . ." She dropped her voice to a conspiratorial whisper. "Nanny believed cinnamon was the meaning of life."

Stepan laughed at that, delighted with her. Fancy Flambeau was a captivating mix of strength and vulnerability, sensuality and innocence, intelligence and beauty.

Fancy deserved more than mistress status. Her endearing qualities demanded an honorable marriage.

The prince and the opera singer? The gossips would chew on that for the next decade. On the other hand, two of his brothers had chosen mates unsuitable for society's approval. Rudolf had married his pickpocket, albeit the daughter of an impoverished earl, and Viktor had married the merchant's daughter. Both had pleased themselves.

Fancy studied the prince, lost in thought. He was no longer a nameless, faceless, despicable aristocrat. Stepan was simply a man, charming and attractive. Very attractive.

How could she prevent herself from falling in love with this irresistible man? She doubted she could discourage him. The prince had the tenacity of a bulldog and refused to take *no* for an answer.

"Tell me about your sisters."

Fancy wondered if telling the brutal, bizarre truth about her sisters and her would discourage him. Either he would dismiss her as a liar or see her as a candidate for Bedlam. In any event, he would trip over his expensively booted feet in his haste to put distance between them. Which was what she wanted. Wasn't it?

Stepan raised his brows at her. "I thought my request rather simple."

Fancy blushed. "Do you want the real truth?"

"I do not want the unreal truth."

"Will you promise not to tell another person?"

"I will respect your confidence."

"So be it, Your Highness." Fancy set the fork on her plate and gave her lips a dainty dab with the napkin. "The truth is my sisters possess special talents, unusual gifts from the Almighty."

His lips twitched. "Explain yourself, please."

"Belle has a gentle soul as well as great beauty," Fancy began, watching his eyes for a sign of disbelief. "Her hands are healing, which makes her an excellent gardener."

No expression of doubt appeared on his face. She was warming to her subject, as her sisters' talents were becoming progressively harder for most people to believe.

"Blaze can communicate with animals and—"

"Is that how she knew Miss Giggles disliked the Tanners?"

"Yes." The prince was not reacting as she had expected. "Bliss loves numbers and sometimes knows what people are thinking, especially if she touches them."

His dark gaze narrowed on her, but he said nothing. Was the prince deciding if she was a liar or crazy?

"God blessed Serena with a perfect operatic voice, a talent for flute playing, and an affinity for the wind,"

Fancy told him. "Sophia, the painter, can judge people by the color of their auras."

A black brow arched. Was he thinking liar or crazy?

"As the seventh daughter of a seventh daughter, Raven has many talents." Fancy gave him her sweetest smile. "She can move objects with her mind."

Stepan burst into laughter. He ceased abruptly, seeing her disgruntled expression.

"You don't believe me?"

"I do not disbelieve you."

Drat. The prince was more tenacious than *two* bulldogs.

"And what about you, Fancy? What hidden talent do you possess?"

"I see and hear and smell and sense what others cannot. And so do you, I think."

"What do you mean?"

Fancy gave him an ambiguous smile but said nothing. Only a special man would still be sitting here instead of running away. Was this a sign from Above? Or Nanny Smudge?

"Tell me about yourself," Fancy said and resumed eating.

"I have led an unremarkable life," Stepan told her. "I am the youngest of five sons, one having remained in Moscow. Princess Amber, my cousin, married the Earl of Stratford."

"What about your life in Russia?"

"I was born, educated, grew into adulthood, and moved to England." Stepan shrugged. "My brothers and I hold interests in many businesses, which allow us a luxurious life. As the youngest, I suffered greatly from my older brothers' teasing.

"My father had no time for us, but an older cousin took us hunting in the wilderness quite frequently. Vladimir, my brother in Moscow, always remained at home with my father, but the four of us enjoyed cooking over a campfire and sleeping beneath the stars.

"One time, Mikhail and I were lying on our backs and gazing at the night sky. He asked me if Moscow or the moon was closer. Of course, my brothers will never let me forget that I chose the moon because we could see it, not Moscow."

Fancy laughed, his amusing reminiscence tugging at her heart, changing her opinion of the man. She had never realized that aristocrats were people with hopes and fears and families. She had never considered aristocrats were human.

"Who is your father?" Stepan asked without preamble.

Her good humor vanished. "A cold-blooded aristocrat."

Stepan reached across the table and covered her hand with his own. "Your father cared for your mother and his daughters."

"My mother loved him," Fancy said, "and he hurt her."

"What about you?"

She gave him a blank look.

"Did you love him, too?"

"I suppose so, but he rode away one day and never returned."

"Your anger stems from your pain," Stepan ventured. "There are worse—"

"I never missed him," Fancy insisted. "He broke my mother's heart, not mine."

"You are prevaricating."

"Je t'emmerde."

Stepan gave her a crooked smile. "You would need to lift your skirt if you wanted a kiss there."

Fancy blushed a vibrant scarlet. "Do you always seduce women by naming them liars?"

"Seduction is the furthest thing from my mind."

"Who is prevaricating now, Your Highness?" Fancy

sighed, reluctant to ruin the evening by bickering. "My father has been generous with his money but not his love."

Stepan shrugged. "If you say so."

"I do."

"Tomorrow evening we will be attending a ball hosted by the Earl and Countess of Winchester, my sister-in-law's relatives," Stepan told her.

"You may attend," Fancy said by way of a refusal, "but do not count on my presence."

"You will accompany me."

"I won't go where I am not wanted."

"I want you with me."

"I meant, society will frown on my accompanying you."

Stepan grinned. "Darling, I am society and promise not to frown at you all evening."

Fancy could not decide if she should smile or grind her teeth. And then an age-old excuse popped into her mind. "I have nothing appropriate to wear."

"Is that all?" The prince patted her hand. "I will take care of that."

"You will *not* buy me a gown."

"Yes, I will."

"Do you always get your own way?"

"Poor, first-born Fancy." Stepan gave her his most winning smile. "The youngest always gets what he wants."

The tenacity of *three* bulldogs: Fancy amended her earlier opinion. On the other hand, the prince would leave her alone once he witnessed society's snub.

"Very well, Stepan. I will attend the ball with you."

"I never doubted it."

A short time later, the royal coach halted in front of the Flambeau residence in Soho Square. The prince climbed out and then lifted her down.

Fancy hesitated, wondering how to end the evening. "Thank you for a surprisingly enjoyable evening."

"I will walk you to your door." Stepan grasped her hand and led her up the three steps. "Hand me your key, please."

"That is unnecessary."

Stepan cocked a dark brow at her and held his hand out. "Give me the key."

Fancy passed him the key. Once the door had opened, Stepan stepped aside to allow her entrance and then followed her into the foyer.

As he'd done the previous evening, Puddles raced into the foyer and leaped at the prince, pinning him against wall. Stepan laughed as the mastiff licked his face.

"Sit," Fancy ordered.

The black-masked, brindled mastiff obeyed, its tail swishing in a warm welcome.

"Good boy, Puddles." Stepan patted the dog's massive head and turned to Fancy. He planted a kiss on her hand and dropped the key onto her palm. "Good night, mademoiselle. May your dreams be pleasant."

Without another word, Stepan slipped out the door and disappeared into his coach.

He had not kissed her good night.

Fancy sat on the stool in her dressing room the next evening and studied her image in the cracked mirror. Why hadn't he tried to kiss her? What was wrong with her?

She had expected the prince to kiss her—respectfully, of course—when he'd delivered her home the previous evening. Though kissing her hand was romantic in the extreme, she had assumed she would be experiencing her first kiss.

For a notorious rake, the prince was taking his sweet time getting down to business. Unless—?

Fancy cupped the palm of her hand in front of her nose and mouth. She inhaled, exhaled, and sniffed her breath. She couldn't smell anything foul, but tried the experiment again just to be sure.

"What are you doing?"

Fancy whirled around. Genevieve Stover stood there.

She gave the other girl a rueful smile. "Checking the scent of my breath."

"I want to thank you for introducing Alex and me," the blonde said. "He is escorting me home tonight, too."

Fancy was pleased for her newest and oldest friends. And then she thought of her baby sister. Raven nurtured an enormous crush on Alex and would be unhappy.

"I am happy you have found each other," Fancy said. "How was your evening with His Highness?"

"Surprisingly enjoyable. Stepan insists I attend a society ball with him after the opera."

The dressing room door opened, drawing her attention. Director Bishop stepped inside, but a furry creature rushed past him.

Fancy scooped the capuchin monkey onto her lap. "How is Miss Giggles tonight?" The monkey covered its ears and eyes and mouth in turn. "We need to teach you another trick."

Director Bishop lifted the monkey off her lap and passed it to Sebastian Tanner, waiting outside. Then the director beckoned to someone else. A middle-aged woman appeared, followed by two younger women carrying boxes.

"Madame Janette has arrived with tonight's evening attire." The director smirked before leaving. "Isn't that exciting?"

In a flurry of movement, Madame Janette rushed into the room and unwrapped the gown. Created in violet silk, the gown matched Fancy's eye color. The assistants showed her the slippers, stockings, undergarments, shawl, gloves, reticule, and fan.

"Oh, you are the most fortunate of women," Madame Janette gushed. "His Highness has spared no expense on his gift."

"I am certain the prince drops many coins in your shop," Fancy said.

"His Highness has never purchased a gift for another woman in my shop," Madame Janette told her. "He insisted your eyes were Persian violets, and he demanded a shade to accentuate their rare beauty."

"He said all that, did he?"

Madame Janette nodded.

"Thank you very much." Fancy gestured around her, saying, "I am preparing for my performance, as you can see."

Madame Janette and her assistants left. Genevieve gave the gown a longing look and followed them out.

Like a woman standing on the gallows, Fancy could feel the prince's noose tightening around her. She refused to relinquish control of her life and end like her mother, a victim of love.

Apprehension about stepping into society swelled within her, making her hands shake. What would she do if her father was also a guest?

Dwelling on this would ruin her performance. Fancy grabbed her Cherubino hat and headed in the direction of the prima donna's dressing room.

Sebastian Tanner opened the door and looked at her in momentary surprise. Then he stepped aside.

Reluctant to enter, Fancy stood on the threshold and waited for the older woman to acknowledge her. Patrice Tanner turned away from her mirror which, Fancy noted, was larger than her own. No cracks.

"What do you want?" The hatred in the woman's

gaze matched the frost in her tone. "Have you come to see the dressing room you covet?"

"I came to apologize," Fancy said. "My behavior was inexcusable, and I hope you will forgive me."

Patrice Tanner stared at her for uncomfortably long moments, inspecting her from the top of her head to the tips of her shoes. Before turning her back in dismissal, the prima donna said, "I will consider it."

Fancy leveled a deadly look on the woman. *Je t'emmerde,* she thought. *Kiss my arse.*

Chapter 4

Fancy stared at the violet silk gown, insidious insecurity stealing her confidence. After her last song, she had returned to her dressing room to await the opera's ending and ponder her unwelcome reception into society. No one would accept her and, least of all, the prince's family.

She felt trapped.

She felt bought.

She felt the urge to escape.

The world closed around Fancy. Her panic swelled to a sickening proportion, making breathing almost painful. Her hands trembled, and nausea gripped her.

I'm sorry, Nanny Smudge, she thought, *but tonight I need to follow my head.*

Fancy changed into her own gown and grabbed her woolen shawl. She peeked outside the dressing room door to verify no one was lurking near and then hurried away, escaping out the stage door.

Suppressing the urge to run, which would only bring her unwanted attention, Fancy distanced herself from the opera house and prayed no one gave chase. The night's sky was clear and the springtime air chilly, neither of which she noticed.

Once past Covent Garden, the crowds grew thinner and thinner. She reached deserted Queen Street but paused at the corner.

The street was eerily silent. The rose-petal murderer popped into her mind, her senses alert to any unusual noise. Adrenaline pumped through her veins, and her heartbeat quickened. She almost cried out in frightened surprise when a coach materialized beside her and halted.

"Here, girl," a man called. "Do you want to make good money?"

Fancy ignored him and started walking. Unexpectedly, a hand grabbed her wrist and whirled her around.

Dressed like a gentleman, he was tall and well built and passably handsome. He reeked of gin.

"What's your hurry, girl?"

"Release me, villain."

He laughed. "Say, aren't you that—"

Fancy tried to yank her hand away, but his superior strength held her immobile. She kicked out, aiming for his groin, but fell when he sidestepped to elude her.

"You'd better come with me." The man started to pull her toward his coach, ignoring her shouted protests.

"Release the lass."

Fancy heard another voice and saw two newcomers standing there.

"Eddie, ye dinna need to drag lassies off the street," the second man said.

Her captor released her as suddenly as he'd grabbed her. He climbed into his coach and fled the scene, leaving her alone with her rescuers.

"Are ye all right, lass?" the first one asked.

His friend helped her off the ground. "Ye shouldna be walkin' aboot at night."

"I'm Douglas Gordon, the Marquess of Huntly," the first man introduced himself.

"And I'm his cousin, Ross MacArthur, the Marquess of Awe," the second man added.

"We canna allow ye to walk home alone," Douglas Gordon said.

Ross MacArthur agreed. "Ye'll need to come with us, lass." He held his hand out to her.

"No, thank you, my lords." Fancy shook her head. "I will be fine now."

Douglas Gordon spoke up. "Our consciences will bother us if we let ye walk aboot alone."

"Aye, 'tis dangerous," his cousin said. "Ye dinna need to fear us, lass."

"Miss Flambeau belongs to me."

Fancy whirled around at the sound of the prince's voice and, breaking free, flew into his arms. Relief surged through her body, weakening her, and she clung to him as if she would never let him go.

Thank God, he had come looking for her. There were worse things in life than stepping into society.

Stepan folded his arms around her. "Are you injured?"

Fancy shook her head.

"Ross and I rescued her from Crazy Eddie," Douglas Gordon said. "Ye shouldna be so careless with yer possessions, Kazanov."

MacArthur nodded. "Aye, Crazy Eddie was draggin' her into his coach when we happened by."

Stepan inclined his head. "I thank you for your assistance."

"Yer a verra bonny lass," Douglas said, looking at Fancy. "Do ye have any sisters?"

"Six."

The Scotsmen looked at each other and laughed.

"Yer da shoulda done the deed with his boots on," Ross said.

Douglas Gordon nodded in agreement. "Aye, that'll turn the trick every time."

With that, the Scotsmen climbed into their coach and continued on their way.

His expression grim, Stepan looked down at her lovely, pale face. "What am I going to do with you, mademoiselle?"

Fancy gazed at him through her enormous violet eyes. "Kiss me . . ."

Stepan obliged her.

Fancy closed her eyes, savoring his sandalwood scent. She felt his heartbeat, his heat, his unyielding strength.

"I have waited forever for this," Stepan whispered, his lips a hairsbreadth from hers.

And then their lips touched, meeting in a gentle first kiss. His lips were warm and firm, undemanding but masterful, stealing all rational thought.

Stepan caressed her back and the nape of her neck, eliciting her sigh. And then he changed the tempo of the kiss, moving his mouth on hers, encouraging her to follow his lead.

Wrapped in his arms, Fancy was powerless against his irresistible invitation. A melting sensation spread throughout her lower regions, inciting her to return his ardor.

Their kiss was long and langorous, the prince capturing her whole being. The world faded away. His body and his lips became her universe.

Stepan flicked his tongue across the crease of her lips, persuading her surrender, staking his claim. She parted her lips, and he slipped his tongue inside her mouth to taste her sweetness.

And then he ended the kiss.

Stepan traced one long finger down her petal-soft cheek. Fancy stared at him in a daze, having had the most erotic experience of her life . . . *her first kiss.*

Stepan held her against his body, and she rested her head against his chest.

"I-I was frightened."

"You are safe now." Stepan looked down at her. "Trust me?"

Fancy stared into his black eyes. The corners of her mouth turned up in a faint smile, and she nodded.

Keeping his arm around her shoulders, Stepan guided her toward his coach but noted her wobbly walking. "Are you injured?"

"My legs are shaking like an earthquake."

"You did experience a frightening misadventure."

"My nerves are running riot from your kiss."

Stepan helped her into the coach and sat beside her. "Miss Flambeau, you should use more coyness in your dealings with the opposite sex. A woman should never give her suitor the advantage of complimenting his kisses."

"Why not?"

"Burgeoning conceit would give the fellow a fat head."

Fancy waved her hand, dismissing that particular problem. "No matter, you already have a fat head."

Stepan grinned. "I appreciate your keeping me humble."

"Soho lies in the other direction. Where are you taking me?"

"My home."

Fancy shook her head. "I refuse—"

"I will feed you supper," Stepan interrupted, "and then we will discuss your actions this evening. Nothing more, I promise."

Ten minutes later, the royal coach halted in front of a

mansion in exclusive Grosvenor Square. Stepan climbed out first, helped her down, and called to his driver, "Harry, I will be going out again in an hour or so."

An unfamiliar pang of jealousy shot through Fancy, but she tried to keep her tone casually unconcerned. "Where are you going after supper?"

Stepan took her hand and led her up the stairs. "I plan to escort you home."

Her face warmed with embarrassment. Thankfully, the night hid her blush.

The front door opened, revealing a tall, dignified, middle-aged man, who stepped aside. The man flicked her a curious glance and murmured, "Good evening, Your Highness."

"Though he gives himself airs, Bones is my opinionated majordomo." Stepan winked at her. "Bones has the most amusing dry wit."

"Better dry than scattered," Bones said, the corners of his mouth twitching with good humor.

Fancy decided she liked the older man. He wasn't the least bit snooty as she would have expected.

"Tell Feliks I want *zakooska* and vodka served in the drawing room."

"Yes, Your Highness." The majordomo disappeared down the corridor.

Fancy flicked a measuring glance around the reception foyer, which was larger than her dining room. The floor was marble, and a graceful staircase twisted to the upper floor.

Stepan gestured toward the stairs. "Shall we?"

Shades of blue with white trimming colored the second-floor drawing room. A Persian carpet covered the floor. Its blue, cream, and gold complemented the various hues of blue throughout the chamber. Oversized sofas and wingbacked chairs sat in small clusters, old friends gathering for a bit of gossip. A round oak table stood in the center of the drawing room, and upon it perched a huge vase of lilacs.

"Did you grow those?"

"We Russians believe lilacs are Heaven's first gift of the year because they signify deliverance from a harsh winter." Stepan led her to the sofa in front of the black marble hearth.

Sitting in the prince's drawing room made Fancy uncomfortable. She had never ventured inside a man's home, and her virtue had been guarded as diligently as that of any society debutante.

Appearances meant everything. Society believed that sitting alone in the prince's home was as immoral as lying in his bed. Her reputation would be ruined if anyone discovered her presence here.

"Relax." Stepan reached over and patted her hand. "Did you apologize to Patrice Tanner?"

"I wasted my time."

"What did she say?"

"Patrice asked if I'd come to see the dressing room I coveted." Fancy gave him a disgruntled look. "I noticed her mirror is much larger than mine and crackless."

Stepan smiled at that. "I am proud of your apology," he said, "but I thought the person receiving the apology was required to accept it."

His puzzlement surprised her. "Your Highness, have you ever apologized to anyone?"

"Hmmm . . ." The prince stared into space for long moments before answering. "I do not believe so. At least, I cannot recall any apologies."

Fancy smiled at his admission, and he returned her smile. She knew he had no idea what was amusing her.

Bones and two men of gigantic proportions marched into the drawing room. All three carried trays, which they set on the table near the sofa. One tray held a bottle of clear liquid, two tiny glasses, and plates with silverware. The other two trays contained bite-sized morsels of food, none of which Fancy had ever seen before, except the bread, cheese, and sausage.

"Thank you, Bones. We will serve ourselves."

"Ahem . . ." One of the men cleared his throat, drawing the prince's attention.

"Fancy, I present Feliks, my chef, who traveled from Russia." Stepan introduced them, and then gestured to the larger of the two. "And this is Boris, Feliks's brother, my sometime bodyguard."

"I am pleased to meet you." Fancy gave both burly Russians a polite smile.

Feliks grinned. "Prince say you sweet songbird, huh?"

Stepan chuckled at her blush. "Miss Flambeau does sing at the opera."

Boris spoke up then. *"Krusseevy dyevuchka."*

"He said 'beautiful girl,'" Stepan whispered, leaning close. "Tell him *spasseeba*, thank you."

"Spasseeba, Boris."

The big Russian grinned at her and nodded. "You good pronounce." Then he followed Feliks and Bones out of the room.

"How difficult life in England must be for Feliks and Boris." When he raised his brows, Fancy added, "I mean, their lack of English limits communication."

Stepan burst into laughter. "After living in London for five years, Feliks and Boris speak English very well. They pretend otherwise when it suits them. Which allows them to eavesdrop on gossip."

"This is vodka." Stepan poured the clear liquid into the tiny glasses. "The food is *zakooska*."

"What does that mean?"

"It means—" The prince shrugged. "Vodka means vodka, and *zakooska* means *zakooska*." He passed her a glass, instructing her, "Do not sip the vodka. Gulp it down in one swallow."

She lifted the tiny glass to her lips, but the prince stopped her. He passed her a wedge of Swiss cheese. "Eat this after you gulp the vodka."

Fancy drank the vodka in one swig, and then regretted it. She coughed and wheezed, the liquid fire stealing her breath and burning a path to her stomach.

"Eat the cheese."

Eat the damn cheese?

Fancy looked at the smiling prince through vision blurred by tears of distress. The coughing and wheezing ceased, but the fire inside left her gasping.

"The vodka does not agree with you." Stepan patted her back solicitously until her gaze cleared and he recognized the murderous glint in her eyes. "Are you hungry?"

Her violet gaze narrowed on him. "Dead women do not eat."

"I apologize for failing to warn you about the vodka's strength." Stepan gave her his most charming smile. "I make amends by giving you the first apology of my life."

Fancy giggled, the vodka relaxing her mood. "I am honored to be the distinguished recipient of your first apology, Your Highness, and will cherish this noble gesture forever."

Stepan spooned pate on a small piece of brown bread and lifted it to her lips. She took a bite of the unknown food.

"Do you like it?"

"Delicious." She ate the remainder of the pate and bread. "What is it?"

"Caviar."

Fancy gave him a blank look. "I don't understand."

"Sturgeon roe."

She arched her brow at him.

"Fish eggs in ovaries."

Her hand flew to her throat as she fought the nausea down. "Do not eat that," she ordered, her gaze on his hand.

Stepan set the pate and bread on his plate. "Caviar is a delicacy." He stared at her a long moment and then asked, "Will you try the jellied eels?"

Her appalled expression was his answer.

"Do you mind if *I* eat the jellied eels?"

She curled her lip at him.

"The salted herring comes from Scotland."

"I misplaced my appetite at the"—Fancy hesitated— "sturgeon roe. I believe now would be the appropriate time for our discussion."

Stepan took her hand in his and waited until she met his black gaze. "Why did you run away tonight?"

I felt trapped.

And bought.

And feared being victimized like my mother.

Her gaze skittered away from his. Those dark eyes seemed to see into her soul and knew her insecurities.

Fancy lifted her chin a notch, proud though she would not look at him. "I would prefer to walk naked down the street than wear a gown purchased by a man other than my husband."

"I would prefer that you walk around naked, too."

She snapped her gaze to his. The prince wore the most wolfish, irreverent grin.

"The problem is I pushed you too soon, not the gown." Stepan cupped her chin. "Whenever you are ready to join me in society, so will I be ready to escort you."

Her heart ached at his unexpected gentility and understanding. She could not, would not, dare not love him. If only—

"Why are you doing this?"

"I am courting my sweet songbird." He kissed her hand. "I forbid you to walk home alone from the theater. Boris will guard you when I cannot be there. That is not negotiable."

Fancy relented, grateful for his concern. "Very well, I will allow Boris to escort me home when necessary."

"Good. Now I will take you home." Stepan offered her his hand. "Do not forget our picnic tomorrow."

"I don't think my sisters will eat caviar or jellied eels."

"I promise, no eels or caviar."

Fifteen minutes later, Stepan climbed out of his coach in front of her home in Soho Square. He helped her down and escorted her to the door.

"Look." Stepan scooped the bouquet someone had placed on her doorstep. "An admirer left you flowers. The pink and white with dark green leaves are oleander, and the reddish, bell-shaped flowers are belladonna." He gave her a worried look. "In the language of flowers, oleander and belladonna mean *beware death.*"

No bigger than an alley, Crown Passage linked King Street and Pall Mall, two of London's busiest thoroughfares. Several shops called the passageway home, as did the French Doves, an unassuming but popular pub for an after-theater supper.

Alexander Blake relaxed in his chair and lazily admired Genevieve Stover's angelic face. The blond opera singer enchanted him, and he counted himself lucky to have been at the Royal Opera House the evening she required an escort home. If he'd attended opening night, he never would have met her.

"So, you really don't mind that Fancy won the role you coveted?"

Genevieve shrugged. "I mind, of course, but Fancy has a powerful voice. I guarantee she will go far in her career."

The waiter served their meals. Sausage and potato for him, baked fish steak with vegetable for her.

"Working with Constable Black must be exciting," Genevieve remarked.

"Contrary to popular belief, a constable leads a boring daily life." Alexander smiled. "The exciting moments come few and far between."

Genevieve leaned close and lowered her voice to a whisper. "Do you think you will capture the rose-petal murderer?"

"I promise we will catch him eventually." Seizing the opportunity to comfort and touch, Alexander reached across the table and covered her hand with his own. "You have nothing to fear if you keep alert."

"How does he kill them?"

"I will not discuss that, but the women don't look as if they've suffered."

"Tell me, how well acquainted are you and Fancy?"

Alexander knew she was interested in him and digging for details of his life. No matter their circumstance, all women possessed certain habits. Digging for details was one of them.

"Fancy and I are almost brother and sister." Alexander noted that detail seemed to relax her. "We have been neighbors our entire lives. Tell me about Genevieve Stover."

"When my parents died," Genevieve said, "my brother and I inherited my house on Compton Street. He moved to another house when he married, and I rent rooms to dancers and actresses. That man over there is staring at us."

Alexander looked across the pub. The well-dressed man worked for his grandfather, and the knowledge that his grandfather was monitoring his activities irritated him.

"Do you know him?"

Alexander shook his head, feigning unconcern. "He must recognize you from the opera. Do you have any free time for me tomorrow?"

Genevieve's smile could have lit the whole pub. "Tomorrow is Sunday, no opera. I will come to your house and cook you lunch."

"I would like that." Alexander mentally rubbed his hands together. A woman offering to cook was definitely interested. He could hardly believe his luck. Beautiful opera singers were usually looking for wealthy protectors, but Genevieve wanted him.

A short time later, Alexander and Genevieve faced each other in front of her Compton Street home. Ever so gently, he touched his lips to hers.

"Good evening, Genevieve."

They broke apart, almost guilty, when another person spoke.

Dressed in red, one of the ballet dancers flounced past them as a coach halted. The coachman climbed down, helped the sultry brunette inside, and returned to his perch.

"That was Phoebe," Genevieve said. "She lost her lover, Lord Parkhurst, and is prowling for another."

Alexander planted another kiss on her lips, murmuring, "Until tomorrow . . ."

Humming a spritely tune, Alexander reached Soho Square fifteen minutes later. He started up his front stairs and stopped short when he spied the person sitting there.

"Where the bloody blue blazes have you been? I've been waiting forever."

Long-legged, blond, and sweet clashed with petite,

ebony-haired, and smart-mouthed. The comparison showed Raven Flambeau in a less than flattering light.

"I need to speak with you." Raven gazed into what she considered the handsomest face in London. "It's urgent."

"Come inside, then." He turned his back to unlock the door.

Raven had sat near her window for hours waiting for him to come home. She knew she could help him with the rose-petal case. Working together would bring them closer, and Alex would notice that she'd grown into a woman. Then he would love her as she loved him.

Alexander lit a night candle, poured himself a dram of whiskey, and gulped it. He faced her, his gaze dropping to her scantily clad body, and then set the glass on the mantel.

Raven smothered a smile. She had purposely dropped her shawl to let him see she was no longer a child. Her gauzy nightgown left nothing to the imagination, and she watched his gaze fix on her breasts and thrusting nipples.

Grabbing the woolen shawl, Alexander wrapped it around her and stepped back several paces. "Tell me what is so urgent, brat."

Brat. That one word told Raven their conversation was starting off on the wrong foot, but she determined to persevere and see her way through.

"I can help you with the rose-petal case," Raven said, dismayed when she heard him chuckle. "I-I had a vision tonight."

"*A vision?*"

"I saw someone sewing what should not be sewn and—"

Alexander pressed one long finger across her lips. "I appreciate your concern, brat, but I cannot go to

Amadeus Black and tell him the case is solved because my slightly daft neighbor had a vision."

"I am not daft," Raven insisted, frustration and irritation mingling within her. "I would never let you down . . . *I love you.*"

Alexander stared at her for long moments, stunned by her declaration. How was he supposed to handle this without hurting her? This Flambeau was everyone's baby sister.

"You don't love me, not as a woman loves a man." He ran his hand through his hair in frustration. "Sweetheart, sixteen is much too—"

Wham! The force of her slap jerked his head back.

"Do *not* tell me what I feel, you arrogant son of a—" His whiskey glass jumped off the mantel and shattered into tiny pieces, drawing his attention. Whirling away, Raven stormed out the door.

"Loves me, loves me not . . ."

The tall gentleman, dressed in formal evening attire, stood beside the Thames River. Here the river's stench assailed his nose and permeated his skin, but he gave no attention to his discomfort.

The gentleman stared at the woman, so lovely in death, giving proof of her peaceful passing. He clutched a handful of rose petals and sprinkled them one by one down the length of her body.

"Are you coming?"

The gentleman turned his head to look at the woman waiting in his coach. "Hardly," he drawled, and scooped another handful of rose petals from his pouch.

"Loves me, loves me not . . ."

Chapter 5

Blue sky, brilliant sunshine, unseasonably warm.

The unusual spring weather combined with the usual Sunday morning peacefulness to create a day that lifted the spirit and made a body glad to be alive. Only two things marred the day's perfection: the smell of low tide and the dead woman covered with rose petals.

Alexander Blake strode toward the two men deep in conversation. He had expected Amadeus Black, but Prosecutor Lowing was an unpleasant surprise. Barney, the constable's aide, was searching the grounds like a mother looking for nits on her child's head.

"Lose one ballet dancer, and another arrives in London," Lowing said. "Only women of dubious virtue need fear the rose-petal murderer. Too bad the populace is so frightened."

The prosecutor sounded like his grandfather. Alexander shot him a look of contempt, disgusted by the man's judging the seriousness of a crime by the victim's station in life. He approached the body, and his mouth dropped open in surprise.

The dead woman, dressed in red, was the sultry

brunette he'd seen the previous evening outside Genevieve's house. She did not appear sultry now.

"I know this woman." Alexander returned to the constable's side. "I saw her last night."

"I'll vouch for your innocence." Prosecutor Lowing chuckled at his own joke. When no one laughed, he added, "I'm surprised your grandfather allows that sort of association."

Alexander ignored him. "Phoebe rents a room in a friend's house."

"Rent*ed*," the prosecutor corrected him.

"Who is this friend?" Amadeus Black asked.

"Genevieve Stover sings in the opera."

"*Humph.* Opera singers are much the same as ballet dancers," Lowing said.

Both men ignored the prosecutor.

"Now I understand the reason witnesses are difficult to find," Alexander said, running his fingers through his hair in frustration. "I watched the victim climb into a coach and ride to her death, but could not tell you who sat inside or even recognize the coach if I saw it again."

Amadeus Black put a hand on his shoulder. "No one expects to witness a crime, and even the best of us cannot remain alert to details every hour of the day."

Barney approached and handed the constable a ring. "I found this over there. It could mean nothing but—" He shrugged.

The ring was heavy and gold, a style appropriate to either man or woman. A scrolled *P* was engraved on the top.

"What do you think?" Prosecutor Lowing asked.

Amadeus Black looked at Alexander. "Would you ask your lady friend if Phoebe owned a gold ring initialed with a *P*?"

He nodded. "Genevieve told me that Phoebe's former lover is Lord Parkhurst."

"A couple connected by the letter *P*," the constable murmured. "One is the victim. Could the other be the perpetrator?"

"I will question Lord Parkhurst," Prosecutor Lowing announced.

Clearly irritated, Amadeus Black turned on the prosecutor. "You will question no one unless I am present, and Parkhurst will not be questioned until Alex asks his friend about the ring." He looked at Alexander. "No one touched the body. Examine it."

Alexander approached the body again and walked around it slowly. No apparent bruises or bleeding. Bloodless slashing across one cheek. Serene expression indicating a painless passing. Whole roses positioned in each ear.

Crouching down, Alexander leaned close to the victim's face. The eyelids and lips had been sewn shut, the same as the other victims.

I saw someone sewing what should not be sewn. Raven Flambeau's words popped into his mind, startling him.

Had the brat actually experienced a vision? Which would prove nothing since visions did not constitute evidence in court. Perhaps she could describe the person sewing what should not be sewn. Assuming, of course, the brat would speak to him after last night.

"What do you see?" the constable asked.

"The perpetrator left us the same calling card."

"How do you think she died?"

Alexander lifted his gaze from the victim's face to Amadeus Black. "A gentle poisoning."

Needing to clear the sight of the murdered ballet dancer from his mind, if only for a little while, Alexander refused a ride to Compton Street and decided to walk instead. Compton Street was located a goodly distance from Tower Hill, but the journey was a direct walk from Byward and Cannon Streets, past St. Paul's to Fleet Street, the Strand, and Charing Cross Road.

Alexander felt a heightened sense of urgency to find the murderer. The latest victim had hit much too close to home. Now he had the unenviable task of giving Genevieve the bad news. Dread sprung to life in the pit of his stomach, growing more pronounced the closer he got to Compton Street.

Genevieve was pure sweetness, amazing in view of her career. Most dancers, singers, and actresses were little better than prostitutes, although the only ones he knew personally were Fancy and Genevieve. Both women were of good character; perhaps the bad reputations were undeserved.

The unwelcome image of a headstrong, ebony-haired smart mouth popped into his mind's eye. Damn Raven Flambeau, her vision, and that flimsy nightgown.

Passing Covent Garden, Alexander vetoed the thought of purchasing Genevieve a bouquet. The beautiful brunette covered in rose petals was too vivid in his mind, and he doubted he would ever again consider flowers a suitable gift for a woman.

The image of every man's ideal maiden, Genevieve wore a petal pink gown with matching shawl. Her blond hair cascaded loosely around her, and her blue eyes sparkled with anticipation.

"Good morning." She greeted him with a smile. "Everyone is still sleeping."

Alexander dreaded stealing the smile from her sweet expression. "May I come inside? We must speak confidentially."

Genevieve stepped aside, allowing him entrance, and led the way into the parlor. "This sounds mysterious."

"Sit, please."

"Why?" He heard the fear in her voice.

"Please do as I ask." When she sat on the settee, Alexander knelt in front of her and held her hands. "Last night, Phoebe fell prey to the rose-petal murderer."

"What?" Stunned surprise drained the color from her face. Tears welled in her eyes and streamed down her cheeks. Her hands shook in his.

Alexander brushed her tears aside. "I must ask you a few questions."

Genevieve nodded once.

"Whose coach did Phoebe climb into last night?"

"I don't know."

"Did Lord Parkhurst end the affair or Phoebe?"

"I suppose Lord Parkhurst since Phoebe was looking for another protector."

"Did Phoebe ever tell you who ended the affair?"

Genevieve shook her head. "I'm sorry."

"You cannot tell me what you don't know." Alexander patted her hand. "Did Phoebe own a gold ring initialed with a *P*?"

"I never noticed one."

"I want your promise never to walk alone at night," Alexander said, "and I will escort you home from the opera."

Her voice was barely louder than a whisper. "I promise."

Alexander kissed the palm of each hand and then stood. "Shall we go?"

"I feel guilty about—"

He pressed a finger to her lips. "Life does not stop for death."

"May we visit a chapel along the way and pray for Phoebe?"

"Of course."

Genevieve gave him a faint smile. "What would you like for lunch?"

"*You.*"

* * *

Huh, huh, huh. Hot air tickled his cheek and neck.

Stepan shifted his black gaze to the seat beside him. The mastiff had rested its head on his shoulder, panting with its tongue hanging out on one side of its muzzle.

Hearing smothered giggles from the opposite seat, Stepan knew the opera singer had purposely sat beside her sister and left him to share the ride with the dog. He put his arm around the mastiff, saying, "We men should stick together."

Fancy and Raven burst into laughter. Stepan looked at them and smiled at his own wit.

"Why am I required to sit with Puddles?"

Fancy gave him a flirtatious smile. "I wanted to admire your handsome face."

He wagged his finger at her. "You are prevaricating, *ma petite*. We could have put Puddles in the coach with the twins."

"My sisters would have been crowded," Fancy said. "Why are Feliks and Boris driving us?"

"Harry takes Sunday as his free day." Stepan scratched the mastiff's neck. "I regret Belle could not join us."

"Baron Wingate was taking her to meet his mother."

"I have a bad feeling about that," Raven interjected.

Fancy rounded on her sister. "You don't like the baron either?"

Stepan spoke, drawing their attention. "You should not disparage a man who could become your brother-in-law."

"Baron Wingate will never marry Belle," Raven said.

"Are you certain?" Fancy asked, concern for her sister etched across her face.

Raven nodded.

"You do not have faith in your sister?" Stepan asked.

"I have faith in Belle, not Baron Wingate," Raven answered.

Stepan shifted his gaze to the opera singer and admitted, "I have never liked the baron."

Fancy leaped on that statement. "Why don't you like him?"

"The few times I met him, Baron Wingate seemed too concerned with appearances," Stepan answered. "He fawned over gentlemen wealthier than he and disdained others who were not. Technically, the baron is the head of the Wingate family but ruled by his mother, a sour woman."

"Where did you meet the baron and his mother?" Fancy asked.

"I attended a recent ball hosted by Lady Drummond," Stepan answered.

"How recently?"

Stepan looked at the singer for a long moment, a smile flirting with the corners of his lips. She sounded a bit jealous, which meant she was beginning to care for him.

"Lady Drummond's ball was three weeks ago." Stepan decided in the next instant that he needed to speak honestly and prepare them for an unhappy sister at home. "Baron Wingate was escorting not only his mother but the baroness's bosom friend, Lady Clarke, and her unmarried daughter, Cynthia."

"That means nothing." Fancy dismissed what he'd said with a wave of her hand. "Belle is the most beautiful woman in London. Why would he want anyone else?"

Stepan cocked a dark brow at her. "After I had danced with Lady Cynthia, the baroness warned me off from the chit, saying she hoped to make a match between Charles and Cynthia. Overhearing this, Lady Clarke told me she was not quite settled on the matter. I believe she would prefer a princess in the Clarke family to a baroness."

"And what do you prefer?" Her expression was stiff and her voice cold.

"I prefer death to marriage with Cynthia Clarke." That brought the smile back to her face. He looked at her youngest sister. "Fancy told me you move objects with your mind. Would you demonstrate for me?"

Raven appeared stunned. She glanced at her oldest sister and then demurred, explaining, "I need the correct emotional state to do that."

Was the prince teasing or tormenting her? Fancy wondered. She had revealed those secrets only to discourage him but now regretted that. She wanted him to think highly of her family and consider them normal.

When had she changed her mind about him? Fancy had no idea, but she wanted him to like her.

Chiswick, their destination, lay along the Thames River an hour's coach ride from London.

Disembarking the coaches, the five younger Flambeaus and Puddles walked to the grassy riverbank. Fancy walked beside Stepan while Boris and Feliks followed with the picnic paraphernalia.

The air seemed cleaner here, no noxious odors to bother them. Birdsong serenaded them, and water lapping the shoreline relaxed them. Wildflowers grew everywhere—blue and white comfrey, palish yellow wild arum, violet cuckoo flowers, white Queen Anne's lace. Like gossiping goodwives, willow trees stood together along the riverbank.

After spreading several blankets, Stepan unpacked the food from the wicker hamper. There were egg and cucumber sandwiches, cold chicken, and lemon cookies.

"Aha, I believe I see a delicacy." Stepan glanced at Fancy and produced a small platter of brown bread and caviar. He spread the caviar pate on the piece of brown bread and popped it into his mouth.

"Do not try to kiss me until you wash your mouth," Fancy drawled.

"Is that an invitation?" he asked.

"No."

"What are you eating?" asked Blaze.

Fancy's tongue was faster than his. "His Highness is eating caviar, which is fish eggs in ovaries."

"Yuck, yuck, yuck." Blaze looked suitably revolted.

Stepan spread the caviar pate on another piece of brown bread and directed his teasing toward the sister. "Fancy tells me you communicate with animals. What is Puddles thinking?"

Blaze gave him a sweet smile. "Puddles thinks he would love to taste the caviar."

At that precise moment, the mastiff stole the bread and pate out of the prince's hand. Everyone, including the prince and his men, laughed.

"Your dappled gray caught a pebble in his shoe," Blaze said conversationally.

Stepan gestured for his man to check the horse. Boris lifted the horse's hoof and picked a pebble out, shooting the prince a surprised look.

Damn, damn, damn, Fancy thought. Now she and her family appeared abnormal.

She touched the prince's arm and sent him an unconsciously pleading look. "We are normal young women, not freakish."

"I assumed the tales of your sisters were meant to discourage me."

"Your assumption was wrong."

"I think not." His smile mocked her. "If you prevaricate, sweeting, your nose will grow."

Fancy said nothing. What could she say? She knew that he knew, and she had never been a good liar.

"I adore nature's colors," Sophia said, breaking the silence.

"Ah, the painter speaks." Stepan gestured to the wildflowers. "In Russia, we believe when a flower's color catches your attention, its fairy is greeting you."

Sophia smiled. "What a lovely thought."

His remark surprised Fancy. In fact, the prince had been a constant source of surprise over the past few days. He did not sound like a notorious rake. Unless that was his ploy.

"I am in a good mood," Serena said, "and this weather is perfection."

"Fancy tells me you enjoy singing, flute playing, and the wind."

"I love nature, especially trees, who love us unconditionally."

"Trees love us?"

"Come with me." Serena led him beneath one of the willow's branches and positioned him with his back against its trunk. "Close your eyes and feel the willow's love and power." When a breeze swished a sweeping branch across his hand, she added, "The willow said hello."

"Be careful the willow doesn't wrap its branches around your neck," Fancy teased him.

Stepan walked toward the opera singer. "I would prefer your branches wrapped around me."

Fancy blushed, her sisters giggling in the background. Ah, that sounded more like the notorious rake.

Stepan caught Bliss's attention and gestured to Fancy. "Touch her and tell me what she is feeling."

Fancy rolled her eyes at their foolishness, but held her arm out to her sister, who told the prince, "She is annoyed by your ridiculing her."

"I beg your pardon, mademoiselle." Stepan grabbed the singer's hand and gently pulled her to her feet. "Dance with me."

"Your Highness—"

"Sometimes my nieces' tea parties are magically

transformed into gala balls. Put your feet on top of mine, and I will demonstrate the way we waltz."

When she did as told, Stepan whirled her around and around in a silent waltz. Her sisters giggling in the background cracked the wall of her irritated reserve.

Fancy laughed, too. "This reminds me of when Papa—" She stopped speaking abruptly, catching herself before she revealed anything too painful.

Stepan lifted her chin and waited until her gaze met his. "What would your papa do?"

Fancy shrugged, unable to mask the anguish clouding her eyes. "What's done is past."

"Belle needs us," Raven said, her voice sounding loud in the silence. "We need to go home."

Fancy heard the beginning panic in her sister's voice. "Damn Baron Wingate."

Slightly less than an hour later, the Kazanov coaches reached Soho Square and halted in front of the Flambeau residence. Without waiting for the prince, Fancy leaped out and ran up the three front stairs. Stepan and Raven were two steps behind, followed by the remaining four sisters.

Fancy stopped short.

Bleeding a river, Belle lay on the foyer floor. Her face had been slashed from beneath her cheekbone to the corner of her mouth.

Stepan looked at Fancy and knew she would be useless. He gestured the others back and knelt beside her sister.

The prince dropped his voice to a soothing tone. "Relax, Belle, we will take care of you and make everything right again."

Stepan began issuing orders like a general to his troops. "Sophia, fetch blankets from the coach. Serena, bring linens. Bliss, boil the thinnest thread and needle you can find. Raven, we need whiskey. Blaze, run next door to the constable's apprentice and tell him what happened." He shifted his gaze to Fancy, staring as if she'd never seen him before, and hoped he would not be hampered by a second patient.

"How did you know?" Belle asked.

Fancy knelt beside her sister and held her hand. "Raven felt you needed us."

"Cover the sofa with the blanket." Stepan leaned close to Belle, saying, "I will carry you to the sofa, and someone will stitch your face."

Gingerly, Stepan lifted her into his arms and set her down on the sofa. Taking a linen from Serena, he covered the slashed cheek. "Fancy, keep this pressed to her cheek until we are ready."

Raven returned with a bottle of whiskey.

"When I lift your shoulders and head," Stepan instructed Belle, "take a big gulp of whiskey."

Belle gulped the whiskey and coughed.

"Good job. Take another. And another."

Fancy watched the prince in action. She could hardly believe that he was an aristocratic rake. He appeared more physician than rogue.

Belle managed ten healthy swigs of whisky, complete with coughing and wheezing. The whiskey seemed to relax her for what would come next.

"Your beautiful face," Fancy moaned, tears streaming down her cheeks. "You will carry a scar."

"Fancy." She heard the prince's warning tone and clamped her lips together.

Stepan leaned close to the injured girl's ear to whisper, "Shall Fancy stitch you?"

"No! Fancy is the worst seamstress in London," Belle said, making him smile. "Raven makes the smallest stitches."

Fancy turned to Raven. Her youngest sister had paled to a deathly white.

"Raven, wash your hands," Stepan ordered. "Belle, will you trust me to get you through this?"

She looked at him through violet eyes that resembled her sister's. "Yes, Your Highness."

Stepan nodded. "Fancy, stand behind the armrest and—"

"Why?"

"Do not argue. Do it."

When the singer positioned herself behind her sister's head, the prince instructed her, "Place the palms of your hands on either side of her head to keep her steady."

"You're much stronger, wouldn't—"

"Do as I say."

Seething but obedient, Fancy did as she had been told. "How is this, Your Highness?" Her voice oozed sarcasm.

Stepan flicked her a cool glance. "This is about Belle, not you."

Fancy reddened at his rebuke, knowing he was right. "Sister, I am sorry."

"Hearing you take orders is almost worth the injury," Belle whispered.

Stepan smiled at that. Apparently, his little opera singer considered herself the boss of her family. She would need to get over that fast.

"Raven, thread the needle and kneel here," Stepan said. "I will nod when she is ready."

His voice low and soothing, Stepan began whispering in Belle's ear. "Close your eyes, and let your muscles loosen. Take a deep breath and exhale. Inhale and exhale. Inhale and exhale.

"Inside your mind, picture a staircase with ten steps leading to a closed door. Do you see it?"

"Yes."

"Climb onto the bottom step, Belle, and feel your

muscles relaxing. Ten, nine, eight, seven, six, five, four, three, two, one. Your legs feel heavy but you can move to the second step."

Stepan guided Belle up the imaginary staircase. "Open the door and walk inside. Tell me what lies beyond the door."

"I see a lush, green woodland," Belle whispered. "I hear the distant sound of gurgling water and smell the perfume of many flowers. Sunshine peeks through the holes between the trees."

"Walk toward the water sounds, and tell me what you see."

"Water is falling into a clear pool," Belle whispered. "Lily pads float on top of the water, a carpet of grass tickles my feet, sunshine warms my face."

"Lie on the grass bed and listen to the rhythmic water noises." Stepan looked at Raven and nodded.

Paler than the walking dead, Raven lifted the blood-soaked linen and, using a fresh cloth, cleaned the wound. Then she raised the threaded needle toward her sister's face.

Fancy snapped her eyes shut against the sight of flesh being sewn. She felt a tiny jerk of her sister's head and knew the sewing had begun.

Holding the injured girl's hand, Stepan kept his lips pressed against her ear. His tone and his words soothed her, inviting relaxation.

Fancy sensed when the stitching had ended and opened her eyes. With droplets of sweat streaming from the crown of her head down her face and neck, Raven looked worse than Belle, whose expression was surprisingly placid.

"There you are," Bliss was greeting someone. "And who is this?"

Fancy saw Alexander and Genevieve standing in the doorway. His gaze had fixed on Raven. She didn't need to see her sister's expression to know how hurt Raven would be.

"Genevieve is a special friend," Alexander introduced her. "She sings in the opera, too."

"Get me a mirror," Belle said.

Fancy vetoed that. "No peeking in mirrors for a few weeks."

"Time will ease its raw appearance," Raven assured her.

"Is she well enough to answer questions?" Alexander asked.

Fancy glanced at Stepan, who nodded. He stood to let the budding constable take his place.

"Tell me what happened."

"I unlocked the door and bid good-bye to Charles," Belle said. "Someone inside the house grabbed me from behind and cut my cheek. His hand covering my mouth prevented me from screaming."

"Was the hand a man's or woman's?"

"A man, I think."

"Did he . . . did he touch you anywhere private?"

"No."

Alexander looked around at the Flambeaus. "Is anything of value missing?"

All the sisters shook their heads.

Which meant someone had targeted her sister, Fancy decided. "How did Baron Wingate's mother receive you?"

"The baroness was gracious and kind. So was his brother."

"You never mentioned him before."

"George doesn't get around easily," Belle explained. "He walks with a cane."

Fancy could not credit the baroness with being gracious and kind to a duke's illegitimate offspring. That did not mesh with what the prince had told them.

"Tomorrow, write down everything you remember," Alexander told Belle. "No detail is too small."

"I would retire now."

Stepan stepped forward. "I will carry you upstairs."

"No, thank you, Your Highness. I prefer to walk upstairs on my own."

Stepan gestured to the twins. "Your sisters will help you."

Belle sat up slowly and, with the prince's assistance, rose from the sofa. She left the parlor, a set of twins on each side of her.

Raven turned to follow them out. "If you will excuse me."

"You will remain here." Alexander looked at Genevieve. "Return to my house, and I'll join you shortly."

"What are you thinking?" Fancy asked.

"If the rose-petal murderer attacked Belle, she would be dead," Alexander answered. "The monster follows a ritual with each victim and would not change his habits now."

"Belle was not raped, robbed, or killed," Stepan said. "Someone wanted to scar her."

Alexander nodded, and then looked at Raven. "Tell me about your vision."

That surprised Fancy, who looked from one to the other. "What vision?"

"Raven visited me last night," Alexander answered. "She'd had a vision about the rose-petal murders."

Raven's voice was colder than the Thames in winter. "Do you believe such things are possible?"

"I will believe anything that helps solve this case."

Raven closed her eyes. "I saw a disembodied red dress and—"

"You saw a red dress?"

She opened her eyes. "That is what I said."

"What does that mean?" Fancy asked.

"Last night's victim wore a red dress." Alexander turned to Raven. "Describe the sewing person."

"I saw hands."

"Man or woman?"

Raven closed her eyes again. "Long fingers."

"Man or woman?" Irritation tinged his voice.

"I heard you the first time," Raven snapped.

"Then answer the question."

Fancy looked from one to the other and then at the prince, who shrugged. Something had passed between her friend and her baby sister.

"I saw long fingers, nothing to distinguish male or female."

"Try again," Alexander ordered.

Raven closed her eyes. "A long finger, an unvarnished nail, a gold ring."

Alexander appeared shaken. "I want to know if you have another vision, the moment you have it."

"Why are you angry with Raven?" Fancy demanded. "She didn't murder anyone."

"What does the gold ring signify?" Stepan asked.

Alexander paused a moment, as if debating something in his mind, and then looked at each in turn. "We found a gold ring at the murder scene this morning. And the sewing . . . the monster sews their eyelids and lips shut. Then he places whole roses in their ears, finally slashing a cheek and covering them with rose petals."

"Mon Dieu." Fancy leaned against the prince, who didn't mind in the least.

Stepan put his arm around her shoulders and drew her against the side of his body. Her reaching for him seemed as natural as breathing, and this pleased him.

Alexander knew what he saw would render most people unconscious. "We believe he does the sewing after the victim has expired."

"That makes me feel so much better," Fancy muttered.

Alexander shifted his gaze to Raven. "Have I sickened you, too?"

"My constitution is stronger than my sister's." Raven opened the door to leave the parlor but paused to look at her sister. "Practice your slingshot."

"Why?"

"I don't know why."

After the door closed behind her sister, Fancy rounded on her friend. "What have you done to Raven?"

"Nothing." At that, Alexander quit the parlor.

Fancy looked at Stepan. "Will you contact Baron Wingate in the morning and tell him about the attack?"

"Shall I bring him to visit Belle?"

"Only if he suggests it."

"A wise decision."

"Where did you learn to take the pain away?" Fancy asked.

"I did not take her pain away, merely redirected it," Stepan explained. "I broke my arm once. While the physician examined and set it, Rudolf did for me what I did for Belle. He had learned it at university." He raised her hand to his lips. "Today has been long and tiring. Au revoir, mademoiselle."

Fancy smiled at him. "Bon voyage, monsieur."

He turned toward the door. Her hand on his arm made him pause.

Fancy threw herself into his arms. "Thank you for being so wonderful with Belle. I don't know what we would have done without you."

"A compliment for me?" Stepan cocked a dark brow at her. "You should seek employment for your free days from the opera."

Chapter 6

"I would speak with Baron Wingate."

The Wingate majordomo raised his brows at the man's attitude and tone. "The family is eating breakfast, the hour entirely too early for calls. If you give me your card—"

"I will not give you my calling card, sir. I demand to speak with the baron."

"Very well, wait here while—"

"I do not wait in foyers."

The majordomo gave him an exasperated look. "Follow me, Mister—?"

"His Highness, Prince Stepan Kazanov."

The blood drained from the majordomo's face. "Your Highness, please accept my—"

"Spare me," Stepan said, his tone purposely haughty. "You have already wasted too much of my time."

"Yes, Your Highness."

Stepan walked down the corridor toward the dining room. One could usually judge the aristocrat by his servants' attitudes. Apparently, the old Russian axiom was true; the worst snobs were always the lowest on the aristocratic scale. The only way to deal with snobbery was to outsnob the snobs, an enjoyable game consisting of a prince and a sniveling, servile sycophant.

"Your Highness, what a surprise," the baroness gushed, her eyes lighting with delight at such an exalted visitor.

Stepan gestured for the two men to remain sitting and smiled at the baroness. "A pleasant surprise, I hope. Tell me how you manage to look so beautiful this early in the morning."

The baroness giggled like a young woman. "I never realized what a flatterer you are."

"Madam, I swear I speak only the truth."

Stepan gave the dining room a sweeping glance. He noted the expensive Worcester Royal Porcelain coffee and tea service on the sideboard and a chipped cup on the dining table. The cushion on the chair beside him looked positively threadbare. The Wingates would probably eat beef stew from Wedgwood china while a true aristocrat would choose filet mignon and caviar served on stoneware.

"Nigel, bring His Highness coffee and a plate of eggs and sausage," the baroness instructed the majordomo.

"Yes, Madam."

"Coffee only, please."

"I don't believe you have met my son George," the baroness said.

Stepan inclined his head to George and then looked at Charles. "I assumed the baron was the eldest son."

"George is my half-brother," Charles explained. "I am the baron's only son."

"I see." Stepan thought that fact did not sit well with George, who appeared unhappy with the circumstances. His younger brother wore the piddling title and controlled the purse strings. What else could a cripple do, though?

"I had no idea you knew where I lived." Charles Wingate smiled at him. "To what do we owe this honor?"

Stepan let the faintest of smiles flirt with his lips while he decided if the baron's words held a note of sarcasm. If so, he would pauperize the fool before summer's end.

"As you may know, I have been courting Miss Fancy Flambeau," Stepan began.

"Courting the opera singer for matrimony?" the baroness exclaimed. "You can't be serious?"

"I have never been more serious in my life." Stepan fixed his dark gaze on the baroness and let her see his displeasure. "The Flambeau sisters are *highly connected.*"

"I have heard wild rumors," the baroness said. "Who *is* her father?"

"Your curiosity will soon be satisfied," Stepan lied, and turned to Charles. "Belle was attacked after you brought her home yesterday."

"What?" Charles Wingate rose from his chair in surprise. "I delivered Belle to her door."

"Sit down," the baroness ordered.

He did as ordered. Which told Stepan a great deal about the baron. If Fancy had been attacked, he would not be sitting here now.

"What happened to the sweet child?" the baroness asked.

"Someone waiting inside the house slashed her face."

"Oh, the poor dear."

"Her beautiful face," Charles lamented, clearly upset.

Stepan glanced at George, who had remained silent. He was ignoring their conversation, unaffected and uninterested in the misfortune of a lower-class woman.

Charles looked toward his mother for guidance. "Shall I go to her?"

"I doubt the child will feel well enough for visitors, my boy."

"I disagree." Stepan rose from his chair. "A visit from Charles will lift her spirits."

The baron stood when he did. "Right, Your Highness, I'll come along then."

"Did you receive Inverary's invitation for his ball this week?" Stepan watched the baroness redden with embarrassed anger. Apparently, she had not received an invitation. "Yours must have been in the pile dropped in a puddle of water. I will tell His Grace to send another along when I meet with him this afternoon." He glanced at the baron. "Shall we leave, Charles?"

Baron Wingate followed him out of the dining room. Together, the two men walked down the corridor to the foyer.

"Riding in my coach will save time," Stepan said.

Baron Wingate touched his arm to stop him. "Your Highness, was Belle violated?"

"Thankfully, no." Stepan decided that, although the baron lived beneath his mother's thumb, the man genuinely cared for Fancy's sister.

"That relieves me," Charles said. "I could never forgive Belle if she had been raped."

Stepan almost tripped down the front stairs at the other man's words. He knew three things for sure. Charles Wingate was an obnoxious arse who deserved to be pauperized and beaten, bringing him to visit Belle was one of the worst ideas he'd ever had, and the baroness's receiving an invitation to Inverary's ball was in doubt.

Alexander Blake and Constable Amadeus Black waited to speak with Lord and Lady Parkhurst. "The

Parkhursts are a strange couple," Amadeus said. "The lady is several years older than her husband."

"Is she the one with the money?"

Amadeus cast him an amused glance. "Your thoughts match mine."

"Where is Lowing?" Alexander asked.

"Unfortunately, Lowing was required to appear in court this morning."

"What auspicious timing."

"I thought so."

"Constable Black." Lady Parkhurst hurried into the drawing room. "My husband will be down directly."

In her forties, Lady Parkhurst was short and decidedly plump. She had plain features but a pleasant expression.

"I present my associate, Alexander Blake."

The lady smiled at him, saying, "Oh, your grandfather—"

"Lady Parkhurst, we are returning your husband's ring," Alexander interrupted. He had no intention of discussing his grandfather with anyone.

Amadeus Black drew the heavy gold ring from his pocket and offered it to her.

Lady Parkhurst stared at the ring for a long moment. "That ring does not belong to my husband."

"Are you certain?"

"Positive."

Lord Parkhurst walked into the drawing room. He was a tall, passably handsome man in his midthirties. "Gentlemen, how may I help you?"

"We would like to ask you a few questions," the constable said.

"Is my wife's presence needed?"

"No, my lord."

Lord Parkhurst looked at his wife. "Run along, dear, and close the door behind you."

The lady hesitated. "Will you need me later?"

"Hardly," Parkhurst drawled.

Amadeus held his hand out. "My lord, do you recognize this?"

"No."

"The ring does not belong to you?"

Parkhurst smiled. "I have better taste than that."

Not in wives, Alexander thought.

"Did the ring belong to Phoebe?"

Lord Parkhurst raised his brows at the constable. "I know no one named Phoebe."

Alexander felt like shaking the truth out of the supercilious lout. "Didn't you conduct an affair with a ballet dancer named Phoebe?"

Parkhurst managed to look suitably shocked. "Sir, I am a married man."

Amadeus inclined his head. "Forgive us for intruding on your day, my lord. Come, Alexander."

"Blake, give your grandfather my regards," Parkhurst said.

Alexander turned to the constable as soon as the door closed behind them. "Parkhurst is lying."

"Calm down, Alex." Amadeus touched his shoulder. "Did you expect him to confess to murder?"

Barney waited in front of the Parkhurst mansion. "Did you learn anything?"

"We learned that Parkhurst is not above lying," Amadeus answered. "Starting today, Barney, you will shadow His Lordship's movements from dusk to dawn, and report to me each morning. And for Gawd's sake, don't let him see you watching."

Standing in her foyer, Fancy looked from Stepan to Charles Wingate. She could not decide if the baron's presence was a good or bad idea. Her sister was a gentle soul in an emotionally fragile condition and could not protect herself if necessary. If the baron should hurt her—

"I'll ask if she wants to see you." Fancy opened the parlor door and stepped inside. "Charles is waiting in the foyer."

Surprise registered on her sister's face. At the same moment, Belle raised her hand to her stitched cheek.

"You don't need to see him," Fancy told her.

Belle met her gaze, the misery of the world clouding her eyes. She shook her head in acceptance of whatever fate decreed. "Send him in."

Fancy opened the door and gestured to the baron. Once he brushed past her, she stepped into the corridor but left the door open a tiny crack.

"Are you eavesdropping?" Stepan whispered.

"I am protecting my sister." Her mulish expression dared him to argue the point.

The prince put his arm around her shoulders, drawing her close. "I will protect her, too."

"Oh, my poor darling," Charles exclaimed. "I feel so guilty."

"You should not blame yourself," Belle said.

"Let me see your lovely face."

"I am no longer lovely and will carry a scar."

"Nonsense, dear heart. Let me see."

Silence.

Fancy looked at the prince and wondered if the baron had grimaced at the raw stitching. Stepan appeared uncomfortably guilty, the silence inside the drawing room emphasizing the enormity of his blunder.

"You will recover, dearest."

The baron's hesitant tone did not inspire confidence in Fancy. She looked at the prince again. He looked uninspired, too.

"I should have escorted you inside," the baron was saying.

"*My sisters were on an outing,*" Belle reminded him. "*Our being alone would have been too much of a temptation. I want nothing to prevent me from coming to you a virgin on our wedding night.*"

Silence again. A prolonged silence.

Alarm shot through Fancy. The baron could not be so cruel as to discard her sister only one day after the attack.

"Do you think the baron is kissing her?" The prince sounded hopeful.

"No." All the hatred for aristocrats she'd harbored for fifteen years shone in her eyes.

"*Well, dearest, the fact is—*" Baron Wingate hesitated. "*My mother believes we are unsuited for each other.*"

"*The baroness was so kind and gracious yesterday.*"

"*She would never behave otherwise,*" Wingate said. "*My mother's true nobility shines, no matter her opinion.*"

"*True nobility?*" Belle said. "*Wasn't her father a vicar and her first husband a squire?*"

Fancy heard the sarcastic edge in her sister's voice. The assailant could not steal her spirit and pride.

"*That is neither here nor there.*"

"*My mother was a countess,*" Belle said, "*and my father is a duke, which makes me more noble than your mother.*"

"*Your parents never married,*" the baron said, a hostile note entering his voice. "*Your bastardy makes you unacceptable.*"

"That sniveling swine." Stepan reached for the door, but Fancy blocked his path. "Step aside so I can kill him."

"Revenge should never be served hot, Your Highness."

"*You should leave now.*"

Her sister's voice ached with emotion.

"*What I meant to say— I need time to persuade my mother that a union between us would be beneficial.*"

"*Take all the time you need, Charles. I will, of course, examine my own feelings about you.*"

By unspoken agreement, Fancy and Stepan hurried

to the foyer. Standing near the door, they tried to appear as if they hadn't been eavesdropping.

Baron Wingate walked into the foyer, his complexion flushed. "I would like to leave now."

Stepan opened the door and gestured to the baron. Wingate stepped outside, but the prince hadn't moved.

"Your Highness, I am rather upset and want to go home," Wingate said.

"I do not chauffeur social inferiors." Stepan slammed the door in the baron's face.

Fancy wrapped her arms around him. "You were wonderful."

"*Merci*, mademoiselle."

And then the heartwrenching sounds of her sister's weeping reached them.

Fancy whirled away, intending to go to her sister's aid. Stepan moved faster, wrapping an arm around her waist, pulling her against his body.

Fancy struggled against him. "Release me."

"Let her grieve in peace," Stepan said. "Nothing will make her feel better. When her tears are spent, she will listen to your counsel."

Fancy opened her mouth to argue.

"How about practicing your slingshot?"

She shook her head. "I have no heart for that today."

"I will let you shoot the apple off my head."

"You will?" Well, that certainly perked her interest.

"No." Stepan smiled at her disappointed expression. "My brothers are expecting me." He gave her a quick kiss and walked out the door.

Fancy appreciated the prince's support during a troubled time, but wished he would refrain from kissing her. At least, without invitation.

She heard her sister in the parlor but decided the prince was right. Belle deserved the privacy to grieve in peace.

A short time later, Stepan climbed the stairs to the Duke of Inverary's second-floor office. He knocked on the door and entered without waiting for permission. When the four men sitting inside dropped their mouths open in surprise, he grinned at each in turn . . . the Duke of Inverary and his three older brothers.

"What are you doing here?" Prince Rudolf asked, the first to find his voice through his surprise.

Stepan made himself comfortable in a roomy leather chair. "I am attending this business meeting."

"Why?" Prince Viktor sounded suspicious.

"Are you in trouble?" Prince Mikhail asked.

"No trouble." Stepan poured himself a whiskey. "A man without a vocation is a man without direction."

Three princes and one duke roared with laughter. Would his brothers ever consider him a responsible adult? Or would they always see him as the small, motherless boy who needed their protection?

"Miss Flambeau believes I need gainful employment."

That brought the men another round of chuckles.

"If you are willing to work," the Duke of Inverary said, "your liaison with Miss Flambeau must be serious."

"Fancy and I do not have an intimate relationship," Stepan admitted, "but I find myself involved in the Flambeau family problems."

Prince Mikhail smiled. "What problems are the Flambeaus experiencing? Indecision concerning gowns?"

"Furs?" Viktor added, falling in with his brother's teasing.

"Could the problem be jewels?" Prince Rudolf asked.

Stepan sipped his whiskey before answering. "Belle Flambeau, the second oldest, was attacked in their home yesterday. The assailant slashed her with a blade."

That killed the good humor and teasing.

"How badly is she injured?" Inverary asked.

"One side of her face required stitches from beneath her cheekbone to the corner of her mouth."

Inverary slammed his fist on the desk. "I suppose the poor girl will carry a scar?"

Stepan gave him a grim nod.

"Perhaps I should send my own physician to examine her."

"That is unnecessary, Your Grace." Stepan sipped the whiskey but wished for vodka. "We treated her as well as any physician."

"You were there?" Rudolf asked.

"I had taken six sisters and their dog on a picnic," Stepan explained, eliciting chuckles from his brothers.

"I suppose a man who loves tea parties would also enjoy picnics."

Stepan ignored his oldest brother's gibe. "We found Belle on the foyer floor, and the youngest sister stitched her face."

"Why didn't she join your picnic?" Inverary asked.

"Belle had had previous plans to meet Baron Wingate's mother." Stepan grimaced, still disturbed by the sister's pain. "The bastard looked at her stitched face this morning and told her he couldn't marry her."

Silence reigned, each man pausing to think about the injured girl.

Stepan broke the silence with a disgusted snort. "Wingate did not name the scar as his reason, of course. He said her illegitimacy made her unacceptable to his mother. Thankfully, she never gave him her virginity."

Rudolf looked astounded. "How do you know this?"

"Fancy and I eavesdropped on their conversation." A smile played on his lips. "When the baron asked for a ride home, I told him I did not chauffeur social inferiors and slammed the door in his face."

All four men laughed, and then their talk turned to business.

"That thoroughbred we bought won its first race," Mikhail said. "I wish we had bet more on the outcome."

"Someone placed a hefty bet on our horse and won a bundle," Rudolf added.

Viktor nodded. "Our longshot proved profitable for at least one gambler."

A tap on the door drew their attention, and the majordomo stepped inside. "Mr. Wopsle has arrived, Your Grace."

"Thank you, Tinker. Send him in."

Bespectacled Mr. Wopsle stepped into the office. The man appeared nervous when he saw the duke was not alone.

"Sit here, Wopsle." The Duke of Inverary gestured to the chair in front of the desk.

Wopsle crossed the office slowly and sat in the assigned chair. Then he pushed his slipping spectacles up with his index finger.

Stepan hid a smile. The poor man sat in the chair as if he were facing the Spanish Inquisition.

The duke smiled at the man. "Would you care for a whiskey?"

"No, thank you, Your Grace."

"I will get straight to the point." The duke lost his smile. "You act as business agent for the Seven Doves Company, which is undercutting our prices."

"Undercutting prices is not against the law, Your Grace."

"We want the owner's identity," Rudolf said.

Wopsle gulped visibly, his complexion reddening. "I am sorry, Your Highness, but—"

"We demand his identity," Viktor said.

"I-I cannot tell you that."

"Cannot or will not?" Mikhail challenged him.

"B-Both, Your Highness."

"Explain yourself," Inverary snapped.

Stepan stretched his long legs out and sipped his whiskey. Intimidation would not get answers from this man. Fright would paralyze his tongue.

"I-I would not break my client's confidentiality," Wopsle said, "even if I knew his identity."

"You don't know his identity?" The duke sounded incredulous, and rightfully so. "How do you conduct your business?"

"We communicate through another business agent."

"I wonder the reason this owner wants to preserve his identity," Stepan said. "On the other hand, who are we to demand his identity?"

Rudolf sent him a silencing look. "Wopsle, what is this other agent's name?"

"I call him Mister *P*," the man hedged.

Stepan laughed. "Is that *P* with an *ea* or double *e*?"

Viktor and Mikhail chuckled at his joke. Rudolf sent him another quelling look.

Stepan decided it was time to take his rightful place in the Kazanov businesses and so ignored his eldest brother's unspoken warning. "Describe the man's appearance."

"He is as tall as yourself with brown hair and well dressed, but not as expensively as you."

"You call him Mister *P*, but you do know his surname."

Wopsle paused a long moment. "Puddles."

An idea was forming in Stepan's mind, albeit a ridiculous idea, and it was no more than a shot in the dark. "Is Alexander his first name?"

"Do you know the man?"

Stepan said nothing, his mind unable to believe what he knew was true. The facts did not lie, however. A company named Seven Doves, an agent named Puddles, and a slip of a girl who loved numbers. His brothers would never believe him.

"Where can we find Puddles?" Inverary was asking.

Stepan could not control his laughter, earning himself a censorious look.

"I don't find Puddles," Wopsle said. "Puddles finds me."

"When you meet this Puddles again, tell him the Duke of Inverary wants a word or two with him."

"Yes, Your Grace."

"You may leave now."

Wopsle wasted no time in escaping.

Rudolf looked at Stepan. "If you want to work, track Puddles and discover the owner of the Seven Doves."

"I know Puddles and the owner*s* of the company."

"Owner*s*?" Rudolf echoed.

"How many?" the duke asked.

"Seven, I believe." Stepan stood, intending to leave. "Conduct your business as usual, and I will take care of this matter." He smiled at his brothers' astonished expressions. "Good day, Your Grace and brothers."

"Miss Giggles." Fancy scooped the capuchin monkey onto her lap. "How is Miss Giggles this evening?"

The monkey stared at her and then performed the now-familiar trick. Hear no evil, see no evil, speak no evil.

"Excuse me." Sebastian Tanner pointed at the monkey.

Fancy passed him the prima donna's pet. She started to close the dressing room door when three people appeared.

"How is Belle feeling?" Genevieve asked.

"She will recover."

Fancy's mind and energy had been fixed on her sister all day. Her only moments of relief had come when she stepped onstage and lost herself in the music. She would probably die if barred from the opera.

Director Bishop cleared his throat. "Genevieve will sing the part of Cherubino tomorrow evening." The blonde gasped, drawing the director's attention. "You may leave, Genevieve."

Fancy flicked a worried glance at the prince, who was lounging against the doorjamb, and then asked the director, "Are you firing me?"

Director Bishop shook his head. "Genevieve will assume your role because you will be singing at the Duke of Inverary's ball."

Fancy looked the director straight in the eye. "I don't work private parties."

"You do if you want employment at this opera."

Fancy closed her eyes against the unfairness of it all. She had expected independence when she won a position in the opera. The reverse was true. She had less freedom than before.

"Very well, I will make this one exception."

"We will debate that another time." Director Bishop left the dressing room.

Looking elegant in his formal evening attire, Stepan cocked his head to one side as if considering her sour expression. "I hope this does not color our evening."

"I dislike being forced into anything." Fancy sighed, and then lifted her violet gaze to his. "I don't feel comfortable attending this exalted duke's society affair."

"Poor, poor Fancy." Stepan cupped her cheek and ran his thumb across her lips. "I will escort you to the party, remain by your side, and escort you home."

"The Inverarys are your brother's in-laws," Fancy said. "Did you put them up to this?"

"I swear I had nothing to do with it. The duchess loves trends, and you are London's most recent trend."

"Success has its drawbacks, I see."

Stepan shrugged. "Many women would gladly change places with you."

"Do you mean millions of women would change places in order to be standing here with you?"

Stepan inclined his head. "There is that, too."

"I am not ungrateful."

"I know that."

Fancy gave him a pleading look. "Will you take me directly home tonight? I am worried about Belle."

"Only if you promise to wear the violet gown tomorrow night."

"I promise."

Stepan saw the budding love shining in her eyes but doubted she realized how much she had softened toward him in only a few days. He would like to strangle that father of hers, who had made winning her love and trust more difficult.

"Will you do me a favor?" he asked.

"Yes."

Stepan planted a chaste kiss on her lips. "Tell Bliss to stop undercutting the Kazanov prices."

"Kazanov prices?" Fancy echoed.

"Do not play the innocent with me," Stepan said. "Your Seven Doves Company is undercutting Campbell Enterprises and Kazanov Brothers."

"I am sorry, but Kazanov Brothers is ancillary damage."

"What do you mean?"

Fancy gave him an ambiguous smile.

Stepan laughed. "Keep your secrets, little songbird."

Chapter 7

Fancy inspected herself in the cheval mirror. She wore the violet silk gown the prince had given her. Its neckline was square, the bodice fitted, and the sleeves off-the-shoulder straps. Matching the gown were a cashmere shawl and satin slippers. Long white kid gloves completed the outfit.

"You-know-who will be there." Fancy rounded on her youngest sister. "What should I do if he speaks to me?"

"Father may not recognize you." Raven looked her up and down and smiled. "You look very different from the girl he saw last."

"You are correct about that. Will you tell the prince I'll be there in a minute?"

"You look like a fairy-tale princess." Raven scooted out the door.

Fancy took a deep breath and exhaled, trying to calm herself. She had no doubt her father would be attending the Inverary ball. If he spoke to her, she would pretend she didn't know their true connection.

And then the scent of cinnamon filled the room. Nanny Smudge was sending advice from beyond the grave.

Listen to your head but follow your heart.

Stepan stood in the foyer and wondered if his song-bird would fly the coop as she had that other night. If she felt trapped or panicked, he had no doubt she would escape out a second-floor window.

"Worrying will give you gray hair," Raven warned him.

"Worry or not, I will get gray hair," Stepan said. "That is the way of the world."

Stepan turned at the sound of Fancy descending the stairs and gave her an appreciative smile before lifting her hand to his lips. "You are lovely, too perfect to be real."

Fancy rolled her eyes. "You have not found employment."

Looping her hand in the crook of his arm, Stepan led her to the door. "I cannot decide which I most admire, your infinite beauty or your sharp wit."

Stepan sat beside her in his coach and held her hand in his. "I love your scent, the softness of rose petals with a touch of sensual vanilla or amber."

Fancy gave him a sidelong look. "Your Highness, you are an incorrigible flatterer."

Park Lane lay a few miles and a world away from Soho Square. Fancy was too nervous for conversation; her hand trembled and her stomach fluttered, her agitation growing when she spied the glamorous society ladies and their escorts entering Inverary's mansion.

"Relax, *ma petite*."

Fancy gave him a tremulous smile. She appreciated the prince's kindness. She could never have come here without him, even if it meant losing her position at the opera.

"Think of this as stage fright." Stepan placed his hand on the small of her back and guided her into the mansion. She looked like a woman meeting the executioner.

"I puke before each performance."

Stepan laughed, drawing curious glances from other

guests. Nearing the ballroom, he said, "Lift your chin and look people in the eye. Remember, your mother was a countess and your father is a duke. The lack of a marriage certificate does not diminish your nobility."

Fancy turned an anguished gaze on him. "I do not want to speak to you-know-who."

"I will remain by your side." Stepan patted her hands. "Besides, your father may not be an invited guest." Then he leaned close to whisper to the duke's majordomo.

"Brace yourself," he warned her.

"Prince Stepan Kazanov," Tinker announced, "and Miss Fancy Flambeau."

Fancy hesitated as guests in the vicinity turned in unison to watch the prince and the opera singer. Like a drowning woman, she clutched his hand. And then Fancy saw her father, his gaze following her progress.

Drawing her attention, Stepan placed his hand on her back and guided her in the direction of a group of ladies and gentlemen. "I want you to meet my family."

"What if they don't approve?"

"Why would they disapprove?"

His question had been spoken in sincerity. That heartened Fancy, who drew strength from the prince's confidence.

The ballroom was enormous and lit by glittering crystal chandeliers. Musicians stood at one end of the chamber and played their instruments. Elegant gentlemen spoke in muted voices and waltzed with ladies gowned in rainbow colors. Priceless gems sparkled on necks, arms, fingers, and ears. Perfume wafted through the ballroom, scenting the air like a lush garden.

"Everyone, I present Miss Fancy Flambeau," Stepan announced when they reached his family. With pride in his voice, he gestured to each relative and friend. "Fancy, I present my oldest brother Rudolf and his wife, Samantha. Meet Viktor, his wife Regina, and Mikhail. Robert Campbell is Inverary's son, and his wife, Angelica. And this is Cousin Amber and her husband, Miles Montgomery."

Fancy greeted each with an ambiguous smile and a regal inclination of her head. She refused to curtsey, regardless of etiquette.

"Oh, my darling Stepan," the Duchess of Inverary gushed, rushing to their side. "I see you have managed to persuade Miss Flambeau to honor us with her presence."

"His Highness did not persuade me," Fancy told the duchess. "Director Bishop threatened my continued employment." The brightness of her smile lessened the bite of her words. She heard husky chuckles from three princes, a marquess, an earl, and the duke, who had joined them in time to hear her comment.

"They are not laughing at you," Stepan assured her. "I believe hearing the truth for a change amuses them."

"You are the veriest sweet child," the duchess added. "No one would dare to insult you, nor would anyone wish that."

"You are too kind, Your Grace."

"I am a superb strategist in dealings with the adorable other gender." The duchess flicked a glance at the prince and returned her attention to Fancy. "Whenever you are ready, I will plot your course."

"I will never be ready," Fancy said, "because I plan never to marry."

"Fancy." The prince's voice held a warning note.

"You would deprive future generations of your beauty?"

Had the duchess been taking lessons in flattery from the prince? "I will consider marriage when the Almighty creates an alternative to men."

"Fancy." The prince sounded distinctly unhappy.

The Duchess of Inverary gave the prince a dimpled smile. "Perhaps I should offer you my strategic expertise."

"I will call upon you at first opportunity."

Fancy smiled at their wordplay and flicked a sidelong glance at the Duke of Inverary. He was watching her. She gave him a polite smile and turned away. She felt conspicuous enough without anyone staring.

"God blessed you with a rare gift," Princess Amber said, standing beside her.

"I appreciate your praise, Your Highness."

"Would you consider singing at my home?"

"I am sorry, but I do not usually perform at private parties."

Princess Amber leaned close to prevent her words from being overheard. "I am not hosting a party. My rose-bush is ailing, and the gift of your voice will revive its spirit."

Fancy laughed, thinking the princess sounded like Belle. "In that case, I accept your invitation. Your Highness, you are not what I expected in a princess."

"What did you expect?"

"An aristocratic snob."

Princess Amber returned the compliment. "You are not what I expected in an opera singer."

"What did *you* expect?"

"A fat lady."

Both women laughed at that, drawing the others' attention. For the first time, Fancy felt she could cope with tonight's society ball. The prince and his cousin were not what she had imagined aristocrats were.

"My lady, may I have this dance?"

Fancy hesitated for a fraction of a moment. "Yes, Your Highness."

Taking her hand in his, Stepan led her onto the dance floor. With one hand at her waist, the prince maintained a proper distance between their bodies and swirled her around and around the ballroom. He moved with the grace of a man who had waltzed hundreds of times, and Fancy forgot her insecurity, losing herself in the man and the music.

"You dance well," Stepan said. "Did your anonymous father hire a dancemaster?"

"No, my sisters and I practiced together each evening," Fancy answered. "We wanted to be ready for Prince Charming when he arrived."

Stepan smiled at her sweet admission. "And here I am."

Prince Rudolf requested her second dance and waltzed as well as his brother. Princes Viktor and Mikhail waltzed with her after that. Mikhail returned her to Stepan's side, murmuring, "I hope you save another dance for me later."

"I need something to drink before I sing," Fancy whispered to the prince.

Stepan put his arm around her waist and escorted her into the next room. "Champagne?"

"I prefer water," she insisted.

"Will you survive if I fetch lemon water from that table?"

"Yes, of course."

"Your presence surprises me." No sooner had Stepan stepped away when Fancy heard a voice beside her. "How is Belle?"

Fancy stared in silence at the baron and then turned her back on him, giving him the cut direct. Stepan and Rudolf stood there. Both men were smiling.

"Miss Flambeau, you are an Original," Prince Rudolf told her.

"Thank you for the praise, Your Highness." Fancy looked from Stepan to his brother, asking, "Do you know what businesses Baron Wingate is invested in?"

Stepan smiled at that.

"Are you planning to pauperize the man?" Rudolf asked.

"The thought had crossed my mind," Fancy answered.

Rudolf narrowed his gaze on her. "One needs capital in order to pauperize other people."

"Yes, Your Highness, I know." Her smile was ambiguous, and she looked at Stepan. "May we step into a more private room while I prepare for my performance?"

Hell, Stepan thought, leading her out of the refreshment room, *I should marry her. My songbird already acts like a princess.*

Stepan brought her into the informal family parlor and passed her the glass of lemon water. Fancy looked around to insure no one else was in the room. She took a swig of water, swished it around her mouth, and then spit it into a nearby vase.

Stepan chuckled at what he had witnessed. "What are you doing?"

"I wet my mouth before I sing," Fancy explained, "but if I swallow, I'll regurgitate."

Prince Mikhail appeared in the doorway. "The duchess is calling for you."

Returning to the ballroom, Stepan escorted Fancy to the top of the room where the duchess waited. The prince kissed her hand, causing a flurry of murmurs, before he left her side.

"Ladies and gentlemen," the Duchess of Inverary said, "I present my special guest, Miss Fancy Flambeau."

"I apologize for my lack of Cherubino's breeches and jerkin," Fancy told her audience, making them smile.

And then she sang *a cappella,* choosing an aria about unrequited love. Her powerful voice captured her audience, wrapping them in emotion, breaking their hearts. When she finished, someone called for her signature song, "Beyond the Horizon," and she obliged them. Enthusiastic applause rewarded her at song's end.

She had done it. She had survived her foray into

high society. Now she could retreat to the refuge of
Soho Square.

"Take me home," Fancy whispered to the prince.

"Supper will be served shortly," he told her. "Wouldn't
you like something to eat?"

"I prefer to leave."

"Then you shall leave."

Stepan and Fancy wended their way to the door slowly.
Some guests wanted to speak personally to London's
latest rage; some guests greeted the prince; some guests
of the female variety slayed her with venomous glares. Especially the blonde standing with Charles Wingate, the
brunette speaking with an older gentleman, and the redhead dressed in the most scandalously scant black gown.

Prince Rudolf caught them at the stairs. "The Duke
and Duchess of Inverary would speak with you in His
Grace's office."

Fancy touched her prince's arm. "Will you take me
home first?"

Stepan looked at his brother. "Tell His—"

"*Now.*" Rudolf stood beside Fancy, trapping her between him and his brother. "I promise you may leave
shortly."

Three people were inside Inverary's office. The duke
sat behind an enormous mahogany desk with a glass of
whiskey in front of him, and the duchess perched in a
chair beside her husband's desk. The marquess leaned
against a bookcase and sipped whiskey.

The ducal office was richly appointed, as befitting an
exalted aristocrat. A Persian carpet hugged the floor,
the hearth was black marble, and the woman in the
portrait above the hearth was attractive but not the present duchess. A chair had been set in front of the desk.

"Your voice is too amazing for words," the duchess
gushed when Fancy walked into the room.

"Roxie." The duke's voice held a gentle warning.

"I cannot contain my excitement." She gave him a dimpled smile. "My nieces' smashing marriages and now—"

"*Roxie.*"

Another dimpled smile. "Sorry, darling."

The Duke of Inverary beckoned Fancy forward. She hesitated, wishing to be anywhere but there. Would this night never end?

"I do not bite, child."

"I *do* bite, Your Grace."

Stepan looked puzzled and, with his hand on the small of her back, nudged her forward until they stood in front of the desk.

No one spoke. A strained silence filled the chamber.

"How about a whiskey?" Rudolf asked his brother, alleviating the tension.

"Any vodka?"

"No."

"Give me the whiskey."

"Miss Flambeau?"

Fancy ignored him, her violet gaze fixed on the duke. "Say what you will, Your Grace, I want to go home."

"Do you know who I am?"

Fancy gave him her sweetest, most insincere smile. "You are the Duke of Inverary, Your Grace."

"I am your father."

Fancy placed the palms of her hands on his desk and leaned forward to look him straight in the eye. She spoke slowly, enunciating every syllable.

"*I have no father.*"

"What is this?" Stepan snapped his head around to look at his brother.

Rudolf chuckled, enjoying the incredible sight of the petite opera singer facing down the powerful duke. "Apparently, Miss Flambeau and her sisters are His Grace's daughters."

Fancy glared at the eldest Russian prince. "I have no father."

"You do have a father, and I am he." The duke gestured to the chair. "Sit and listen."

She refused to stay in this room. He had relinquished his right to be heard fifteen years earlier.

Pale and trembling, Fancy turned to the prince. "I want to leave now."

"The sooner you sit and listen," Stepan said, "the sooner we can leave."

Staring into the prince's black eyes, Fancy knew that he would support and comfort her, no matter the circumstance, but insisted she sit for as long as she could. Fancy surrendered to the inevitable and sat in the chair facing the duke. Stepan stood beside her, lending her his strength.

Fancy sent him a grateful look and then spied the marquess and the eldest prince smiling at each other. She didn't know what they had to smile about. She found nothing amusing in the situation.

"Darling, you cannot imagine the plans I—"

"Roxie, enough."

"There is no need for rudeness, Magnus."

Fancy stared straight ahead, unfocusing her gaze. She would sit here until the duke stopped talking and then escape.

"Fancy, you are sitting but not listening." His tone was a gentle, fatherly rebuke.

"Call me Miss Flambeau."

The duke inclined his head. "I know you have good reason to distrust me—"

"I hate you."

"She doesn't mean that," the duchess gasped. "Her anger is speaking."

"I understand that, Roxie." Inverary stared at Fancy

for several long moments. The longer he watched her, the more agitated she grew.

"Let me begin again." He gestured to the two men standing together. "Robert Campbell and Prince Rudolf Kazanov are your half-brothers."

Fancy looked at Prince Rudolf in surprise.

He raised his whiskey in a toast to her. "I am pleased to have made your acquaintance, *Sister.*"

Fancy rounded on her prince, dawning horror in her expression.

"Rudolf and I have different fathers," Stepan assured her. "Trust me, we do not share bloodlines."

The Duke of Inverary cleared his throat. "I want you to know that, in my own way, I did love your mother."

"You loved her so much your neglect put her in an early grave."

"I could not marry Gabrielle." The duke leaned forward in his chair. "I had a wife."

Fancy leaned forward, too, challenging him. "You should have stayed home with her and left my mother in peace."

"I do regret my youthful selfishness."

"Thirty years old is hardly youthful."

"Damn it, Gabrielle became pregnant whenever I got close."

"Ah, I see. So the blame for my mother's pain and misery rests with herself." Fancy gave him a look of supreme contempt, the first the duke had received in his entire life. "Abstinence prevents pregnancy."

"I accepted my responsibilities," her father defended himself. "You wanted for nothing and—"

"I didn't need your money," Fancy cried, bolting out of her chair. "I needed—" She broke off, unable to finish her thought, and held her hand out to ward off his words.

No one spoke, the silence becoming almost intolerable. Fancy tried to swallow the raw emotion rising in her throat. She turned her back on the duke. "I want to leave now." Her voice was barely louder than a whisper.

"What did you need?" the duke asked in a quiet voice.

Fancy fought to control her emotions, her bottom lip quivering in the struggle. She looked at the prince through violet eyes mirroring her misery, festering bitterness consuming her.

"Tell me what you needed, Fancy."

Her small hands balled into fists, and she rounded on her father.

"*I needed you.*" Her voice cracked with emotion, and her chest heaved visibly with dry sobs.

"Oh, dear God," she heard the duchess exclaim softly. She sensed her prince gesturing the others away, and then his arm went around her.

Fancy leaned against him, her gaze on her father's expression of guilt and regret. Fifteen years' worth of scathing recriminations slipped from her lips. "You went away and never returned. I stood at the window every day and watched and waited and listened to my mother's weeping.

"Nanny Smudge couldn't budge me from that window with a crowbar. Finally, Nanny told me you were dead and would never visit again."

The Duke of Inverary winced visibly. He gulped his whiskey, as if to fortify himself for the emotional flogging.

"I grieved for you. When spring arrived, I persuaded the boy next door to take me to pick flowers for your grave. Alex knew the truth, though, and brought me to Hyde Park to show me.

"I saw you, hale and hearty, riding along Rotten Row. You were laughing and flirting with a beautiful lady. Not the woman in that portrait over the hearth."

A bitter smile touched her lips. "I thought God had blessed me with a miracle. Thankfully, Alex held me back.

"You saw me and turned away. I am a bastard by birth, Your Grace, but you are a bastard by nature."

Her father found his voice through his misery. "I know I deserve your contempt."

"You deserve worse than my contempt."

"You will not believe me," he continued, "but I suffered fifteen years of nightmares after that day."

"So did I." Fancy gave the prince a pleading look. "Take me home."

Prince Stepan looked from her to the duke and then back again. He appeared undecided about what to do.

"I know she is hurting, Stepan, but let it play out." His brother broke the silence. "The wound cannot heal until the poison is gone."

"I want to make amends and acknowledge you now," her father said.

"I am no longer a child and do not need a father." Noting his stricken expression, Fancy went in for the kill. "I will never forgive or acknowledge you."

"Forgive me or not, my daughters will live here with me," the duke continued, as if she hadn't spoken. "Roxie and I will sponsor you in society"—he glanced at the prince—"and make suitable matches for all of you."

"I wouldn't live here to save my soul." Fancy headed for the door, calling over her shoulder, "Come now, Your Highness, or I will walk home."

"Do not open that door." The duke sounded exasperated, stern, and unused to defiance.

Prince Rudolf moved then. He stepped in front of the door, blocking her escape.

"I have the power to ruin your career," her father threatened.

"Magnus." Now the duchess's voice held a warning tone.

"What do you want from me?" Fancy rounded on him. "I can never love or forgive or even respect you. I despise all aristocrats"—she glanced at her prince— "almost all aristocrats. I loathe the ground you walk upon, the air you breathe, the—"

"Such hate is a heavy burden for one tiny woman to carry," Rudolf said, cutting off her scathing speech.

Fancy ignored him. "Do you want me to announce my paternity after my next performance?" Her voice dripped sarcasm. "Or shall I give an interview to that *Times* reporter?"

"I admit I have made a grievous mistake," Inverary said, "but I have seen my errors and want my daughters."

"We do not want you, Your Grace." Fancy cringed inwardly at his stricken expression, surprising herself that some part of her still cared for the man who had hurt her most.

"Do you speak for your sisters?"

"My sisters could not recognize you if they tripped over you in the street. If you want to ruin my career, do your worst." Fancy showed him her back, her expression demanding that Rudolf step aside. When he did, she reached for the doorknob.

"Belle would not have been slashed if she'd been living here."

That stopped her as no threat could, and she dropped her hand to her side. Her father had spoken truthfully. He could protect her sisters.

"You can take my sisters," she said, her gaze still fixed on the door. "Not me."

"Will they move without you?"

"My sisters will do as I say." Fancy turned around. "Blaze will not come without her dog. She is the redhead, in case you didn't know."

Fancy felt grim satisfaction when her father flushed. Ignorance of his own daughters' names *should* embarrass him.

Her father inclined his head. "The dog can live here, too."

"Belle requires a garden, both flower and herb," Fancy told him. "Serena plays the flute and sings and loves trees, especially willows. Sophia will need canvas and paint. Bliss would appreciate mathematics books."

"What about the youngest?"

"Raven wishes for everyone else's talent instead of her own."

"What is her talent?"

"I will let you discover that yourself." Fancy glanced at the duchess, a faint smile flirting with her lips. "If I were you, I would hide my fragile treasures."

She looked at her father. "When do you want them?"

"Tomorrow?"

"I will deliver them in the afternoon." Fancy turned away, the need to escape overwhelming. She didn't know how much longer she could control fifteen years' worth of heartache, bitterness, and insecurity. Weeping in front of her father was not an option.

And then he spoke, nearly felling her with his words. "I regret the coach ride that never happened."

Fancy steeled herself against his misery. Her back stiffened with pride, and she reached for the doorknob.

"I hope none of your children ever reject you."

She wanted to shout that he had rejected her, but aching emotion made speaking too difficult. She flicked a stricken glance at her prince, yanked the door open, and escaped the office.

Stepan caught up to her in the corridor. "I swear I had no knowledge of this."

Tears blurred her vision and rolled down her pale cheeks. "Please take me home."

Stepan passed her his handkerchief. "Go into the ladies' retiring room and freshen your face first."

The retiring room was empty. Staring into the mirror, Fancy wiped her cheeks and dabbed at her eyes. Her hand was shaking, and she needed to steal a moment to compose herself. A darkened corner beckoned her, a retreat where no one entering would notice her.

Fancy sighed and closed her eyes. Her sisters would do well at their father's since they did not share her bad memories. She would miss them, of course, but could not live with a father who had once turned his back on her.

And her mother.

Many nights Fancy had awakened to the pathetic sound of her mother's weeping. The Duke of Inverary had consigned her poor mother to an eternity of mourning a lost love. And he wanted her forgiveness? She would see him in hell first.

"Did you see Lady Clarke's expression when Stepan kissed the opera singer's hand?"

A throaty laugh. "Lady Clarke appeared ready to die from apoplexy."

Fancy opened her eyes when she heard the prince's name. A brunette and a redhead had walked into the retiring room but could not see her where she sat.

"For once, I hope perfect Lady Cynthia will not be given her heart's desire," the brunette said.

The redhead agreed. "Cynthia will need to set her sight on something less than a prince."

"Charles Wingate and his domineering mama," the brunette replied. "What do you think of the opera singer?"

"The prince will make her his mistress," the redhead answered. "Stepan will bed the little bastard but marry society."

The two women left the room, leaving Fancy alone in her misery.

Their cruel words had been a jolt from Above. What, in God's holy name, did she think she was doing? She had vowed never to become involved with an aristocrat.

She was outdoing her mother. If the duke refused to marry the woman who had borne him seven children, would a prince consider a woman who refused to bed him?

Fancy knew she was beginning to love the prince, but her pride refused to allow surrender. She would never marry or bed him. The daughter had learned hard lessons from the mother.

Loving but resisting. *Mon Dieu*, she felt like a fly entangled in the spider's web.

Fancy stood and crossed the room to the mirror. She dabbed at her eyes again, preparing to rejoin the prince.

A hand touched her shoulder. "May I help you, Miss Flambeau?"

Fancy looked at Princess Amber and shook her head. "I have had a disturbing interview with my long-lost father."

The princess gave her a blank look. "I do not understand."

"Though my mother was a French countess and my father an English duke, they never married," she explained. "My mother passed away several years ago, and now my father—who ignored us for fifteen years—wants us to live with him."

"Us?"

"I agreed to send him my six sisters, but I will be alone without them."

"I understand loneliness because I have been alone my whole life," the princess said. "The life of a princess is not as wonderful as it appears. Come, my cousin is worried about you."

Princess Amber returned to the ballroom with her husband. Stepan and Rudolf stood in the corridor.

The prince took her hand in his. "Are you feeling better?"

"Yes." She managed a faint smile. "Will you help me move my sisters tomorrow?"

"I was planning on it."

"Miss Flambeau . . ."

She looked at Rudolf. "You may call me Fancy."

"Thank you, Fancy. Very soon, we must have a long conversation." He looked at his brother. "Until then, take good care of my sister." And then he returned to the ballroom.

"I will take you home now." Stepan ushered her toward the stairs.

"I don't want my sisters to know I won't be moving with them," Fancy said. "If I tell them in advance, they will refuse to go, too."

Stepan wrapped his arm around her shoulder. "We will get through this together, I promise."

Chapter 8

Fancy sat at the head of the table, facing the windows, and watched her sisters at breakfast the next morning. Never again would they sit together like this. Life would change when she delivered them to Park Lane.

A breeze flirted with the French lace curtains, giving her a glimpse of a wren in flight. Carried on the wind, the flower garden's perfume wafted into the dining room.

The table was laden with a special breakfast, egg-batter fried bread with blueberry preserves. Sausage, kippers, and coffee accompanied the main dish.

Fancy looked at Raven on her right. "Why did you make us this delicious breakfast?"

"Do I need a reason?" Her youngest sister shrugged, a meaningful look in her eyes. "I awakened early and decided to treat my sisters this morning."

"Raven, you are a treasure," Blaze called from the other end of the table. "Puddles loves your sausages."

Fancy looked at each sister and knew she had made the right decision. Her father was correct. They would be safe at Park Lane. Belle would not have been injured if they had sought his protection. As the oldest, she should have visited her father's solicitor to ask for that protection after Nanny Smudge had died. She had failed in her duties, and her sister had paid the price.

Now her responsibility was to get her sisters moved with the least amount of resistance. To that end, Fancy decided to pretend to move with them. She would pack her clothing and unpack when she returned to Soho Square.

Setting her fork on the plate, Fancy cleared her throat and pasted a bright smile on her face. "Sisters, I have exciting news to share."

All six sisters looked down the table at her. Leaping onto the chair at the opposite end of the table, Puddles cocked his massive head to one side as if giving her his attention.

"Dogs do not sit at the dining table," Fancy informed her sister.

Blaze looked confused. "Is that the exciting news?"

Everyone, including Fancy, laughed at that. Puddles raised his head and howled, eliciting more laughter.

"I spoke with our father last night," Fancy announced, "and he wants us to live with him."

That grabbed their attention.

"Pack your clothing and valuables, but leave everything else for another day." Fancy managed to smile at their stunned expressions. "Prince Stepan will move us to Park Lane this afternoon."

"Park Lane?" Belle echoed, sounding impressed.

"Our father lives in a mansion on Park Lane. He will acknowledge us and—and—etcetera."

"What do you mean by etcetera?" Blaze asked.

"Father plans to launch us into society and find us husbands worthy of a duke's daughters."

"Who *is* our father?" Raven asked.

Fancy shifted her gaze to her youngest sister. How

sad for their father to sire seven daughters, six of whom had no knowledge of his identity.

Her gaze wandered to each sister before answering. "Magnus Campbell, the Duke of Inverary, is our father."

Serena smiled. "That explains his kindness to us the night of your debut."

"How strange to speak with a man but remain ignorant of his true identity," Sophia remarked.

"How sad." Belle's words echoed Fancy's thoughts. "Why does he want us after all these years?"

"His Grace regrets neglecting us," Fancy explained, "and he blames Belle's injury on his neglect."

"His Grace?" Raven murmured. "Is that what we call him?"

Fancy shrugged. "I do not know his preference."

"I'll call him Grace," Blaze announced, making her sisters laugh, "and we'll call his wife Gracie."

Belle appeared worried by the reminder of his duchess. "Will his wife welcome us?"

"Her Grace is his second wife, married after Mother passed away." Fancy hoped her smile was encouraging, though her face was beginning to hurt from the strain. "The prospect of our living there excited her. I gather she has no children of her own."

"What about Puddles?" Blaze asked.

"Puddles is moving with us."

"What will happen to the Seven Doves?" Bliss asked.

"Our plan for revenge stands." Fancy looked at each sister, her expression challenging them to disagree. "Alex comes to the theater each night to escort Genevieve home. I will give him our instructions then."

Serena laughed, drawing their attention. "We can eavesdrop on his business meetings and steal his secrets."

"This move could prove financially sound," Bliss said.

"Will Grace buy me a horse?" Blaze asked. "I'd love a monkey like Miss Giggles, too."

Blaze's question broke the dam of their surprise. Everyone started talking all at once.

Fancy felt a hand touch her arm.

"Practice your slingshot," Raven advised her. "I don't know the reason yet."

"What is troubling you?" Sophia asked. "You are not as happy as you want us to believe."

"Nothing troubles me." Fancy wished her sisters were not so talented. Almost nothing escaped their notice.

"Your secret sadness will affect my mood," Serena warned, "and then we'll be moving in the rain."

"Grace is a stranger to us," Belle explained, "but Fancy cannot forget he is the father who abandoned her."

Fancy needed to divert their attention. "I have more news." She looked around at their expectant expressions. "We have two half-brothers."

"Brothers?" six voices echoed.

"Robert Campbell, the Marquess of Argyll, is the duke's legal son and heir. Prince Rudolf Kazanov is his son born out of wedlock."

"Grace liked the ladies in his younger days," Serena said.

"You mean *loved*," Sophia corrected her twin.

"Grace had a roving eye for the ladies," Bliss said. "Many men do."

"Humph." Blaze looked at her twin. "Grace had more than an eye to produce seven daughters and one son on the wrong side of the blanket."

"Do you think there could be others?" Raven asked.

The sisters grew silent, even Fancy. How many children *had* the duke sired?

Raven broke the silence. "I will miss Soho Square."

Fancy looked around at her sisters. "We enter a new world this afternoon."

"I like the old world," Raven said. "What if I don't like the new world?"

Fancy raised her hand and gestured that problem away. "We still own our home in Soho Square."

"Technically, Grace owns it," Bliss reminded her.

"What if he won't let us come home?" Raven asked.

"We will worry about that another day." Fancy felt her irritation rising. She needed to move her sisters with as little trouble as possible. Her father would blame her if they refused to go, and she cared too much to let him down in spite of her bad memories. If only she could erase the past from her mind.

"I think we should worry before we move," Blaze was saying.

Raven nodded. "That will save us the return trip."

"Our father will not keep us prisoner," Fancy assured them.

Blaze would not quit, though. "What if he does?"

Fancy's temper flared. "What if the sky falls? What if the earth opens to swallow us? What if the Thames rises up to drown us?"

Silence greeted her outburst.

Belle touched her hand. "Sister, all will be well."

Looking as miserable as she felt, Fancy met each sister's troubled gaze. "I am sorry." She took a deep breath to regain her composure. "How do *you* feel today, Belle?"

"My face hurts but I will live." Belle looked across the table. "Thank you for the excellent stitching."

"Thank you for being my sister." Raven's voice sounded hoarse with emotion.

Tears threatened Fancy. She moved to rise from her chair, but her youngest sister reached out and stayed her.

"May we forever be as close in our hearts as we are at this moment," Raven said.

"Amen," six voices chorused.

Fancy stood then. "We need to pack."

"Good afternoon, Tinker." Prince Stepan greeted the ducal majordomo and led his charges into the foyer.

"Good afternoon, Your Highness."

Fancy gave the man a nervous smile when he shifted his gaze to her, saying, "Good afternoon, Miss Flambeau."

Stepan turned to the Flambeau sisters. "Meet Tinker, your father's majordomo." Then he gestured to each and told the man their names. "Belle, Bliss, Blaze, Serena, Sophia, Raven. Puddles, of course, is their dog. So what do you think, my good man?"

Tinker raised his brows. "I think my life is changed forever."

Stepan winked at the man. "The fun begins now."

"Do you always open the door?" Blaze asked.

"Yes, miss."

"Are we forbidden to open the door?"

"You may open the door to your heart's content," Tinker drawled, his lips twitching at her unsophisticated questions. "Their Graces"—the sisters giggled—"are waiting in the parlor. Come with me, please."

Tinker led the way upstairs, the sisters falling into a single line like ducklings following their mama. Holding hands, Stepan and Fancy walked behind them. Their *oohings* and *aahings* at the opulence of the mansion embarrassed Fancy.

"How are you holding up?" the prince whispered.

"I don't think I could survive this without you."

That made him smile.

but not *those* gifts. You must demand jewels, not books and animals."

"Roxie, shall I fetch you the hartshorn?" Robert Campbell teased his stepmother.

The Duchess of Inverary gave him a dimpled smile. "You are almost as impertinent as your father."

"I do not want you to call me Papa until you feel it in your heart," the duke was saying to Blaze. "I will give you a horse, but we will debate the monkey another day."

Blaze gave her father a smile brighter than her name. "Thank you, Papa."

Everyone laughed, including Fancy and her father.

"What is your dog's name?"

"Puddles." Blaze looked around, murmuring, "Where did he—*oh, no.*"

The mastiff had wandered across the parlor. True to his name, he lifted his leg and made a puddle.

The duchess gasped and appeared ready to swoon.

"Don't worry," Blaze rushed to explain. "Puddles is marking his territory."

Robert, Rudolf, and Stepan were nearly howling with laughter. The duke's shoulders shook with silent amusement.

Fancy covered her face with her hand. She had envisioned a different, more genteel scenario than this humiliating fiasco.

"Puddles will remain outside," the duchess announced.

"If Puddles remains outside," Blaze told her, "I will remain outside."

The Duchess of Inverary rolled her eyes and looked at her husband for support. He was rubbing his forehead, as if suffering a headache.

"I am too old for this," the duke muttered, and then cleared his throat. "Puddles is on probation. We will

consider that"—he gestured across the chamber—
"an accident."

Her father moved closer to her youngest sister. "And
this is my baby."

Raven considered the father she had never seen.
"Yes, Sir."

"And what is *your* heart's desire?"

Raven gave her oldest sister a sad glance. "I wish to
stop time so my sisters and I could forever remain as
close as we were this morning."

Her wistful remark silenced everyone, casting a bittersweet spell over all. Fancy felt tears welling in her
eyes, and the prince gave her hand a gentle squeeze.

"A most worthy wish," her father said, and then
peered at his oldest daughter. "I wish I could *reverse*
time and correct my mistakes."

Fancy dropped her gaze to the carpet, her father's
sentiment tugging at her heart, confusing her resolve.
Feeling the prince's hand on her back, she lifted her
eyes and read his expression, urging her to make
peace with her father. She looked away in refusal.

The Duke of Inverary approached his sons. "And
now daughters, I present your two half-brothers,
Robert Campbell, the Marquess of Argyll, and Prince
Rudolf Kazanov."

Blaze shook her head in exaggerated confusion.
"What the hell do we call them?"

"Blaze." Fancy decided she *would* throttle her sister.

"Call me Robert," the marquess said, "and call him
Rudolf."

"If you are a prince," Blaze asked, "does that mean
I am a princess?"

"You are a poor relation," Fancy said.

Blaze looked at the prince for verification. Rudolf
shrugged and smiled.

Fancy should have known her sister would not let

the matter rest. Once this sister grabbed hold of an idea, she refused to let go.

"I don't wish to remain a poor relation," Blaze announced. "Papa, will you take me to the thoroughbred races?"

"Keep those lips shut." Fancy could not mask her growing irritation.

The duke looked from one sister to the other. "Why do you want to go to the races?"

Blaze threw Fancy a sullen look. "Never mind."

Drawing Belle with her, the Duchess of Inverary rose from the settee. "Come, darlings. We will settle into our bedchambers and then return here for tea."

Raven approached Fancy. "Do not fail to practice your slingshot."

"You know?"

"Yes."

"What does she know?" Blaze asked.

Fancy took a deep breath. "I will not be living here with you."

Ready for battle, Blaze rounded on her father. "Why can't she live here?"

"I chose to remain in Soho Square."

Blaze whirled around. "We need you."

Fancy closed her eyes against her sister's pain, knowing the others would be wearing the same expression. She opened her mouth but could not find the words to soothe them.

Her father rescued her. "Fancy needs more time but may change her mind in a few days. She knows she is welcome here."

The sisters marched across the parlor to hug Fancy. Even Puddles gave her a good-bye lick.

"I promise to visit," she told them, "and want you to visit me."

Fancy watched the duchess usher them out of the

parlor. She didn't know whether to laugh or cry when she heard the two voices drift into the room from the corridor.

"Puddles sleeps with me," her sister said.

"Oh, dear Lord above." The duchess's appalled horror was apparent. "How will we ever find you a husband?"

"I would prefer a monkey."

Robert and Rudolf looked at each other and laughed.

"Roxie may have met her match," Robert said.

"I think you are right," Rudolf replied.

The Duke of Inverary glanced at the three younger men. "I want to speak privately with my daughter."

"Listen to what he says." Stepan touched her cheek. "I will wait in the foyer."

The duke approached and took her hands in his. "Will you change your mind?"

Fancy wanted to forgive him, but that long-ago day in Hyde Park prevented her from accepting his offer of love. Though her heart ached, she forced herself to refuse. "I can't do that."

Regret flashed across his expression. To his credit, her father banished the look and drew her across the parlor. "I want you to see this." He gestured to the portrait hanging on the wall.

Her own mother's image stared down at her. This was a mother she had never seen, a woman whose innocence clung to her like a sensual perfume, her eyes alight with coy invitation.

"She's so young and carefree." Fancy shifted her gaze from the portrait to her father. His gaze had fixed on her mother, his eyes clouding with warmth, longing, and regret. Perhaps he *had* loved her mother.

"I commissioned the portrait six months after we began our affair," her father told her, a smile of remembrance touching his lips. "After my first wife died, I brought Gabrielle here. Throughout the years, I have sat here wishing circumstances had been different, wishing I hadn't abandoned her and my daughters to the care of others, wishing I could unravel the damage I had done.

"Your mother would have been a countess in France. Her heart never mended from losing her whole family in the Terror."

Her father looked at her. "Your mother was pure aristocrat. She came to my bed a virgin and remained faithful her entire life. If I had been free, I would have married her."

"Thank you for telling me that." Raw emotion clogged her throat.

He lifted her hands to his lips. "I ask that you think about my offer and join your sisters here."

"I will consider it." That was the best she could do.

"Whenever you are ready."

"What if I am never ready?"

"I will still love you." Her father put his arm around her shoulder and led her toward the door. "May I inquire about your relationship with Prince Stepan?"

"I don't have a relationship with the prince."

The Duke of Inverary smiled at her. "Prince Stepan appears to believe you share more than a friendship."

Fancy shrugged. "I cannot control what the prince believes."

"Do you have tender feelings for him?"

"Stepan has been kind," Fancy admitted, "but princes do not marry opera singers."

Her father gave her a sideways hug. "Princes *do* marry the daughters of dukes."

Chapter 9

Stepan leaned against the banister, his arms folded across his chest, and worried about what was happening upstairs. If only she would make peace with her father, Fancy could make peace with herself, but he could not force her to see reason. Her emotional scars would last a lifetime, as his own did, but refusing to forgive meant the wound would fester.

Magnus Capmbell carried the burden of many sins on his own wounded soul. Not only had he hurt the mother but also his oldest daughter. The duke would always live with the anguish of guilt and regret unless his daughter forgave his trespasses.

His brother and the marquess loitered in the foyer and talked business. The ducal majordomo had resumed his duties nearby.

"My baby brother is behaving like a man in love," Rudolf remarked.

"Or an expectant father," Robert Campbell said.

"Ah, the agony and the ecstasy of true love," the majordomo murmured, eliciting chuckles from the marquess and the oldest prince.

Feeling like a baited bear, Stepan gave his brother and the marquess a grim stare. He heard a muffled squawk, but when he looked at the majordomo, the man's expression was somber.

Stepan heard footsteps on the stairs. With his arm around her shoulders, the father escorted the daughter to the foyer. That seemed encouraging, until he lifted his gaze and saw her expression. His songbird had the dazed look of a fledgling warrior in the midst of his first battle.

"Wopsle will attend us the day after tomorrow," the Duke of Inverary said to the three men.

Stepan glanced at Fancy. Her gaze pleaded for silence.

"This Alex Puddles has that dog's name," Robert Campbell said.

"Let us pray he did not earn his name as the dog did." Rudolf looked at Stepan. "I thought you were taking care of this matter."

"I spoke with the Seven Doves Chairman." Stepan struggled against a grin. "A cartel of seven owns the company."

"Where did you see him?" Rudolf asked.

"We met at the opera." Stepan flicked a glance at Fancy, who appeared ready to explode with laughter.

"What did the bloke say?" the marquess asked.

Stepan shifted his gaze to his brother. "Kazanov Brothers is ancillary damage."

"Do you mean this cartel wants to pauperize me?" the Duke of Inverary asked.

"Yes, Your Grace, the Seven Doves has targeted you."

"Who are these damn people?"

"I cannot answer that question."

"Cannot or will not?"

Stepan met the furious duke's gaze and shrugged his shoulders in a helpless gesture, which incited the man to a growl of anger.

"Where is your loyalty?" Rudolf demanded. "This

cartel is undercutting Kazanov Brothers. More important, the enemy of our friends is our enemy, too."

"I warned the chairman to cease undercutting prices," Stepan said. "If my warning does no good, Kazanov Brothers has two choices. Either we divest ourselves of our interests with the Campbells"—he gave the duke an apologetic grin—"or we pauperize the Seven Doves Company."

Fancy cleared her throat, drawing their attention. "I will be late for the opera if we don't leave now."

Stepan nodded at the three men and escorted Fancy out of Campbell Mansion. He helped her into the coach and then sat beside her.

"Thank you for your silence."

"I believe the Seven Doves will soon review its pricing policy." Stepan placed his arm on the leather seat behind her. "Until then, Kazanov Brothers can afford to lose a few coins."

Fancy remained silent for a long moment and then turned to him. "My mother's portrait hangs in his parlor. I-I think he loved her truly but fate—" She shrugged.

"Can you forgive him?"

"No."

"You are a stubborn wench, *ma petite.*"

"I am what I am." Fancy gazed out the coach's window. "Tell Harry he took the wrong turn. I am going directly to the opera house."

"I believed you would not feel well enough to perform," Stepan said. "I contacted Bishop for another night off."

"You are not my keeper." His acting on her behalf without her knowledge made her feel controlled, which irritated her. She had lived for many years without a man telling her what to do and intended to retain her independence. "You had no right to speak with Bishop on my behalf."

Stepan grinned. "Have I mentioned how adorable you are when angry?"

The prince was a condescending swine. Fancy opened her mouth to give him a verbal flogging, but he was faster.

"I was teasing you."

Fancy narrowed her violet gaze on him. "I need to sing tonight."

Stepan raised his brows.

"Performing exhilarates me," she explained. "The audience loves me, and I love the audience."

Stepan gave her a long look. "Have you considered their fickleness? An audience that loves you tonight may despise you tomorrow." He slid a finger down her petal-soft cheek. "Do not confuse illusion with enduring emotion."

Fancy remained silent, her gaze sliding away from his. The prince sounded like a man in love.

That frightened her. She knew he could never make her a permanent part of his life. Princes did not marry opera singers. If she surrendered to him, she would end her days like her mother.

Reaching Soho Square, Fancy led the way to her front door. She paused a moment, searching for her key, stalling before entering the empty house. Only Gabrielle Flambeau, Nanny Smudge, and she would reside here now. More spirits than living bodies.

"Allow me." Stepan reached around her and unlocked the door.

"Where did you get that key?"

"Belle had no further use for it."

Fancy walked into the foyer, her lips a grim line of displeasure. "Leave the key when you go."

Stepan gave her a boyish smile. "I think not."

Fancy opened her mouth to argue when the sounds of his coach departing registered. "Are you walking to Grosvenor Square?"

"Harry is fetching my retainers, who will serve us supper." Stepan closed the front door. "I assumed you would not want to dine out tonight."

Fancy stared at him as if the prince had suddenly turned purple. She could not credit that he'd instructed his servants to cook dinner and serve them here. "I would have cooked us supper."

"I knew I had chosen well." Stepan gestured toward the parlor. "Finding a woman willing to cook for her man is difficult, if not impossible."

Fancy gave him a rueful smile. "You are not my man."

"I consider you my woman."

"I belong to me."

Fancy prevented his reply by turning her back on him, her gaze scanning the foyer. Without her sisters, the house seemed empty. She even missed the mastiff barreling down the stairs to greet her. Loneliness would rule her life from this day onward.

"The silence hurts my ears," Stepan said, his words echoing her thoughts. "How will you bear the silence after living with a crowd?"

Unfastening his cravat, Stepan sauntered into the parlor. The prince tossed his jacket and then his cravat onto a nearby chair. Making himself comfortable on the sofa, he lifted his legs and rested them across the coffee table.

"Sit with me." Stepan patted the spot beside him.

Surrendering to the inevitable, Fancy plopped onto the sofa. The prince was an irritating, tenacious bulldog too accustomed to getting his own way, but she would be completely alone if he hadn't forced himself into her heart and her home.

Her heart? Did that mean she loved him? Sitting so close his thigh touched hers, Fancy inhaled his arousing sandalwood scent. It comforted her, as did the heat emanating from his body.

"I do not want you alone tonight." Stepan slipped his arm across the back of the sofa behind her. "I will remain with you."

"You can't sleep here," Fancy exclaimed, her expression appalled. "If you insist, I-I-I'll fetch the authorities to make you leave."

"I do not plan to seduce you, merely to pass the night to ease your transition from living with a crowd to being alone." Stepan cocked a dark brow, teasing her, "I hope you are not planning *my* seduction?"

Fancy blushed but fell in with his drollness. "I do not plan seducing any prince at the moment"—she shrugged—"but if I changed my mind, I would choose you."

Stepan gave her an easy smile, his gleaming dark eyes mesmerizing her. "Being the chosen one flatters me."

Fancy longed to throw herself into his arms, press her body against his heated strength, surrender all she was into his care. Her mother had walked down that path and died unhappily. Even her seven daughters could never console her. Their combined hearts and love would never equal what she had felt for Magnus Campbell.

"You may sleep in my sisters' bedchamber for one night only. I will lock my chamber door, and you must promise to leave at dawn."

"I promise." Stepan winked at her. "Shall I also cross my heart and hope to die?"

Fancy smirked. "That will be unnecessary."

Stepan heard someone banging on the front door. "My retainers have arrived."

Smiling to himself, Stepan walked down the hallway toward the foyer. His songbird wanted him but feared soaring to the heights of love. In view of her mother's unhappy history, he could not fault her skittishness.

Even he was not unaffected by his childhood. His own lack of parental attention and his mother's sad history colored his adult behavior. Which was one reason he savored his brothers' children and had never contemplated using a woman for his own purposes.

His songbird believed he was an unscrupulous rake. He *was* a mind-bogglingly wealthy and incredibly handsome aristocrat. That much was true, but wealth and good looks did not make him a libertine. Though, if pressed, he would admit he was no saint.

Stepan yanked the door open, allowing his retainers entrance. Bones, Feliks, and Boris bustled into the foyer, leaving Harry guarding the prince's coach. Each man carried several covered serving platters.

"Follow this corridor to the kitchen," Stepan instructed them, "which opens onto the dining room." He returned to the parlor. "Shall we dine?"

Fancy rose from the sofa. Hand in hand, they walked through the French doors to the dining room.

Leaving the head of the table for himself, Stepan led Fancy to the chair on his right. He realized the symbolism had not escaped her.

Fancy looked from the side chair to the head of the table and then at him. "This is not my place."

His songbird needed to overcome this tendency to rule. There could be one head of their household, and he intended to be that person.

Stepan startled himself with the thought of living with her. Was he actually contemplating marriage?

Stepan gifted her with his most charming smile. "Surely, you do not begrudge your guest his choice of seats?"

Fancy looked from the side chair to the head chair. Settling the matter, she sat in the side chair.

Stepan sat at the head of the table. Their relationship was definitely progressing.

Feliks and Boris walked into the dining room with their dinner of grilled tenderloin steak with béarnaise sauce and asparagus. Behind the two Russians came Bones, carrying a bottle of chilled champagne and two crystal flutes.

The burly Russians nodded and grinned a hello to Fancy before leaving. Bones remained long enough to open and pour the sparkling white wine.

Stepan lifted his glass in salute. "To the sweetest songbird England has ever heard."

Fancy touched her glass to his, sipped the champagne, and giggled. "The bubbles tickle my nose and throat."

They ate and drank in comfortable silence for a time. And then, as Stepan knew it would, her conversation concerned her missing family.

"I wonder how my sisters are faring at Park Lane," Fancy said. "Do you think they will miss me?"

"I am certain they are thinking of you now." Stepan refilled her champagne flute. "My sympathy lies with the duchess, who may not survive your sisters."

"Blaze was already rebelling against authority." A smile lit her disarming violet eyes. "You don't think there's a chance the duchess will return them to me?"

Stepan shook his head. "Rudolf mentioned the prospect of mothering your sisters and you excited the duchess. You knew she raised her three nieces?"

"She never had children of her own?"

"None. Though, the Duke of Inverary is not her first husband."

Fancy cut a tiny piece of steak and chewed it slowly. Then she reached for her champagne and looked at the prince.

Stepan crooked a finger at her, beckoning her

closer, and leaned toward her at the same time. He touched his lips to hers, his tongue flicking out to lick the corner of her mouth.

Fancy pulled away, a blush rising on her cheeks. "What . . . ?"

"I adore béarnaise sauce," Stepan drawled, "and you had a dot clinging to the corner of your mouth. Besides your spirited innocence and brutal honesty, what I love about you is your ardor. Most society ladies are shallow, but you erupt with passion like a volcano."

Fancy stared into his dark eyes. "I do hope searching for employment appears on your agenda for tomorrow."

"Only you would insult a man for offering you flattery."

"How would a society lady respond to your compliments?"

"The young lady would flutter her eyelashes at me. Like so." Stepan demonstrated as he spoke, her laughter filling the dining room. "Then she would lift her chin to expose her swanlike neck, perhaps in the event I proved a vampire. The married and widowed ladies would *accidentally* brush their breasts on my arm."

"What sluttish behavior."

"My opinion matches yours."

Fancy relaxed in her chair, her gaze on the remains of their meal. "I could easily become accustomed to servants cooking and cleaning for me."

"You have only to ask, and I will grant your wish." Stepan smiled at her skeptical expression. "By the way, Rudolf is expecting us at his ball tomorrow night."

"Us?" Fancy arched an ebony brow.

"Do not feign ignorance."

"I have nothing to wear."

"That problem is easily solved. Expect Madame Janette to deliver another gown with accessories to your dressing room."

"I am not welcome in your social circles." Fancy shifted her gaze to the French lace curtains ruffled by the evening breeze. She could not force her way where she was not wanted. Getting the cut direct would humiliate her.

When the prince remained silent, curiosity got the better of her. She slid her gaze to him.

"I welcome you into my social circle." Stepan moved his arm in an expansive gesture. "My brothers and their wives welcome you. The Duke and Duchess of Inverary welcome you. The duchess's nieces and their husbands welcome you. My cousin—"

"I get the point." Fancy had no defense against his logic and, for once in her life, accepted defeat with grace. "Purchase a blush pink gown, if possible, no ruffles or other adornments."

"You give orders like a princess." Stepan stood and gestured toward the parlor, asking, "Shall we?"

Fancy sat on the sofa and wondered how they would pass the hours between now and bedtime. That disturbing thought both frightened and interested her.

"I want to lock the door behind my men." Stepan headed for the corridor. "Make yourself at home until I return."

"This *is* my home."

Stepan glanced at her over his shoulder and gave her an exaggerated wink, which made her smile.

When he returned, Stepan sat beside her and rested his arm on the back of the sofa behind her. Fancy stiffened, physical awareness of the man heightening her extreme nervousness.

The prince reeked of masculinity. His sandalwood scent, his body heat, and his muscled strength made her weak with longing. He was the handsome hero of her maidenly dreams and her worst nightmare rolled into one man.

Stepan dropped his hand to her shoulder. "Relax, songbird."

"I am relaxed."

"If you were any stiffer," he said, laughter lurking in his voice, "you would already have been dead for several hours."

Fancy looked into his dark eyes, anticipation flaring to life and flooding her body. Resisting his magnetic pull, she dropped her gaze to his lips. His hand on her shoulder began a slow caress, a delicious shiver tickling her spine.

She wanted to kiss his invitingly shaped lips.

She wanted to glide her fingertips across the warm flesh covering his hard muscles.

She wanted to forget her unhappy mother, who prevented her from losing herself in the prince.

"Do not think," Stepan murmured. His handsome face inched closer, her nerves rioting in response.

Instinct surfaced, vanquishing her shyness and her resolve. She lifted her face, her lips meeting his, and pressed her body against him.

His arms surrounded her and pulled her tighter. Her arms glided up his chest to entwine around his neck.

Their kiss deepened. He flicked the tip of his tongue across the crease of her lips, coaxing them open, and slipped inside to taste her sweetness.

His lips were warm and firm, his tongue coaxing her surrender. His heat and his strength enveloped her, his gentle touch persuading her trust.

The world faded away. Her body and her mind and her soul centered on him, and he became her whole universe.

Fancy returned his kiss with equal ardor. They fell back on the sofa, his hard muscles covering her soft curves.

Sliding her hands inside his shirt, Fancy reveled in his unyielding planes, gloried in his strength. She became lost in the fog of exciting sensation, never feeling the cool air on her naked breasts.

Stepan worshipped her with his lips, sliding down her delicately boned throat to capture a pink nipple. He sucked and licked and kissed the nub and then lavished his attention on her other breast.

Fancy purred low in her throat. The sexy sounds of her own pleasure were a dash of cold water to her senses.

"No." She pushed against him.

His dark eyes glazed with desire, Stepan lifted his head and stared into her eyes. He groaned in unsatisfied protest but lifted himself off her.

Fancy yanked her gown up, covering her nakedness. He had broken his promise not to seduce her. Her violet gaze judged him guilty.

Stepan ran a hand through his black hair. "You promised not to seduce me," he said. "Perhaps I should lock *my* door tonight."

"What?" Fancy could not believe what she was hearing. How dare the royal swine accuse her of seduction when she'd never even kissed a man.

Stepan gave her a wolfish smile. "I apologize for getting carried away. I never meant . . ." He shrugged.

Fancy realized he had reacted to her response. Both shared the blame for being swept away.

"I forgive you," she said, "and consider the fault partially mine."

"You are too generous, love, because a man should exhibit self-control." Stepan gave her a long look. "Surely, you can see from our behavior that we belong together."

Fancy scooted back on the sofa, putting more distance between them. She did not understand what he wanted from her. "I-I don't want to discuss this tonight."

"Then I will respect your wishes. Shall we retire?"

"Together?" She heard her own high-pitched squeak.

Stepan smiled at her panic. "I will sleep in another bedchamber tonight."

After showing him to his room and bidding him goodnight, Fancy locked herself in her bedchamber. She changed into her nightshift and plopped down on the bed, her troubled thoughts keeping her awake.

She had almost succumbed to the weakness of loving a man and become her mother. She needed to guard her heart more carefully.

With a deep sigh, Fancy realized it was too late to save herself heartache. She'd done the unthinkable— fallen in love with an aristocrat.

All was not lost, though. She could still refuse him her body, saving an unborn baby from the anguish she had suffered.

Fancy lay back on the bed. Knowing the prince slept two doors down made relaxing difficult. She tossed and turned and fell into a light doze.

Until— Fancy awakened in the small hours of the morning. Darkness shrouded the world, and she realized a noise had disturbed her. Was the prince looking for a way into her chamber? Had a thief broken into her house? Even worse, was the intruder the one who had left the threatening flower message on her doorstep?

And then Fancy heard the faint sounds of weeping. With a heavy heart, she padded across the chamber and stepped into the corridor. The weeping grew louder here.

Fancy passed the prince's chamber on the way to her mother's. She inched the door open and stood on the threshold.

Gabrielle Flambeau lay across the bed and wept for

her lost love, the sound of her mother's heartbreak tearing Fancy into pieces. Her father may have loved her mother, but he had still abandoned her to misery.

A hand touched her shoulder, and the weeping ceased abruptly. Fancy jumped and whirled around. The prince stood mere inches from her. She slid her gaze from his face to his bare chest, her breath catching in her throat. A matting of black hair covered his magnificent muscles and ended in a *V* that disappeared inside his breeches.

"What are you doing?" Fancy demanded, her voice a harsh whisper.

Stepan cupped her cheek. "I heard you weeping and worried."

First the prince had smelled her nanny's cinnamon. Now he heard her mother's weeping? He needed to know the truth. "This chamber belonged to my mother. You heard her weeping, not me."

Stepan raised his brows at that, the hint of a smile touching his lips. "I do not commune with spirits, sweetheart. I drink them."

"Loves me, loves me not . . ."

Dressed in formal evening attire, a tall gentleman stood on the deserted grounds of St. Bartholomew's Fair at Smithfield Market. He gazed through the predawn mist at the woman lying at his feet, so peaceful in death. The man sprinkled a handful of rose petals one by one the length of her body from head to feet.

"I'm cold," complained a hoarse voice.

Like a striking snake, the gentleman backhanded the short, plump woman who stood beside him. "Return to the coach. I need to make one more stop." He grabbed another handful of rose petals.

"Loves me, loves me not . . ."

* * *

Fingers of gold-orange light in the eastern horizon reached for the world, announcing another dawn. Slashes of pink and mauve streaked across the sky, darkening to indigo in the west.

In spite of the early hour, Fancy sat in silence at the dining room table and sipped coffee. As dawn had neared, she'd risen from her restless bed and cooked the prince breakfast.

Stepan sat at the head of the table and devoured eggs and sausage and biscuits. He wore breeches, boots, and his unbuttoned shirt. Glimpses of his bare chest made Fancy's mouth water for him, not food.

"Delicious," Stepan said. "You are the only woman in thirty years who has cooked for me."

"That distinction honors me," Fancy said, her tone dry. "Your failure to have breakfast delivered surprises me."

Stepan smiled at her humor and changed the subject. "I will see Madame Janette this morning. Later, I am engaged for a tea party."

That brought a smile to her lips. The prince would make an excellent father, taking special joy in children.

"What will you do today?"

Fancy shrugged. "I suppose I'll nap and then practice my slingshot."

"You are not planning another revenge on Patrice Tanner?"

"No, I am following my baby sister's advice."

"Take *my* advice, love. Do not mention your mother's haunting to anyone."

"I would not wish to vacation in Bedlam."

"Good." Stepan lifted his cup for a last sip of coffee

and then buttoned his shirt. "Life must be wonderfully private for commoners in love."

Fancy rolled her eyes. "I doubt the wives who cook and clean feel especially blessed."

"Harry will be waiting." Stepan shrugged into his waistcoat without buttoning it. After slinging the cravat around his neck, he grabbed his jacket and hooked it over his shoulder.

"Walk me to the foyer," he said, rising from the chair, "and lock the door behind me."

When she stood, Stepan pulled her into a sideways hug and dropped a kiss on the crown of her head. Hand in hand, they walked down the hallway to the foyer.

The prince opened the front door. "Someone left you roses." He bent to scoop them in his hand but then leaped up and shouted, "*Yadrona mysh' svinya.*"

"What did you say?"

"I said, mouse-fucker pig." Stepan pointed to the doorstep. "Someone gave you *decapitated* roses."

Fancy gasped, her complexion paling to a sickening white, and raised her gaze to his. "You don't think the rose-petal murderer did this, do you?"

"I do not approve of your living alone." Stepan passed her the decapitated roses. "Either move to Park Lane or come home with me."

Fancy dug in her heels like a donkey. "I will do neither."

"I cannot live every minute of every day fearing for your safety," Stepan argued. "You need protection."

"I will report this to Alex later this morning," Fancy promised. "Perhaps Constable Black will investigate."

Stepan gave her an unhappy look. "I warn you, Fancy. I will not hesitate to put you in my protective custody."

"I am no criminal."

"I will not allow you to play a madman's games. Now lock the damn door."

Chapter 10

He was late.

The sun raced across the sky toward noon by the time Alexander Blake unlocked his front door. He rubbed the dark stubbles on his chin. Shaving and changing his suit would make him even later. Leaving a few essentials at Genevieve's would be wise.

Alexander opened the parlor window and inhaled the warm, spring air. A breeze flirted with the curtains. Exhausted from a night of lovemaking, he poured a dram of whiskey and dropped onto the sofa.

Did he love Genevieve? She was sweet and oh so sensuous. He had almost proposed marriage last night, but something had held his tongue.

Alexander sipped his whiskey, closed his eyes, and then regretted it. His mind conjured another image.

Ebony hair. Violet eyes. Ripe breasts, playing peek-a-boo beneath that flimsy nightgown.

Raven Flambeau was too young to consider. Good God, she was the baby sister he'd never had. If he truly loved Genevieve, why was he imagining Raven in her nightgown?

He would propose to Genevieve after they apprehended the rose-petal murderer. If she fell pregnant before then, he would marry her immediately.

Banging on the front door drew his attention.

Alexander rose from the sofa and, pushing the curtains aside, peered out the window. The Duke of Essex's coach stood in front of his house. A visit from his grandfather foreshadowed a miserable day.

With great reluctance, Alexander opened the front door. Longtime adversaries, he and his grandfather stared into each other's eyes.

"As I live and breathe," Alexander imitated his late mother's Irish lilt. "Top o' the mornin' to ye, Bartholomew Blake."

"Do not be impertinent," the Duke of Essex said.

"What do you want?"

"I want to come inside."

Squelching the urge to slam the door in the old man's face, Alexander stepped aside to allow him entrance. Then he slammed the door.

Leaning on his cane, the Duke of Essex limped into the parlor. He inspected his grandson from stubbled cheeks to wrinkled suit, unfastened shirt, and cravat slung around his neck. "You look like a bedraggled tomcat."

"Thank you, Your Grace."

The duke's sharp gaze scanned the parlor, his expression saying he found it lacking. "I don't understand him living here after *she* died."

Alexander could cheerfully have smashed the cane over the old man's head. Instead, he poured himself a dram of whiskey. "Would you care for a drink, Your Grace?"

"No." His grandfather raised the cane and struck, sending the glass flying out of Alexander's hand. "And neither do you."

Alexander stood motionless, his gaze boring into his

grandfather's. "Would the cane be the same one that scarred my father?"

The Duke of Essex said nothing. "Soho Square is no proper residence for the Marquess of Basildon."

"I do not acknowledge the title."

"Your parents were legally wed."

Alexander could not contain his bitterness. "You disowned my father because he married my mother."

Regret clouded the old man's eyes. "As my only living relative, you will inherit all one day in the not too distant future."

"I refuse to acknowledge you," Alexander said. "All you possess will go to the Crown. Remember my words on your lonely deathbed."

The Duke of Essex banged his cane on the coffee table. "You will accept the title, the land, and the wealth even if I must cram it down your throat."

Their dark gazes clashed, the resemblance heightened by their anger. The grandfather could still outstare the grandson.

Alexander shifted his gaze. "Is there a point to this visit?"

"You have no financial need to work with Constable Black."

"I enjoy investigating crimes."

"How bourgeois," the duke drawled, his voice filled with contempt. "What is your relationship with this opera singer?"

Alexander raised his brows at the old man. "Genevieve is none of your business."

"The girl is unsuitable," his grandfather said. "Even one of those Flambeau sisters will do, especially now."

Alexander drew a blank. "Explain yourself."

"Inverary acknowledges paternity, has moved them into his home, and will be sponsoring them into society," the duke said. "Those girls may have been born out of wedlock, but their mother was a countess. Aristocratic blood runs in their veins."

"How do you know this?"

The Duke of Essex gave him a long look. "I know everything worth knowing." He turned and limped toward the foyer. "You must take your rightful place, marry, and produce an heir. I won't live forever."

Making no promises, Alexander opened the door for his grandfather. Constable Amadeus Black stood there, his hand raised to reach for the knocker.

The constable looked from Alexander to his grandfather. "Good day, Your Grace."

The Duke of Essex nodded at the constable and looked at his grandson. "When you change your mind—"

"I won't."

Alexander watched the duke hobble toward the ducal coach. His grandfather seemed so old and alone. He couldn't help feeling sorry for the old man.

He could not imagine living with such weighty regret. No man should disown his son for marrying the woman he loved. His grandfather should have swallowed his disapproval for the young Irishwoman who had captured his son's heart.

The old man had lived to regret his actions. Too late, though. Both his father and his mother were dead.

Amadeus Black followed him into the parlor. "What was that about?"

Alexander dropped onto the couch. "His Grace has decided I must take my rightful place in society." He gestured to the broken glass and whiskey on the rug. "The old man has tantrums."

"You should consider it," Amadeus said, surprising him. "The Marquess of Basildon would have entrance into society and expand our investigation."

"Do you believe Parkhurst is guilty?"

"Barney lost Parkhurst last night," Amadeus said, sitting in the high-backed chair, "and we have another victim. The perpetrator made his first mistake by dropping the body near Smithfield Market. Apparently, the gentleman is ignorant of the early hours required of apprentices."

Alexander perked up. "Do we have a witness?"

"An apprentice noticed a coach near the market," Amadeus said. "A tall gentleman struck a plump lady, who then hid in the coach. When they left the area, our apprentice investigated and found the victim."

"Can this apprentice identify the gentleman?"

"No." Amadeus inspected his disheveled appearance. "Are you ill?"

Alexander flushed. "I passed the night with Genevieve."

Constable Black smiled, "Ah, lovesick."

Fancy Flambeau, appeared in the doorway, bringing both men to their feet, and gave them an apologetic smile. "Your door is unlocked."

"Fancy Flambeau, meet Constable Black."

"Look." Fancy held the decapitated roses out. "Someone left these on my doorstep during the night. Could he be the rose-petal murderer?"

"Or someone imitating him." Amadeus lifted the decapitated roses out of her hands."

"You didn't move to your father's?" Alexander asked.

Fancy lifted her chin. "I refuse to forgive him."

Alexander ran his hand through his hair. Her vendetta against her father could cost her life. "If your father is acknowledging—"

"I refuse to abandon my mother's memory and do not acknowledge him."

"I do not recommend living alone," Amadeus warned. "Do you have a dog?"

"His Grace is acknowledging Puddles, too."

Amadeus looked puzzled.

"Puddles is the Flambeaus' mastiff," Alexander said.

The constable's lips quirked into a smile. "Very generous of His Grace."

"Fancy, listen to reason," Alexander pleaded. "You cannot—Whoever left those could have broken into your house and hurt you."

"Prince Stepan passed the night at my house." Fancy blushed. "Not in my bed."

Alexander did not know how to make her understand the danger. She was more stubborn than a donkey and, if pressed, more cantankerous than a camel.

"Move with your sisters to Park Lane," Alexander advised her. "I will worry myself sick if you don't."

"You sound like Stepan." Fancy looked at the constable. "Did Alex tell you my sister could help with your investigation?"

"*Fancy.*" Alexander's tone warned her to silence.

"Your sister can help the investigation?" the constable echoed.

Fancy nodded. "God blessed Raven with special talents."

Amadeus cocked a brow at her. "Explain."

"Raven knows things."

"The twit has visions," Alexander explained, "but she did know certain unreported facts like the sewing."

"Raven can touch objects to facilitate her visions," Fancy added.

Alexander rolled his eyes. "She professes to move objects with her mind, too."

"Schedule a meeting with Raven, preferably here," Amadeus instructed. "I would not wish to inhibit her talents by meeting elsewhere."

That surprised Alexander. "Are you serious?"

"Successful investigators keep open minds while other men solve fewer cases." Amadeus Black turned to the opera singer. "Either move to your father's or hire a bodyguard. Living alone is flirting with danger."

He was late.

Stepan banged on the door. When his brother's majordomo opened it a moment later, he brushed past the man, saying, "Good afternoon, Bottoms."

"Your Highness, the princesses worried that you might miss today's tea party," Bottoms said. "They await your pleasure in the drawing room."

Stepan smiled at that. They had begun their tea parties in the dining room, but his nieces had argued about who would sit at the head of the table. Keeping the peace, Bottoms procured a round table and set it in the drawing room each week.

This equality did not impede his oldest niece, though. Princess Roxanne dominated the proceedings in the tradition of her namesake, Roxanne Campbell, Duchess of Inverary.

Wearing an apologetic smile, Stepan rushed into the room and sat in his usual place across the table from Roxanne. The four younger princesses took turns sitting on either side of him. Lily and Elizabeth, the four-year-olds, sat beside him today while Sally and Natasia, the five-year-olds, sat on either side of Roxanne.

"You are late," Roxanne said.

Stepan looked at each princess in turn. "I apologize for being detained elsewhere."

Drawing their attention, Bottoms entered the drawing room with the tea cart. The majordomo placed cucumber sandwiches and lemon cookies on the table. He served each princess a glass of lemonade, brought the prince a pot of tea, and left the room.

Stepan ate a cucumber sandwich, sipped his tea, and looked around the table. Paying homage to the undisputed queen of these proceedings, he said, "Princess Roxanne, what is the gossip this week?"

Roxanne set her lemonade on the table, as did the other girls. "Captain Crude insulted Princess Sunshine."

Stepan feigned horrified surprise. "What did the captain do?"

Roxanne glanced at her sisters and cousins. "I dare not say."

Stepan chuckled at that. His watching nieces giggled.

"Darling, Princess Sunshine was not smiling," Roxanne embellished, eliciting more laughter. "The Earl of Goodness defended her, of course. Goodness and Sunshine are an item, if you know what I mean."

"Uncle," Lily whispered, "what does she mean?"

Stepan leaned close to his niece. "Goodness and Sunshine love each other."

"Lady Snoot gave Princess Sunshine the cut," Natasia told them.

"How shocking," Stepan exclaimed.

"Uncle," whispered Elizabeth, "what is the cut?"

"Lady Snoot refused to speak with Sunshine."

"Lord Vexing danced with Lady Fast *five* times," Elizabeth said.

"Is Lady Fast ruined?" Stepan asked.

Elizabeth shrugged. "I'll tell you next week."

"Appearances mean everything in this town," Roxanne drawled.

Stepan grinned. "Who told you that?"

"Aunt Roxie."

"I thought so." Stepan looked at Viktor's daughter. "Do you have any news for me?"

Sally nodded. "Lord Badboy and Lady Reckless 'loped to Greta Green."

"You mean *e*loped to Gret*n*a Green?"

"Who's Greta Green?" Lily asked, her expression bewildered.

Stepan chuckled. "Badboy and Reckless ran away to marry in a town called Gretna Green."

Lily's expression cleared. "I know gossip."

Stepan leaned close. "What is your gossip, sweetheart?"

"The Earl of Rotten bought a ticket to Tyburn!"

Stepan shouted with laughter. "Who told you that?"

"My daddy told me," Lily answered. "My daddy knows everything."

"Do you have gossip for us?" Roxanne asked.

Stepan looked at each of his nieces. All five were staring at him with rapt attention. "I was late today because I needed to purchase a gown for my friend, Fancy Flambeau."

"Is she a princess?" Lily asked.

"No."

Elizabeth tugged on his sleeve. "A duchess?"

"No."

"She must be a countess," Sally said.

"No."

Natasia spoke up. "A baroness?"

Stepan shook his head. "No."

Roxanne lifted her chin, secure in her superior knowledge. "Are you saying she is merely a lady?"

"No."

"What the blue blazes is she?" Lily demanded.

"Did your daddy teach you about blue blazes?"

"My mummy taught me blue blazes," Lily answered. "My mummy knows more than my daddy."

Stepan grinned at her. "Fancy Flambeau is an opera singer."

"Do you love her?" Lily asked.

Stepan scanned the five faces watching him. "I suppose I do."

"Did you tell her?" Elizabeth asked.

"No."

"Why not?" Natasia asked.

Stepan shrugged. Typical females, his nieces adored gossip and love stories.

"Does she love you?" Sally asked.

"I do not know."

Lily touched his hand. "Ask her."

"Then you will know," Elizabeth agreed with her cousin.

"Uncle Stepan will never ask her." Roxanne shook her head in disapproval. "Aunt Roxie said silly boys need to be handled, and Uncle is a boy."

"You hurt my feelings," Stepan said.

"You are naughty." Lily shook her finger at her eldest sister. "Uncle Stepan is not a boy."

Roxanne rolled her eyes. "Uncles *are* boys."

"I love you," Elizabeth whispered, touching his arm.

Stepan smiled at Mikhail's shy daughter. "I love you, sweetheart."

"I love you lots," Lily told him.

"And I love you lots." Stepan made a sweeping gesture with his hand. "I love you and you and you and you and you."

Roxanne gave him a feline smile. "Which one do you love the most?"

Stepan understood Paris's dilemma when facing Hera, Athena, and Aphrodite. Unlike foolish Paris, he ignored the question by changing the subject. "So, all of you believe I should tell Fancy I love her?"

The five little girls bobbed their heads in unison.

"What if she does not love me?"

"Trust me." Lily pointed her finger at him. "She loves you."

Stepan smiled at the four-year-old. Laughter from the doorway drew his attention. He stood and offered his sister-in-law the seat. "I heard you know more than Rudolf."

"That is true." Princess Samantha sat in the offered chair, her eyes sparkling with merriment. "Will Miss Flambeau attend the ball this evening?"

"I guarantee her presence." Stepan glanced at his nieces and then asked his sister-in-law, "What is your opinion of this love business?"

"You should definitely tell her." Samantha winked at him. "No woman can resist a prince in love."

"That is settled then." Six-year-old Roxanne assumed control of the gathering. "Uncle, you will tell us the gossip next week if not sooner."

"I promise." Stepan told his sister-in-law, "Your aunt has certainly influenced her namesake." He circled the table, as was his custom, and gave each niece a peck on the cheek before leaving.

"Uncle!" Lily caught him at the door.

Stepan crouched eye level with her. The four-year-old wrapped her arms around his neck and touched her nose to his.

"Tell the lady *I love you.*"

"I promise." Stepan kissed the tip of her nose. "I love you, too."

"Bring the princess here next tea party."

"Fancy is not a princess."

"All girls are princesses." Lily gestured to her mother, her sisters, and her cousins. "We are princesses."

Stepan traced a finger down her cheek. "Fancy will become my princess when I marry her . . ."

He was late.

Waiting in her dressing room at the opera house, Fancy tapped her foot in growing agitation and wondered where the prince was. She would have paced the room if it hadn't been a pigeonhole. Making her operatic debut had not made her this nervous. She would prefer facing a standing-room- only audience to stepping into society.

Madame Janette had delivered an exquisite blush silk gown. The bodice's rounded neckline hinted at cleavage, the sleeves short and puffed. Blush silk slippers, embroidered silk stockings, and elbow-length white kid gloves completed the ensemble. The modiste had even included a Barege shawl and a mother-of-pearl mirror fan, the latest rage.

Keeping her appearance simple, Fancy had woven her hair into a knot at the nape of her neck, but a few ebony wisps escaped to soften the look. She wore no jewelry, which accentuated her natural beauty.

Seeing her image in the tiny cracked mirror proved impossible. Perhaps if she inspected herself in sections?

Fancy pinched her cheeks for color and then looked at each side of her face. She turned around and glanced over her shoulder, trying to see the back of her head.

Next, Fancy studied the gown's neckline. The hint of cleavage appeared sophisticated and modest.

Deciding to inspect her backside, Fancy stood on her stool. She twisted her body this way and that like a contortionist but failed to see—

"What are you doing?"

Fancy whirled around, nearly toppling off the stool. Her cheeks bloomed rose red.

Stepan leaned against the doorjamb. Laughter gleamed in his dark eyes.

Fancy stepped off the stool. "I was trying to inspect my appearance in that contemptible mirror."

"You look beautiful," Stepan said, "but your red complexion clashes with the pink gown."

Fancy smiled. "Thank you for the gown."

"I will purchase you a proper mirror tomorrow."

"Please don't do that." Fancy sighed, wishing she

could accept the gift. "I am trying to keep the peace with Patrice. Why are you late?"

"Did you miss me?"

"I've been holding my tears at bay."

"How encouraging."

"I suppose you're growing on me."

"Like a wart?"

Fancy batted her eyelashes at him. "You are more handsome than a wart."

Stepan grinned. "Thank you, I think."

"You didn't answer my question."

"I found Miss Giggles wandering," Stepan told her, "so I decided to charm the prima donna."

"How diplomatic." Fancy slipped her hand through the crook of his arm. They left her dressing room and walked through the empty opera house to exit on Bow Street.

The coach ride to Montagu House, Prince Rudolf's residence, passed too quickly. The closer they got to the ball, the more nervous Fancy became, and the worry sickened her.

Coaches lined both sides of Great Russell Street. The spot in front of the mansion had been left vacant for arrivals.

Fancy touched his arm. "You won't leave me?"

"I will stick with you like a bee on a flower." Stepan gave her a reassuring smile. "Unless a gentleman invites you to dance."

Fancy smiled. "The three of us waltzing would seem odd."

Prince Rudolf's footmen greeted them at the door. Stepan ushered Fancy across the foyer and upstairs to the ballroom.

"Prince Stepan Kazanov," the majordomo announced, "and Miss Fancy Flambeau."

"I wish he hadn't done that," she whispered, making the prince smile.

Fancy saw a sea of faces turn in their direction and felt more conspicuous than the night she had sung at the Inverary ball. Some guests stared at them; other guests whispered to each other; a few ignored their arrival.

The ballroom looked similar to that of the Duke of Inverary. An orchestra played at the top of the ballroom. Chairs and small tables hugged the walls, leaving the expanse in between for loitering and gossiping.

"Ready?"

Fancy felt the prince's hand grasp hers. She looked at him and nodded.

"Good evening," Prince Rudolf greeted them.

"We're pleased you could attend," Princess Samantha greeted Fancy. She slid her gaze to the younger prince's. "The girls are looking forward to next week's tea party."

"Lily told me her father knew everything," Stepan said, "but her mother knew more."

Prince Rudolf smiled and looked at Fancy. "My four-year-old daughter adores her Uncle Stepan."

"Your brothers are at the far end of the ballroom," Samantha said. "Do not forget what you promised your nieces."

Fancy looked at Stepan. "What did you promise them?"

"I will tell you later." Stepan led her away. "Let us greet my brothers."

Fancy felt interested gazes following her across the ballroom. She refused to look at anyone, knowing she would see their disapproval.

"You remember Viktor, his wife Regina, and Mikhail," Stepan said.

"Sally spoke endlessly about you after returning from the tea party," Princess Regina told her.

"My Elizabeth also spoke of you," Prince Mikhail added.

"How would they know me?" Fancy glanced at the prince, who looked flushed.

"I mentioned you to my nieces," Stepan answered. "Shall we dance?"

Fancy and Stepan stepped onto the dance floor. He drew her into his arms, one hand on her waist. They swirled around the ballroom, the man and the music mesmerizing her.

"Why did you speak about me to your nieces?"

"I was telling them about the opera." Stepan gave her his boyish smile. "My nieces invite you to attend next week's tea party."

"I would love that. So, inviting me to their tea party was your promise to them?"

The music's ending precluded the prince's reply. He ushered her back to their group, now joined by the Duke and Duchess of Inverary.

"Darling Fancy," the Duchess of Inverary exclaimed, giving her an air kiss. "I am so happy to see you among us."

"Roxie, there's no need to gush," the Duke of Inverary said.

The duchess rolled her eyes. "My sweet Belle refuses to see anyone."

"My sister needs time to heal," Fancy said. "Her scars go deeper than skin."

"She refused to go shopping," the duchess said, her tone filled with horror.

Fancy bit her lip to keep from laughing and glanced at the prince. He had turned slightly away, probably to stifle his laughter.

"That problem is easily solved," the Duke of Inverary told his wife. "Invite the shopkeepers to Park Lane. By the time she's ready to come out, Belle will have a complete wardrobe."

The duchess gave him a feline smile. "Magnus, only your intelligence rivals your startling good looks."

Now the Duke of Inverary rolled his eyes. "I'm going to see what's happening in the card room."

Fancy watched him walk away. She thought that he and his wife made a good match.

"Good evening, Stepan."

Fancy turned toward the female voice. A redhead in a daringly low-cut gown was smiling at the prince.

"Meet Lady Veronica Winthrop," Stepan said to her. "Lady Veronica, I present—"

"I know who she is," Veronica interrupted, ignoring Fancy. "Your brother's expectation that we socialize with opera singers surprises me."

Fancy felt the prince grasp her hand. Though he and his family accepted her, she should not have come and inflicted her presence on others.

"Miss Flambeau is Inverary's daughter," Stepan said.

Veronica Winthrop looked at Fancy, the accusation *bastard* stamped across her expression. She returned her attention to the prince. "I'll see you later."

Fancy watched the redhead turning away. She had just been given the cut direct.

"Veronica, darling, I love the gown." The Duchess of Inverary shook her head. "Though, that particular blue combined with your red hair reminds me of the Union Jack."

Fancy coughed to cover a laugh. Veronica Winthrop glanced at her and then curled her lip at the duchess before walking away.

The Duchess of Inverary touched Fancy's arm. "Wise women appear cool and calm, no matter the provocation, and we always hit back. You must learn the fine art of insult."

Prince Rudolf approached her. "Miss Flambeau, may I have this dance?"

"Yes, Your Highness." Fancy placed her hand in his and stepped onto the dance floor. This prince danced as well as his brother, with the grace of a man who had waltzed hundreds of times.

"How is my secret sister this evening?" His smile reminded her of Stepan.

Fancy gazed into his dark eyes so reminiscent of those of his youngest brother. "Stepan promised to stay by my side unless a gentleman invited me to dance. I thought three of us waltzing would seem odd."

Prince Rudolf laughed at that, drawing curious gazes from those around them. "Relax and enjoy the evening. You are among friends."

Fancy gave him a rueful smile. "I doubt Lady Veronica considers me a friend."

"My youngest brother is a wealthy, eligible prince, much chased by society ladies."

"That explains his aversion to the word *no.*"

"Babies of the family believe themselves irresistible," Rudolf said. "The eldest—like us—shoulder the burden of responsibility. Though, since he met you, Stepan has requested more participation in Kazanov Brothers."

Fancy smiled, pleased with herself. Apparently, she was influencing the prince for the better.

Prince Rudolf escorted Fancy back to their group when the music ended. Her spirits dropped, though, when she saw an older woman and a young blonde, gowned in white silk, speaking with Stepan and the duchess.

"Fancy, meet Lady Clarke and her daughter Cynthia." The duchess made the introductions.

"I am pleased to make your acquaintances," Fancy said.

Both mother and daughter gave her a polite smile. Their blue eyes were ice crystals.

"Your Highness," Lady Clarke addressed the prince. "You haven't danced with Cynthia."

"Your thoughts mirror mine," Stepan said, oozing smooth sophistication. "Lady Cynthia?"

Instead of being embarrassed by her mother's interference, Lady Cynthia preened beneath the prince's invitation and placed her hand in his. She cast Fancy a smug smile and headed for the dance floor.

The surge of jealousy that swept through Fancy surprised her. And then she realized the prince had had no choice except to dance with the twit. Refusing would have been too cruel.

"Miss Flambeau?"

Fancy turned around.

Prince Mikhail Kazanov stood there. "May I have this dance?"

"Yes, you may." The prince's brothers were certainly welcoming her presence among them.

Fancy and Mikhail stepped toward the dance floor but heard Lady Clarke say to the duchess, "Your niece's choice of guests surprises me. A gentleman bringing his mistress into respectable society makes me uncomfortable."

"Poor darling," the duchess commiserated. "If you feel uncomfortable, perhaps you should leave."

Fancy had never felt more humiliated. Her complexion colored a deep scarlet, and she would have preferred leaving to waltzing.

"Do not let her remarks bother you," Mikhail said. "Lady Clarke is angling to catch my brother for a son-in-law."

"Many women are angling for Stepan."

"My brother is in no danger of being caught by that woman. Stepan has been hooked already."

Fancy caught his gaze. "What do you mean?"

"For the first time in his life, Stepan has fallen in

love," Mikhail answered. "The gossips are already spreading the news."

Her expression mirrored her confusion.

"My advice is this," Mikhail said. "Keep him dangling a bit longer and then reel him into marriage."

Fancy laughed. "You can't be serious."

"I would never joke about affairs of the heart."

Mikhail escorted her off the dance floor. Cynthia Clarke was clinging to the prince's arm. His expression registered polite resignation.

"Cynthia, darling, why do you always wear white?" the duchess asked.

Lady Clarke flicked a glance at Fancy and then answered for her daughter. "Cynthia's white gowns symbolize her maidenly virtue."

"Cynthia will never attract a husband." The duchess shook her head. "The blond hair, pale skin, and white gown make her disappear into the background."

Lady Clarke and her daughter left soon after that remark. Retreating to the safety of another group seemed wise.

Stepan looked at the duchess. "Your tongue draws blood."

She gave him a dimpled smile. "Thank you, darling."

"Do you consider my sisters and me a challenge?" Fancy asked her.

"How refreshingly direct you are, my dear."

"You did not answer my question."

"Your stubbornness reminds me of your father." The duchess smiled to soften the scolding. "Darling, I consider finding husbands for my stepdaughters a new, hopefully short-lived project."

Fancy opened her mouth to argue.

"I felt the same about my three nieces," the duchess added.

Fancy shut her mouth, postponing the argument.

"Your daughters have arrived, Your Grace," Tinker announced.

The Duke and Duchess of Inverary rose from the settee in front of the hearth. Standing nearby were Robert Campbell and Rudolf Kazanov.

The Campbell family parlor was warm and invitingly comfortable. The walls were painted a cream ochre, the perfect background for artwork and portraits. A Persian carpet in gold, red, black, blue, and cream covered the polished hardwood floor. Groups of sofas, chairs, and settees in jewel colors clustered together, and lilacs scented the air from various vases. Above the white marble hearth hung a portrait of the present duchess.

"Oh, my precious darlings." The Duchess of Inverary rushed across the parlor to put her arm around Belle and escort her to the settee. "My poor sweeting. How frightened you must have been."

Fancy watched Belle redden with embarrassment. Her sister did not need to be the focus of attention. She wished she had sent the duchess a message to ignore her sister's injury, if only for a few days.

With a welcoming smile, the Duke of Inverary walked across the parlor in his wife's wake and greeted her sisters. Her father was a charming man, a little too accustomed to others accepting his orders without question, but she had no doubt her sisters would soon feel at home.

"This is Grace," Bliss whispered to her twin.

The duke turned to Bliss, who stepped back a pace. "Who is Grace?"

"We named you and your wife Grace and Gracie," Blaze told him. "You know, Your Graces."

Fancy glanced at the prince. Stepan struggled against laughing out loud, his shoulders shaking with the effort. Across the parlor, the duke's sons were not so discreet and were laughing openly. Tinker exploded in a muffled squawk of amusement, drawing the duke's attention.

"See to their belongings," the duke ordered.

"Yes, Your"—Tinker chuckled—"*Grace.*"

Her father stared at her offending sister, his expression grim. "Blaze, is it?"

Blaze had the good grace to blush. "Fancy called you 'His Grace,' and we asked her if that was the name we called you. She didn't know, so we nicknamed you Grace and Gracie." She gave him a bright smile as if that settled the matter of her impertinence.

"You may call me Papa when you are ready," he announced. "Until then, call me Sir or His Grace. My wife is Roxie, Madam, or Her Grace."

"I like Grace and Gracie better," Serena whispered to her twin.

"So do I," came Sophia's reply.

The duke's sons were laughing again, as was the prince. Even the duchess's dimple showed.

Fancy struggled against the urge to laugh. If their ignorance had not been so embarrassing, she would have found the whole situation humorous. There was nothing funny about her sisters not knowing how to address their own father.

The duke gestured to the cluster of chairs and settees near the dark hearth. "Come and sit with us."

Fancy felt the prince squeeze her hand and lifted her eyes to his questioning gaze. She shook her head, indicating they would remain standing.

The Duke of Inverary took Belle's hand in his. "I am sorry I failed to protect you."

"I thank you for the kind words, but the blame does not belong to you."

The duke patted her hand. "Fancy tells me you love

to garden. Consider my gardens yours, both here and at my country estate."

"Thank you, Your—Sir—*Papa*."

The duke flicked a glance at Fancy and then spoke to her sister again. "Your forgiveness humbles me. I regret neglecting you."

"I regret only your neglect of my mother," Belle said.

"I regret that, too."

Fancy knew his words were meant for her. She wished she could forgive him as easily as her sisters. They did not share the memory of his turning his back on that long-ago day in Hyde Park.

"You are Sophia, the artist?" her father was asking.

Her sister nodded.

"What part of creating do you favor?"

"I love colors," she answered. "I can see people's—"

"*Sophia*." Fancy's tone warned her sister to silence.

The Duke of Inverary looked from one daughter to the other. "Canvas and paint will be delivered in the morning."

Sophia smiled, her eyes gleaming with excitement. "Thank you, Your—*Papa*."

"And this is Serena?"

Her sister wore a placid expression. "I am Sophia's twin."

Her father's expression changed, a faraway look on his face. "I remember how surprised I was to learn Gabrielle had delivered a second set of twins. At first opportunity, I want to hear your flute playing and your singing."

Fancy noted and appreciated his skill at making each daughter feel special. Too bad he had waited fifteen years to do that. She could not believe in his sincerity.

"I own hundreds of mathematics books," he was telling Bliss. "How do you apply mathematical knowledge to your life?"

Bliss smiled. "Well, Papa, we own—"

"*We own,*" Fancy interrupted, and then heard her prince laughing. "*We own* many recipes requiring mathematical ability, not to mention drapes and whatnot."

"I see." The Duke of Inverary shifted his gaze from Fancy to Bliss. "I think there is more to mathematics than recipes and drapes, but I will wait for the story."

Escaping his attention, Bliss gestured to the redhead. "This is my twin."

"Blaze loves animals," the duke said, "and your red hair marks you the cuckoo in my nest."

"I'll call you Papa if you buy me a horse and a monkey," she told him.

"*Blaze.*" Fancy wanted to throttle her sister.

The duke's sons and the prince burst into laughter. The duchess broke into a dimpled smile, but Blaze's sisters looked appalled.

The duke smiled at his cuckoo in the nest. "Do you believe I should bribe you to call me Papa?"

"Bribery?" Blaze had never looked more innocent in her life. "A gift is an expression of good faith."

The laughter from the duke's sons grew louder.

"Sister, that isn't nice," Bliss said.

"Gee, I didn't hear you refusing those boring mathematics books," Blaze countered.

"Papa offered the books," Bliss defended herself. "I didn't ask for them."

"You got what you wanted."

"That is different."

"It's *always* different for you."

"*Enough.*" The duke's stern voice silenced the twins.

"Welcome to fatherhood, Your Grace." Sarcasm laced Fancy's voice.

"Your education has been lacking," the duchess exclaimed, entering the fray. "Accepting gifts is expected

"Miss Flambeau, may I have this dance?"

Fancy smiled at Prince Viktor Kazanov and accepted his invitation. She glanced at Stepan, who followed her with his eyes.

"I have waited a long time for this moment." Viktor winked at her. "The sight of my brother so smitten pleases me."

Fancy blushed and stepped into his arms. "Mikhail advised me to let him dangle."

"Stepan is our favorite target for teasing."

Fancy smiled at that. These Kazanov brothers treated each other as commoners would.

As Viktor and Fancy swirled around the ballroom Fancy noted Stepan waltzing with a sultry brunette gowned in red.

Viktor's gaze followed hers. "Lady Elizabeth Drummond wants Stepan for her lover. She married a man old enough to be her father."

Fancy had never heard of anything so scandalous. Surprise etched itself across her delicate features.

"Stepan would never consider a married woman," Viktor said, "nor has he kept a mistress. Though, my brother is no saint."

Viktor and Fancy returned to their group when the music ended, and Stepan joined them, sans Elizabeth Drummond. The Duke of Inverary had returned from the card room and stood with his wife.

"Fancy?" Her father turned to her and offered his hand. "Will you honor me with this dance?"

Fancy didn't know what to do. She dropped her gaze from his face to the offered hand, a tense silence descending on the others.

"I understand your reticence." He started to turn away.

Acting on instinct, Fancy reached out and placed

her hand in his. He closed his fingers around it and led her to the dance floor.

Fancy stepped into his arms, her daydream of dancing with her father at a grand ball becoming reality. They waltzed in silence for a time, keeping their gazes fixed on each other. She didn't know what to say or even the reason she had accepted his invitation.

"I have dreamed of this moment for a long time," her father told her. "I pray my daughters allow me to escort them down the aisle to their husbands, though I do not deserve the honor."

Fancy gave him a sparkling smile. "We will need to find grooms before that can happen."

The duke returned her smile. "I do not anticipate any problems with that."

Her father escorted her off the dance floor and paused to lift her hand to his lips. "Thank you, Fancy." He looked at the prince. "My daughter is yours, Your Highness."

Chapter 11

"I appreciate the confidence, Your Grace." Stepan acknowledged the unspoken message. The duke was trusting him to protect his daughter and approving a match between them.

Stepan touched Fancy's hand, a smile on his lips. "May I have this dance?"

"Yes, Your Highness."

Stepan led her onto the dance floor and drew her into his arms. Exuding sophisticated grace, he swirled her around and around the ballroom. His gleaming black gaze held hers in thrall.

"Your beauty shames every woman here."

Her lips twitched into a smile. "I see you have found no employment."

Stepan laughed, drawing curious glances from nearby couples. "Loving you is a full-time career."

Fancy missed a step. "What did you say?"

His words had been a mistake. "Merely a figure of speech, *ma petite.*"

When she relaxed in his arms, Stepan knew to beware. This particular beauty distrusted men of his ilk, especially those who professed love as her father had.

Stepan suffered the feeling that she would never

accept his proposal of marriage. If only he knew how to win her trust, the love would surely follow.

"Princesses Roxanne, Natasia, and Lily Kazanov," the majordomo announced.

Stepan slid his gaze to the stairs where his brother's three daughters stood in their nightgowns. Their little faces shone with amazement at the glamourous sight of society in their finest.

"I want you to meet three of my nieces." Stepan ushered her off the dance floor and headed toward the stairs.

Fancy glanced around and saw most of the guests smiling. Prince Rudolf and Princess Samantha had already reached the stairs. Rudolf held the youngest in his arms while Samantha clutched her older daughters' hands.

"Uncle," Lily called.

"Miss Flambeau, I present Princesses Roxanne, Natasia, and Lily," Stepan introduced them.

Fancy smiled at the three girls. "I am pleased to make your acquaintances. Your uncle has spoken of you."

Natasia stared at her. "You look like a princess."

"Uncle said she is not a princess," Roxanne corrected her sister.

"She's Cinderella," Lily exclaimed.

Everyone, including Fancy, laughed at the four-year-old. Lily yawned at their appreciation.

"Say good night," Rudolf told his daughters.

"We didn't say hello," Lily said. "How can we say good night?"

Rudolf glanced at his wife. "This is *your* daughter." He looked at his older daughters, asking, "Where is Nanny?"

"We tied her up," Roxanne answered.

"And gagged her," Natasia added.

"We tiptoed down the stairs," Lily finished.

Princess Samantha looked at her husband. "Those are *your* daughters."

Natasia turned to Stepan. "Did you tell her, Uncle?"

"No."

Fancy watched, fascinated, as the prince's complexion reddened. She wondered what embarrassed him.

"I told you boys were silly," Roxanne said.

"I want to dance," Lily said.

"Princess Lily," Stepan said, "may I have the honor of this dance?"

Lily smiled and nodded, but Roxanne placed her hand on her uncle's arm. "Darling, the eldest dances first."

The Duke of Inverary looked at his wife. "She sounds like you."

The duchess gave him a dimpled smile. "Isn't darling Roxie the sweetest?"

Stepan escorted the six-year-old onto the dance floor. Roxanne stood on top of his shoes, and their waltz began.

A hand touched Fancy's arm. She smiled at Natasia.

"Uncle will make you a princess," the girl said in a loud whisper.

"Will Uncle give me a crown?" Fancy asked.

"Uncle will marry you."

Lily spoke up. "Uncle loves you."

Fancy blushed and glanced at the adults. "I-I don't think—"

"Uncle said he loves you," Natasia insisted.

"Uncle never lies," Lily said. "Do you love Uncle?"

Her complexion heating with embarrassment, Fancy did not know what to say with the prince's relations waiting for her answer. His return with Princess Roxanne saved her from responding.

She watched the prince circling the dance floor with Natasia. Clearly, his nieces adored him, and he adored them. The prince had all the makings of a wonderful father.

Lily touched her hand. "Do you love Uncle?"

"I-I . . ."

"She loves him, darling," Princess Roxanne drawled, sounding exactly like her great-aunt. "She can hardly speak."

Fancy felt her face flaming when the adults laughed at the six-year-old. What had the prince said about her at the tea party? Had he really professed his love for her?

Stepan returned for Lily. He lifted the four-year-old into his arms and waltzed her around the ballroom, her laughter making the other dancers smile.

"Come along, girls," Princess Samantha said when the dance ended. "Let's untie Nanny."

Prince Rudolf carried the four-year-old. Lily waved and called, "Good night, Cinderella."

Fancy waved at the girl and then noticed two gentlemen advancing on their group. Ross MacArthur and Douglas Gordon had saved her from Crazy Eddie the night she'd walked home. She listened to them greeting the Duke of Inverary and realized they were her father's kinsmen.

"Well, here's a familiar face," Douglas Gordon said, his gaze on her.

"I'm glad to see ye, lass," Ross MacArthur greeted her. "And where are these sisters of yers?"

"If they're half as lovely as you," Gordon added, "I'm smitten already."

"Fancy and her sisters are my stepdaughters," the Duchess of Inverary told the Scotsmen. "I guarantee each girl is a beauty."

"Is that so?" Gordon said.

"I dinna think Her Grace would fib us," MacArthur said.

"You would enjoy meeting Bliss and Blaze," the duchess said. "Come to dinner one night next week."

"Aye, we'd like that," MacArthur said.

"I canna think of anythin' I'd like more," Gordon agreed.

"I'll send a note confirming which evening." The duchess gave them a feline smile as the Highlanders drifted away. Then she turned on her husband. "Magnus, darling, you should have reminded me of those two when we discussed possible matches."

"I was hoping to become acquainted with my daughters before you haul a big catch," the duke said, a smile tempering his words. "I'll need to start honing my matchmaking skills."

"I didn't know you had any," his wife replied.

Fancy swallowed a laugh. She looked at the prince, who also seemed to be struggling against laughter. Insulting the duchess by laughing was unwise.

Stepan winked, grasped her hand, and drew her away from their group. "I need a glass of champagne," he said. He ushered her out of the ballroom down the corridor to the refreshment room.

"Champagne or lemon barley water?"

"Champagne, I think."

Stepan raised his brows. "What are you celebrating?"

Her expression was pure innocence. "Nothing special, Your Highness."

"What did you discuss with my nieces?" Stepan asked, handing her the champagne flute.

"We spoke about tea parties." She gave him an ambiguous smile, but her blush made him suspicious.

Stepan did not doubt his nieces had talked about tea parties, but he knew the conversation had not ended there. His songbird's smile made him uncomfortable. She knew a secret and dared him to question her.

They left the ball before supper was served.

Relaxing in the coach's leather seat, Stepan rested his arm behind her. He studied her delicate profile and savored her scent of amber, rose, and feminine sensuality. No one who saw her would guess how stubborn and cantankerous she could be, but he enjoyed every moment passed in her company. If they married, would he feel the same in ten or twenty years?

Stepan climbed down when they reached Soho Square and then lifted her out. He waved at Harry, put his arm around her shoulder, and ushered her toward the front door.

"What are you doing?" Fancy asked.

"I am passing the night here." When she opened her mouth to protest, Stepan added, "Someone left you decapitated roses, and I refuse to risk your well-being."

Stepan unlocked the front door and followed her up the stairs to the second floor. Outside her bedchamber, he lifted her hand to kiss her palm and then leaned close to press a kiss on her lips.

What he wanted more than anything else was to make love with her, feel her soft nakedness against his bared flesh. Stepan did not want to frighten her or lose her trust and so held himself in check.

Fancy gazed at him through her disarming violet eyes. "Do you love me?"

Now Stepan knew what his nieces had talked about. He traced a finger down her rose-petal cheek. "Do you want me to love you?"

"I don't know."

His thumb caressed her lips. "Ask me again when you do know."

Leaving her there, Stepan headed for the bedchamber he had used the previous night. He stripped down to his peacock blue silk drawers and opened the window a crack. Then he lay on the bed, his arms pillowing his head.

His songbird was a temperamental twit, but he loved her. Their relationship was progressing.

Stepan would have kissed her into oblivion if she hadn't been set against his sleeping here. No matter what, he would never stop protecting her even if she ordered him out of the house.

The next morning Stepan dressed and walked downstairs. He could hear Fancy humming to herself as she prepared breakfast, the scent of coffee brewing calling out to him.

They were behaving like married commoners. He liked that.

Stepan opened the front door to verify no threatening gifts had been left during the night. He waved to his coachman, who had returned to drive him home.

Apparently, Harry had left the morning *Times* on the doorstep. His man had opened the paper to the page three society column.

Cutting through the parlor to the dining room, Stepan sat at the head of the table and read the column.

> *One of London's most eligible foreign royals was seen yesterday morning leaving a certain opera singer's residence.*

Stepan set the paper aside when he heard a certain opera singer carrying their breakfast into the room. "Good morning." He greeted her with a smile.

Fancy placed their breakfast on the table. "You have stolen my seat again."

"I am a guest. Remember?"

"Your presence speaks more of a tenant behind on his rent."

Stepan laughed. "You cannot imagine how much I admire your wit and intelligence."

Her lips twitched at his compliment. "Will you be seeking employment today?"

"I plan to attend a business meeting at your father's," Stepan answered. "After that, I belong only to you until your Tuesday performance."

"Are you my jailer or protector?"

Stepan sipped his coffee. "You brew the best."

"Do not become accustomed to its taste." Her gaze fell on the newspaper. "Is that the *Times*?"

"Harry left it for me on the doorstep," Stepan answered. "There is nothing of importance."

Fancy grabbed the newspaper and turned to page three. "Damn that reporter," she exclaimed.

"Do not worry about gossip," Stepan said. "I will marry you and save your reputation."

Fancy stared at him for a long moment. "If the society reporter saw you leaving at dawn, do you think he saw the person who left those decapitated roses?"

A slow smile spread across his face. "I will investigate that possibility."

Raven stood in her father's garden and watched Puddles searching for the proper spot to conduct business. She and her sisters rotated taking the mastiff out every two hours in an attempt to keep the duchess happy.

The garden was an oasis of tranquility with its blooming trees and dark green shrubs and primary-colored flowers. Overhead, powder-puff clouds meandered across a bluebell sky.

Closing her eyes, Raven inhaled the mingling scents and then called to the dog. "Come, Puddles."

The mastiff galloped across the garden. She opened the door and followed the dog inside.

The duke's majordomo stood in the foyer. The mastiff raced past him and disappeared up the stairs.

Tinker moved when someone knocked on the door. Raven stopped, hearing Alexander Blake's voice.

"I want to speak to Raven Flambeau."

"I am uncertain if she is receiving visitors today." Tinker flicked her a sidelong glance. When she nodded, the majordomo opened the door and allowed him entrance. "The lady will see you."

Alexander and a short middle-aged man stepped into the foyer. Raven met his smile without expression, a new trick she'd learned from the duchess.

"What can I do for you?"

Alexander gestured to his companion. "Barney assists Constable Black, too."

Raven slid her gaze to the older man. "A pleasure to meet you, Barney."

"Constable Black requests you meet him at my house tomorrow," Alexander said.

Raven arched an ebony brow at him. "Does the constable suspect—?"

"Amadeus thinks you could help with the investigation," Alexander told her.

My, my, my. Her hocus-pocus could solve a crime. How satisfying to know Alex was forced to swallow his words and his contempt for her.

"Will you help us?"

Raven gave him a feline smile, another trick learned from the duchess. She placed an index finger across her lips as if pondering a weighty matter. His irritated expression pleased her.

"What time?"

"Two o'clock?"

Raven inclined her head like a queen granting her courtier a favor. "Two of the clock, it is."

Alexander gave her a long look and walked out the door. The older man smiled at her and the majordomo.

"Nice place," Barney said before leaving.

"We like it," Tinker drawled.

Raven turned away to start up the stairs. She hoped the remainder of her day was as satisfying as the past few minutes.

The majordomo's voice stopped her. "You are a fast learner, Miss Raven."

She turned around. "Learner at what?"

"The most effective way to torment men."

"The duchess is giving us stepdaughters the accelerated class."

"Her Grace excels at relationship strategies."

Raven laughed and hurried to the third floor. She paused at Belle's door, uncertain if she should knock. And then she heard her sister's weeping. Belle needed to heal herself, and no one could help her.

Turning away, Raven almost crashed into two sisters. Bliss and Blaze stood there.

"Thank you for taking my turn with Puddles," Blaze said. "He loves your company because you let him romp longer than anyone else."

"He told you this?"

Blaze smiled and nodded.

"Will you do me a favor?" Bliss asked.

"What is it?"

Bliss held up pencil and paper. "Hide inside the duke's office and take notes on the business meeting."

Blaze rolled her eyes. "Our darling stepmama insists on shopping for more appropriate gowns."

"The duchess has two prospective gentlemen coming to dinner next week," Bliss added.

Raven looked from one sister to the other. "Prospective what?"

Bliss passed her the pencil and paper. "Suitors for us."

"Highlanders." Blaze feigned a horrified expression. "We have a plan, though."

The twins looked at each other and laughed.

"You can take the Flambeau out of Soho Square," Bliss said.

"But you can't take Soho Square out of the Flambeau," Blaze finished.

Raven laughed. "I can hardly wait for the entertainment."

"The Kazanovs will arrive soon," Bliss said. "Hide while you can."

Raven walked downstairs to the second floor. Reaching the duke's office, she tapped on the door to be sure no one was within. Silence. She slipped inside and walked to the far side of the room to make herself comfortable on the oversized chair, its back to the ducal desk.

While she waited, Raven let her thoughts drift to Alex. She could hardly believe he wanted her help but worried her emotions would inhibit her talent. What she'd revealed to him that night mortified her still.

The Duke of Inverary would not be pleased with that tidbit of gossip about Fancy. Though she hadn't been named, Stepan realized that all of London would assume the prince's and the opera singer's identity. A damage-control strategy eluded him.

"Good afternoon," Stepan greeted the majordomo. "Am I late?"

"Good afternoon, Your Highness," Tinker returned the greeting. "Your brothers arrived a few minutes ago."

Stepan took the stairs two at a time, his long strides

eating the distance to the duke's office in record time. He knocked on the door but entered without waiting for permission.

The Duke of Inverary and his son as well as his own three brothers relaxed in leather chairs around the ducal desk. Five heads swiveled in Stepan's direction when he burst into the office.

"I apologize for my tardiness." Stepan crossed the office to sit in the vacant chair beside Mikhail near the window.

Rudolf's smile boded ill. "Baby brother, His Grace desires a word with you."

"Several words," Viktor added.

"A few more than several," Mikhail murmured.

Stepan pasted an expression of mild inquiry on his face. "How may I help you, Your Grace?"

The Duke of Inverary gave him a long look. Then he slammed a folded newspaper down on the desk. "Explain this."

Stepan glanced at the newspaper. "What is that?"

"You know damn well what it is."

Stepan glanced at his brothers. All three were smiling at him.

"Fancy and I have shared no intimacies." Stepan ignored his brothers' chuckling. "Since she is living alone, I wanted only to protect her."

"You're ruining her reputation," the duke growled.

"I want to marry her," Stepan said, "but persuading her into matrimony could take months. You know she dislikes aristocrats."

The Duke of Inverary had the good grace to flush. He knew his daughter's opinion of him and others of his ilk.

"I heard no woman can resist a prince in love," Rudolf teased him.

The men laughed at that. Except Stepan.

"Your daughters talk too much," Stepan complained. "Fancy asked me if I loved her."

"What did you say?" Viktor asked.

Stepan gulped his whiskey before answering. "I asked if she wanted me to love her."

Mikhail smiled. "And does she?"

"She doesn't know."

"What did you reply to that?" the Marquess of Argyll asked.

"I told her to ask me again when she did know."

Rudolf grinned. "And we thought you were short on sense."

Stepan let that remark slide. "I need one of you to speak with the *Times* reporter and ask him if he saw anyone else loitering in the vicinity of the Flambeau residence."

"Is there a Peeping Tom in Soho?" Rudolf asked.

Stepan shook his head. "Someone left decapitated roses on the doorstep."

"Someone means Fancy harm?" the duke exclaimed.

"That was not the only threat left on the doorstep," Stepan added. "If the reporter saw someone—"

"I will speak to the man," Rudolf said.

"I can do that," Viktor offered.

"Both of you tend to threaten people to get what you want," Mikhail said. "I will speak with him."

Rudolf smiled. "The three of us will speak to the reporter."

"That should relax him," Stepan said.

And the discussion turned to business matters.

"Our beer and ale cartel with Ginger Evans is making a healthy profit," Viktor said.

"You mean, Ginger Black," Stepan corrected. "She married the constable."

Viktor looked at him. "The Evans Smith Company belongs only to Regina and Ginger."

Mikhail stood to stretch his legs and wandered to the window overlooking the ducal garden. Stepan joined him there as Rudolf spoke about other joint ventures.

"The damn Seven Doves Company is still undercutting our prices," the Duke of Inverary remarked.

"Brother, I thought you would speak to the Doves' owners and persuade them against this suicidal plot," Rudolf said.

Stepan looked at the others and shrugged. "Six agree to cease this nonsense, but the seventh is determined to pauperize the duke."

Magnus Campbell banged his fist on the desk. "I want to know the bastard's name."

"I am truly sorry, Your Grace, but I have given my word."

Mikhail spoke then. "Is that one of Inverary's daughters?"

Stepan peered down at the garden. "Belle Flambeau."

Mikhail looked over his shoulder at the duke. "Your daughter seems sad and lonely—"

The Duke of Inverary rose from his chair and stood with the brothers at the window. "Belle lost her suitor because of the damn scar. Even Roxie cannot perk her up. Belle refuses to see anyone and even declines her pin money. She says she doesn't need money because she isn't going anywhere."

All the men fell silent. When a woman refused money, she suffered a severe problem.

"Belle is a beauty," Stepan said, "but the slash on her cheek cut into her soul."

Mikhail touched his brother's shoulder and then turned to the duke. His words stunned everyone. "My daughter needs a mother, and the women I have met are unsuitable. I will marry her."

The Duke of Inverary looked surprised. "You want to marry Belle?"

"Mikhail would never joke about marriage," Stepan assured the duke. "He always considers other people's feelings."

The Duke of Inverary nodded. "I will speak to Belle about your offer."

"No."

Raven watched the men turn in her direction. She had caught them off guard if their expressions proved the matter. Bliss popped into her mind, but nothing could be done for being found out. Belle needed her help more than Bliss.

The duke walked toward her, a confused smile on his face. "What are you doing here?"

Raven gave her father a bright smile. "I was eavesdropping and taking notes for Bliss."

Prince Stepan was laughing, drawing the men's attention. "Your Grace, I present one of the owners of the Seven Doves Company."

The duke looked at her. "My daughters are my business rivals?"

Raven shrugged and nodded. "I apologize for our costing you money."

Her father put his arm around her and ushered her across the study to a chair near his desk. Then he sat down, too. "Start at the beginning and tell me everything."

Raven wet her lips, gone dry from nervousness. She looked at each of the men, who did not seemed surprised by women owning businesses. Which surprised her.

"Fancy is angry with you," Raven told her father. "Her method of retribution is pauperizing you."

"I know Fancy is angry," the duke said, "but I don't understand how my seven daughters formed a viable company."

"Bliss is a mathematical genius," Raven explained. "She studies commodities and such and then decides where our financial investments will profit most."

"Bliss reminds me of Ginger Evans," Stepan interjected.

"Where did you get the money to start investing?" Prince Rudolf asked.

Raven glanced at him and then her father. "We invested the money we won at the races."

"What races?" the duke exclaimed.

"I will tell you everything," Raven said, "but you must promise not to punish anyone."

Her father stared at her a long moment. "I do not bargain with my children. Tell me all, and I will decide if anyone deserves punishment."

Raven hoped her sisters, especially Fancy, would forgive her. "Blaze talks to animals"—she ignored the men's smiles—"and she knows what animals are thinking and feeling. Bliss and Blaze dress like boys, and Alex—"

"Alex?" her father interjected.

"Alexander Blake."

"The Marquess of Basildon?"

"Yes."

"What are you saying?" Prince Stepan asked. "Blake is your neighbor and works with Constable Black."

"That is true," Raven said. "Alexander Blake is also the Duke of Essex's grandson, but Alex refuses to recognize the connection."

"Continue," her father said.

"Alex, Bliss, and Blaze attend the thoroughbred races," she went on. "Blaze walks by the stables and communes with the horses. Then she tells Alex who will win the race, and Bliss decides how much to bet."

"Is there more?"

"Alex places the bet, the horses race, and we collect

our winnings." Raven gave her father another bright smile. "Then Fancy calls a company meeting, and Bliss explains the best investments. After that, Fancy gives us our pin money."

The men laughed at that. Even her father chuckled. Perhaps no one would be punished.

The Duke of Inverary relaxed in his chair. "Has Blaze ever chosen a loser?"

Raven shook her head. "She always picks the winner."

The duke looked at his son and the princes. "I believe Blaze will be attending the races with me this year."

"I would like to join you," Prince Rudolf said.

"Of course, you are welcome."

Prince Stepan drew her attention. "What is your objection to Mikhail's proposal?"

"I have no objection," Raven said, "but Belle will never agree unless you go about this the correct way." She looked at Mikhail. "If she believes you pity her, she will refuse."

"Then I will meet her by accident," Mikhail said.

"Belle refuses to see visitors," she reminded him.

"My wife still owns the cottage on the other side of Primrose Hill," the duke said. "Roxie will persuade Belle to go there for a few days."

"Belle will believe His Highness pities her," Raven said. "Unless he can get her to believe he loves her in spite of her scar."

"I will pretend to be a commoner set upon by robbers," Mikhail said. "I will feign temporary blindness and memory loss. I will beg her for help."

"That could work," Raven said. "What will prove you were set upon by robbers, though?"

"We will be happy to batter him," Rudolf said. "A few well-placed bruises."

"That could work," Raven said. "Fancy is a problem."

"I will get Fancy out of London and take her to Rudolf's estate on Sark Island," Stepan offered. "Mikhail's plan will work, and Fancy will be out of harm's way."

"My sister won't go willingly," Raven said. "I know herbs that promote sleep. You must contrive to get them into her body."

"Upon returning to London, you will need to marry her," the duke warned him.

Stepan smiled at his future father-in-law. "You may announce our betrothal as soon as we sail away." He looked at Raven. "Your Grace, did you know that this daughter can move objects with her mind? Give us a demonstration."

The prospect of performing held no appeal for Raven. "I never participate in vulgar displays." She dropped her gaze to the glass of whiskey on the desk in front of him. The glass tipped on its side, sending its contents onto the royal lap.

Stepan leaped out of his chair. Too late, he found that whiskey had soaked his trousers.

Raven caught his eye. "Oops . . ."

Chapter 12

What he wanted was within his reach. Soon the object of his desire would be within his grasp.

Pleased with the day's events, Stepan slipped into the deserted opera box during the second act. He stretched his long legs out and relaxed in the chair to await the end of tonight's performance.

Stepan had delivered Fancy to the opera house and returned to the Flambeau residence. Using his own key, he had let himself into the house and packed her possessions, including slingshot and pellets. She would forgive him if she had her belongings.

Fancy was so wonderfully predictable. That could be used against her.

He would invite her to his country estate. Of course, she would refuse. Then he would invite her to supper at his house. She would accept that one because she had already refused his first invitation.

After the final curtain call, Stepan walked downstairs to the lobby. He spoke to several acquaintances along the way, giving Fancy time to remove the theater cosmetics and change into her gown.

"Your Highness," a woman called.

The voice belonged to Lady Clarke, which meant Lady Cynthia would be standing with her mother.

Stepan managed a smile for them. "A pleasure to see you."

"I didn't notice you during intermission," Lady Clarke said.

"I arrived late this evening."

"Will you be attending the Randolphs' affair tonight?" Lady Clarke asked.

"Regretfully, no."

That answer did not sit well with the daughter. Her eager smile became forced.

"Will we see you at Lord Wilkins' tomorrow evening?" Lady Clarke asked.

"I do plan to attend."

"Alone?" Cynthia asked.

"I am an unmarried man," he hedged. "Will you save me a dance?"

Cynthia gave him a flirtatious smile. "Yes, Your Highness, I will save you a dance."

Stepan turned away, planning to find Director Bishop. The man needed to be informed that Fancy would be gone for a few weeks. And then he spied an unlikely duo headed in his direction.

Veronica Winthrop and Elizabeth Drummond. Apparently, these two had joined forces to entrap him.

The red-haired Veronica flicked a curl away from her face. "Stepan, will you—"

"I have a prior commitment tonight," he said. "I will see you tomorrow at the Wilkins' affair."

"And will you also see me at the Wilkins' affair?" Elizabeth Drummond asked, her voice smoother than silk against flesh.

Stepan dropped his gaze to her daringly low-cut gown. "Elizabeth, I am seeing you tonight."

The sultry brunette laughed throatily. The woman

was appealing, but he never tarried with other men's wives.

"Ladies, if you will excuse me? I must speak with Director Bishop."

Stepan did not want the *Times* reporter gossiping about his speaking with other women. He wanted nothing to upset Fancy.

"Bishop." Stepan shook the man's hand. "I am taking Fancy away for a couple of weeks."

The opera director did not look happy. "With all due respect, Your Highness, could this trip be postponed until after the season?"

"Someone has been threatening Fancy," Stepan explained. "I think taking her out of town for a few days is best."

"I understand."

"When we return," Stepan added, "I will be marrying her."

If the director was surprised, he did not show it. "Fancy never told me."

"She does not know."

Bishop laughed. "Will she be returning to the opera?"

Stepan shrugged. "I plan to discuss that when she accepts my proposal."

"Wasting her beautiful voice seems sinful," the director said. "I have never heard another singer who could wrench such strong emotions from her audience."

"I believe a younger sister sings."

Director Bishop brightened. "I will look into that possibility."

"The Duke of Inverary has moved his daughters into Park Lane," Stepan told him. "You will need his permission."

Stepan left the director and walked through the deserted theater to the backstage area. Unexpectedly, the prima donna's pet darted out of her dressing room.

Laughing, Stepan scooped the monkey into his arms. "How are you, Miss Giggles?"

The capuchin monkey covered its ears, eyes, and mouth.

"Good girl," Stepan praised her. He passed the monkey to the prima donna's husband. "Miss Giggles needs a new trick."

Sebastian Tanner smiled. "I keep telling Patrice the same thing, Your Highness."

Reaching Fancy's dressing room, Stepan opened the door without knocking and walked inside. Fancy turned around and gave him a smile filled with true affection.

His songbird painted a living picture of sultry vulnerability. Her heart-shaped face, generous lips, and disarming violet eyes with their fringe of black lashes combined in perfect symmetry to create a haunting beauty.

Stepan loved her. Of that, he had no doubts. She incited many tender feelings in him.

She belonged to him. He belonged to her.

His task was to convince her of that.

"Are you ready?" Stepan asked, answering her smile with his own.

Fancy rose from the stool. "Ready for what?"

"Since your next performance is Tuesday," Stepan answered, "I thought we could pass the weekend at my country estate."

"I think not."

Stepan assumed a disappointed expression. "Will you sup with me at my house?"

"That sounds wonderful."

Stepan smiled, pleased with himself. Apparently, the best way to handle his songbird was always to offer her two choices, an unacceptable choice and what he really wanted her to do.

Half an hour later, the royal coach halted in front of the prince's residence. Stepan climbed down first and then assisted Fancy. Bones opened the door before they reached it.

"Good evening, Your Highness," the majordomo greeted them. "And a good evening to you, Miss Flambeau."

Fancy greeted the man, "Good evening, Bones."

"Feliks is preparing a delicious supper," Bones said. "I will serve you directly, Your Highness."

Fancy looked at the prince and lost her smile. "How did Feliks know we would be supping here?"

"I-I . . ." Stepan searched for a plausible excuse and then realized she would believe the truth. "I thought you would not want to travel to my estate and left word for Feliks to prepare us supper."

"Will we eat in the dining room?"

Stepan relaxed. "The dining room is this way."

After helping her into the chair beside his, Stepan sat at the head of the table. He watched her scanning the chamber and tried to see the room through her eyes.

The rounded-end mahogany table sat twenty. A glittering chandelier hung over the table. Fine porcelain and crystal goblets and silverware waited for them on the table.

Bones served them from the sideboard and then left the dining room. As promised, Feliks had cooked them a light supper of vegetable souffle, potted ham, and toast.

"I am relieved not to see that disgusting caviar," Fancy said, making him smile. "Since I am your guest, Your Highness, shouldn't I have been offered the seat at the head of the table?"

"Have I mentioned how much I admire your wit?"

"You have mentioned it several times." Fancy spread potted ham on a small triangular piece of toast. "You mention my wit to avoid a direct reply."

Stepan avoided that remark by asking, "Will you join me in a glass of wine?"

"I don't want to get drunk," she declined.

"You do not sing until Tuesday," he coaxed her. "Surely, you will join me for a rare drink."

"Very well," she agreed. "How did your business meeting go?"

Stepan walked to the sideboard to pour them wine. "Your father is concerned about the Seven Doves Company."

"He can afford to lose a few coins," Fancy said. "Especially since his loss brings me pleasure."

Stepan slipped the sleeping draught into her wine and stirred it. He returned to the table and set the crystal goblet in front of her. "You are the most vicious songbird. Some vile crow must have married with one of your ancestors."

"Thank you for the praise." Fancy lifted her goblet in a salute and then drank the wine.

"How was your evening at the opera?" Stepan asked.

"Patrice has been less hostile."

"Is it possible you have misjudged her?" Stepan finished his wine.

Fancy drank when he drank. "I did not misjudge the prima donna." She yawned and giggled. "The wine was delicious. Perhaps I'll have another."

"One is enough, princess."

Fancy yawned again. "I feel tired tonight."

"You have endured an anxious week." Stepan took her hand and drew her to her feet, saying, "Come here." He pulled her onto his lap, his arms encircling her. "Rest your head on my shoulder."

Fancy closed her eyes and snuggled against him.

"You are a comfortable pillow, Your High—" She dropped into sleep.

Success.

Stepan cradled her in his arms and rose from the chair. He left the dining room and found his major-domo lurking in the corridor.

"Did Harry bring the coach around back?"

"Yes, Your Highness."

Bones fell into step beside him and opened the doors along the way. The two of them cut through the garden to the alley in back of the mansion where Feliks and Boris waited.

Stepan grinned at his majordomo's anxious expression. "What worries you?"

Bones shook his head. "May God have mercy on you when the lady awakens."

"Come, Puddles."

Raven opened the door for the mastiff and followed him inside. The drudgery of escorting the dog into the garden was grating on her nerves. Between favors and swaps, she was beginning to feel solely responsible for the mastiff, and now she had promised her sister to assume her turns with the dog for a week.

Sophia could read other people's emotions from the color of their auras, so Raven had asked her sister to accompany her to Soho Square. She wanted the companionship and the knowledge of Alexander's and the constable's emotions. If she knew their emotions, she would know their thoughts. Or so she supposed.

Raven found her sister waiting for her in the corridor and chatting with Tinker. "Let's go, Sophia."

Her sister smiled at the majordomo. "I am glad you feel happy today."

"I am in the pink," Tinker drawled.

Raven and Sophia walked east on Upper Brook Street to Regent Street. Soho Square was one mile from Park Lane. Though a respectable address, Soho Square lacked the money and exclusivity of Park Lane.

That late spring day had been created for outside activities. The temperature was comfortable for walking, and marshmallow clouds dotted a bluebell sky.

The idyllic day did nothing to calm Raven. If her talents failed her today, no one would believe her again.

"Relax."

"I am relaxed."

"You cannot lie to me," Sophia said. "The speckles of dark red in your colors indicate agitation."

Raven gave her sister a sidelong glance. "I invited you along to tell me how others feel."

Sophia ignored the comment. "Life does not seem the same without Fancy. Shall we visit her afterward?"

"Fancy won't be home," Raven answered. "Prince Stepan and she made plans for today."

The sisters reached Soho Square and walked directly to the Blake residence. Both gave their old home a wistful look, their former lives seeming years in the past.

Genevieve Stover answered their knock. Apparently, the blonde was spending her free time with Alexander.

Raven had not thought of that. She blushed with embarrassed dismay and wondered if Alex had shared her declaration of love with the blonde. She hoped that her concentration would not be impaired because of it.

Genevieve opened the door wider. "Alex and the constable are waiting for you."

Raven walked into the Blake residence, her sister following behind. Being invited into a house she had once considered her second home did not sit well with her.

"You remember Sophia." Raven glanced at her sister.

Wearing a strange expression, Sophia was staring at the blonde. Raven could not imagine what was wrong.

Sophia recovered her composure. "A pleasure to meet you again."

"How is Belle's recovery progressing?" Genevieve asked.

"Belle is improving slowly," Raven answered. "She is resting at our father's country estate."

"Thank you for asking," Sophia said.

"Do either of you sing like Fancy?" Genevieve asked, leading them down the hallway toward the parlor.

"I paint," Sophia answered.

"What about you, Raven?"

"I have no talent."

Raven noticed the blonde behaved like the mistress of the house. Her spirits plummeted even lower. Winning Alexander's love would never happen if that was true.

Genevieve stopped at the parlor door. "Can I bring you coffee or tea?"

"No, thank you."

The blonde left them at the parlor door and walked toward the kitchen at the back of the house.

"Genevieve seems at home here," Sophia whispered, her gaze fixed on the blonde.

Raven gave her a disgruntled glance.

Her sister touched her arm. "Lose your temper and lose your gift."

Raven took several deep breaths. "Are my colors better now?"

"The red is gone," Sophia said, "your gold glitters like the sun, and your white is brightening."

Raven and Sophia walked into the parlor without knocking. Alexander and Constable Black rose from their seats. Dressed in somber black, the constable appeared a no-nonsense man.

"Constable Black, meet Raven and Sophia Flambeau," Alexander introduced them.

Raven looked at the constable. "I hope you don't mind Sophia accompanying me."

"Your sister is welcome," Amadeus Black said. "Do you enjoy the same talents as Raven?"

"My talents lie elsewhere."

"Please sit," Alexander invited them.

Raven sat on the sofa, thinking she'd never needed an invitation to sit in the Blake house before today. Sophia sat beside her.

"Alex told me about your visions," the constable said, "and Fancy insisted your holding objects could facilitate them."

"That is true." She peeked at Alexander, who wore a skeptical expression.

"How do you know things?" Constable Black asked.

Raven fixed her violet gaze on him. "I know because I know, just as I breathe without thinking."

Amadeus Black nodded. "I understand what you mean."

"You understand her?" Alexander could not keep the surprised disbelief out of his voice.

"Some talents exist," the constable answered. "We do not know the why or the how of them."

Alexander opened his mouth to argue.

"Do you believe in God?" Constable Black asked.

"Of course, I do."

"How do you know He's there? You've never seen Him."

"I know because I know."

"Precisely my point."

Alexander looked at Raven. She gave him a smug smile.

"I've brought several objects from different crime scenes," the constable said. "I will appreciate whatever you can tell me."

Raven held her hand out. "Give me one."

Amadeus Black passed her a glass container with dried, decaying rose petals. "The petals covering the body were fresh when we found her."

Raven opened the container and shook a few petals onto her lap. Closing her eyes, she relaxed and fingered the dried petals.

She waited and waited and waited. Nothing came to her. If she didn't perform, Alexander would never let her forget it.

Her sister touched her arm. "Relax and invite the visions into your mind."

Raven took several deep breaths and forced herself to calmness. Still, no image or thought popped into her mind.

She opened her eyes. "I'm sorry but—"

"Hogslop, I told you," Alexander said.

Raven ignored the insult. "Are the rose petals placed on the victims before or after death?"

"I believe he kills them elsewhere and drops the bodies where we find them," Constable Black answered. "If that is true, he covers them after death."

Relief surged through her. "Their souls had already departed this world," she explained. "That is the reason for my failure."

Alexander looked disgusted. "Do you expect us to—?"

"Be quiet," Raven snapped.

Her order surprised him. He clamped his lips shut.

Constable Black winked at her. "I could not have phrased that any better."

Raven took the next object, a long white glove. The feelings slapped her senses as soon as she touched it. Holding the glove in both hands, she leaned back and closed her eyes.

"Dark hair and blue eyes . . . white gloves worn with a pink gown . . . an actress, optimistic about the future, seeking advice from someone knowledgeable . . . drowsy, eyelids too heavy . . . drifting away from life like an oarless boat in calm waters."

Raven opened her eyes. All three were staring at her. The two men wore surprised expressions.

"Your identification of the victim is correct," Amadeus Black verified.

"She did not identify the killer," Alexander scoffed.

"Alex, your hostility is unattractive," Sophia scolded him.

"You mentioned the victim's drowsiness," the constable said.

"She never knew when her heart stopped beating," Raven said. "A gentle poisoning with no pain."

Amadeus Black was silent. "I wonder what—"

"Five drops of *acqua toffana* in wine or water deliver a painless death in a very few hours," Raven informed him.

"What is that?"

"*Acqua toffana* is a mixture of arsenic and cantharides," she answered. "The murderer probably mixed it with a sleeping draught."

"How do you know this?" Alexander asked.

Raven leveled a cold look on him. "I know because I know."

Constable Black laughed at that. "You mentioned advice."

"She trusted the murderer to help her career in some way."

Amadeus and Alexander exchanged glances. Only a wealthy gentleman could help a young actress's career.

"This is the last object." Constable Black passed her the gold ring, initialed with *P*.

Dread seeped into her from the spot on the palm of her hand where the ring sat. Bleak misery spread, chilling body and heart and soul.

Raven looked at the constable. "This belongs to the murderer, not the victim."

Amadeus Black leaned forward. "Tell me more if you can."

Raven wanted to toss the ring away. Instead, she leaned back and closed her eyes.

"Loves me, loves me not . . . tall, lean gentleman in formal evening clothes . . . a short, plump woman . . . faces jumbling, merging together . . . he looks like her, she looks like him . . ."

Raven opened her eyes and returned the ring. "His soul is corrupt, decaying like the rose petals."

"What did you mean by he looks like her and she looks like him?" Constable Black asked.

"I saw vague female and male features merging into one face."

"Can you identify the faces?" Alexander asked.

"No." Raven shook her head. "Sometimes my visions are symbolic."

Alexander turned to the constable. "What do you think it means?"

"I would have said two parts to one person," Amadeus answered, "but our witness saw a man and a woman." He looked at Raven. "Will you help us again?"

"Send for me," she agreed, albeit reluctantly, "and I will come."

Raven and Sophia stood to leave. Alexander and Constable Black stood when they did.

"You look pale," the constable said. "May I drive you to Park Lane?"

Raven shook her head. "I need to feel the sunshine."

Raven and Sophia left the Blake residence, retracing their steps to Park Lane. They walked in silence for a time.

"You look disturbed," Raven said. "What are you thinking?"

Sophia turned a troubled expression on her.
"Genevieve Stover had no aura."

Fancy awakened but resisted opening her eyes.
She'd had a delightful sleep, the best rest since meeting the disconcerting prince. When she realized
falling asleep again would not happen, she opened
her eyes. The light streaming into the room said the
hour was late.

Sitting up, Fancy noted three things. The chamber
was not hers, she was still wearing her gown from the previous evening, and the prince dozed in a chair near the
bed.

Memory failed her, though. What had happened?
Was she upstairs at the prince's mansion?

The bedchamber was richly appointed, its furniture
and textiles colored pink, gold, and antique white.
The windows were high and arched with built-in seats.

Fancy rose from the bed. She glanced at the dozing
prince and then padded across the chamber to peer
out the window.

Green lawns and hedges, adorned with beds of
primary- and pastel-colored flowers, carpeted the
grounds. A row of trees stood like silent sentinels in
the distance. Beyond the trees, sky and water met in
the same amazing shade of blue.

She was not in London anymore.

"Do you like the scenery?"

Fancy whirled around. "Where am I?"

"Rudolf's estate on Sark Island." Stepan rose from
the chair. "We arrived on one of the Kazanov ships last
night."

"Why don't I remember?"

"I slipped a sleeping draught into your wine."

"You drugged and abducted me," she accused him.

"I sedated and rescued you," he defended himself.

Fancy marched across the chamber to stand in front of him. "I want to go home."

"I will grant whatever you wish except that."

She curled her lip. "*Je t'emmerde.*"

"If I kissed your arse, *ma petite*, you would bludgeon me to death."

"I do not find you amusing."

"Calm down," Stepan said, "and enjoy a few days of leisure."

"How few?"

"Two or three weeks, perhaps."

"That is unacceptable," Fancy said. "I must return to the opera."

"Bishop understood and accommodated the need for you to get out of London."

"How do you dare—?"

Stepan traced a finger down her cheek. "Have I mentioned how adorable you are when angry?"

Fancy suffered the urge to bite his finger. The prince was the most infuriating man.

"Am I your prisoner?"

"An honored guest." Stepan dropped into his chair. "Sit down, and I will explain everything."

Fancy sat on the edge of the bed. There was nothing the prince could say to earn her forgiveness.

"As you know, my brothers and I attended a business meeting at your father's yesterday." Stepan leaned forward. "During the course of the meeting, we discovered your youngest sister hiding behind a chair and taking notes on our business discussion."

That made her smile.

"Raven admitted that you have been trying to pauperize your father," he continued.

Fancy could not believe that. Raven would not—

"Did my father enlist your aid in getting rid of me in order to control my sisters?"

Stepan stared at her for a long moment, making her squirm mentally. His expression announced his irritation.

"The world does not revolve around your hatred for aristocrats."

"I never said the world—"

"Be quiet," Stepan ordered, his voice stern. "Listen to me."

His tone surprised her. This was a side to the affable prince that she had never seen.

"Mikhail saw Belle sitting alone in the garden," Stepan told her. "He offered to marry her."

That surprised Fancy. Her sister needed a man to cherish her, but she would dismiss him if she felt pitied.

"Why does your brother want to marry her?"

"Mikhail needs a mother for his daughter and a wife to give him an heir," Stepan answered. "Typical society ladies do not impress him. Your sister is a beauty in spite of the facial scar."

"I don't understand the reason you abducted me."

"You have ruled your sisters like a temperamental queen." Stepan smiled, softening his words. "Raven worried that you would ruin our plans for Belle. She gave me the sleeping draught."

Fancy could not believe Raven would think that she could ruin Belle's possible happiness. Her sisters had never complained about her bossing them. How could she know their feelings? She wasn't a mind reader. Every family needed a leader, and she was it in the Flambeau family.

"I did not intend to hurt your feelings," the prince said.

"My feelings are not hurt." Fancy fixed her gaze on his. "What is the plan?"

"Your father has sent Belle to recuperate at the duchess's cottage on the far side of Primrose Hill," Stepan answered. "Mikhail will pretend to be a commoner suffering from amnesia and temporary blindness."

Fancy smiled at that. "How did he suffer those maladies?"

"Rudolf and Viktor will give him a few bruises."

Fancy winced at the thought. If Mikhail was willing to allow his brothers to beat him, then he was worthy to marry her sister.

"For your sake, I am missing out on the fun," Stepan added.

"Does my father know you have taken me away?"

"Yes." He would not tell her about their impending marriage. Even now all of London was reading about their betrothal, and the duchess was planning the wedding.

She arched an ebony brow. "My father trusts you?"

"My mother is playing the chaperone."

"Your mother?"

"My mother lives here." Stepan stood and crossed the chamber to the door. "Your belongings hang in the armoire. Freshen up and join us for lunch."

Fancy stared at him. She had no idea what to think about this complication. Yet, the idea of meeting the prince's mother appealed to her curiosity.

"Songbird?"

She focused on him. Their gazes met and locked.

"My mother is . . . unwell. Please say nothing to upset her."

"I promise."

Chapter 13

"Here she is, Mother, the woman I love."

Fancy stopped short, poised on the threshold of the garden room. She stared in surprise at the prince. Had his nieces spoken truthfully? Did the prince love her?

He had shocked her, of course. How could she have foreseen the prince professing his love for her to his mother? She had never imagined he had a mother, though everyone did. In her mind, the prince had materialized from nowhere with no earlier life or childhood.

"Will you join us?" Stepan smiled at her, his arm encircling a middle-aged woman. "My mother has waited all morning to meet you."

The prince's mother was an attractive woman, though streaks of gray lightened the black hair at her temples. Her smile was warm and welcoming, curiously childish.

Stepan gestured her into the room. Fancy moved then, approaching mother and son.

"Mother, I present Fancy Flambeau," Stepan introduced them. "Fancy, meet Princess Elizabeth."

"I am honored to meet you, Your Highness."

"What a lovely young woman." Princess Elizabeth reached for Fancy's hand to prevent her from curtseying but spoke to her son. "You have chosen wisely,

Stepan. I am relieved you will not die without knowing true love." She looked at Fancy. "Knowing true love is worth any pain it causes."

Stepan escorted them to the small dining table set on one side of the room. He assisted them into their chairs and then sat between them.

"I am the thorn between two roses."

Princess Elizabeth smiled. "I am more dried flower than dewy rose."

Stepan lifted his mother's hand to his lips. "You will always be a dewy rose to me."

The byplay between mother and son fascinated Fancy. The prince's gentleness with his mother brought unshed tears to her eyes. He loved his mother the way she had loved her own. She blinked back her tears before either of them noticed.

Part sitting room and part dining area, the garden room had glass walls which gave the impression of being outside. The sole departure from a true solarium was the lack of a glass roof; a more traditional ceiling hung overhead.

Boris walked into the room to serve their first course of oyster soup. He grinned at Fancy while he poured their lemon water.

"Pretty songbird sleep long time, huh?" the big Russian said.

"I did sleep a long time." Fancy glanced at the prince. "I had help, though."

"Prince Stepan is fox, huh?"

"The prince is more wolf than fox."

Boris laughed, his voice booming. "I think little songbird tame wolf, huh?" At that, the Russian quit the room.

"I do love oyster soup," Princess Elizabeth gushed, her eyes sparkling with joy. "Do you, Fancy?"

"I like it very much." Fancy smiled at the prince's

mother and wondered at the lady's state of mind, her comment seeming too girlish for a society lady of her age.

"Fancy sings with the opera," Stepan told his mother. "The *Times* named her 'London's Fancy' because her voice is the best anyone has heard in years."

"How exciting." Princess Elizabeth looked at her. "I always loved the opera but haven't seen a performance in years."

"I will sing for you later if you like."

Princess Elizabeth laughed and clapped her hands together. "Oh, I would love that. Wouldn't you, Stepan?"

The prince patted his mother's hand. "I will enjoy the performance almost as much as you."

Fancy shifted her gaze from the mother to the son. The prince's dark eyes glistened with unshed tears at his mother's happiness in a simple song.

Could she have been mistaken about aristocrats and this one in particular? His love for his mother ran deep. She had misjudged the prince on the basis of his wealth and his title. Was she guilty of the snobbery she'd attributed to him?

Boris returned to clear their plates. His brother Feliks served them celery and crab salad along with a platter of cheeses and fruits.

"Your wife will sing sweet lullabies to your children." Princess Elizabeth looked at Fancy. "Stepan always wanted a lullaby before he went to sleep." She frowned then and asked the prince, "Who sang you to sleep when I—when I . . . ?"

"Rudolf sang me to sleep, Mother."

Princess Elizabeth brightened at the mention of the eldest prince. "Why isn't Rudolf eating with us?"

"Rudolf remained in London," Stepan explained, his voice a balm, his patience limitless. "Everyone will come to Sark in August and enjoy a long visit with you."

"Not Vladimir, I hope." Princess Elizabeth looked worried. "I don't like Vladimir."

"Vladimir lives in Moscow and will not visit England," Stepan assured her. "Even Cousin Amber will be coming to visit this year. Next year, she will be busy with her firstborn."

His mother smiled at the news. "Sweet Amber married an Englishman?"

"You remember, Mother, Amber married the Earl of Stratford."

Fancy could not take her eyes off the prince. His sensitivity astonished her. Again, she wondered about the princess's confusion.

"Fancy comes from a large family," Stepan said, drawing his mother's attention to a new topic.

Princess Elizabeth looked at her, her expression clearing. "Tell me about your family."

"Mummy passed away a few years ago," Fancy said, "and Nanny Smudge died last year. My six sisters and I have lived our whole lives in Soho Square with our dog, Puddles."

The princess laughed at the dog's name. "Where is your father?"

Fancy hesitated, embarrassed that this woman had also been her father's paramour. She looked at the prince, who noted her obvious distress.

"Magnus Campbell is Fancy's and her sisters' father," Stepan told his mother.

"Oh, Magnus? Are you Rudolf's sister?" She looked at her son. "Is she Rudolf's sister?"

"Yes, Mother. Rudolf is her half-brother."

Unaccustomed to visitors, the princess quickly tired during the luncheon conversation. She retired to her chamber for a rest after the meal.

Stepan stood when his mother rose from her chair.

Once the princess had disappeared inside, the prince turned to her. "Let me take you on a tour of the grounds."

They left the manor and stepped into the formal gardens. Nature's vibrant colors startled Fancy, who had never ventured far from London.

The lawn was a green carpet leading to a cobblestone wall, separating the grass from a formal rose garden. Here were the undisputed queens of every garden from deep reds to pristine whites and sugary pinks. A topiary garden stood behind the roses, and then the land sloped down to a beach.

Fancy inhaled the mingling scents of sensuous roses and ocean-salted air. Blue sky touched blue ocean in the distance.

"Look at the horizon." Fancy raised her arm and pointed toward the ocean. "Sky and water are one."

Stepan touched her shoulder. "Your land beyond the horizon lies there."

She smiled at that. "Is England the magical land beyond the horizon?"

"Each soul must find his own utopia."

"What's that?"

"Utopia is a land of perfection," the prince explained.

Fancy stared at him for a long moment. "I can't imagine why I considered you frivolous."

"I am frivolous and thoughtful and generous and loyal and a host of other things." Stepan took her hand in his. "Come, I want you to see the rest of the grounds."

They walked around the side of the mansion. Creeping greenery softened the manor's stone walls, and wisteria grew against the building.

Stepan led her across the lawn to a structure built of glass and opened the door. Fancy stepped inside. Everywhere she looked grew potted plants and shrubs. The air was more humid than the dog days in London.

Fancy shifted her gaze to the prince, who stood close to her. His sandalwood scent teased her senses.

"What is this place?"

"My brother's hothouse," he answered. "I work here in the mornings whenever I visit."

"Ah, the gardener."

"Gardening relaxes a person. You should try it."

She gave him a puckish smile. "I have murdered every plant I ever adopted."

Leaving the hothouse behind, they entered the rear gardens, and Fancy recognized the view from her window. A gigantic oak stood alone at the edge of the lawn. A lofty treehouse circled its proud girth, trusting its strong branches. A curving stairway led up, up, up into the tree's arms.

"A treehouse," Fancy exclaimed, her violet gaze sparkling with excitement.

"Come." Stepan grasped her hand and escorted her up the stairs.

The treehouse offered the Kazanov children luxury. A roof covered the house, providing shade, and slats could be lowered to protect the inhabitants from inclement weather. On one side of the treehouse stood a daybed, large enough for several children. A sturdy-looking table and chairs had been placed on the opposite side.

"The older children sleep here on hot nights." Stepan sat on the daybed and patted the spot beside him. When she accepted his silent invitation, he put his arm around her shoulders.

"Your gentleness to your mother impresses me." Fancy gave him a searching look, hoping he would confide in her.

"Does this mean you like me?" he teased her.

Her smile was flirtatious. "Your gentleness persuades me to *tolerate* you better."

Stepan gazed into her disarming violet eyes and pressed a kiss on her temple. "I think you would like to know about my mother."

"If you want to tell me."

"My mother was carrying Rudolf when she married Fedor Kazanov," Stepan began. "My father knew she carried another man's baby, and he never let her forget she had come to the marriage tarnished. Fedor pretended to the world that Rudolf was his son but despised him.

"Though she loved Magnus Campbell, my mother was a dutiful wife and bore my father four sons. Vladimir is Viktor's older twin."

Apparently, her mother had not been the Duke of Inverary's only victim. How many lives had her father ruined because he could not control his urges?

"Why doesn't your mother like Vladimir?"

"Fedor poisoned Vladimir against my mother." Stepan stared into space, his words in the present, his mind in a faraway time. "My father named Vladimir his heir and ignored the rest of us.

"When Mother passed her childbearing years, Fedor locked her in an insane asylum. There she remained for fifteen years until Rudolf rescued her and brought her to England. My brothers and I followed them."

Speechless with shock, Fancy could only stare at him. Tears welled up in her eyes, her horror written across her expression.

Stepan wiped a stray tear off her cheek. "My mother has flourished on Sark Island. Strangers frighten her, but she does enjoy her grandchildren's visits."

Fancy sat in stricken silence. How could she comfort the prince, a man who'd witnessed life-altering cruelty to his mother? At least her father had protected her mother and sent them Nanny Smudge.

Stepan gently turned her face toward him. "Weeping cannot change the past."

Fancy gazed into his black eyes, raw emotion sticking in her throat. "There are worse things in life than being an abandoned bastard."

Dying in winter was preferable to dying on a day like this.

Alexander leaped out of the hackney and walked toward the men gathered on the banks of the Thames River. Sunlight heated his face, but his coldly grim expression mirrored his mood.

Wanton summer had arrived that Sunday in London. The air swelled with a sultry humidity, and the sun shone in a near cloudless sky, baking the earth and its inhabitants. A salty high tide mingled with the river's stench.

Standing near a blanket-covered lump, men spoke in muted voices. Beyond them stood a growing crowd of the curious. Once again, Barney was searching the grass for nits of evidence.

Alexander realized he should have gone to Park Lane first and brought Raven Flambeau. He had decided to wait for the constable's instruction because he didn't have the strength to see Raven twice in one day.

When he looked at her, Alexander saw Raven as she had appeared in her flimsy gown that night. If he loved Genevieve, why did Raven parade across his mind's eye?

Alexander nodded at the constable. "Should I fetch Raven?"

Christ have mercy, was that eagerness he heard in his own voice? What kind of man made love to one woman and thought about another?

Amadeus gave him a long look. "Inspect the victim and tell me if we need Raven."

Walking toward the lump, Alexander yanked a pair of black leather gloves from his pocket and pulled them on. Being careful not to disturb possible evidence, he drew the blanket off the body slowly.

With his gaze fixed on the victim, Alexander walked around the body. At first glance, this beauty seemed like all the others with rose petals sprinkled on her from head to toe. Instinct told him something was different.

Alexander dropped to his knees beside the victim's upper torso and head. The murderer had not placed whole roses in the woman's ears. An oversight due to an intruder? He didn't think the perpetrator would change his calling card now.

Leaning close to the body, Alexander stared hard at the woman's eyelids. No sewing. He glanced over his shoulder, sending the constable a questioning look.

Amadeus Black raised his eyebrows in answer. Pleased with his protege, the constable sent him an almost imperceptible nod.

Alexander returned his attention to the victim. Her lips had not been sewn. Deep bruises marked her neck, and her face was a dark red, a sure sign of occluded vessels.

This woman had not been poisoned. She'd been strangled.

Alexander stood and, pocketing his gloves, walked back to the constable. "This one is different."

Constable Black gestured to a heavyset man standing a short distance away. The weeping man was being comforted by friends.

"The husband found his missing wife." Amadeus Black turned his back on the crowd. "I guarantee he saw his chance to get rid of her and blame the rose-petal murderer."

Alexander flicked a glance at the grieving husband. "He's not much to look at. Why rid himself of a pretty young wife?"

"She would have fared better if she'd been plain."
The constable shook his head. "Married or not, pretty
women get attention from men. If she succumbed to
temptation, the husband would not want her."

Alexander could not mask his shocked expression.
"Would he stoop to murder?"

"Only the wealthy can afford to divorce," Amadeus
answered. "The rest of us are stuck with *until death do
us part.*" The constable rubbed his darkly stubbled
cheek in a weary gesture. "We must find our rose-petal
murderer, or we could be flooded with imitations."

Alexander nodded in understanding. If one unhappy husband had copied the rose-petal murderer,
there must be hundreds of others considering the
same action.

"We need to investigate Parkhurst," Amadeus said.
"I want you to accept your grandfather's offer and take
your place in society."

Alexander opened his mouth to argue. Constable
Black placed his hand on the younger man's shoulder.

"Your pride refuses to acknowledge your own flesh
and blood," Amadeus said, "but your instinct urges a
different action. Believe me. Whatever emotional pain
you inflict on the old man is nothing compared to what
he inflicts on himself. You needed a reason to make
amends, and now I give you one."

Nothing created inner conflict better than divided
loyalties. He needed time to gather his thoughts and
stifle his guilt at betraying his parents' memory.

Walking to Park Lane instead of riding, Alexander
paused when he saw the Duke of Inverary's mansion.
Raven deserved his apology. He hadn't meant to be so
rude. How could he explain his reason for his bad behavior? Keeping her at bay cooled the heat he'd been
feeling for her.

Park Lane smelled like money. Hyde Park and

impeccably maintained mansions lined the street. The mingling scents of myriad flowers and manicured grass wafted through the air. Indeed, life was good for the wealthy.

And then Alexander stood in front of his grandfather's mansion and told himself making amends with the old man was necessary to catch a killer. More important, the old man had hurt his parents and ended by hurting himself more.

The Duke of Essex was a lonely old man. His own father would understand making amends.

Alexander took a deep breath and climbed the stairs. He banged the knocker on the door and waited.

The door swung open, revealing an older man, his grandfather's majordomo. "Good afternoon, my lord. Do come inside."

The welcome and easy admittance surprised Alexander, who'd never ventured near this mansion before today. "Do you know who I am?"

"Don't *you* know?" the majordomo drawled.

"I know who I am." Alexander gave the man a lopsided grin. "And you are?"

"Twigs." The majordomo gestured toward the stairs. "Come along. His Grace is taking tea in the parlor."

Alexander followed Twigs up the stairs and down a corridor to the informal family parlor. Along the way, he noted the decor's understated elegance. Nothing garish for old money like his grandfather's.

"Your Grace," Twigs announced, "the Marquess of Basildon requests—"

"I can see who is there," the duke interrupted.

Twigs looked decidedly unhappy. "The killjoy could have let me finish," the majordomo muttered, turning to leave. "I hadn't announced anyone in months."

Alexander looked from his grandfather to the departing majordomo. "Twigs?"

The majordomo paused and turned around. "Yes, my lord?"

"Bring me a cup of tea, please."

Twigs burst into a smile. "Yes, my lord."

Alexander crossed the parlor. Without waiting for an invitation, he sat in the high-backed chair opposite his grandfather.

"You should not coddle him," his grandfather grumbled. "The attention will go to his head."

Alexander suppressed the urge to laugh in his grandfather's face. Instead, he said, "I've changed my mind about the inheritance."

"Humph, I deduced as much."

"Would you prefer I didn't?"

"Did I say that?"

Twigs returned with the tea. He lifted the porcelain cup and saucer off the tray and then set the small pot on the table, too.

"I've brought you cucumber sandwiches," the majordomo said, and set that dish on the table.

"Thank you, Twigs."

"You are very welcome." Twigs leveled a disgruntled look on his employer and left the parlor.

Alexander sipped his tea and lifted a cucumber sandwich off the plate. "I warn you," he said, "I plan to marry Genevieve Stover and will not listen to your rantings about that."

The Duke of Essex gave a weary sigh. "I don't give a damn if you marry the flower girl at Covent Garden."

"You accept my wishes?"

"Do I have a choice?"

"No."

"I traveled that road with your father and lived to regret it," his grandfather admitted. "Do not marry the girl to spite me, though. You will be married a long time, Alexander. If you make the wrong choice, you will suffer for it."

"Genevieve Stover is not the wrong choice," Alexander insisted. Thoughts of an ebony-haired, violet-eyed witch popped into his mind, but he banished her to the shadows.

"Take yourself to Bond Street tomorrow," his grandfather was saying. "Purchase more appropriate clothing."

"There's nothing wrong with—"

His grandfather banged his cane on the floor. "Your attire is appropriate for investigating murders, not society functions."

Alexander inclined his head. "I stand corrected."

"Humph, it's about time you admitted a lack of knowledge," his grandfather said. "Now, tell me how the investigation is going."

"Are you interested?"

"Would I ask if I weren't?"

Alexander smiled at the old man. "You would have made an excellent criminal."

"Why do you say that?"

"You have acquired a habit of answering a question with a question," Alexander said. "We could never trick you into a confession."

The hint of a smile touched his grandfather's lips and then disappeared. "If I didn't need this cane, I might embark on a life of crime."

"Speaking of crimes," Alexander said, "I came here from Mill Bank near the Vauxhall Bridge. We discovered a body covered with rose petals. The husband tried to rid himself of his wife and blame the rose-petal murderer."

"Did the man confess?"

Alexander shook his head, "Constable Black will have no trouble when he questions the man."

"The Earl and Countess of Winchester are hosting a

ball this week," his grandfather said. "I want you to attend with me."

"Very well." Alexander stood to leave.

"May I ask why you changed your mind about accepting the inheritance?"

Alexander stared at his grandfather and saw a lonely old man who had lived with regret for many years. The choice between hurting him with the truth or glossing over it was no choice at all.

"Constable Black advised me to make peace with you."

His grandfather inclined his head. "I am grateful for his interference."

"I will see you tomorrow after I visit Bond Street."

His grandfather narrowed his gaze on him. "Drop the pity. I dislike that emotion."

Alexander gave his grandfather a cold stare. "Why should I pity the no-good son of a bitch who hurt my father?"

The older man gave him a broad smile. "You do remind me of me."

Alexander returned the smile. "If you insult me like that again, *I* will disown *you.*"

His grandfather threw back his head and shouted with laughter.

Fancy paced her bedchamber at midnight while the household slept.

She had misjudged the prince. True, Stepan was not the most responsible man in England in terms of employment. Outrageous compliments slipped from his lips like sweets given to children.

The prince was no aristocratic rake as her own father had been. He liked women; his compliments were designed to make the recipient feel special,

whether duchess or maid. Saving time each week for
tea with his nieces was extraordinarily loving, and his
gentle patience with his mother tugged at her heart.

Fancy paused at the window and gazed at the night.
A full moon shone against the backdrop of a black
velvet sky, casting the world into light and shadow. In
the distance, the treehouse waited for its children to
return.

The scent of cinnamon filled the bedchamber.
Fancy knew her nanny was near to guide her, and
those famous words popped into her mind.

Listen to your head, child, but follow your heart.

Her head was warning her to keep her distance
from the prince lest she become her mother. Her
heart was urging her to rush into his arms, trusting his
love to keep her safe.

Fancy knew one thing for certain. She did not want
to die without knowing love.

Dare she sneak into his bedchamber? Should she
wait for the morning and tell him—

Tell him what? She loved him? She hoped he loved
her? She wanted what she had previously refused, a
place in his bed?

Fancy stared out the window, uncertainty riding her
hard. She would follow her heart, but which path
should her heart take?

And then she saw him. Wearing only breeches, the
prince sauntered in the direction of the treehouse.

Fancy watched him climbing the twisting stairs until
he disappeared inside. Desire loved darkness as much
as she loved the prince.

Wearing only her nightgown, Fancy padded on bare
feet across the chamber and slipped out the door.
Shining through the window panes, the full moon lit
her way to the stairs.

Fancy reached the first floor without mishap. Again,

the moon lit her path to the door. She lifted the bottom edge of her nightgown and dashed across the lawn until the twisting wooden staircase stood in front of her.

Pausing a moment, Fancy took a deep breath and then climbed the stairs. She reached the top, stepped into the treehouse, and hesitated.

The prince stood with his back to her. She savored the sight of his naked back. Broad shoulders. Strong, sinewy muscles. Tapered waist. Lean hips.

"Stepan?"

He whirled around. *Mon Dieu*, his naked chest with its matting of dark hair was even more beautiful than his back.

"What are you doing here at this hour?"

"I-I . . ." Fancy flicked her tongue and wet her lips. "What are *you* doing here at this hour?"

"I was trying to avoid temptation," Stepan said, "but you followed me."

Fancy heard the smile in his voice. Summoning her courage, she crossed the treehouse until mere inches separated their bodies.

"Do you love me?"

Chapter 14

Her question surprised him. "Do you want me to love you?"

"Yes."

Anticipation surged through him. "Why?"

"I love you."

She loved him. She was his. He had won her love.

Stepan slid the palms of his hands up her bare arms. "I love you more than my own life."

In silent answer, Fancy slid her palms up his naked chest to entwine around his neck. Their bodies touched from chest to thigh.

"Kiss me," she breathed.

Stepan dipped his head, his lips claiming hers. Mingling with sensual amber, her soft rose scent and her promise of love seduced his senses.

Their kiss was long and langorous. His tongue caressed the crease of her lips, which parted for him, allowing him entrance to the sweetness of her mouth.

Fancy trembled in response, her tongue swirling with his in a mating dance. She pressed herself against him, her breasts heavy and her nipples tightening with the wanting.

His arms encircled her body, one hand holding the

back of her head steady. One hand cupped her buttocks through the gauzy nightgown, pressing her against his arousal.

Stepan had never known a woman could be this sweet. She was an innocent, and he did not want to frighten her.

"Will you make love with me?" Stepan gazed into her hauntingly lovely face and willed her to acquiesce.

Fancy looked at him through disarming violet eyes. "I thought we were making love."

"There is more," he whispered. "So much more, princess."

"I want all your love, my prince."

His mouth captured hers in a slow, soul-stealing kiss. That melted into another. And another.

Lifting his lips from hers, Stepan stepped back a pace and rested his hands on her shoulders. "You are certain you want this?"

The full moon bathed her face in light, showing him the love in her expression. "I am sure."

"Belonging to a prince means forever," he warned her.

"I want you. Stop wasting time."

That made him smile. When his little songbird made a decision, no one could persuade her otherwise.

Stepan slipped the straps of her nightgown off her shoulders, letting it pool around her feet. His breath caught in his throat at her beauty, his hands drifting from her shoulders to her breasts down her body to her waist and hips. Gently rounded hips, fashioned to carry his babies. His hands retraced their path up her silken body. His thumbs teased her nipples, aroused into buds.

For the first time in her life, Fancy felt a man's hands on her body, and she liked it. She loved the strength and the gentleness of his hands gliding across her flesh, worshipping her softness. Her breath caught raggedly when he caressed her aroused nipples. And the hidden place between her thighs began throbbing.

"Undress me," Stepan whispered.

"You want me to—?"

Stepan heard the surprise in her voice. "Draw my breeches down and touch me."

"Where shall I touch you?" she squeaked, her panic rising.

Stepan ignored her alarm. "Wherever you desire."

Fancy touched the waist of his breeches, dragging them down until they pooled at his feet. Bypassing his privates, she slid her fingertips across his chest, feeling his muscles. Pressing herself against him, she rubbed her breasts back and forth across his matting of black hair.

"You feel good," she whispered. "Your hair teases my nipples."

"Why do you not touch below my waist?"

"I'm afraid."

The prince did not laugh as she'd expected. He offered her his hand instead. "Come to my bed, and I will cure your fear."

She hesitated.

"Trust me, princess."

Fancy placed her hand in his. Stepan closed his fingers around it and drew her toward the daybed.

They lay facing each other, their flesh and lips pressing together. She looped her arms around his neck, and he held the back of her head while caressing the slender column of her back and her rounded buttocks.

Stepan rolled her onto her back and gazed into her face. Lowering his head, he teased the crease of her lips with his tongue and then kissed the corners of her mouth.

"Beautiful songbird," he murmured.

Stepan sprinkled feathery light kisses on her cheeks, her temples, her eyelids. Sliding lower, he flicked his tongue across her delicately boned throat and heard her purr of pleasure.

"So much more, princess." Stepan kissed the swell of each breast. His mouth latched onto one nipple while his fingers played with the other, catching it between two fingers and running his thumb across its tip.

Flaming sensation shot from her beaded nipples to the folds between her thighs. She held his head against her breast and arched herself into his mouth.

"Your breasts are sensitive." And then Stepan slid his hand across her fluttering belly and slid one long finger down and up her moist crease.

Fancy gasped at this new, even more exciting sensation. How could she ever have imagined such exquisite torment?

Stepan slipped a finger inside her, whispering, "Easy, princess."

Fancy moved her hips, meeting his finger's rhythm. "I want you."

Stepan claimed her lips, pouring all his love into that stirring kiss. "Shall I make you mine, princess?"

"Please . . ." Her whisper pleaded for his possession, telling him she would die without it.

Stepan spread her legs and knelt between them. Lifting her buttocks, he positioned himself and pushed the head of his shaft into her moist heat.

Feeling her tense, Stepan stopped and let her become accustomed to him. Then he pushed forward an inch.

"All your love," she whispered.

And Stepan thrust deep inside her, breaking her maidenhead. She gasped in surprise and then relaxed, arching her hips in silent invitation.

With long strokes, Stepan fanned her passion into

wild flames. She met him thrust for thrust, holding him while he rode her hard.

"Deeper," she panted.

"Like this?" Stepan ground his groin against hers. His strokes became fierce. "And this?"

Paradise caught her by surprise. Throbbing waves of exquisite sensation washed through her, and she cried out.

Stepan's strokes became shorter, faster, urgent. Then he shuddered, spilling his seed, his groan of pleasure mingling with hers.

Stepan floated to earth first and rolled to her side. Intending to cuddle, he tried to pull her against him.

Fancy turned her back on him. Then she burst into tears.

"What is this?" Stepan forced her to face him and held her close while she sobbed against his chest, a wrenching sound that tugged on his heartstrings.

"I am sorry, princess." Stepan stroked her back to soothe her. "I did not intend to hurt you, but a woman feels pain when she gives her virginity."

The word *virginity* made her sob harder. "Y-You d-didn't h-hurt m-me."

Stepan felt confused. Was she crying because he didn't hurt her? Or was she crying because she had given him her virginity, never to be reclaimed?

"Why are you weeping, sweetheart?"

"I have become my mother," Fancy wailed.

Stepan squelched the urge to laugh. She would never forgive him if he laughed.

"You are not your mother." Stepan tightened his hold on her. "I love you, princess."

"M-my f-father t-told my mother he l-loved her," she sobbed.

"Your father told my mother he loved her, too."

Fancy wailed louder at that.

Stepan swallowed his laughter. His little songbird was the strongest-willed woman he had ever met. Yet, engaging in sexual relations had reduced her to weeping insecurity. Which benefited his plans for her.

"You are not your mother or mine," Stepan assured her. "I want to marry you."

"What?" That stopped her tears.

Stepan planted a kiss on the crown of her head, rose from the daybed, and then knelt on one bended knee. "Miss Flambeau, will you do me the honor of becoming my wife?"

Fancy said nothing, merely stared at him. For one awful moment, Stepan thought she would refuse.

"I promise to love and to honor you each day of my life," he coaxed her, "*and* I will let you shoot the apple off my head."

Her smile could have lit the whole island. "Yes, Your Highness, I will marry you."

Stepan lifted her hands to his lips. "Which swayed you, the apple or my love?"

"Both."

Stepan growled and pushed her back on the bed. Hovering above her, he smiled and dipped his head to claim her lips in a lingering kiss.

He would impregnate her before returning to London. His songbird could not change her mind when faced with the prospect of a child.

"Some day in the future," Stepan said, "you will tell our grandchildren how I knelt naked before you and proposed marriage."

Fancy laughed. "I don't think that would be proper."

"Forget proper." Stepan yanked her into his arms and kissed her again. "I want a dozen daughters and one son."

"Thirteen is an unlucky number."

"A baker's dozen daughters," he amended.

She traced her silken fingertips down his stubbled cheek. "You have all of London fooled, Your Highness, but you are no rake."

"I do enjoy cultivating that false reputation." He turned his head and kissed her hand. "Rakes are more interesting than family men in the making."

Stepan sat up and dragged his breeches up his legs. Then he reached for her nightgown and drew it over her head.

"Come, princess." Stepan stood and offered her his hand. "I want to sleep beside you in bed and promise to return to my chamber before anyone awakens."

Fancy placed her hand in his and let him pull her off the daybed. She hesitated and glanced over her shoulder. "Take the blanket, and I will wash the blood spots off."

"Leave it," Stepan said, drawing her toward the spiral stairs. "Someone will wash it in the morning."

Fancy felt her face heating with embarrassment. "I do not want the maids to see my virgin's blood."

"I work in the hothouse during the early hours," Stepan told her. "I will take care of the blanket then."

Fancy awakened alone the following morning. She yawned and stretched and smiled, her thoughts on her prince. Before dawn, Stepan had kissed her and returned to his own chamber.

Rising from the bed, Fancy looked out the window at another glorious day. Her spirits soaring with the prince's marriage proposal, Fancy dressed and shoved the slingshot into her pocket. She walked downstairs to the garden room and poured herself a cup of coffee.

"You eat egg?" Boris asked. "Feliks cook special egg for songbird."

Fancy shook her head. "I'll wait for lunch. Where is His Highness?"

"He work flower house."

Fancy finished her coffee, pocketed an apple, and walked outside. She strolled around the manor to the hothouse.

The extreme humidity hit Fancy when she stepped inside, followed by mingling flower scents. The sight of the prince's bare back halted her in her tracks. She paused to admire the well-honed muscles moving as he worked. And then he spoke.

"That did not hurt," Stepan told the rosebush, plucking its dried leaves. "Don't you want to grow as big as your family and join them outside next summer?"

The prince treated the plants as gently as he did his mother, his nieces, and her.

"Stepan?"

He turned around. The warmth in his smile registered, but her gaze fixed on his muscled chest. Memories of the previous night melted inside her and made her ache.

Fancy walked down an aisle lined with potted plants and stepped into his embrace. She looped her arms around his neck and drew his face toward her, capturing his mouth in a hungry kiss.

"I missed you."

Stepan smiled. "I missed you more."

"You were talking to that rosebush."

"Were you spying on me?"

"I was admiring your naked back."

"Oh, stop . . . you will make me blush."

Fancy gave him a flirtatious smile. "If you didn't blush last night, you will never blush."

"Have I told you today how much I admire your wit and your beauty?"

"I would prefer hearing you profess your love."

Stepan nuzzled the side of her neck. "I love you, princess."

"And I love you, my prince."

"Then we are even." Stepan hooked an arm around her waist. "I want you to meet some friends."

"Would these friends be plants?"

Stepan pointed to a plant with nodding violet blossoms. "The Persian violet reminds me of your beautiful eyes."

"I will think of your compliments whenever I see a Persian violet," Fancy said.

"I hope you will think of me more often than that," he said.

"I promise to think of you every minute of every waking hour of every day."

Stepan looked disappointed. "Is that all?"

Fancy laughed. "I will dream about you, too."

Stepan slid his hand up the front of her body to cup her breast. "Then we are even." He gestured to the potted rosebush and changed the subject. "This rose is a temperamental queen. Did you know that every culture since ancient times has valued the rose?"

She shook her head. "I know nothing of flowers."

"I will teach you," he said, "and you will help me in my own hothouse."

"If I were you, I would never let me near your plants." Fancy gave him a mischievous smile. "My touch murders plants, but my voice can heal them. What a wonderful way to practice for the opera."

Stepan stared at her. His beloved could not be serious, could she? Singing in the opera was unsuitable for his wife. Not only would she become a princess but the mother of princes and princesses.

"Is there something wrong?"

Grabbing his discarded shirt, Stepan stalled by pulling it over his head. Did he want to argue about this now? Getting her with child before returning to London would be wiser than arguing. Once she had a babe to nurture, Fancy would forget about the opera.

"The woman I love loves me." Stepan winked at her. "What could be wrong in God's universe?"

When they left the hothouse, Fancy saw the tree-house and remembered the blood-spotted blanket. "Do we need to wash the blanket?" She blushed. "My virgin's blood, you know."

Stepan waved her worry away. "I took care of the problem."

"You washed the blanket?"

Her question surprised him. "Princes do not wash blankets."

"You said you took care of it."

"I instructed Boris to wash the blanket."

"*Mon Dieu.*" Her complexion darkened into tomato red.

"You did not want the maids to see your virgin's blood," Stepan reminded her.

"I would have preferred the maids to Boris."

"You should have said that." Stepan shook his head at her foolishness. "I will tell Boris I cut myself."

"No! You are purposely embarrassing me," she accused him.

Stepan ran a hand down his face and counted to ten. "Your virgin's blood should not embarrass you."

"You are being obtuse."

He grinned. "Thank you, but what is this *obtuse*?"

Fancy stamped her foot in frustrated anger. How could she rant and rave if he refused to participate? "I did not want anyone seeing my virgin's blood."

Stepan laughed, which did not endear him to her. "The deed is done, princess."

Fancy turned her back on him and took several deep

breaths. Facing him again, she managed a smile and reached into her pocket. "Are you ready for the apple?"

Stepan narrowed his dark gaze on her. "You lack the proper mood to attempt shooting an apple off my head."

"My mood enhances using the slingshot."

"Give me the apple." Stepan held his hand out. "I promise to leave you the blood washing next time."

Was this his idea of a joke? The prince was either very brave or very foolish.

"There will never be a next time," she said.

He flashed her a wicked smile. "Ah, yes. A woman can lose her virginity only once."

Fancy handed him a fallen leaf. "Hold this out straight away from your body for my practice shot."

"You need more practice?" The prince sounded alarmed.

"I meant my warm-up shot."

"Why do you need to use the slingshot?" Stepan asked. "I will protect you."

"Raven told me to practice," Fancy answered. "I trust my sister's feelings."

Stepan knew he would not change her mind. Accepting defeat, he held the leaf as she'd instructed.

Fancy marked off ten paces and took the slingshot from her pocket. Next came the pellet. She aimed, and the pellet flew toward the prince.

The force of the shot ripped the leaf out of his hand. "You did it."

Did he need to sound so damn relieved? "I know I did it. Balance the apple on your head."

The minx wanted him to prove his love with the damn apple. Stepan gingerly set the apple on top of his head.

Risking injury proved his love. Fancy hoped she didn't hurt him.

"Close your eyes just in case."

"What do you mean *just in case*?" The apple fell off his head.

Fancy gave him a smile meant to encourage. "I was joking."

Stepan did not look convinced but scooped the apple off the grass. Love set it on his head again.

With her focus on the shot, Fancy studied the difference in height from the level of his outstretched arm to the top of his head. She pulled the pellet from her pocket and placed it in the slingshot's flexible tubing.

Whoosh. Fancy sent the pellet hurtling toward the prince. The apple tumbled off his head.

Stepan opened his eyes when he felt the apple fall. He scooped it up. The pellet was embedded in its core.

"I knew you could do it."

"Don't move." Fancy hurried to a shrub and amputated a twig. Returning to the prince, she placed it in his hand. "Stand sideways and hold the twig between your lips. I will go—"

Stepan threw back his head and shouted with laughter. Tossing the twig down, he started walking toward the manor.

Fancy hurried after him. "Where are you going?"

"I want to wash before lunch."

"Does this mean you won't hold the twig?"

His laughter was her answer.

"Don't you love me?"

"Not *that* much."

Gawd, but she dreaded tonight.

Raven walked down the corridor to Sophia's bedchamber and tugged her long white kidskin gloves into place. Having lived her entire life sharing a bed-

chamber with sisters, she could not accustom herself
to sleeping alone.

After knocking, Raven entered the chamber and
stopped short. Serena and Sophia were playing cards
instead of dressing for the Winchester ball. Puddles lay
on his back on top of the bed, his tail wagging at her
entrance.

"You aren't dressed." Raven stated the obvious. "The
duchess will pitch a fit."

"Stepmama has given us permission to stay home,"
Serena said. "Dearest Sophia is painting my portrait,
and we are much too busy to socialize."

"That isn't fair," Raven said.

"Don't be upset," Sophia said. "Stepmama has invited several gentlemen to dinner next week to make
our acquaintances."

"If the duchess has her way," Raven said, "all seven
of us will be wed by Christmas."

"You look beautiful tonight," Serena said.

"Thank you." Raven crossed the chamber to inspect
her appearance in the cheval mirror. She wore a petal-
pink silk gown with a modestly scooped neckline and
puffed shoulder sleeves. The duchess's maid had woven
her hair into a knot at the nape of her neck, allowing
wispy ebony tendrils to escape.

"You don't think I look too young in pink?"

"Darling," Serena drawled, imitating the duchess,
"you *are* young."

Raven looked at Sophia. "Have you thought about
the reason Genevieve Stover had no aura?"

Sophia shrugged. "Perhaps some people don't have
colors."

"Have you ever seen anyone who did not?"

"No."

Raven left her sisters and walked downstairs to the

foyer. A violet-gowned Bliss and a pale yellow-gowned Blaze stood with the duchess.

"Don't you think I am too young for such activities?" Raven asked.

"The Countess of Winchester is my niece," the duchess said, "so your attending is perfectly acceptable."

The duchess inspected their appearance and smiled with satisfaction. "Remember, my darlings, not all men are annoying. Some are dead."

"Don't teach my daughters that, Roxie." Dressed in formal evening attire, the Duke of Inverary was walking down the stairs.

The duchess feigned innocence. "Magnus, my love, you know I don't mean you."

"Do not make manhaters of my daughters," the duke said, gesturing to the majordomo to open the door. "The world belongs to men, and I want my daughters to navigate safely and happily through their future marriages."

"I intended to caution them only," the duchess said. "You know how devilish the young swains are nowadays."

The Duke of Inverary turned on his daughters, his expression worried. "Do *not* believe a word any gentleman says until you marry. Then you may trust your husband."

The Duchess of Inverary rolled her eyes. "Trust within reason, of course." She glanced at her own husband. "I merely caution them, dearest."

Several hundred guests filled the Winchester ballroom. A small orchestra consisting of a cornet, a piano, a cello, and three violins stood at the far end of the rectangular chamber. A rainbow of colors swirled around the dance floor as brightly gowned ladies waltzed with gentlemen in formal evening attire.

"The Duke of Essex," the Winchester majordomo announced. "The Marquess of Basildon."

Raven watched the two men descending the stairs. In his formal evening attire, Alexander Blake had never looked more handsome. His presence with his grandfather surprised her, though. Had he accepted his grandfather's offer of inheritance? Did that mean the old man accepted Genevieve Stover for his granddaughter-in-law? Or had Alexander dropped her the way her father had dropped her own mother?

Surrounded by eager aristocrats, the Duke of Essex introduced his grandson to society. Debutantes and their grasping mamas seemed especially interested in this new, handsome, wealthy aristocrat destined for dukedom.

And then the Duke of Essex reached their group and introduced Alexander to the Duke and Duchess of Inverary. Next came Princes Rudolf and Viktor and their wives.

The Duchess of Inverary drew Raven forward. "I believe my stepdaughter and you are already acquainted, my lord."

"Good evening, Raven," Alexander greeted her, for once using her given name instead of the word *brat.*

Raven wished her sisters weren't dancing. "I never expected to see you here."

Alexander grinned at her. "I never expected that either." He hesitated for a fraction of a moment and then asked, "Would you care to dance?"

Raven recalled the evenings of her childhood when Alexander would visit and waltz with her. They had pretended the kitchen was a grand ballroom in one of the great mansions.

Her smile chilled him. "No, thank you. I don't care to dance."

"Of course, she wants to dance." The Duchess of Inverary laughed. "Raven, darling, don't be shy."

Alexander offered her his hand. "Dance with me. *Please.*"

Everyone was watching them. What else could she do?

Raven placed her hand in his and let him lead her onto the dance floor. Alexander drew her into his arms and waltzed her away from her relatives.

"This feels like the old days, doesn't it?"

"Quite." Raven fixed her gaze on an imaginary point behind him.

"I believe light conversation is customary," Alexander said, a smile in his voice.

Raven shifted her gaze to him and then wished she hadn't. Her peace of mind suffered from his too-handsome face, and she'd already made a fool of herself once.

"I was beginning to think I was invisible."

She said nothing. Her lips twitched with the urge to smile.

"Why do you dislike me, brat?"

"I do not dislike you. I do not think about you at all."

Having reached the far end of the ballroom, Alexander escorted her off the dance floor. Had she deflated his enormous conceit? She certainly hoped so.

"I want to speak with you privately," he said.

Raven inclined her head. "I will not miss this candlelit hell."

Smiling at her words, Alexander led her around the ballroom. He gestured to the duchess that they were going to the refreshment room.

"Let's walk in the garden," Alexander said, once they'd left the ballroom.

"This sounds mysterious."

Stepping into the garden, Raven felt a surge of relief at the reassuring sight of other couples catching a breath of air. Torches lit the area, and the mingling perfumes of flowers scented the air.

Raven wished she hadn't agreed to come outside. She had already played the fool once and worried about saying something she'd regret later.

"Constable Black advised me to make peace with the old man," Alexander told her.

"You do not need to explain yourself."

"I am telling, not explaining." Alexander slipped her hand through the loop of his arm and led her off the path to stand beneath a silver birch tree. "We need to investigate Lord and Lady Parkhurst from inside society. Will you help?"

Raven leaned back against the birch's white trunk, its solidness a comfort. "Why do you need my help?"

Which was precisely the problem, Alexander thought. He'd brought her outside on a pretext. He loved Genevieve, but fighting his attraction for this petite ebony-haired witch was proving impossible.

Alexander lifted a hand and traced a finger down her cheek, savoring its softness. "You look delicious in pink, like a tempting confection."

His compliment startled Raven speechless. She froze in alarm, realizing his face was inching closer and closer. He was going to kiss her. What the blue blazes should she do with her hands?

Their lips touched in a sweet kiss. His were warm and moved against her with confidence. Hers were cold with insecure fright.

"Lord Basildon?"

Alexander turned toward the voice. A footman stood near them, his gaze discreetly averted.

"Mister Barney in the foyer requests a word with you," the footman said.

"Thank you." Alexander grasped her hand, and they followed the footman inside.

With hat in hand, Barney stood in the foyer. "The constable needs you," he said. "We've got another body."

"The constable may want my perceptions," Raven said. "I'm going with you."

Alexander nodded and turned to the footman. "Inform the Duke of Essex and the Duke of Inverary that Raven Flambeau suffers from a headache, and I am escorting her home."

"Yes, my lord."

Twenty minutes later, Barney halted the coach outside Battersea Fields across the river. Alexander leaped out and then helped Raven.

"Barney, go to the opera house," he instructed, "and escort Genevieve Stover home."

"Your home or hers?"

"Hers."

A dozen men stood around lighting the night with torches. In their midst lay a blanket-covered lump.

"I'm glad to see you, Raven, though you may not be up to this." The constable touched her arm. "She is not a fresh kill, which means she isn't a pretty sight. Stand with me until Blake gets a look at her."

Alexander approached the lump. He drew the blanket off her and walked around the body slowly. Crouching beside the body, he inspected her face and then nodded at the constable.

"Raven, I don't think you should see this," Alexander said. "I think you should wait for the next one."

Wait for the next one? If seeing this unfortunate woman saved another from becoming the next one, Raven would reserve her horror for later.

"I insist." Raven walked toward Alexander and stared at the decomposing body. Her heart ached at the sight of the once-beautiful woman decaying without burial. Rose petals and ravenous flies covered the corpse.

A demon had done this, a monster masquerading as human.

"I need to kneel," Raven said, unable to take her sickened sight off the corpse.

Alexander removed his jacket and set it on the ground beside the body. Raven knelt, but when she reached to touch the body, Alexander grabbed her hand and shook his head.

"Let me touch a rose petal," she said.

Alexander put on gloves and lifted a petal. He dropped it into the palm of her hand.

Raven closed her eyes. "Evil has two faces."

"We know a man and a woman are working together," Alexander said.

"Which is the man?" Raven dropped the rose petal. "And which is the woman? Their confusion is confusing me."

"Do you mean they don't know their own genders?" Constable Black asked.

"The monsters know what they are," Raven answered, "but their faces merge, blurring the differences between them." She sighed in defeat. "I'm not much help, am I?"

Alexander touched her shoulder. "No one commits a perfect crime. We will find them."

Raven glanced at the corpse. "Is she wearing any jewelry I could touch?"

Constable Black inspected the victim and then unfastened a bracelet. He placed the delicate gold chain in the palm of her hand.

Raven closed her fingers around it and felt something. Opening her hand, she spread the gold bracelet out and traced a finger from top to bottom on both sides.

"What is it?" Constable Black asked.

"I feel several strands of hair caught in the links." Raven looked at the constable and then at Alexander. "The hairs do not come from any human."

Chapter 15

Four weeks on Sark Island passed faster than a sunny day in London.

Fancy stared out the cabin's porthole at the rain while waiting the Kazanov ship's turn to dock. Making love, tending the garden, and singing for the prince's mother felt like another lifetime. A gloomy mood settled over her like the fog hugging the top of the Thames.

These had always been her favorite days. The rain had brought her father's visits and her mother's smiles. The rain did not cheer her today, though.

Fancy wished she and the prince could have lingered on the island. She had felt like a princess every day for four weeks.

On the other hand, Fancy yearned to step onstage again and bask in the audience's love. There was no feeling in the world like a standing ovation following a well-sung opera.

Having felt under the eaves for a few days, Fancy hoped her stomach ailment had passed, and her nausea on the return journey had merely been seasickness. Though she had to admit, sailing from Sark Island to London wasn't exactly adventuring on the wide expanse of ocean. When she became so famous that the

Continent's capitals begged for her voice, she would only cross the Channel from Dover to Calais, and travel everywhere else by coach.

Fancy turned around when the door opened. Carrying a tray, the prince walked into the cabin and shut the door with his foot. His smile sent the butterflies in her belly fluttering with excitement.

"How do you feel?" Stepan set the tray on the table.

Fancy crossed the cabin to meet him there. "The seasickness stole my energy."

"I have cooked you tea and toast," Stepan said. "Docking will take another hour or two."

Fancy sat across from him. "*You* cooked tea and toast?"

"I am a man of many talents."

"I know." Fancy gave him a flirtatious smile. "I appreciate every one of them."

Stepan laughed and reached for a piece of toast. He watched her nibble on her toast and sip the tea. "You can nap before we dock if you want."

"Perhaps."

"Are you happy to return to London?"

"I wish we were back on Sark Island," she answered, "but I'm eager to return to work."

Stepan nodded but said nothing for a long moment. He refused to argue about the opera before their marriage had taken place. She could not back out of it now; she was carrying his child but too inexperienced to realize it yet. He wondered why the thought did not occur to her that her singing career would end with the words *I do*.

"My mother enjoyed our visit," Stepan said. "We must visit her again soon."

"Princess Elizabeth is a most appreciative audience." Fancy dropped the half-eaten piece of toast on the plate and then pushed the plate away. "Too bad crowds frighten her. She would enjoy attending one of my performances."

"Have I over- or undercooked the toast?" Stepan asked, staring at her plate. "Spread too much butter?"

"The boat ride made my stomach weak."

"This is a ship, not a boat."

"The *vessel* has turned my stomach." Fancy sipped her tea.

"You may as well wait until next week before returning to the opera," Stepan said. "Today is Friday, and Genevieve Stover can finish the week playing Cherubino."

"That sounds like a good idea." Fancy yawned and then smiled. "Your tea relaxed me."

"Come here."

Fancy walked around the table and sat on his lap. Stepan wrapped his arms around her, and she rested her head against his shoulder.

"What are you thinking?" she asked.

"I hate rainy days."

"Why?"

"Nothing good ever happened in the rain."

"My father visited on rainy days," she murmured, her eyes closing in sleep, "and my mother always smiled . . ."

Wrapped in a cloak, Fancy stepped on deck two hours later. The river's salty stench hit her hard. Which surprised her since the Thames's stink had never bothered her before.

Fancy clamped a hand over her mouth to keep from vomiting and turned distressed eyes on the prince. Stepan led her a few feet away and held her while she gagged.

"There go the tea and toast." He sounded almost cheerful.

Was His Highness happy with her illness? His mood was less than sympathetic.

"How embarrassing," she moaned.

"You should not feel embarrassed." Stepan wrapped the cloak tightly around her and then scooped her into his arms. With a nod to the captain, he carried her off the ship.

Stepan helped Fancy into the coach and then climbed inside. "Park Lane," he instructed the driver.

Fancy turned to him as the coach moved into traffic. "I want to go home to Soho Square."

"Your sisters will want to see you."

"I'll see them tomorrow."

"Do you want to know how Mikhail and Belle fared?"

"Very well, we'll stop at Park Lane." Fancy rested her head against the prince's shoulder and promptly fell asleep.

Nothing good ever happened on rainy days, Stepan thought. And the worst was still to come with Fancy. Their coming confrontation loomed like a storm cloud over his head. She was his but resisted depending on anyone except herself.

How would Fancy react when she learned the truth about her position? She was cantankerous on her good days, and pregnancy was making her even more cranky. Perhaps truth—like vodka—should be swallowed in small doses.

Thirty minutes later, the coach halted in front of the Duke of Inverary's mansion. Stepan nudged Fancy awake, climbed down, and then lifted her out of the coach.

Fancy yawned, making him smile. "I can't imagine why I am so tired."

"You have been ill this week." Stepan put his hand on the back of her waist and guided her toward the stairs.

Tinker, the duke's majordomo, opened the door. They stepped into the foyer and removed their cloaks.

Puddles materialized from nowhere and ran down the stairs. The mastiff leaped at the prince, knocking him back against the door.

Stepan laughed. "Sit, Puddles." The dog sat and wagged its tail.

"Master Puddles knows it's time for his garden constitutional," Tinker said. "Their Graces are taking tea in the family parlor."

"I know the way." Stepan put his arm around Fancy and ushered her up the stairs to the second floor. "We will share the news of our forthcoming marriage."

"How forthcoming will it be?"

"Soon."

"We will need to plan the ceremony around my opera schedule."

"Bishop will be flexible."

"But I—"

Stepan stepped into the family parlor, precluding further discussion. The Duke and Duchess of Inverary sat in chairs near the hearth. With them were two of the prince's brothers, Rudolf and Mikhail.

The parlor was as Fancy remembered from her previous visit, warm and inviting and furnished in jewel colors. There was her mother's image hanging on the wall, her eyes still lit with coy invitation. Clustered in vases, summer roses scented the air in place of spring's lilacs.

"Oh, my darling," the duchess gushed, "you cannot imagine how excited I am."

"Roxie, calm yourself," the duke said.

Fancy gave the prince a questioning look. He raised his brows and shrugged.

Stepan sat on the sofa and drew Fancy down beside him. "Mother is well," he told his brothers. "Fancy's singing entertained her."

"She must have enjoyed the performance," Mikhail said.

Feeling awkward, Fancy stared at her hands folded in her lap. She avoided looking at her father, and his wife confused her. Why was the duchess excited?

"I enjoyed my visit to your lovely estate," Fancy said to Rudolf.

Stepan grinned and put an arm around her. "She loved the treehouse."

Blushing scarlet with guilt, Fancy gave him a quelling look and tried to change the subject. She turned to the other prince. "Where is Belle?"

Prince Mikhail did not look especially happy. "Upstairs, I suppose."

"You said you wanted to marry her," she accused him.

"I proposed and she refused," Mikhail said. "Your sister believes a scarred wife will ruin my life."

"I will speak to her."

"I was just telling him that we will solve Belle's problem after Monday," the duchess said. "I have the prettiest bedchamber prepared for you." She looked at the duke. "Think, Magnus, all your daughters will be sleeping beneath your roof tonight."

Fancy shook her head. "I am returning to Soho."

"You can't do that," the duchess cried. "You must stay here until the wedding. What will society think?"

Her knowledge surprised Fancy. "How do you know Stepan proposed?"

Tinker arrived at that moment, saving the duchess from answering. The majordomo set a pot of tea and two cups on the table in front of the sofa. Cucumber sandwiches and boiled oysters on toast accompanied the tea.

Fancy saw the boiled oysters, her stomach lurching

like the pitch and roll of a ship at sea. She clamped her hand over her mouth.

"You have nothing in your stomach." Stepan put his arm around her. "Take deep breaths."

Fancy pointed at the offending oysters. Then she averted her gaze.

Stepan grabbed the plate of oysters and slid it under the sofa. "Is that better?"

"I know it's there."

"You cannot see the"—she shook her head at him— "the food you dislike."

"Are you ill?" The duchess sounded alarmed. "Magnus, send for the physician."

"Fancy does not require a physician." Stepan held her close against the side of his body. "She has been feeling under the eaves for a few days." He smiled at the duke, who wore a suspicious expression. "Nothing serious."

"How does Her Grace know you proposed?"

Stepan groaned inwardly. This was not happening as he had envisioned. His brothers' presence and the duchess's enthusiasm were making the situation difficult.

"You did not tell her?" Rudolf shook his head with theatrical disapproval.

"Tell me what?" Fancy demanded.

Stepan looked from Rudolf to Mikhail to the duke. All three were struggling against smiles.

"When we left London," he told her, "your father announced our betrothal."

"I don't understand." Fancy glanced at her father, her expression mirroring her confusion. "How could he—?"

"Our wedding is scheduled for Monday," Stepan interrupted. "You will remain here until then."

Fancy bolted off the sofa and stared at him. "I can't marry you Monday and return to the opera Tuesday."

Stepan patted the sofa. "Sit with me."

"I will *not* sit with you."

"Baby brother, did we not teach you to tell the truth?" Rudolf laughed, and Mikhail joined him.

Fancy rounded on them. "You be quiet." She faced Stepan. "There will be no wedding on Monday."

"The wedding is planned, the invitations sent, the gown commissioned," the duchess cried. "We need only fit the gown to you."

Ignoring the duchess, Fancy addressed her father directly for the first time. "You cannot force me to stay here or marry that sneak."

"I am a man in love, not a sneak." Stepan stood, his size intimidating, and pointed at the sofa. "Now sit."

"How romantic," the duchess murmured, eliciting chuckles from the three watching men.

"*I said sit.*"

Fancy plopped down on the sofa. She leveled a disgruntled look on him and lifted her nose into the air.

"You have no choice but to marry me," Stepan told her.

"I *do* have a choice." Fancy moved to rise from the sofa.

"*Sit.*"

Fancy sat.

"Look at me." When she did, Stepan said, "You are carrying my child."

"Oh, how wonderful," the duchess gushed.

"I did not approve her seduction," the duke growled, making the two older princes laugh.

Fancy had never been more humiliated in her life. This was even worse than vomiting on the ship's deck. "I am not *that.*"

Stepan took her hands in his. "We have been living like a married couple for a month, and you have suffered nausea for a week."

"What does that prove?" Fancy could not believe they were discussing this in front of an audience.

Stepan ran a hand through his hair. "Listen—"

"I will not listen to this nonsense."

The Duchess of Inverary took charge of the situation. "Rudolf and Mikhail, please leave us for now."

"Do we really need to leave?" Rudolf asked.

"We are coming to the most interesting part," Mikhail complained.

When the two disappeared out the door, the duchess asked. "Darling, when did you last have your menses?"

Fancy gasped at the question, her complexion reddening. This interview was unendurable.

And then she paled, realizing its implications. She had not had her menses since before going to Sark Island.

Fancy hid her face in her hands and began to weep. Stepan said nothing, merely gathered her into his arms, and let her cry.

"Roxie, those are not tears of joy," the duke growled. "If she doesn't want to marry him, she and the baby can live in the country."

Fancy wailed louder at that. She had indeed become her mother.

"My child will be born in wedlock." Stepan lifted her chin and gazed into violet eyes brimming with tears. "You do not love me?"

"I do love you."

"Then what is the problem?"

"I feel trapped."

"Forgive me."

Fancy sighed and leaned heavily against him. "Some blame belongs to me."

"I wanted to marry you so much," Stepan said, "I thought you would not change your mind if I got you with child."

"I will take more time off from the opera."

Stepan stroked her back and sent the duke and duchess a warning look. Fancy did not understand the reality of her situation, and he did not have the heart to tell her that her opera career was over.

Nausea would prevent her from singing, and when that passed, she would be too big with child. Once she had their baby, Fancy would decide to retire from the opera permanently.

At least, he hoped so.

Fancy was too tired to argue about where she would sleep. "Very well, I will stay until Monday."

"You look exhausted." The duchess rose from her chair. "Come with me, darling, and take a nap."

Stepan planted a chaste kiss on her lips. "Sleep well, and I will see you tomorrow."

"Princess Samantha has taken your sisters shopping," the Duchess of Inverary said, escorting her out of the parlor. "Except for Belle and Raven, who declined the invitation. I did not want your sisters in the vicinity of our meeting."

Fancy nodded. "I understand."

"I will instruct the maids to leave you a slice of bread which you must eat before rising." The duchess led her to the third floor. "The bread will help with the morning sickness."

"My morning sickness lasts all day."

"That happens sometimes."

Well and truly trapped, Fancy thought. And she hadn't lasted through one season, caught in less time than her mother.

She loved Stepan, but she wasn't stupid. At some point, the prince would insist she leave the opera. And then what would happen?

She needed to sing. She needed the audience's love. She needed to retain her independence.

"Here we are." The duchess showed her into a bedchamber decorated in blues, cream, and gold. "Shall I send your sisters for a quick visit before you nap?"

"Thank you." Fancy sat on the edge of the bed and managed a weary smile. "I would like that."

Belle and Raven rushed into the bedchamber a moment later. Both sisters laughed and hugged her and sat on the bed.

"Stepan and I will marry on Monday," Fancy told them, inciting more hugs. "I am pregnant." She looked at Belle. "Prince Mikhail wants to marry you."

"I cannot ruin his life," her sister said. "He needs a wife to take into society."

"Why don't you let the prince make his own decision about what he needs?" Fancy asked.

"I told her the same thing," Raven agreed.

"Let me see your face." Fancy inspected the injured cheek. Though much improved, a scar ran down one side of her sister's face. "My theater cosmetics will cover that nicely. Then you can hold your head up high and dance with the prince at my wedding."

"I don't know if—"

"I *do* know," Fancy interrupted. "Tomorrow, I will fetch my cosmetics from the opera house."

"I will reserve judgment until I see how much it covers." Belle looked anxious. "How does being pregnant feel?"

"I feel nauseous, tired, and cranky."

Raven turned to Belle. "You have been nauseous and tired."

"You need to tell Mikhail," Fancy said. "I do admit I did not tell Stepan. He told me what my illness was."

"You are the only ones who know," Belle said. "Don't tell anyone. *Please.*"

"We promise," Raven said.

"For now," Fancy amended. "Eating a slice of bread

before rising in the morning will help the nausea. Or so the duchess said."

After her sisters left, Fancy changed into a nightgown and crawled beneath the coverlet to sleep. A tapping on the door awakened her, and she opened her eyes to the growing dimness in the chamber.

The door opened to reveal the duke carrying a tray. He crossed the chamber, setting the tray on the bedside table. Then he lit a night candle and pointed to the edge of the bed. "May I?"

Fancy sat up and leaned back against the headboard. Her father sat on the bed.

"Bland fare for a queasy stomach," he said.

"You did not need to—"

"I *wanted* to bring you supper. I want us to speak privately."

"Yes?"

"Stepan and I worried for your safety," her father said. "Which is the reason we engineered your vacation."

"I enjoyed my visit to Sark Island." Fancy blushed, recalling how much she had enjoyed the intimacies shared with the prince.

Her father patted her hand. "I will give you whatever you want if it's within my power."

His words saddened her. She had treated him badly when all he wanted was to make amends for his earlier neglect. Hurting her father had not eased her pain.

"Do you want to marry Stepan?"

"I love him and the child I carry but—I need my independence."

"Do you fear becoming as dependent as your mother?"

"I want to be happy. Will you hold me, Papa?"

Her father reached out and gathered her into his arms, cradling her against him. She rested her head

against his chest while he patted her back in a soothing motion.

"Remember, your mother had suffered the loss of
her entire family, and that colored her whole life." Her
father set her back and, lifting the tray off the table, set
it on her lap. "Your baby needs nourishment even
when you don't want to eat."

"Thank you, Papa." Fancy lifted the spoon to taste
the soup.

Her father crossed the chamber to the door. "Stepan
is a good man and will understand your special needs."

He would never understand her even if he lived a
hundred years.

How best to tell Fancy that she would never sing with
the opera again? This was one situation where his
brothers could not help. Hence, his procrastination.

The best course of action was no action. At least,
until after the wedding.

Why did Fancy need the opera? She had him. She
had his love. She had his baby growing inside her. What
more could she want?

Stepan walked into the exclusive White's Gentlemen's Club. He spotted his brothers sitting around a
table and waiting for him.

"I need vodka." Stepan dropped into a chair.

Rudolf poured him a dram of vodka and pushed it
toward him. "My wife is suffering the headache from
entertaining your future sisters-in-law."

Stepan was in no mood for teasing tonight. He
cocked a dark brow at his brother. "You mean *your* half-
sisters?"

"Samantha with a headache is frightening, especially
when pregnant, as she is now."

"Congratulations." Viktor raised his glass in salute.

"Regina is pregnant, too, and I wish she would cease writing that book."

"I thought you approved," Stepan said.

"I do approve, but pregnancy makes her cranky," Viktor said. "Crankiness affects her writing, which makes her more cranky. Home becomes hell."

"Fancy is pregnant," Stepan said, eliciting his brothers' laughter, "but I shudder to tell her the opera career is over."

"Baby brother," Rudolf said, "will you ever learn?"

Mikhail grinned. "Do you want us to take care of this problem for you?"

Stepan slanted a glance at him. "I do not find you amusing."

"Let Fancy sing with the opera until her pregnancy prevents her," Viktor suggested. "Then you will not be walking into an argument."

"I can do that," Stepan said, "if you allow Regina to sit onstage in front of the audience while she writes her book."

Viktor nodded. "I understand."

"What is the problem?" Rudolf asked. "Patrice Tanner is married and she sings with the opera."

"Sebastian Tanner is a toad, not a prince."

"Let her sing for a few weeks," Mikhail advised him, "and she will quit of her own accord."

"If you are such an expert on women," Stepan asked, "why could you not persuade Belle Flambeau to marry you?"

Mikhail gulped his vodka and eyed his younger brother. "The difference between you and me is I have time to persuade Belle because she is not pregnant."

Stepan smiled at him. "Your powers of persuasion must be slipping if you did not share intimacies at that cottage."

"Of course we shared intimacies." His words sounded like a growl.

"Then how can you be certain she is not pregnant?"

"Belle would have told me."

"Perhaps Belle—like her sister— does not know she is pregnant." Stepan smiled with satisfaction when his brother bolted out of the chair, his intent written on his face.

"Sit down, Mikhail," Rudolf ordered.

Viktor reached out and forced Mikhail into the chair again. "You cannot barge into Inverary's home and demand to know if you have made his innocent daughter pregnant."

"Thank you, brother." Stepan could not erase the grin from his face. "Taunting you has lightened my mood."

"I am glad to have been of service." Mikhail raised his brows and returned the smile. "So, when did you plan to tell Fancy her operatic career is over? I would like to place a wager in the betting book."

Without another word, Stepan stood and walked out of the club. His brothers' laughter followed him to the door.

Chapter 16

How had her mother traded the theater's excitement for the love of a man?

Fancy looked out the coach's window on its way to the Royal Opera House. She wondered at the life her mother had chosen, depending on a man for survival.

Perhaps her father was right. Losing her family in the Terror had colored her mother's whole life. Her mother had needed love and security, but Fancy knew she needed more. Had her mother's unhappiness with her married lover colored her own life? Was that the reason she craved the audience's adoration?

The prince had not mentioned the opera. Yet. When the moment arrived, would she quit the opera? *Could* she quit the opera?

The Inverary coach halted in front of the opera house. The coachman appeared, opened the door, and helped her down.

Fancy walked into the deserted lobby and headed straight for Director Bishop's office. The director smiled when he saw her and stood.

"I need to retrieve my cosmetics."

Director Bishop inclined his head. "Best wishes on your forthcoming marriage."

"How do you know about that?"

"His Highness sent me a note this morning."

Her anxiety grew and her spirits sank. Had the prince sent the director her resignation? If she mentioned returning to work, she would learn the answer to that.

"My wedding is scheduled for Monday," Fancy said, her smile forced, "but I can sing later in the week. Do I still have a job?"

Director Bishop hesitated. "Well, yes . . . Do you have the prince's permission?"

"I do not need anyone's permission to do anything."

Fancy left the director's office and walked through the deserted auditorium to the backstage. She opened her dressing room door and stopped short.

Genevieve Stover sat in *her* dressing room on *her* stool and looked into *her* cracked mirror. Surprise, jealousy, and anger shot through her. She felt like an outsider, alone and adrift in dangerous waters. The other girl was stealing her life.

The blonde leaped off the stool when she spotted her in the cracked mirror. "I'm so happy for you."

Fancy managed a smile but decided Miss Stover was happy for herself. "I see you are keeping my seat warm."

Genevieve blushed. "I hope you don't mind."

"Of course, I don't mind," Fancy lied. Now she knew how Patrice Tanner felt. "I need to retrieve my cosmetic case."

"I put it here out of the way." Genevieve grabbed the case from a dark corner.

Out of the way like me. Fancy reached for the case. "Will you come to my wedding Monday morning at Grosvenor Chapel?"

"I would love to see you married," Genevieve

hedged, "but mingling with society would make me uncomfortable."

"My sisters and I are not society."

"I make no promises," Genevieve said. "Did you know Alex has accepted his grandfather's inheritance?"

Nothing could have shocked Fancy more. "Alex always said he would never forgive the old man."

"They reconciled." Genevieve did not seem pleased.

"If I don't see you at the wedding," Fancy said, turning away, "I'll see you later in the week."

"Where?"

"I am returning to the opera at the end of next week."

Genevieve looked surprised. "Did the prince give you permission?"

Fancy's irritation grew. "I do not need his permission."

"If you say so."

"I do."

Fancy walked out of the dressing room and saw Miss Giggles running toward her. She dropped her case and lifted the monkey into her arms.

"How are you, Miss Giggles?"

The capuchin monkey covered its ears, eyes, and mouth. Then it began chattering.

"Oh, you're back."

Fancy passed the monkey to Patrice Tanner, who handed it to her husband. "I'm marrying the prince on Monday."

"We'll miss you," Patrice drawled, her tone oozing sarcasm.

Fancy gave the prima donna her sweetest smile. "I will be singing at the end of the week."

"Do you have the prince's permission?"

Irritation ballooned into anger. "I do *not* need his permission."

Patrice Tanner shrugged and headed for her dressing room, calling over her shoulder, "Come, Sebastian."

Fancy lifted her cosmetic case and watched the unlikely couple walk away. She pitied Sebastian Tanner. His wife dominated him in more ways than height.

Three people had asked if she had the prince's permission to return to the opera. Did they know something that eluded her?

Fancy could not resist walking onstage. She stood downstage center and set the case on the floorboards.

The auditorium seemed lonely without people. Something wonderful was slipping away from her. She wanted to hold on desperately.

Would she stand on this stage again? Would she ever bring the audience to their feet? Or make them weep? Could she live without the audience's adoration? Was the prince's love enough?

Her violet eyes glazed, and she conjured a standing-room-only crowd in her mind's eye. And then she sang, bidding the empty seats farewell.

Fancy sang *her* song about the land beyond the horizon. Robust in her singing, she attacked the song with every fiber of her being, pouring heart and soul into its lyrics and melody, trying to freeze this moment in time.

When the last bittersweet words slipped from her lips, Fancy heard rousing applause behind her. She whirled around and curtsied to her audience of stagehands and chorus dancers.

Lifting the cosmetic case, Fancy left the stage and started down the aisle toward the lobby. Applause and whistles stopped her. Tears welled in her eyes when she turned to see almost the whole cast and crew clapping for her. Only Patrice Tanner and Genevieve Stover were missing.

Panic hit her hard. Her colleagues were behaving as

if she would never work with them again. She managed a smile and raised her arm in a farewell salute.

Director Bishop and Prince Stepan were watching from the rear of the auditorium. Her prince did not look happy. In fact, he seemed damn disgruntled.

"What are you doing here?" she asked.

"What are *you* doing here?" he answered.

"I asked first."

"I asked second." Stepan gave her a lopsided grin. "Tinker told me where you had gone."

Fancy lifted the case high. "My cosmetics may cover my sister's scar."

Stepan lifted the case out of her hand. "I will take you home now."

"I have a coach."

"I sent it away." Stepan turned to the director. "Call for the auditions, and we will discuss the financing next week."

Fancy looped her hand through the crook in the prince's arm. They walked through the deserted lobby to the street.

Once inside the coach, Fancy turned to him. "Will auditions for an opera begin next week?"

Stepan patted her hand. "Probably so."

Fancy could not contain her eagerness. "Which opera?"

"*The Maid of Milan.*"

"I don't know that one."

Stepan put his arm around her shoulders and drew her close against him. "You have never heard this opera because it is new."

Her violet eyes lit with barely suppressed excitement. "Who is the composer?"

"Bishop."

"He never mentioned it to me."

"You are a singer, Miss Flambeau, not a patron," Stepan said. "Bishop wants me to finance the production."

"Will you finance it?"

"Probably."

"Oh, I am so excited," Fancy exclaimed, her gaze on his. "Patrice Tanner is too old to play a maiden."

Ignoring her remark, Stepan placed his palm against her belly. "How is the newest Kazanov today?"

She gave him a rueful smile. "He does not like mornings."

"You mean *she*."

"Loves me, loves me not . . ."

A tall gentleman stood on the summit of Primrose Hill during the night's darkest and quietest hours. He stared at the woman, serene in death, and sprinkled rose petals one by one the length of her body from head to feet.

"When will this end?" asked the woman standing behind him.

The gentleman did not bother to turn around. "This will end when I catch that opera singer."

"Which opera singer?"

"You know the one." He took another handful of rose petals from his leather pouch. "Loves me, loves me not . . ."

The monster's date with the hangman had been delayed for too many days. Lord, he would love to wrap his hands around the man's throat and squeeze the breath from his body.

Alexander Blake rested his head against the back of the hackney and closed his eyes. He would have enjoyed sleeping late for a change, especially since Genevieve's irritation grew each time he was called away.

Thankfully, the traffic to Park Lane was nonexistent. Only a blinking idiot would be up and about at seven on a Sunday morning. If only those dandies hadn't chosen Primrose Hill for their duel at dawn, he would be sleeping, too.

Guilt consumed him then. What was the loss of a little sleep when a young woman had been murdered?

The hackney halted in front of Inverary House, and Alexander climbed out. "Wait for me," he told the driver. Alexander reached for the duke's doorknocker, but the door opened before he could even touch it. The majordomo stepped aside to allow him entrance.

"Good morning, my lord," Tinker greeted him. "We have been expecting you."

Alexander gave the man a blank stare. How could the man have known? *He* hadn't known until Barney showed up at his door.

Raven sat in a chair. "I've been waiting."

"How could—"

"I dreamed last night."

"There are more things in the universe, my lord constable, than are thought of in your limited logic," Tinker said.

"You are misquoting Shakespeare," Alexander said.

"I *meant* to misquote the Bard."

Alexander looked at Raven. "I have a hackney waiting."

She stood and crossed the foyer to the door. "If anyone asks—"

"You mean Grace or Gracie?"

Her lips twitched. "Tell them something plausible. Use your imagination."

"I will lie through my teeth for you," Tinker promised.

Alexander helped Raven into the coach and sat opposite her. "Primrose Hill," he instructed the driver.

Folding his arms across his chest, Alexander stared at Raven. *Startling violet eyes . . . small, delicate nose . . . courtesan lips.*

"So." Alexander cleared his throat, struggling against the urge to drop his gaze to her breasts. "Who are Grace and Gracie?"

"The Flambeau sisters' nicknames for the Duke and Duchess of Inverary."

"I see Blaze's fine wit in that."

Primrose Hill stood more than two hundred feet high on the far side of Regent's Park. Long denuded of its trees and undergrowth, the hill was a popular site for illegal dueling.

"I hope you don't mind walking up the hill." Alexander lifted her out of the hackney. "If I were younger, I would carry you piggyback style."

"I think I can manage the climb," Raven said. "What is Barney doing over there?"

"Searching for nits." When she looked at him in surprise, Alexander grasped her arm and guided her toward the constable. "Barney is scouring the ground for evidence."

Constable Black took her hand. "I'm glad you could come at such an early hour."

"She was dressed and waiting," Alexander said.

Raven looked at the lump covered by the blanket. "Do you know who she is?"

"Our victim dances in the opera's chorus," the constable answered.

Raven approached the lump and gestured to Alexander to uncover the body. The young woman had been a beautiful redhead.

"Do you want to get closer?" Alexander asked.

Raven nodded. He placed his jacket on the grass, and she knelt beside the body. "Do you have anything of hers I can touch?"

Crouching beside the woman, Alexander pulled the silk scarf from her neck and passed it to Raven. He watched her closing her eyes, her features assuming a serene expression. Except, of course, for those courtesan lips. He wondered how—

"Two indistinct faces are merging," Raven spoke, drawing his attention. "Lift her gown."

"What?" Her order startled him.

"Something bit her leg." Raven turned her disturbing violet gaze on him. "Lift the bottom edge of her gown to her knee."

Alexander and Amadeus leaned close to the victim's leg. They studied the purplish bite mark.

"Look at the dried blood," Alexander said.

The constable nodded. "Something bit her before death claimed her."

"Poison killed her," Raven said.

Alexander looked at the constable. "Do you think a snake?"

For once, Constable Black look baffled. "I suppose—"

"The bite did not kill her," Raven said.

"How do you know?" Alexander asked, shifting his gaze to her.

Raven leveled a displeased look on him. "I know because I know."

Alexander scowled. "You just said—"

"The poison did not enter her body through the bite," Raven interrupted. "She drank it."

"I see a miracle."

Fancy caught her sister's gaze and smiled at her in the cheval mirror. The cosmetics had covered the facial scar almost completely.

Belle whirled around and hugged her. Tears welled in her eyes, threatening to spill over.

"If you weep, Sister, I will need to refresh the cosmetics."

"What a selfish sister I am to think of myself on your day," Belle said. "How will I repay you?"

"You can begin by telling Prince Mikhail about the baby."

"I will tell him when the moment is right," Belle assured her. "I do not want to live our mother's life."

"The prince needs a wife and a mother for his daughter," Fancy said. "Don't wait too long lest he look elsewhere."

"I promise." Belle positioned her in front of the mirror. "You look like a princess."

Fancy stared at her own image. She *did* look like a princess.

Her form-fitting gown had been created from silk and lace, its neckline scooped and its long sleeves bell-shaped. She wore her ebony hair cascading down her back and covered it with a sheer veil held in place by a crown of orange blossoms.

Something old. Something new. Something borrowed. Something blue.

Fancy remembered the old superstition and took stock of herself. New gown. Blue garters borrowed from Rudolf's wife. Her mother's lace handkerchief brought from France all those long years ago.

"The cosmetics are yours," Fancy told her sister. "I can purchase replacements before returning to work."

Belle looked at her in surprise. "Do you have the prince's permission?"

A bolt of annoyance shot through her. Why did everyone think she needed her husband's permission? They would be surprised when he financed the new opera, and she became the maid of Milan. Patrice

Tanner did not know it, but her prima donna days were almost finished.

The door flew open, drawing their attention. "Oh, my dearest, you must leave that unflattering expression behind," the duchess said, "or the prince will escape out the back door."

Belle giggled. Fancy managed a smile for the duchess, but the stress of uncertain career, society marriage, and first pregnancy grated against her nerves.

"Think happy, my darling." The duchess waved her arm in the air like a fairy godmother bestowing blessings. "Happy, happy, happy . . ."

Thirty minutes later, Fancy stood beside her father in the rear of the Grosvenor Chapel. Two hundred of the Inverarys' closest relatives and friends filled the pews. Hundreds of candles lit the chapel, eerie shadows dancing on its walls, while two violinists played from their perches in the choir loft.

"If this wedding is small," Fancy whispered, "I'll eat my veil."

"Roxie loves making a grand entrance," the duke said. "Look at her, leading your sisters to the front pew."

"They remind me of ducklings following their mother."

Her father tilted her chin up and gazed into her violet eyes, so much like her mother's. "I wish Gabrielle could see you today."

He *had* loved her mother. No one would ever persuade her differently.

"I love you, Papa." Her voice cracked with emotion.

"I always have and always will love you," her father said. "No matter the circumstance, you have a place in my home."

"Thank you, Papa."

"Escorting you to the prince is the biggest honor of my life."

"We did not have much time together."

Her father lifted her hand to his lips. "I regret that."

The violinist stopped playing, and the organist signaled the bride's arrival. The wedding guests stood and faced the center aisle.

"Are you ready?"

Fancy answered by placing her hand on his. Ignoring the unknown faces, she fixed her gaze on the prince waiting at the end of the aisle, who had eyes only for her.

Fancy and her father reached the altar. He placed her hand on the prince's and then backed away.

Stepan lifted her hand to his lips. "Thank you, my love, for making this the happiest day of my life."

The Flambeau sisters in the front pew sighed audibly. On the opposite side of the aisle, the sighs of the Kazanov nieces joined her sisters' sighs. Her lips twitched into a smile when she heard them.

"You have not found employment?"

"Alas, my love, a prince has few marketable skills."

She winked at him. "I will gladly recommend you."

"Will you marry me first?"

"Yes, I will."

Together, they turned to the bishop. The ceremony lasted less than thirty minutes. Which suited Fancy, who never attended Sunday services.

Stepan faced her at ceremony's end and brushed his lips against hers. He recognized the love shining at him from the depths of her violet gaze and knew all would be well.

She was beautiful. She was his. She carried his baby. A happily-ever-after future beckoned them.

"Are you ready to begin your new life, Princess?"

"You have made all my girlish dreams come true."

"I thought you disliked aristocrats," Stepan whispered, guiding her down the aisle.

"You persuaded me otherwise." Fancy gave him a coy smile and dropped her gaze below his waist. "Very persuasive."

A short time later, with harpists playing in the background, Stepan and Fancy stood in Inverary House's ballroom to greet their guests. With them stood the Duke and Duchess of Inverary as well as Prince Rudolf, the official heads of the Campbell and Kazanov families.

"You have met Cousin Amber and her husband, the Earl of Stratford," Stepan reminded Fancy.

"You never sang for my roses," Princess Amber said.

"I will sing for your roses," Fancy said, "whenever my operatic schedule allows."

Princess Amber looked confused and shifted her gaze to Stepan. He hoped his cousin would not comment on his wife's career.

"On behalf of my roses," Amber said, recovering herself, "I appreciate your generosity."

Lady Althorpe, the duchess's crony, stood before them. "So," the older woman said, "this beauty caused your misbehavior on the opera's opening night."

Stepan heard Rudolf chuckling. He flushed when his bride looked at him.

"Your husband's adoration created near pandemonium in the boxes," Lady Althorpe told her. "I could scarcely hear the singing."

"How interesting," Fancy murmured. "I promise my husband will behave from now on."

"I do not doubt that with you beside him," Lady Althorpe said, and then moved on.

Stepan squelched the urge to throttle the old crone. Beating an old lady would not suit for a prince.

The Duke of Essex and his grandson, the Marquess

of Basildon, offered their best wishes. Alexander Blake lifted his longtime friend's hand to his lips.

"I thought you weren't interested in inheritances," Fancy said.

Alexander grinned. "And I thought you disliked aristocrats."

"I was very persuasive," Stepan said. "Or so my bride tells me."

"You proved me wrong." Alexander offered the prince his hand in friendship. "I'm glad you did."

Stepan shook the marquess's hand. "I am glad I did, too."

When the Blakes left to find their seats, Rudolf whispered, "Here comes trouble."

Stepan grinned at his nieces' smiles.

"You have not met all my ladies," he told his bride. "Princess Zara, at the venerable age of twelve, is Rudolf's oldest, and these young ladies holding hands are Sally and Elizabeth, Viktor's and Mikhail's daughters, respectively."

"I am pleased to make your acquaintances," Fancy said. "Now that your uncle and I are married, we will look forward to hosting a tea party."

Stepan crouched down, eye level with his nieces. "What happened while I was away?"

"The Earl of Goodness ruined Princess Sunshine," Natasia informed him.

Stepan feigned horrified dismay. "How did he—?"

"They loped," Elizabeth said.

Sally nodded. "To Greta Green."

"Uncle, darling," Roxanne drawled like the duchess, "Sunshine needed a husband, if you know what I mean."

Stepan laughed and then gave his attention to the smallest. "What do *you* say about this?"

"Lady Gossip talked too much and lost her voice."

Lily wrapped her arms around his neck. "I love you, Uncle."

"And I love you, sweetheart."

"What about us?" Roxanne demanded.

"I love you and you and you . . ." Stepan pointed at each niece and declared his love. He stood then and drew his bride into his arm. "I love you most of all."

"I love you, too." Fancy planted a kiss on his lips to the music of little girls' giggling.

Once the guests had been greeted, Stepan and Fancy took their seats for the meal. The head table had been set along one of the rectangular chamber's short walls. Two long tables, each seating one hundred, stood perpendicular to the head table.

Prince Rudolf stood to speak and lifted his champagne flute for a toast. "The newest Kazanov princess is beautiful, loving, and forgiving. Fancy will need the last trait in order to live with my baby brother. To the bride."

Stepan stood next to address the guests. "The first time I met her, Fancy said I needed gainful employment." He waited for the laughter to die. "I decided the only position I wanted was that of her husband." He smiled at her and lifted his champagne flute. "To my beautiful bride."

After the toasts, Tinker directed the footmen in serving the meal. Their Graces had ordered a lavish feast, suitable for the marriage of a prince and a duke's daughter.

Stepan leaned close, resting his arm on the back of his bride's chair. "You are not eating, my love."

"I have never attended a wedding." The excited gleam in her eyes reminded him of his nieces. "When can we leave without raising eyebrows?"

Stepan brushed his lips against her ear. "You are eager to begin our married life?"

"I am eager to pleasure my prince."

"You do realize I married you for the workings of your mind?"

"We make a winning team," Fancy said. "London's newest prima donna and her adoring patron."

Damn, Stepan thought, keeping his expression placid. He had blundered by ignoring the subject of her returning to the opera. Why didn't she realize singing onstage was inappropriate for a princess? Was she waiting for him to say the words? He refused to ruin his wedding night with the first argument of their marriage.

"We do make beautiful music together." His black gaze smoldered with desire. "We can leave now if you like."

Her smile was invitingly coy. "I like . . ."

Chapter 17

Wanting to leave and walking out the door proved entirely different.

Custom required that the bride and groom stay longer than meal's end. Custom required that the happy couple dance. Custom required that they make the rounds and thank the guests.

Or so the Duchess of Inverary insisted.

Fancy did not see the need to thank the guests for attending. They *had* enjoyed a free feast.

In the end, Stepan masterminded their escape. He whispered in the duchess's ear that the babe sickened his bride, and she needed to retire.

"If I had known the magic excuse"—Fancy stepped out of the coach in front of her husband's Grosvenor Square mansion—"I would have slumped over the poached salmon."

Stepan laughed and, without warning, scooped her into his arms. He set her down inside the foyer where members of his small household staff waited to greet them.

"On behalf of the staff, I wish you felicitations on your nuptials," the majordomo said.

"Thank you, Bones."

The majordomo gestured to the footmen and maids to return to their duties.

Stepan put an arm around Fancy. "Bones will be interviewing applicants for lady's maid, and you will choose from the finalists."

"I don't need a maid."

"A princess without a lady's maid is unseemly," Stepan said. "You will accustom yourself to the life in no time at all." He ushered her across the foyer toward the stairs, saying over his shoulder to the majordomo, "You will advertise for nannies once the lady's maid is employed."

"Yes, Your Highness." Then Bones added, "We have plenty of time to consider nannies."

"We have less than nine months."

Fancy felt the blood rushing to her face. She peeked at the majordomo, who was gaping at his employer.

"Serve us a light supper in the connecting bedchamber later." Stepan gave Fancy a wolfish smile. "I will give you the tour tomorrow, my love. We have more important activities scheduled at the moment."

"Will there be anything else, Your Highness?"

"Privacy."

Bones blushed. "Yes, Your Highness."

The master bedchamber was as masculine as the man. Drawing the eye first was an enormous curtained bed spacious enough for a tall man like the prince. The blue brocade bedcurtains matched the coverlet, and a chaise of carved oak perched at the end of the bed. Its matching sofa and two chairs stood in front of a black marble hearth. Bay windows faced west over the garden.

"I will play the lady's maid today."

Stepan unfastened the gown's buttons and ran a finger up the delicate column of her spine. He felt her trembling from his touch already, their three-evening forced separation having affected her the same as it did him.

Stepan thought there was something to be said for seducing the bride before the wedding. No fears and no tears made for a happy groom.

Leaning close, Stepan pressed his face against the heavy curtain of her hair. He loved her scent. Lifting her hair, he tickled the nape of her neck with his tongue.

She sighed and leaned against him. He wrapped his arms around her and cupped her breasts.

"Did you remember that old superstition?"

Fancy turned in the circle of his arms and kissed him. She pushed him toward the chaise and, when he sat down, lifted her right leg onto the chaise beside him.

Stepan suffered her teasing with an appreciative smile. His bride lifted the edge of her gown slowly and pulled a lace handkerchief tucked under a blue garter. After waving it in front of his face, she said, "Something old." Then she dropped it on the chaise.

"I want my lips where the handkerchief was." His voice was husky.

"Soon, husband."

"Tell me, princess." Stepan relaxed back to enjoy the show. "How do you wipe your nose on French lace?"

"A French lace handkerchief is a lady's accoutrement, not a nose wiper."

Stepan laughed. "Please continue undressing."

"Something new." Fancy stepped out of her wedding gown and set it across the sofa. She posed in front of him wearing only her chemise, silk stockings, and blue garters.

And a seductive smile.

Stepan loved her air of sultry vulnerability. Especially the sultry.

"Something borrowed." Fancy placed her right leg on the chaise again and rolled the garter and silk stocking down. She lifted her left leg onto the chaise and rolled that garter and stocking down. "Something blue."

Stepan stood and drew her chemise-clad body into

his embrace. He kissed her lingeringly, savoring her scent and her taste, the feel of her in his arms and the sound of her purr. When he broke the kiss, her chemise dropped to the floor.

"Your breasts are heavy." He cupped them in his hands and caressed their tips with his thumbs. "Your nipples are large and dark. Already, our baby is changing your body."

Fancy wrapped her arms around his neck. "I want you inside me, husband."

Stepan kissed her, her sexy words inciting his emotions. "Sweetheart, I am still dressed. Sit on the bed and let me disrobe for you."

Sitting naked in front of him did not embarrass Fancy. She loved her husband and would bare her heart, her mind, her soul.

Her prince was walking temptation. She had known that from the moment he appeared in her dressing room on opening night.

Stepan shrugged out of his jacket and waistcoat. "Something old," he said, making her smile.

After unfastening his cravat, Stepan tossed it over his shoulder and winked at her. "Something new."

Stepan lost his shoes and hose next. He held her gaze captive while unfastening his shirt and then tossed it aside.

Fancy dropped her gaze to his chest. His magnificent chest with its matting of black hair.

"Something borrowed." Stepan reached into his trouser and produced a gold pocket watch. "Compliments of Rudolf." He placed it on the bedside table.

"And something blue." Stepan gave her an exaggerated wink and dropped his trousers. There stood her husband wearing peacock blue silk drawers.

Fancy shrieked with laughter and fell back on the

bed. A moment later, having lost his drawers, Stepan lay on top of her.

"Good fortune will favor us, *ma petite.*"

Fancy placed the palms of her hands on his cheeks. "Fortune smiled at me the day you walked into my life."

"I love you, wife."

"I love you, husband."

He moved onto his back. And she moved with him.

Fancy lay on top of the muscled planes of his body and sprinkled dozens of kisses across his face, his lips, his chin. Lower and lower, she slid to press her face against his groin.

Her husband groaned. Which sounded like music to her.

Fancy held his growing erection in her hand and then took it inside her mouth. She sucked on it, swirling her tongue around its head. When he grew too big to take inside her mouth, Fancy flicked her tongue out and licked it up and down, down and up.

Stepan grasped her upper arms and pulled her on top of him. He traced a long finger between her buttocks.

"You have such sweet etcetera." Gently, Stepan rolled her onto her back. He kissed her face, her neck, her breasts. Brushing his lips down her fluttering belly, Stepan pressed his face between her thighs.

"I love your scent." He flicked his tongue out, separating her lips, and slashed upward in sweet torture.

"I want you," Fancy moaned. "Please."

Stepan rose and gently pulled her to the edge of the bed. Lifting her legs, he hooked them over his shoulders and slowly pushed himself inside her until their groins touched.

"I do not want to hurt the babe or you." His voice was hoarse with desire and the struggle to control himself.

"You won't hurt us."

Stepan moved then, slowly at first. He caressed her moist heat with long strokes and then ground himself against her.

Fancy met him thrust for thrust, stroke for stroke. Her nerves were rioting with the exquisite pleasure of possession.

"I love you . . ." Fancy pulled him down and kissed him. She flew over pleasure's precipice, her soft, wet heat contracting around him.

Stepan groaned and shuddered, pouring his love inside her. He fell to the side and pulled her into his arms.

And then they slept.

The sound of knocking awakened Fancy. She opened her eyes and, judging from the chamber's dimness, knew that twilight was aging into night.

Muttering indistinct words, Stepan rolled out of bed and shrugged into a bedrobe. He shut the bed-curtains, protecting her from prying eyes.

Fancy heard low voices but could not understand the words. The door clicked shut.

"Supper awaits us in the next chamber." Stepan sat on the edge of the bed and traced a finger down her cheek. "Are you hungry?"

"I'm famished." Fancy smiled drowsily and sat up. "I need something to wear."

Stepan dressed her in her chemise and set the crown of orange blossoms on top of her head. Taking her hand in his, he led her into the connecting chamber.

Bones had placed a small table near the open window. A gentle breeze flirted with the curtains and perfumed the room with summer's fragrances.

Uncovering platters revealed buttered lobster casserole and stuffed artichokes. Another plate contained cheeses, nuts, and cubed fruit.

"What does our daughter want to eat?" Stepan asked.

Fancy made a show of inspecting each offering. "Our daughter wants to taste everything."

Stepan filled her plate before helping himself. "Do you want wine or lemon water?"

"Lemon water," she answered. "I do not want to risk giving birth to a drunkard."

"I am glad you love our daughter as much as I do."

"This will make an excellent newborn nursery," Fancy said, "and once our daughter is weaned, we can move her to a big-girl nursery with the nanny we hire."

"This is your bedchamber."

"That is my chamber." Fancy pointed in the direction of his room. "I want to care for my own newborn."

Her husband looked surprised. "All day?"

"Most mothers do."

"Those mothers are poor. I am thinking of your comfort."

"I feel comfortable caring for my own baby."

"Whatever you want, princess." Stepan could not help thinking his wife considered her opera days finished. After all, she could not care all day and night for their baby and sing onstage. He lifted a velvet box from the pocket of his robe. "Happy wedding day, my love."

Fancy opened the box and stared in surprise at her gift. The matching necklace, bracelet, and earrings had been created in oval-cut sapphires and diamonds set in platinum.

"How beautiful," she whispered.

"The beauty of these jewels cannot compare with yours," Stepan said smoothly. The outrageous compliment sounded sincere coming from him. "You will wear these when we attend the opera."

Fancy lifted her gaze from the sapphires and diamonds to him. Was there a message in his statement? She had no desire to argue on her wedding night and would put her response aside until the end of the week.

"I have a gift for you in my case," she said. "Where did Bones hide it?"

"Look in the dressing room." Stepan watched her walking across the bedchamber and admired the natural sway of her hips. He could hardly wait to see her heavy with his child and waddling around the house.

Fancy reappeared with a package the size of a small painting. "Open it."

Stepan looked from her excited expression to the package. He could not recall the last time a woman had given him a gift. Not since before his mother . . . That was not a good memory for his wedding day.

After removing the wrapping, Stepan set the framed document on the table. He stared at it for a fraction of a second and then shouted with laughter. Inside a gold frame was a letter of recommendation from his wife, a calligrapher's artistry apparent.

"I thought you could use that."

"Come here." Stepan pulled her onto his lap and wrapped his arms around her. Then he read part of the framed letter. "'What His Highness lacks in experience and skill is mitigated by his enthusiasm' . . . This is the most wonderful gift I have ever received. I love you."

Fancy rested her head on his shoulder. "And I love you."

"I love you more."

She touched his dark, stubbled cheek. "I love you the biggest number in God's universe."

"I love you the same amount." His lips twitched into a smile. "Plus one . . ."

Heavy rains cocooned them from the outside world. The master bedchamber became their universe. The enormous bed was their kingdom.

On Tuesday morning, Fancy awakened to her husband's hand caressing her buttocks. She opened her eyes to find him sitting on the edge of the bed.

"Good morning, Princess."

She gave him a drowsy smile.

His hand traced the curve of her hip. "I brought you bread."

"How did you—?"

"The duchess told me what to do," Stepan said. "As did Rudolf, Samantha, Viktor, Regina, and Mikhail."

Fancy nibbled on the bread. "What a helpful family you have."

Stepan gestured to the window. "It is raining."

After finishing the last crumb of bread, Fancy tugged at his robe's belt and rubbed the palm of her hand across his chest. "I don't need sunshine, husband."

They fell back on the bed, he on top of her. . . .

Stepan awakened on Wednesday morning to the rhythmic beating of rain against the windows and the exquisite feeling of his wife's silken fingertips caressing his chest. He opened his eyes to find her sitting on the edge of the bed, noting her nightgown and bedrobe.

"I ate my bread and ventured into Feliks's domain." Fancy pointed at the covered dishes on a tray sitting on the bedside table.

"You cooked me breakfast."

"Just like poor people."

Stepan pulled the belt of her robe. "You are wearing too many clothes."

Fancy rose from the bed and shrugged the robe off. Catching his eye, she pushed the nightgown's straps off her shoulders and let it drop to the floor.

"That is much better." Stepan reached out and caressed the heat between her thighs.

Fancy crawled on the bed and pressed her nakedness to his. She lay on top of him. . . .

The sound of pelting rain awakened Fancy on Thursday morning. She opened her eyes and found her husband peering down at her.

"Good morning, Princess."

"Good morning, Prince."

"I am beginning to like the rain." His smile was boyishly charming. "I hope the sun shines tomorrow on the men's golfing and the duchess's luncheon."

"I wouldn't mind another day or two of rain."

"So, Princess, what would you like to do on this third morning after our marriage?"

She gave him an inviting smile.

"You naughty, naughty girl." Stepan leaned close, dipping his head to her breasts, his lips latching on to her sensitive nipple.

Fancy purred low in her throat. "I love indoor activities . . ."

Dressed in her robe, Fancy sat on the edge of the bed and nibbled her bread. Silently, she cursed the sunshine, a feeling of gloom settling on her shoulders.

Stepan stood across the chamber at the porcelain basin and looked into the mirror while he shaved. Even from this angle, her husband was incredibly sexy wearing only black breeches. She missed the sight of his chest, but his back was muscular and his buttocks rounded.

"I am sorry the sun is shining," Stepan said, without turning around.

"So am I." Perhaps she should feel grateful that nausea had not draped her over the chamber pot.

"After the golf match, my brothers and I will stop at White's," Stepan told her. "Wait at your father's, and I will fetch you on my way home."

Four days married, Fancy thought. Four days without their important discussion regarding her career.

"Don't bother about me." She forced a light tone

into her voice but fixed her gaze on the floor. "I will take a hackney to the opera."

The razor dropped with a clink into the basin. Her husband's black shoes appeared in front of her.

"You are my princess and the mother of my child and will *not* sing in the opera."

Well, now she knew what he thought of her continuing career. If only he had not commanded her, she could have negotiated their differences, allowed him to persuade her to his thinking.

She loved her husband and their baby, but refused to feel cornered into her mother's dependency. Misery lay at the end of that road.

Yes, Stepan loved her. Her father had loved her mother, too.

Fancy stood, meeting his challenge. "Why didn't you mention this preference *before* we married?"

"I gave you an order, not a preference," Stepan said. "You would have refused to marry me if I had made stipulations."

"You're damn right about that."

"Guard your tongue." Stepan ran a hand through his hair. "I would never permit the stigma of bastardy to stain my child. Of all people, you should appreciate how hurtful bastardy is."

Fancy felt as if he'd struck her. He tossed the word *bastard* at her at the first dissent.

"You tricked me into conceiving," she accused him.

"*I* tricked *you?*" Stepan laughed without humor. "Your memory is failing if you cannot recall that *you* followed *me* to the treehouse."

"I did not follow you to the treehouse," Fancy lied, needing someone else to blame, her voice rising in anger. "I *found* you there."

"You offered yourself to me," Stepan reminded her.

"You were not thinking about the opera that night. Or do you consider cries of pleasure soprano practice?"

Fancy felt the telltale heat of scarlet embarrassment. What he said was true, but she would never admit it.

Fancy turned her back on him, her lip quivering with the struggle to control her emotions. She could never win with him. Why trouble herself trying?

"Fancy, please—"

"Do not bother to fetch me," she cut off whatever he would have said. "Even a dog can find her own way home."

"Then I will pass the entire evening with my brothers."

"I don't care."

Silence filled her ears. She wondered what he was doing. The door clicking shut echoed louder than cannon fire.

Fancy longed to throw herself on the bed and weep herself to sleep. She squelched that urge lest her husband return to their chamber and catch her in a weak moment.

After calming herself with a deep breath, Fancy decided she would do what she wanted. And damn that conniving cock.

White's Gentlemen's Club on St. James Street was a bastion for London's elite. Oversized sofas and chairs cushioned wealthy posteriors, bringing peaceful refuge from flighty female company.

Stepan slouched in a leather chair, drank whiskey, and listened to his brothers' conversation with half an ear. His thoughts had never left his wife all day, wreaking havoc on his golf game. How ignominious to win the championship one year and to place dead last the next.

"I suggest daily practice," Mikhail needled him.

"Someone needed to place last," Viktor said.

"Did you know the Lord Mayor is calling for an investigation on how you managed to win last year?" Mikhail asked.

Viktor looked at Mikhail. Both men laughed.

"Do not let them bother you," Rudolf said. "I explained to the Lord Mayor your muscles were sore from riding your bride this week."

Now the three oldest Kazanov brothers laughed.

"My brain is sore from your combined babblings," Stepan growled, eliciting more chuckles.

"Why are you sitting with us while your bride—?" Rudolf shouted with laughter, drawing the room's attention. "You have already argued with your wife?"

Viktor turned to Mikhail. "Check the Betting Book."

Mikhail crossed the room to the Betting Book. He found the entry and wrote something that drew laughter from those around him.

Though he appeared relaxed, Stepan felt every nerve and muscle coiling in preparation for attack. His morning irritation had heated to noontime aggravation and then late-afternoon anger. The taunts of his brothers had ignited simmering anger to the boiling point.

"You win," Mikhail told Rudolf. "I will pay you tomorrow."

Viktor sent Stepan a look of extreme disappointment before turning to Rudolf. "So will I."

Stepan bolted out of his chair. "You wagered on when my wife and I would argue?" He looked at each brother in turn. "You sicken me."

Without another word, Stepan walked away. He had almost reached the door when his brother caught him.

"Give over, brother." Rudolf grabbed his right arm. "We mean nothing by it."

Stepan whirled around, his left hand clenched into

a fist. He struck hard, catching his brother's right cheekbone, sending him crashing to the floor.

All conversation ceased. Heads swiveled to watch this unusual and interesting scene.

"I bet a hundred pounds Kazanov raises a black eye," a voice said into the heavy silence.

"Who wants to bet the youngest is a dead man?" asked a second voice.

"Kazanov won't kill his brother," a third voice said.

"Want to wager fifty pounds on that?" the second voice asked.

Stepan looked at his fallen brother. "Stay away from me."

Cupping his injured cheek, Rudolf gave him a confused stare. "Are you left-handed?"

"Ambidextrous."

Stepan sent his coachman away and walked to Grosvenor Square. He needed time to cool his anger before he saw his wife. Making peace would be impossible unless he calmed himself.

Bones opened the door. "Welcome home, Your Highness."

Stepan grunted a greeting and walked toward the stairs.

"Her Highness has not returned," Bones said.

Stepan stopped short and turned around. "Did Harry drive her to Inverary's?"

"I believe so, Your Highness."

Stepan retraced his steps across the foyer. "Tell Harry to bring the coach around."

"Yes, Your Highness."

A few minutes later, Stepan climbed into his coach. Driving two blocks to Park Lane seemed obscene, but he did not want Fancy walking after being up and about all day. Her pregnancy exhausted her, and he would not risk her health or their child. Hopefully, the duchess had persuaded her to nap.

Tinker opened the door. "Good evening, Your Highness."

Stepan nodded at the majordomo. "Fetch my wife, please."

"I don't believe Her Highness is visiting."

Stepan took the stairs two at a time and marched into the parlor. "Where is my wife?"

The Duchess of Inverary stood in alarm. "Fancy never came to the luncheon. I assumed the babe had sickened her."

The Duke of Inverary stood beside his wife. "Are you thinking foul play?"

"I am thinking Royal Opera House."

Walking into the theater's lobby, Stepan saw Director Bishop, who gave him a helpless shrug. Wild applause and whistles erupted inside the auditorium.

"She just stepped onstage for the first time," Bishop said.

Stepan walked upstairs to the Kazanov opera box. He sat in the back out of sight, watching his wife's every movement, listening to her voice.

Fancy sang like an angel, a voice the world should hear. She was more than a perfect voice, though. She was a woman, his wife, a mother-to-be.

Stepan knew his wife needed this almost as much as he needed her love. The cruel reality was that she could not be all things to all people.

Fancy had chosen wife and mother when she had come to him at the treehouse. She knew that, too. Struggling against fate would not change the truth.

And he would not allow her to forget her duty to their child.

Chapter 18

Fancy sat in her dressing room, exhilarated and exhausted. Before stepping onstage, she had not realized how much the babe depleted her energy.

She wished she could put her head down. She wished she were home in bed. She wished she had listened to her husband.

The door crashed open, startling her. She whirled around and saw her husband advancing on her.

"Who is the *sneak* now?" Stepan asked.

Fancy bristled at his tone. Instead of admitting he'd been right, she refused to back down from his challenge.

"You are a pregnant princess and have no business prancing around on that stage," Stepan said, his tone scathing. He leaned close, backing her against the dressing table, and placed his hands on either side of her, his arms effectively imprisoning her. Almost nose to nose with her, he asked, "What if that bitch trips you into the orchestra pit again? Are you willing to risk our child?"

A ferocious pounding began in her temples and spread to the crown of her head. She was miserable enough without his interference. "Go away."

He straightened and looked down on her. "Will you come with me?"

Fancy wanted to leave with him more than anything else. Unfortunately, leaving in the middle of a performance was unacceptable.

"I can't do that."

"So be it." Stepan looked at her for a moment longer and then headed for the door, adding, "I may never forgive you for this."

Fancy stared at the empty doorway. Then she put her head on the table and wept.

A hand touched her shoulder. She looked up and saw Genevieve Stover.

"I heard the prince," the blonde said. "Are you all right?"

"I will survive." Fancy reached for a linen to dab at her tear-streaked face. "Will you and Alex drive me home?"

"Yes, of course."

Fancy finished the performance, but the audience's enthusiastic applause sounded hollow now. Her husband was correct. Audiences were notoriously fickle. Hadn't they adored Patrice Tanner at one time? Applause could warm her heart but never keep her warm at night.

Listen to your head, child, but follow your heart.

Her head told her that security lay in independence and an operatic career. Her heart insisted only her husband's love could bring happiness.

Fancy walked with a weary step to her dressing room. She wiped the cosmetics from her face and changed into her gown, pausing to look around her dressing room for the last time.

Patrice Tanner stood in the open doorway. Behind the prima donna stood Sebastian Tanner holding a diapered Miss Giggles.

"I heard about the prince." Surprisingly, the hate had vanished from her expression. "I'm sorry."

"Are you sorry or worried I will be named the 'Maid of Milan'?"

"Never mind." Patrice turned away.

"I apologize." Fancy touched the other woman's arm. "The babe upsets me."

"You're pregnant?" The prima donna looked stunned. "No wonder the prince was madder than a hornet." She shook her head and made a sweeping gesture with her hand. "This is illusion. Go home, make peace with your husband, be happy."

"Thank you for the advice."

"Come, Sebastian." Patrice paused, asking, "Do you need a ride home?"

"I've made arrangements."

Fancy watched the Tanners walk away. Perhaps Patrice wasn't as bad as she had thought. The prima donna had no children and had buried three husbands. The only constant in her life was the opera.

Fancy did not want merely to exist. She paused for a brief moment and stared at the stage. Then she walked down the deserted auditorium's aisle and never looked back.

An hour later, Fancy climbed the front stairs of the Grosvenor Square mansion. And then she realized she had no key.

How humiliating to feel like a guest at her own door. Or was it really her door? The prince might toss her out. Perhaps she should walk to Soho Square where she belonged.

The door opened while Fancy stood there and wondered where to go. Bones stepped aside to allow her entrance.

"Welcome home, Your Highness," Bones greeted her. "His Highness was looking for you."

"He found me."

"Your Highness?" Bones followed her across the foyer to the stairs.

Fancy turned around. "Yes?"

"His Highness left you a message," Bones said.

"What is the message?"

"Do not wait for his return."

Let his wife worry about his whereabouts.

Stepan climbed out of the coach in front of the Flambeau residence in Soho Square. He held a bottle of whiskey in one hand and a bottle of vodka in the other.

"Harry, return for me at noon tomorrow," Stepan called to his driver. "Do not tell anyone where I am."

"Yes, Your Highness."

Stepan set the bottles down and searched his pockets for the key. After unlocking the door, he reached for his bottles and shut the door behind him with his foot.

The house was dark, but Stepan managed to find his way to the parlor. After setting the bottles on the table, he lit two night candles and then dropped on the sofa.

Without the Flambeau sisters, the house seemed sad yet oddly welcoming. He leaned his dark head back and closed his eyes for a moment.

This was a good house. One need never feel alone here.

Stepan stood and, taking a candle along, headed for the kitchen. He found two shot glasses and returned to the parlor.

Opening the two bottles, Stepan poured vodka into one glass and whiskey into the other. First he gulped the vodka and followed that with a whiskey chaser.

Stepan shuddered from the alcohol's kick. Then he repeated the process. Several times.

Damn her. How could she have chosen the opera

before him and their child's health? Had his tone been too forceful? Accustomed to ordering her sisters about, his wife disliked taking orders from anyone herself. Perhaps he should have tried gentle persuasion.

Stepan felt the hair rising on the back of his neck like hackles. Someone else was here. He shifted his gaze to the doorway, almost expecting to see a ghost. Alexander Blake stood there.

"How did you get in?"

"I could ask you the same thing." Alexander dropped his gaze to the bottles. "The Flambeaus gave me a key in case of emergency. I saw the light from your candles and decided to investigate."

"I am punishing my wife," Stepan said. "Fetch a couple of glasses and join me in a drink."

Alexander grabbed a night candle and left the parlor. He returned a few minutes later with two shot glasses and sat in the chair opposite the sofa.

Stepan poured vodka and whiskey into the glasses. "Drink the vodka in one gulp and chase it down with the whiskey."

"You're kidding?"

"I do not kid you."

Alexander gulped the vodka and then downed the whiskey. He shuddered like a dog shaking off rain.

"Well?"

Alexander nodded. "I like it."

Stepan refilled their glasses and then raised his vodka in toast. "*Za druzhbu* . . . to friendship."

Alexander raised his vodka. "To happiness."

Both men gulped their vodka and immediately chased it down with the whiskey. Then they smiled at each other.

Again, Stepan poured the vodka and the whiskey. "*Za zhenschin* . . . to women."

Alexander added, "To health."

Again, both men drank the vodka in a single gulp and followed it with whiskey. Dizzy with drink, Stepan looked at Alexander, who gestured for another refill.

Stepan obliged him and raised his own glass. "*Za yadrona mysh*'. . . to mouse-fuckers."

Alexander shouted with laughter. "To mouse-fuckers."

"I did not like you the first time we met," Stepan said, refilling their glasses.

"I didn't like you, either."

"Everyone loves me," Stepan said, surprised. "Except my wife."

"I worried that you would hurt her."

"You should have worried about her hurting me." Stepan burst into song. "There was a girl from London *town*. At all aristocrats Fancy did *frown*. I gave her a wedding *gown*, but she let me *down* . . ."

Stepan stared into space for a long moment, and when he spoke, drink had deteriorated his English. "I gots big problem."

"Wass problem, princey?" Alexander asked, his own words slurring.

"I gots no more word rhyme wit *town*."

Alexander laughed and gestured for more drink. Stepan grinned and obliged him . . . again and again and again.

"My anger punch brother," Stepan told him. "Never hit man before."

Alexander shrugged. "Tings . . . sappen."

"Rudolf gots black eye."

"He will rec-rec-get better."

Stepan made a fist and demonstrated. "Smash him."

Alexander nodded in understanding. "Very angry."

"Nobody forgots Rudolf on floor . . . *in White's co-co-common room.*"

Alexander threw back his head and shouted with laughter.

* * *

Fancy awakened at midmorning. She rolled over and saw the bed beside her had not cushioned her husband. No slice of bread awaited her awakening.

Stepan was punishing her by sleeping in another chamber. If her husband had bothered to speak to her last night, there would be no problem now.

Rousing herself, Fancy washed and dressed in a white morning gown. She opened the connecting door before going to breakfast. Her husband had not slept in that bed, either.

Masking her pain, Fancy breezed into the dining room. "Good morning, Bones."

"Good morning, Your Highness."

Fancy walked to the sideboard and chose scrambled eggs, a ham slice, and dry toast. "Bring me tea, please."

She sat at the table and looked at the majordomo when he served her tea. "Has my husband eaten?"

"No, Your Highness."

Fancy arched an ebony brow at the man. "Is he gone out or still out?"

Bones hesitated. "Still."

"He never came home last night?"

"No, Your Highness."

Fancy wanted to put her head down and weep. Instead, she gave the majordomo a brave smile of dismissal.

She sat for several long moments trying to compose her emotions. Since that long-ago day in Hyde Park when her father had rejected her, she had never allowed others to see her pain and would not give her husband the satisfaction by starting now.

What had her husband said last night? *So be it.* Which sounded like an appropriate motto to live by.

Fancy wondered if the gossip column in the *Times* would give any indication of where her husband had gone after leaving the opera. Unfortunately, she did not possess the inner strength to read the worst possible scenario.

She stood to leave.

"Your Highness, you haven't eaten," Bones said. "Are you ill?"

"I am not as hungry as I thought." Fancy forced herself to smile at him. "Thank you for your concern."

Upstairs, Fancy walked into the connecting bedchamber and took her bag from the dressing room. She packed a few simple gowns, a shawl, and other necessities.

Fancy felt surprisingly calm when she walked into her husband's bedchamber. She knew what she wanted and where to find it.

Peacock blue silk drawers. A souvenir from her one and only late marriage.

Fancy slipped her wedding band off her finger. She crossed the chamber to the marriage bed and placed it on her husband's pillow.

Downstairs, Fancy approached the majordomo, whose gaze had fixed on her bag. "I thank you for all your help. Please tell His Highness I left him something on his pillow."

"Is that all?" Bones looked alarmed. "Where shall I tell him you've gone?"

"Do not concern yourself with me." Fancy opened the front door and walked out. In the background she heard the majordomo calling, "Boris! Feliks!"

Soho Square or Royal Opera House?

Fancy decided to go to the opera house first. Once she made herself comfortable at home, the babe would put her to sleep, and she needed to speak to the director.

The walk was long, but the day was fair. Brook Street would take her to Regent Street and then Piccadilly Circus and Covent Garden.

An hour later, Fancy entered the Royal Opera House and headed for the director's office. Wearing a puzzled smile, Bishop rose from his desk when he spied her and then checked the time on his pocket watch. "Auditions for the new opera don't begin for a couple of hours."

"I am quitting the opera," Fancy told him. "I will not perform again."

"I am sorry to hear that," Bishop said, "but you are making the correct choice."

"I must think of my child first." Fancy hesitated for a moment and then forged ahead. "My sister Serena sings if you are searching for the perfect maid of Milan."

"Does Serena sing as well as you?"

"Much better than I." Fancy felt her heart breaking, but losing the opera was nothing compared to losing her husband. "Serena plays the flute, too."

Director Bishop could not quite mask his excited expression. "Serena is living with the Duke of Inverary?"

"You will need to appeal to my father in order to get to her." Fancy stood on tiptoes and planted a kiss on the director's cheek. "Thank you for giving me the pleasure of performing."

"Best wishes to you and His Highness."

"I am quitting His Highness, too."

Fancy turned her back on the director's shocked expression and, without another word, left the opera house to walk to Soho Square. She and her baby would live in the Flambeau residence. The Seven Doves Company provided her with enough money to live comfortably, if not luxuriously.

She would never sing again. Nor would she give her heart to another man. She had indeed become her mother but, unlike her mother, refused to allow the pain to crush her.

So be it, Fancy thought, unlocking the door to her home. *So be it.*

Fancy dropped her bag in the foyer and walked down the corridor to the kitchen. There would be time enough later to unpack. What she needed was a pot of tea and a nap.

How would she ever fill the empty hours until her baby arrived? Next week she would begin to decorate a nursery. Perhaps her father would loan her a coach when she shopped for baby necessities.

And then what? Perhaps she could teach herself to cook and stitch as well as Raven. Too bad, she hated cooking and sewing. She might plant a garden to rival Belle's, but she hated getting her hands dirty. She would not even consider wallowing in paint like Sophia. Well, whatever she did, she would not be singing again.

She had begun the opera season with so much promise, only to be led astray faster than her father had seduced her mother. What did she have to show for her trouble? No opera, no husband, no love.

Fancy had not become her mother. Gabrielle Flambeau had fared better than she.

Walking into the parlor, Fancy set the tray on the table. She poured steaming tea into her cup and raised it to her lips, blowing gently on the tea before sipping.

Fancy placed her cup and saucer on the table and lay back on the sofa. She closed her eyes and willed herself to relax, breathing in and out.

For the first time in her entire twenty years, Fancy was completely alone. The feeling was quite pleasant and peaceful. That is, if one liked grating silence.

Fancy fell into a light doze, the scent of cinnamon growing stronger until she awakened. Opening her eyes, she glanced around the parlor. She saw nothing, but still the scent grew stronger.

"I know you're here," Fancy called to the empty room, sitting up. "I followed my heart, Nanny Smudge, and look where I am. *Go away.*"

The cinnamon scent dissipated slowly, almost reluctantly. And then someone banged on her front door.

Fancy yawned and then stood to walk to the foyer. When she opened the door, Rudolf Kazanov stood there.

"Will you invite me inside?" he asked.

She noted his bruised cheek and blackened eye. "Did Stepan send you to speak to me?"

"I came to speak about my brother, not for him."

Fancy stepped aside to allow him entrance. Then she gestured in the parlor's direction.

Rudolf dropped his gaze to her bag. "I will follow you, dear sister."

Fancy led the way into the parlor and sat on the sofa. Rudolf took the chair opposite her.

"Would you like anything?"

"Answers."

Her expression became mulish. "My marriage is no business of yours."

"When my brother does me bodily harm," Rudolf said, leaning forward, "his marriage becomes my business. Now tell me why my brother is sitting at Grosvenor Square, and you are sitting at Soho Square."

"Stepan deceived me," Fancy told him. "He abducted me from London, seduced me into his bed, and purposely made me pregnant. Unfortunately, he failed to inform me that marriage meant no opera career. He stole all my choices."

Rudolf nodded, as if understanding and sympathizing with her grievances. "What would you have chosen if he had not stolen your choices?"

"What?" Fancy had no idea what he meant.

"Would you have chosen a different life?" Rudolf fixed

his dark gaze on hers. "Or are you rebelling against the fact that my brother knew what you wanted in life?"

Fancy narrowed her violet gaze on him. Sounding oh so reasonable, this sneaky prince was even smoother than his brother.

"We will never know the answer to that," Fancy hedged, pleased with his suddenly disgruntled expression.

"Will you sing and care for my brother's child?"

"I quit the opera this morning."

The prince relaxed. "Stepan does not know this."

"I quit him, too."

"If you separate," Rudolf told her, "English law states the child belongs to the father."

Fancy felt a twinge of alarm. She had not known what the law on child custody stipulated. Why should she? Nobody she knew had ever been divorced.

"My influential father will not let that happen."

"He is a duke, not a magician," Rudolf countered. "His Grace wants you settled and married and will never try to use his influence to dissolve your marriage."

"My father owes me."

Rudolf shook his head. "Nobody owes anybody anything in this life, little girl. Learn that truth, or suffer the consequences."

"My husband never came home last night," Fancy snapped. "I cannot countenance an adulterer."

That certainly surprised him. "I will investigate his whereabouts but doubt he committed adultery."

Fancy said nothing. Her husband had deserted her at the opera and slept somewhere else. She loved him, but if he wanted her, Stepan would need to crawl back and beg her forgiveness. And she could not imagine her husband in a subservient position.

"I want to explain my brother," Rudolf said, "and then I will leave you to enjoy your solitude."

Fancy sighed. "Tell me what you came to say."

"Viktor, Mikhail, and I had enjoyed our mother's love for years before she was taken to that asylum," Rudolf began. "My father's heir, Vladimir, basked in my father's love.

"Being the baby, Stepan needed at least one loving parent, and my mother adored her youngest. Stepan was only four years old when my father took her away. He clung to her skirts for dear life, and Fedor dragged him, kicking and screaming, away from her. My father actually pried my brother's fingers, one by one, off my mother's skirt."

Fancy felt her heart wrench at the thought of any child torn from his mother. Imagining her husband as that little boy made it worse.

"Stepan cried day and night," Rudolf was saying. "Finally, Fedor lost patience and beat him whenever he cried."

Fancy gasped. Fedor Kazanov sounded like Satan himself. Oh, what she would do if only she could get her hands around the monster's neck.

"Stepan declared war on Fedor." Rudolf smiled at the memory. "My father suffered snakes in his socks drawer and ants in his bed."

Fancy smiled at that, too.

"Since Fedor hated me already," Rudolf said, his tone dry, "I shouldered the blame."

"Thank you for that." Her voice sounded hoarse, and tears blurred her eyes. Her own father's neglect paled beside Fedor Kazanov's cruelty.

"Stepan grew to adulthood with brothers for parents," Rudolf continued. "Though he is no angel, he has never been seriously involved with another woman." He stood then. "Will you think about what I have told you?"

"Yes."

Fancy walked with him to the foyer and touched his

arm before he could disappear out the door. "What was the weather on the day your mother was taken away?"

Rudolf looked confused by her question. "I-I . . . it rained that day."

Nothing good ever happened in the rain.

Her husband's words hit her with the impact of an avalanche.

Fancy returned to the parlor and lay on the sofa. She wept for her husband, for the little boy he'd been, and for herself. Her weeping wearied her into sleep.

The house was dark when she awakened. Rousing herself, she lit a night candle and went to the kitchen. There was nothing to eat in the house, and her baby needed nourishment.

Hearing footsteps in the hallway, Fancy whirled around. In a panic, she grabbed a knife and waited.

Alexander Blake appeared in the doorway. He seemed surprised to see her. "I came to investigate the light. What are you doing here?"

"I own the house," Fancy reminded him. "Do you have any food at your house? I'm hungry, but there's nothing here."

Alexander turned around, his footsteps sounding on the wood floor as he retraced his steps. Ten minutes later, he returned with a pot of soup and bread and cheese.

"Sit down," Alexander said, slicing the bread and the cheese. He set a plate in front of her, ordering, "Eat this while I warm the soup."

Fancy did as she was told. Nothing had ever tasted as delicious as the plain bread and cheese. She hadn't eaten all day. Her stomach rumbled, and she wondered if her baby was enjoying the meal, too.

Alexander set a bowl of soup and pot of tea on the table. Fancy started spooning the soup into her mouth.

"Good soup, Alex."

He sat down. "Do you want to talk about it?"

"The soup?"

Alexander smiled. "Do you want to talk about whatever is bothering you?"

Fancy shoveled another spoonful of soup into her mouth and then gave him a sidelong glance. "I quit the opera today."

"Your husband will be happy."

"I quit him, too."

Alexander touched her hand. "Listen, Fancy—"

"I do not want to discuss it," she said. "Rudolf stopped by today, and I am talked out."

"You know where to find me if you need a friend." Alexander checked the time on his pocket watch. "Damn, I am late to fetch Genevieve. Come, lock the door behind me."

Fancy walked him to the foyer and then locked the door. After cleaning the dishes, she sat on the sofa and closed her eyes.

The minutes passed slowly, peacefully. And then the house's atmosphere felt different. She shivered, though the night was warm. Someone was in the house with her.

Fancy opened her eyes. Genevieve stood in the doorway.

"Where's Alex?"

Genevieve gave her a sad smile. She raised her hands and covered her ears, her eyes, her mouth. Then she placed an invisible crown on her head, touched her heart, and pointed toward the door.

Fancy was confused. "What are you—?"

Genevieve dissolved into nothing.

"Mon Dieu, Genevieve—"

Fancy leaped to her feet. She needed her father. He could send men to find Alex.

After extinguishing the night candle, Fancy staggered in the dark to the foyer and grabbed her still-packed bag. She stepped outside, locked the door, and hurried down the street. She did not think about the distance to Park Lane or the dangers in the night.

A strong hand grabbed her upper arm. Fancy whirled around and opened her mouth to scream.

"Boris? What are you doing?"

The big Russian grinned. "Prince say Boris guard little songbird."

"I need my father," Fancy told him. "I need to go to Park Lane."

Boris pointed to the coach a few houses down. "Come, songbird. I take you."

When they reached Park Lane, Fancy climbed out of the coach. "Go home, and tell the prince I am with my father."

Fancy banged on the door and rushed inside when it opened. "Where is my father?"

"Good evening, Your Highness," Tinker greeted her. "Their Graces are in the parlor."

Dropping her bag, Fancy raced across the foyer and, lifting her skirt, ran up the stairs. Her stomach rolled with queasiness, baby and fright and emotional upheaval taking their toll.

"Fancy?" The Duke of Inverary stood in surprise when she flew into the parlor.

She burst into tears. "Papa, send footmen to find Alexander Blake. Something bad has happened. And send a man to Amadeus Black, too."

The duke sent his wife a puzzled look and told his daughter, "I will gladly send my footmen out if only you tell me why."

Fancy raised her violet gaze to his, misery etched across her expression. "I made Alex late, and now she's dead."

The Duchess of Inverary gasped. "Who is dead?"

"Genevieve Stover is dead . . . *murdered.*"

Chapter 19

Raven rose early that Sunday morning. She'd had another dream the previous night and knew the constable would send for her.

After grabbing a shawl, Raven peered out the window. Gray clouds drooped in a low overcast. A brisk wind slapped the trees in the garden, sending green leaves fluttering to the ground, but the day was dry.

Raven walked down three flights to the foyer. She sat on the bottom stair and waited.

The majordomo appeared. "Good morning, Miss Raven."

"Good morning, Tinker."

"Shall I bring coffee while you wait?"

She shook her head. "There isn't time for coffee."

The knocker banged on the door, surprising the majordomo.

"It's for me." Raven crossed the foyer and opened the door. Barney stood there instead of Alexander. "There's been another victim."

The little man dropped his mouth open in surprise. "You know?"

Stepping outside, Raven walked down the front stairs. She wondered what had kept Alexander away and realized he'd most likely passed the night with Genevieve.

"Where is Alex?" Raven asked, getting into the coach.

Barney climbed in after her. "Ah, Alex went directly to the crime scene from home."

Raven heard the hesitation in the man's voice. She stared at him, making him fidget, but he told her nothing more.

The coach halted at Riverside Gardens along Mill Bank near the Vauxhall Bridge. Raven climbed down, draped her shawl around her shoulders, and looked in the direction of the men.

Constable Black stood alone near the blanket-covered lump. Oddly, Alexander stood a short distance away and stared at the Thames.

"Thank you for coming this morning," Amadeus greeted her. "Prepare yourself."

Raven looked at him in alarm, his warning frightening her. Why was this victim different from the others?

Amadeus Black drew her closer to the lump. Leaning down, he pulled the blanket off the victim.

"Oh, God," Raven gasped.

Genevieve Stover lay at her feet, her expression peaceful as if asleep. Rose petals covered the blonde from head to toe.

Constable Black darted a glance at Alexander. "She was carrying his child."

Raven closed her eyes against the horror. Poor Alex had lost his lover and his child. How shocked he must have been to arrive at the crime scene to find this.

Placing her shawl on the ground, Raven knelt beside the body on the dew-moist grass. Genevieve looked the same as the others. Eyelids and lips sewn shut. Bloodless slash on one cheek. Rose petals covering her body.

And then Raven noticed one difference. A note had been attached to the gown. She leaned close and read:

Neglect your precious possession, Mister Constable, and lose her.

Raven did what she had never done before. She touched the dead woman's arm. Closing her eyes, she told the constable what she sensed.

"Two indistinct faces merging into one. No pain. Heavy eyelids closing and peaceful sleep. She never guessed what was happening until her soul left her body. Genevieve knew her killer."

Raven opened her eyes. "That is all."

"Thank you." Amadeus Black helped her to her feet. "We will begin by questioning family, friends, colleagues."

Raven glanced at Alexander, her indecision apparent. She felt the constable touch her shoulder, and when she looked at him, he nodded.

Raven approached Alexander. She longed to reach out, to touch, to comfort. "Alex?"

His back stiffened.

"I am sorry for your loss."

Alexander did not look at her. "Genevieve would be living if I hadn't gone late to the opera. She was—" He broke off, unable to continue.

Raven felt his pain. "If there is anything I can—"

Alexander whirled around, his expression grim. "Can you tell me who did this?"

Raven shook her head slowly. "She knew her killer, though."

That surprised him. "Did the others know the man?"

"I speak for Genevieve only."

* * *

This was the end.

Stepan sat in his rarely used office at his Grosvenor Square mansion. He rested his booted feet on top of his desk and studied the wedding band he'd found on his pillow.

His marriage was probably the shortest in history. Would circumstances have been different if they had discussed her opera career before the wedding?

A knock sounded on the door, and Bones entered before he could send the majordomo away. "This arrived by courier, Your Highness."

"Thank you." Stepan opened the missive. It read:

> *We must discuss our marriage on neutral ground.*
> *Meet me at Patrice Tanner's residence in Portman*
> *Square at two o'clock.*

His wife wanted to settle their differences. Was this a good or bad omen? Why would Fancy consider Patrice Tanner's neutral ground? Unless she and the prima donna had made peace . . . which meant his wife had quit the opera.

Stepan checked his pocket watch. He stood then, a relieved smile on his lips, and left the study to bring his wife home.

"So Stepan did not return home that night." Fancy sat in the dining room with two sisters that Sunday afternoon.

"His staying out does not mean he slept with another woman," Raven said.

"I agree," Blaze spoke up. "The prince went to a lot of trouble to marry you. I doubt he would behave badly."

"I plan to return to Grosvenor Square later." Fancy

gave her sisters an impish smile. "Worrying about my whereabouts will do my husband a world of good."

Puddles placed an enormous paw on Fancy's lap, drawing her attention. She scratched behind the mastiff's ears and fed him a slice of ham from her plate.

"That dog travels from lap to lap trying to catch a crumb," Raven said.

"Puddles knows not to beg when Grace and Gracie are eating," Blaze added. "Fancy, did we tell you what Puddles did the day Lady Althorpe visited?"

She shook her head. She could use a funny story to lift her spirits.

Blaze burst into laughter at the memory and couldn't continue. She gestured to her sister.

"Lady Althorpe and the duchess were sharing tea and gossip in the drawing room." Raven's lips twitched in an effort to hold her laughter back. "They did not know Puddles was sleeping behind the sofa." Now Raven dissolved into giggles, too, and gestured for her sister to continue.

"Puddles expelled silent and stinky gases," Blaze said, making Fancy giggle. "Lady Althorpe eyed the duchess with suspicion."

Fancy's giggles grew into laughter.

"The duchess eyed Lady Althorpe in the same manner," Raven said.

Fancy laughed so hard tears streamed down her cheeks. Her sisters were also laughing uproariously.

The majordomo walked into the dining room. "My, this is a happy group."

"Tinker, remember the day Puddles behaved badly during Lady Althorpe's visit?" Blaze asked.

A squawk of laughter escaped the majordomo. "Indeed, I do remember," Tinker drawled. "The staff savored that story." He passed Fancy a box. "A courier delivered this for you."

Wearing a puzzled smile, Fancy opened the box and found lilac blue flowers lying inside. "There's no card."

Raven peered into the box, her expression becoming grim. "Those are sweet scabious. In the language of flowers, sweet scabious means widowhood."

Fancy stared at her sister in surprise. Who would send her that message?

"Do you have anything of Stepan's with you?" Raven asked.

"Upstairs, in my bag."

"I'll fetch it." Blaze disappeared out the door and returned a few minutes later.

Fancy opened the bag and dug deep. She produced her husband's peacock blue silk drawers.

Raven stared at her. "What is that?"

"My husband's underwear. Don't worry. It's clean."

Raven lifted the blue drawers out of her sister's hands and closed her eyes. "Stepan is in danger."

"Where is he?" Fancy bolted out of the chair. "We need to warn him."

"Sit down," Raven ordered.

Fancy sat, surprising her sisters by obeying an order for the first time in her life.

"Tell me again what Genevieve Stover did when she appeared," Raven said.

"You think the rose-petal murderer is threatening Stepan?" Blaze asked.

"Yes." Raven looked at Fancy. "Well?"

"Genevieve covered her ears, eyes, and mouth," Fancy answered. "Then she placed an invisible crown or hat on her head, touched her heart, and pointed to the door."

"The crown, heart, and door refer to Stepan," Raven said. "She was advising you to return to your husband." She shook her head. "I cannot say what the other part means."

"Oh, my God!" Blaze cried. "I know the murderer's identity. Miss Giggles covers her ears, eyes, and mouth."

Fancy rolled her eyes. "Miss Giggles could not possibly poison anyone."

"Patrice and Sebastian Tanner *could* poison those women," Blaze countered. "Miss Giggles has been communicating their secret."

"That won't fit," Raven disagreed. "The man is tall and the woman is short."

"I beg to differ, dear sister," Blaze said. "The Tanners could disguise themselves as the opposite sex."

Fancy and Raven bolted out of their chairs. Proud of her deductive powers, Blaze rose more slowly and assumed a decidedly satisfied smile.

"Have you been practicing your slingshot?" Raven asked.

Fancy nodded. Her hand shook as she searched her bag for the slingshot and ammunition and then pocketed both.

The three sisters hurried down the corridor to the foyer. The majordomo stood there to accept calling cards from visitors.

"Where are the duke and duchess?" Raven asked.

"Their Graces have gone out for the afternoon."

"Send footmen to find Alexander Blake, Constable Black, and the Kazanov princes," Fancy said, taking charge of her husband's rescue. "Tell them to meet us at Patrice Tanner's in Portman Square if they want to catch the rose-petal murderer."

"And tell them to bring weapons," Blaze added for good measure.

Tinker looked alarmed. "Perhaps you should wait—"

The sisters dashed out the door. They hurried down Park Lane and crossed Oxford Street. Portman Square was one block away.

Fancy paused at the corner of Baker and Seymour Streets. "Hers is the last house on the right."

"We cannot ring the doorbell," Raven said.

"We'll cut down the alley," Fancy decided. "We can sneak into the house through the back door."

"What if the door is locked?" Blaze asked.

"We'll cross that threshold when we come to it," Fancy said. "Besides, Patrice has nothing to fear from the rose-petal murderer."

Circling the block, the sisters walked down the alley behind the town houses. They halted at the last one.

"We will maintain silence," Fancy said.

"What if the Tanners employ servants?" Blaze asked.

Raven shook her head. "The Tanners could not murder anyone with servants in the house."

"What if they murder their victims somewhere else?" Blaze persisted.

"Do you believe the Tanners would disguise themselves if they employed servants?" Raven asked.

Blaze shrugged. "I suppose not."

Fancy led her sisters into the garden. They skirted the perimeter and, finally, reached the rear door.

Fancy touched the knob and turned it slowly. She pulled the door and, realizing it was unlocked, opened it inch by excruciating inch.

Then Fancy removed her shoes and gestured to her sisters. Blaze and Raven removed their shoes, too.

The sisters slipped into the house and, on silent feet, tiptoed up the stairs until they reached the first floor. Hugging the wall, they started down the corridor.

Fancy looked down and stopped short. Rose petals covered the hallway floor.

Voices drifted into the hallway from the dining room.

Recognizing her husband's voice, Fancy peeked into the dining room and then drew back out of sight.

Patrice Tanner, dressed in a gentleman's formal attire, sat at the head of the table and pointed a pistol at Stepan. He sat on the prima donna's right, his hands tied behind his back. Dressed in a woman's gown, Sebastian Tanner sat on his wife's left and cut slices of apple with a paring knife. Miss Giggles sat on the chair beside Stepan's and stared at him.

"I prefer a gunshot to poison," Stepan was saying.

"Why do you prefer gunshot?" Sebastian asked.

"Poison is a woman's death," Stepan drawled. "I can see that you would prefer poison, though."

"Dying is dying, Your Highness," Patrice said.

Ignoring that, Stepan said to the husband, "Of course, poison is preferable to wearing a dress."

"Now see here," Sebastian began to protest.

"Stifle it, Sibby."

Silence.

Fancy drew the slingshot and pellet from her pocket. She had no hope of shooting the pistol out of the prima donna's hand, but if she hit her eye, Patrice would drop the pistol.

Fancy placed the pellet on the flexible tubing and waited for the right moment. Her hands shook, but she willed the mild tremors to stop. Her husband needed her, and if she failed, he would die.

"I will save the poisoned wine for your lovely bride," Patrice said. "If she isn't too dense to understand my message, she should arrive shortly."

Fancy stepped into the doorway. "Here I am."

When the prima donna looked at her, Fancy let the pellet fly. Swoosh! The pellet hit Patrice's right eye, and the pistol fell to the floor.

"Get the pistol," Patrice ordered her husband.

Miss Giggles was faster, though. The capuchin monkey scooped the pistol up.

"Here, Giggles." Blaze knelt in the doorway and

opened her arms in welcoming invitation. "Bring it to me."

Miss Giggles ran across the room. Blaze passed Fancy the pistol and lifted the monkey into her arms.

"Good girl, Giggles," Blaze was crooning. "I'm taking you home to meet Mister Puddles. You'll like him."

Fancy pointed the pistol at Sebastian. "Slowly and gently, place the paring knife on the table and slide it to this end."

"You little bitch," Patrice shrieked, one hand covering her injured eye. "I knew you would cause me trouble."

Fancy ignored her. "Raven, unfasten my husband."

Stepan was smiling. He stood, rubbing his wrists, and started toward her.

"Stay where you are." Fancy pointed the gun at him, making her sisters gasp. "Hold your hands high, too."

Losing his smile, Stepan raised his hands into the air. "Sweetheart, pointing pistols is dangerous."

"Darling . . ." Fancy gave him her most adoring smile, her fingers still on the trigger. "Where did you sleep the night before last?"

"He was with me."

Alexander Blake walked into the room with Constable Black. Behind them came the other three Kazanov princes.

"You slept with Alex?"

All the men laughed at that.

Stepan lifted the pistol out of his wife's hand. "Blake and I drank ourselves into a stupor at your house in Soho." He passed the constable the pistol and warned, "Don't drink the poisoned wine."

Raven stood at the end of the dining table. "Patrice and Sebastian are the rose-petal murderer."

"I wish you had not endangered yourselves by rushing to the rescue," Constable Black said, looking at each of the sisters. "Your folly could have cost your lives."

"You need not worry about the Flambeau sisters." Stepan drew Fancy into his arms. "My wife is deadly with her slingshot."

Alexander Blake turned to the prima donna, his expression murderous. "My deepest regret is we can hang you only once."

"I won't hang!" Patrice shrieked with hysterical laughter. "I'm crazy! They don't hang crazy people."

Sebastian Tanner bobbed his head up and down. "She is crazy."

"Crazy people go to Bedlam, not the hangman," Patrice taunted.

Fancy heard Raven gasp and shifted her gaze to her youngest sister. Raven was staring hard at the discarded paring knife on the table in front of her.

The knife shook and then slid slowly. Picking up speed, it became airborne.

The paring knife flew toward the prima donna's throat and caught it dead center. Patrice gurgled sickeningly, clutching at the knife, and then slumped facedown on the table.

"Ooops," Raven whispered.

All gazes swiveled to her. No one spoke, merely stared in surprise at the youngest Flambeau.

"Come, Miss Giggles." Unaffected by the execution, Blaze turned to leave the room, the monkey cuddling in her arms. "Mama Blaze will take you home to play with the duchess. Won't that be fun?" She disappeared out the door.

"I'll walk with her," Raven said.

"Do not move," Alexander ordered. "I want to speak with you."

Raven paled. "Am I arrested?"

"If you leave, I will take you into custody."

Fancy leaned against her husband. "Why did you come here?"

Stepan pulled the note out of his pocket, showed it to her, and passed it to the constable. "I thought you wanted to speak to me."

"That isn't my handwriting."

Stepan steered her toward the door. "I have never seen your handwriting."

"You would never forget it if you had."

"Chicken scratch?"

"Worse."

Stepan and Fancy walked out the front door and down the steps. "Where are your shoes?" he asked.

"I took them off when I sneaked into the house."

Stepan scooped her into his arms and carried her to his brother's coach. He helped her up and climbed inside. "Grosvenor Square," he called to the driver.

"How will your brothers get home?"

"Let them walk." Stepan yanked her into his arms. "I love you, princess."

Fancy looped her arms around his neck. "I love you more."

"I love you as much as the biggest number in God's universe," Stepan said.

Fancy kissed his throat, whispering, "I love you the same . . . plus one."

"*Plus two* . . ."

Eight months later

The girls made their debut on the first day of spring, the same evening their Aunt Serena made her operatic debut in *The Maid of Milan*. Princesses Gabrielle and Genevieve captivated their parents from the first moment of their arrival.

On the second day of spring, Fancy and Stepan were closeted with the girls in their bedchamber. Cradling Gabrielle in her arms, Fancy sat in bed and leaned against the headboard. Stepan sat beside her and cradled Genevieve in his arms.

"It's raining," Fancy said.

Stepan could not drag his gaze from the daughter in his arms. "Sometimes good things *do* happen in the rain."

"Let me hold Genevieve now." Fancy passed him Gabrielle and took Genevieve into her arms. "What happened to your face?"

Stepan moved Gabrielle to his left arm. "You slugged me last night."

"That never happened."

"I offered to redirect your pain, and you slugged me."

"Oh, how sweet . . ." Fancy smiled at her daughter. "Genevieve is yawning."

"And Gabrielle is scrunching her little button nose."

"Let me see." Fancy smiled and then asked, "How was Serena's debut?"

"I do not know."

"Didn't we get the *Times* this morning?"

"Holding my daughters was more important than reading your sister's review." Hearing a tap on the door, Stepan crossed the bedchamber and opened the door.

Bones's voice.

Stepan looked at her over his shoulder. "Several guests have arrived to meet their newest cousins."

Fancy smiled at that. Her husband's nieces had been sick with excitement for the past few months. She had no heart to make them wait another moment.

"Send them up." Stepan left the door open a crack and

returned to perch on the bed's edge. Moments later, the sound of more tapping on the door. "Enter."

Grinning with excitement, the nieces filed into the bedchamber and lined up for the viewing. Raven and Blaze followed the little girls into the room.

"Oh, Uncle and Aunt, how darling the little ones are," Roxanne gushed.

"I cannot believe we got *two* cousins," Natasia said.

"I found that difficult, too," Fancy said.

Her sisters smiled. Her husband chuckled.

Sally and Elizabeth, Viktor's and Mikhail's daughters, held hands and stepped closer.

"I love Gabrielle and Genevieve," Sally said.

"I love them, too," the soft-spoken Elizabeth said.

Fancy looked at Elizabeth. "You will soon have a baby brother or sister."

Elizabeth nodded. "Daddy said the baby is coming tomorrow because Mama Belle has pains in her belly."

Lily peeked at Geneveive. "I love her."

"Both Gabrielle and Genevieve will love you," Stepan said.

"What about me?" Roxanne demanded.

"They will love you, too," Stepan said. "And you—"

"—and you and you and you," his nieces chimed.

Lily gazed into her favorite uncle's dark eyes. "Uncle, how does the baby get out of the mummy's belly?"

"I do not know precisely." Stepan cleared his throat. "Your daddy tells me he knows everything. Ask him."

"Rudolf will not appreciate your helpfulness," Fancy said.

"If my brother can tell her the Earl of Rotten bought a ticket to Tyburn, he can tell her how the baby gets out of the mummy's belly."

"Aunt," Lily drew her attention, "why are Gabrielle and Genevieve wrinkled?"

"All babies are wrinkled," Fancy answered, "but the skin smoothes out as they grow."

"Princess Sunshine had a baby, too," Lily announced.

Sounding like the duchess, Roxanne drawled, "Darling, this is the year for babies."

"You must return here next week for Gabrielle's and Genevieve's first tea party," Stepan invited them.

"Are we invited to the tea party?" Raven asked.

"My husband is in charge of tea parties," Fancy said, "but I know he will invite you."

"What about me?" Blaze asked.

"You can come to our tea party tomorrow," Lily said.

"Will you invite Miss Giggles?" Blaze asked.

"Who is she?"

"Miss Giggles is my monkey."

"How exciting!" Lily clapped her hands together. "Can we go home with you now and meet her?"

"Yes, of course."

The five little girls squealed with excitement. Genevieve howled her dislike of the noise, inciting her sister to howl with her.

"New babies need sleep," Raven said, herding the girls toward the door. "We should leave now."

Before following them out, Blaze placed a newspaper on the bed. "I brought you a copy of Serena's review."

Stepan moved, sitting beside his wife, and leaned against the headboard. "We will need another nanny or two or three."

"Read my sister's review."

Stepan opened the *Times* to page three and read:

> "*Serena Flambeau delighted the opening-night crowd at the Royal Opera House. Young Serena stepped into the lead role in The Maid of Milan and proved as talented as her older sister, who retired upon her marriage.*

*This Flambeau sings and plays the flute. Per order of
her distinguished father, several enormous bodyguards
kept society's eager swains at bay."*

"*Her older sister*? That nasty reporter did not even
write my name."

Stepan slipped his free arm around her shoulder.
"Does Serena's success bother you? Bishop would love
to take you back."

Fancy looked at him. "You would approve?"

"If singing in the opera makes you happy," Stepan
answered, "I will agree, not approve."

Fancy pressed a kiss on his cheek. "Thank you, my
love."

"Will it make you happy?"

"I could not possibly be any happier than I am at this
moment," Fancy answered, her love shining in her
eyes. "What we hold in our arms is better than a good
review."

His gaze returned her love. "A good review cannot
hug you or miss you or—"

"—or keep you awake at night crying to be held,"
Fancy finished.

Stepan brushed his lips across her temple. "Believe
me, love. You sing like an angel, much better than
your sister."

She gave him a sidelong smile. "You still haven't
found a job?"

"Loving you is my vocation."

"A worthy profession." Fancy gave him a flirtatious
smile and moved her hand to caress his groin.

"What are you doing, princess?"

"Pleasuring my prince."

Please turn the page for

an exciting sneak peek of

Patricia Grasso's next historical romance

DESIRING THE PRINCE

coming in April 2007!

London, 1821

He smelled her fear.

Shrouded in darkness and swirling fog, he watched her glancing over her shoulder when she reached the sickly yellow glow from the gaslight. She knew he was there. Somewhere. He loved the hunt, especially when his quarry knew he was lurking, watching, waiting.

Rejecting him had sealed her fate. An insulting laugh and a seductive toss of her ebony curls had answered his proposition.

When she rounded the corner, he cut through the next alley to get ahead of her and leaned against the stone wall. Footsteps approached, heightening his anticipation.

She was almost here.

She would be his.

She would regret refusing him, if only for a moment.

Leaping out as she passed, he grabbed her from behind and slashed the blade across her throat. He pushed her to the ground and stood over her. The gurgling sounds of her struggle to breathe lessened, each beat of her heart pumping the life out of her.

He dipped his finger in her blood and painted a

cross on her forehead, as if she'd been anointed by
the devil. Then he pressed a shiny, gold sovereign into
the palm of her hand and closed her fingers around the
coin.

"Thank you for an enjoyable evening, my dear."

The unmistakable aroma of horse droppings floated
into the garden on a gentle breeze.

Belle Flambeau stood in her blossoming domain
and sniffed the air, a smile touching her lips. The odor
of horse dung from Soho Square shouted springtime.

Wisteria trees bloomed purple against the red brick
house while yellow tulips conspired with purple crocus
to startle the eye with vibrant color. A fragrant lily of
the valley ground cover reclined in front of the silver
birch tree guarded by lilac, gardenia, rose, and pussy
willow shrubs. Forsythia nodded in the breeze at their
old friend, the purple pansy that lived in the shade beneath the oak tree.

The garden goddess promises minor miracles.

The clever business slogan pleased Belle. Her success
in reviving plants had spread to the great mansions the
previous season. Already, gardeners for those wealthy
aristocrats had requested her services.

Belle narrowed her violet gaze on the pansy and
walked toward the oak tree. The pansy's failure to
thrive troubled her. Each day she snatched the pansy
from death's grip but found it wilted again the next
morning.

"Sister."

Belle glanced over her shoulder and saw one of her
sisters walking across the grass. Bliss looked disgruntled.

"Why does Fancy insist on keeping the duke's identity a secret?" Bliss demanded, her voice shrill with
anger.

"To which duke do you refer?"

"Our father, of course." Bliss rolled her eyes. "Investing would be easier if I knew which companies he owns." Her sister waved in the direction of the house. "The duke has always supported us in style. Why does our company need to pauperize him? If he retaliates, the Seven Doves will fail, and we will live in the poor house."

Belle placed her hand on her sister's shoulder. "Calm yourself."

Bliss took several deep breaths and then asked, "Is your touch making me feel better?"

Belle gave her an ambiguous smile. "Fancy will never forgive Father because, as the eldest, she remembers the relationship they shared."

"You're only a year younger," Bliss said. "Don't you have memories?"

"When I think of Father," Belle answered, "I see a tall, dark-haired gentleman holding Fancy on his lap."

"Did he never hold you?"

"At first I was too young to share his lap with Fancy." Belle shrugged. "When you and Blaze arrived, I suppose I was too old. The man could only hold one baby in each arm."

"Being born between the oldest and a set of twins is not the most auspicious position," Bliss said. "Being ignored could not have been pleasant."

"I enjoyed Nanny Smudge's attention." Belle lifted a rectangular gold case from the basket looped over her forearm. "Search for the duke with the initials *MC* and a boar's head crest."

Bliss shook her head. "Admitting ignorance of one's father's identity is humiliating. Does your illegitimacy bother Baron Wingate?"

Belle paused before answering, squelching the rush of irritation. None of her sisters could resist the opportunity to insult her future husband. "Charles understands that we cannot control our origins."

"I worry the baron will hurt you."

"I appreciate your concern." Belle watched Bliss disappear into the house and turned to the ailing pansy. All thoughts of healing the flower vanished with her sister's concern.

I refuse to become love's victim, Belle told herself, *like my mother.*

Gabrielle Flambeau, the daughter of a French aristocrat, had escaped the Terror when the citizens slaughtered her family. A penniless countess, her mother had won a position in the opera and caught the eye of a married duke. Together, her mother and her anonymous father had produced seven daughters.

The Flambeaus had wanted for nothing, except the duke's love and attention.

The daughter had learned hard lessons from the mother, though. She refused to die broken-hearted.

Charles Wingate loved her and accepted that she intended to go to her marriage bed a virgin. She would never consider becoming any man's mistress.

Turning her thoughts to the pansy, Belle knelt in the dirt and set her wicker basket beside her. She reached for the white candle and its brass holder. Next came a tiny bell, followed by the *Book of Common Prayer.*

Finally, she lifted the gold case engraved with the initials *MC* and a boar's head. The case contained Lucifer matches and sandpaper to light her healing candle.

Belle traced her finger across the initials *MC.* A gentleman's accoutrement, the case had been left behind fifteen years earlier, and her father had never returned for it. A wealthy duke could easily replace one gold case, and she had cherished this momento of her father.

Hearing the door open again, Belle saw Blaze and Puddles, the family's mastiff, entering the garden.

Blaze headed in her direction while Puddles raced around sniffing for a particular place.

"Are you practicing your hocus pocus for the season?" her sister asked.

Belle smiled at that. "The garden goddess cannot perform minor miracles without a bit of showmanship."

"Good Lord, the stench from Soho seems stronger than usual today," Blaze remarked, pinching her nostrils together for emphasis. "What is wrong with that sorry-looking pansy? Is it choking from dung stink?"

Belle shrugged. "I revive the pansy every afternoon and then find it wilted again by morning."

"The garden goddess fails to save a flower's life?" her sister teased. "This could ruin your business."

The black-masked mastiff loped across the garden toward them. Reaching the oak tree, the dog lifted its hind leg perilously close to the pansy.

"Puddles, no." Down came the leg, and Belle rounded on her sister. "Tell Puddles to conduct his business against the stone wall, not near my pansy."

"Sorry." Blaze gave her a sheepish smile and then knelt in front of the dog. She stared into the mastiff's eyes for a long moment and then patted its head. Puddles bounded across the garden to the stone wall and conducted his business there.

"Thank you." Belle relaxed and teased her sister, "If my pansy dies, I will consider you and Puddles its murderers."

Blaze crouched down beside her. "Listen, Puddles dislikes Baron Wingate."

Belle gave her a rueful smile. "Charles has disliked your dog since the day—"

"Puddles lifted his leg to the baron because he doesn't trust the man."

"I will not listen to another word against Charles." Her sisters' disapproval of the baron irritated Belle.

"None of you, including Puddles, needs to like Charles since I am the one marrying him."

"If you say so." Blaze returned to the house, the mastiff following behind her.

Banishing all disturbing thoughts, Belle gave her attention to the pansy. She lifted her right hand to make the beginning blessing but heard the door slam behind her.

Another visitor? Her pansy would expire before she could revive it. Perhaps ignoring whoever—

"Belle." The voice belonged to her youngest sister, who did not sound especially happy.

Raven plopped down on the grass beside her. "I need your advice."

Belle leaned back on her haunches. "What is the problem?"

"Constable Black asked me to use my special gift to help with that slasher investigation."

"Do you mean the one the newspapers have dubbed the Society Slasher?"

Raven nodded. "My problem is Alex," she said, referring to their neighbor, the constable's assistant.

Belle waved her hand in a gesture of dismissal. "A brick is more sensitive than Alexander Blake."

"I want to help the constable," Raven said, "but Alex makes me feel . . . *young*."

"You *are* young." Belle studied her sister for a long moment. "You told him you loved him, didn't you?"

Raven nodded, her misery etched across her face. "How do I behave around Alex?"

"Men want what they cannot have." Belle touched her sister's hand. "Treat Alex with chilly politeness and icy disdain."

"Be careful with Baron Wingate," Raven said before leaving. "I cannot trust the man."

Belle took a deep, calming breath and hoped her

other three sisters did not interrupt. Then she prepared to heal the pansy.

As Nanny Smudge had taught her, Belle began with the magic blessing. She touched her left breast, her forehead, her right breast, left and right shoulders; finally she touched her left breast again.

Removing a Lucifer match and sandpaper, Belle lit the white candle. Then she waved the tiny bell above the pansy, its tinkling sound breaking the garden's silence.

Belle placed her fingers against the pansy. "Ailing, ailing, ailing. Pansy, my touch is sealing, and thy illness is failing. Healing, healing, healing."

Taking the *Book of Common Prayer*, she held it over the pansy and whispered, "It is written. It is so."

Belle extinguished the candle's flame and made the magic blessing to complete the ritual. The pansy perked up almost immediately.

A hand touched her shoulder.

"Enough interruptions," Belle exclaimed, whirling around. "Charles, what a surprise."

Baron Charles Wingate stared at her, amusement lighting his brown eyes. "What are you doing?"

Belle blushed at being caught kneeling in the dirt. "My pansy needed tending."

The baron offered his hand to help her rise. When she reached for it, he dropped it to his side. "Your hands are dirty."

"This is dirt, not dung."

Charles shook his head in disapproval. "Playing in the dirt is unseemly behavior for a baroness, not to mention whispering to flowers."

"Ooops, you just mentioned it," she teased him, rising without his assistance.

"I do not consider that amusing. Once we marry—"

"Really, Charles, you are much too particular." Belle

put her hands on her hips. "Do not forget we met when your gardener hired me to revive that rosebush."

"Darling, I don't mean to scold." He smiled, suddenly amenable. "Your meeting with my fastidious mother concerns me."

"Concerns or worries?" Belle touched his arm, trying to soothe him. "I will behave properly."

"Promise you won't mention working for money."

Belle smiled. "I promise."

"Do not mention gardening, either."

"My lips are locked." She pretended to button her lips together.

"Above all else, do not mention your sister singing in the opera. Mother dislikes such women."

Belle lost her good humor. Fingers of unease curled around her spine. Was he embarrassed by her family?

"If you cannot be expensively attired," Charles continued, "then be certain your gown is modest."

Belle narrowed her violet gaze on him and brushed an ebony wisp off her forehead. "Are you implying—"

"I have a sterling idea," Charles interrupted. "We could contrive to mention your father."

Belle gave him a blank stare. Was he serious? Or had he bumped his head, rattling his brain?

"You know, sweetheart, the duke?"

"That could prove awkward," Belle said, "since I do not know which duke sired me and my sisters."

"Doesn't His Grace support you and your sisters?" He sounded annoyed. "His Grace's barrister must mention him when he delivers your monthly allowance."

"Percy Howell calls my father *His Grace.*"

"You said your sister knows the duke's identity."

"Fancy refuses to name him."

"Then we will mention your deceased mother was a countess, albeit a penniless French refugee," Charles decided. "We can only pray that your anonymous noble bloodlines and your incredible beauty sway Mother into approving our union."

Belle's irritation rose, inciting her to sarcasm. "I will pass the whole evening in prayer."

"I must leave now," Charles said, reaching for her hands, "Mother doesn't like waiting." He lifted her hands to his lips but dropped them again when he saw the dirt.

"Where are you going?" Belle asked, when he walked in the direction of the alley exit.

"That disreputable dog growled at me." And then he disappeared into the alley.

The baron's blond good looks reminded Belle of sunshine, but his snobbishness made her uneasy. She feared his mother was worse; after all, the woman had raised him. Beneath that haughty exterior beat the heart of a decent man. If only she could snatch him away from his mother's influence.

Belle sighed, knowing that was impossible. She only wished Charles was not so concerned with appearances.

One mile and a world away from the Flambeau residence stood the great mansions in Grosvenor Square. Offensive street odors did not dare assault aristocratic nostrils in this enclave of the wealthy. Here, fragrant gardens masked the occasional whiff from passing horses.

Prince Mikhail Kazanov sat at his thirty-foot dining table set with the finest porcelain, crystal, and silver. Perched on the chair beside him was his four-year-old daughter, Elizabeth.

Mikhail stared at his plate, his grim expression mirroring his mood. Instead of beef, the prince saw his former sister-in-law's coy eagerness. The roasted potatoes bore a striking resemblance to his former mother-in-law's determined look.

He felt hunted.

His year of mourning had ended the previous month. Lavinia, his late-wife's younger sister, had made her come-out two weeks earlier and immediately targeted him for her husband.

Even his former mother-in-law had become dangerous company. At the opera the previous evening, Prudence Smythe had reminded him that Lavinia had come of age and then proceeded to extol her virtues.

He had barely escaped entrapment. Thankfully, his brother Rudolf had seen his panicked expression during intermission and interrupted the woman's dialogue.

Lavinia and Prudence Smythe were not alone in their matrimonial ambition. Every maiden and widow in London desired a prince for her husband.

He wanted a wife to give him an heir, and his daughter needed a loving stepmother. The society ladies of his acquaintance were shallow and greedy, unfit to mother his daughter.

"Daddy, your elbows are resting on the table."

"Excuse my lapse in manner, Bess."

Mikhail sliced a piece of beef, raised it to his lips, and then glanced at his daughter. Elizabeth had stabbed a piece of beef with her fork and raised it to her lips.

He winked at her; she winked in return. Slowly, he chewed the beef and swallowed. His daughter did the same.

Mikhail set his knife and fork on his plate and reached for his wine goblet. Elizabeth set her fork on the plate and reached for her lemon water.

Lifting his napkin, Mikhail dabbed at each corner of his mouth. His daughter lifted her napkin and dabbed at her mouth.

Mikhail leaned close to her and puckered his lips.

Elizabeth puckered her lips, too, and gave him a smacking kiss.

"Thank you, Bess. I needed that kiss."

Elizabeth gave him a dimpled smile. "You are welcome, Daddy."

"What should we do before visiting Uncle Rudolf?"

"I want to go to Bond Street."

Mikhail smiled at that. "What do you want to purchase?"

"I want a mummy," Elizabeth said, her disarming blue eyes gleaming with hope. "Cousin Sally got a new mummy, and I want one, too."

His heart ached for his only child. "The Bond Street shops do not sell mummies."

Her expression drooped.

Mikhail lifted her tiny hands to his lips and proceeded to kiss each of her delicate fingers. Then he pretended to gobble them, eliciting her giggles.

"Daddy, does the stork bring mummies?"

A smile flashed across his features. "Who told you about storks?"

"Cousin Roxanne said storks bring babies so I thought—" Elizabeth shrugged.

"Come Bess, sit on my lap." When she did, Mikhail wrapped his arms around her. He wanted to protect her and make her dreams and wishes come true. "Tell me about this mummy you want."

"The best mummies know lots and lots of stories," Elizabeth said.

"Bedtime stories *are* very important." Mikhail nodded in agreement. "Anything else?"

"My new mummy will like laughing and playing in the garden."

Except for his brothers' wives, no lady of his acquaintance played in the dirt. Finding this mythical mummy could take years.

"My mummy will make tea parties for me." Her blue eyes sparkled with excitement as she warmed to her topic. "And happiness cakes, too."

"Happiness cake?" he echoed.

"Cousin Amber makes happiness cakes for her little girl." Elizabeth placed the palm of her hand against his cheek. "Mummy will love me."

Mikhail turned his head and kissed the palm of her hand. "I love you, Bess."

"I love you, Daddy." She smiled into his dark eyes. "Mummy will love you, too."

Julian Boomer, the prince's majordomo, appeared in the doorway and hurried to his side. "Your Highness?" The man shifted his gaze to the little girl and then arched a brow at him.

"Bess, tell Nanny Dee you will be leaving in a few minutes." Mikhail kissed her cheek and let her slip from his lap.

"Nanny Dee is gone for the day."

"Tell Nanny Cilla to wash your face," he instructed her. "I will wait in the foyer."

Mikhail watched his daughter disappear out the door. Then he looked at the majordomo.

Boomer passed him a calling card. "Ladies Prudence and Lavinia request an interview."

Mikhail groaned, his expression long-suffering. He was not safe in his own home. His daughter's mythical mummy had better appear soon, or he would fall prey to the hunters.

Boomer cleared his throat. "I told them you had left for a business meeting, and Princess Elizabeth had gone with you to her tea party."

Mikhail grinned at the man. "You are worth your weight in gold."

"Thank you, Your Highness," the majordomo drawled. "Would that gold be literal or figurative?"

Mikhail laughed, rose from his chair, and clapped the man on the back. "Boomer, I do see a hefty raise in your future."

Belle Flambeau sat alone in the coach that Sunday afternoon and fumed, her anger directed at the baron and his mother. Charles knew she felt nervous but had opted to send his coach instead of escorting her himself, and Belle had no doubt his mother had done this purposely to prove her influence over her son.

Shallow, insensitive, and disrespectful were the most appropriate words to describe Charles Wingate at the moment. Sending his coach insulted her. She would tell him that when they were alone.

Knowing she had one chance to make a good impression, Belle had taken more than an hour to dress for the occasion. Her high-waisted, white gown had been embroidered with pink flowers beneath her bosom and around the hem. Her sisters had decided she appeared pleasingly virginal.

Belle ran her palm across the worn leather seat cushion. She wondered why the baron did not refurbish his carriage or purchase another.

The coach halted in front of a town house in Russell Square, a section more familiar with barristers than barons. The liveried coachman opened the door and helped her down.

When she banged the knocker, the majordomo opened the door. He stared at her, his expression haughty.

"I am Miss Flambeau," Belle said. "Baron Wingate is expecting me."

The majordomo stepped aside to allow her entrance. "The family is taking tea in the drawing room."

Belle gave the foyer a quick scan. She had expected something more lavish, but this foyer was lacking when compared with her own. She followed the servant to the stairs.

"You will wait here," the majordomo ordered, whirling around.

Belle looked at him in surprise. The servant's attitude stoked the flame of her simmering anger.

Would the Wingates keep a countess, a duchess, or a princess waiting in the foyer? The baron's mother had engineered this to make her feel inferior, and if that was true, she doubted this meeting would have a happy outcome.

Making a good impression did not seem so important now. Self-respect demanded she return insults in kind.

"Come now, miss," the majordomo said, returning to the foyer. "Do hurry. The baroness dislikes waiting."

"*I* dislike waiting, especially in foyers."

When she stepped inside the doorway, Charles smiled and crossed the room. "I'm glad you've come." He escorted her across the room. "Meet my family."

A man resembling the baron sat in a highbacked chair. His long legs stretched out, and a cane rested against the side of the chair. His expression registered boredom.

The middle-aged, blond woman on the settee was another matter. Mild distaste had etched across her face.

"Mother, I present Miss Belle Flambeau," Charles introduced them. "Belle, my mother and Squire Wilkins, my half-brother."

"I am pleased to make your acquaintances." Belle looked from the mother to the half-brother who was perusing her body.

Lifting his gaze to hers, Squire Wilkins rose from the chair and reached for his cane. "A pleasure to meet you, Miss Flambeau." With that, he left the drawing room.

"Please be seated."

Belle glanced at his mother and then chose the highbacked chair. Charles sat beside his mother on the settee.

The drawing room held an air of genteel shabbiness. Age had yellowed the armchair's doily, and the chair beneath it appeared threadbare. Even one of the teacups was chipped.

The Flambeau residence was more comfortably and expensively furnished. Her anonymous father had taken good care of them.

"My son did not exaggerate your beauty," the baroness said.

"Thank you, my lady." Belle sent Charles a serene smile, masking the knot of nervousness gripping her body.

"Beauty fades," the baroness said, "and couples—"

"Indeed, beauty does fade," Belle agreed, giving her a pointed look. She knew the baroness would not appreciate that comment, but the woman's expression screamed disapproval. Belle did not appreciate being treated like an inferior, and self-respect demanded reciprocity. Perhaps she should leave now before the situation worsened.

The baroness flushed but quickly regained her composure. "As I was about to say, couples need more than love for a successful marriage."

Belle flicked a glance at Charles and wondered at his silence. "I would agree with you," she said, "but riches do not guarantee a happy marriage."

The baroness gave her a frigid smile that matched the coldness in her eyes. "Tell me about your family."

Belle had prepared herself for this particular topic. "My late mother was a French countess, and my father is an English duke."

"Can you prove that?"

Belle had not prepared herself for that unexpected question. "I do not carry birth or baptismal certificates in my reticule."

"How about a marriage certificate?" the baroness asked, her tone sneering.

"Mother, I object to this," Charles found his voice. "She cannot help—"

"Be quiet, Charles. This needs discussion." Then the baroness looked at Belle. "Your parents never married which makes you—"

"—the daughter of a French countess and an English duke," Belle interrupted.

"Please Mother," Charles whined.

The baroness ignored him. "I mean no disrespect."

"Of course you don't," Belle drawled, her voice dripping sarcasm. She could not decide who was more despicable, the mother or the sniveling son.

"Mother," Charles whined again, "I asked you to—"

"Be quiet," Belle snapped, surprising him. Ready for battle, she refused to cower or retreat. "What about your family, my lady?"

The baroness dropped her mouth open in surprise.

"I mean no disrespect," Belle said, "but my blood is a mingling of the French and English aristocracy, which I would not wish to dilute." She looked at the baron. "Didn't you tell me your maternal grandfather was a vicar and your mother's first husband a squire?"

The older woman found her voice. "You impertinent piece of baggage. How dare you—"

Belle bolted out of her chair, startling the other woman. "Charles, I want to leave. *Now.*"

"The coachman will drive you home," his mother said.

Charles had stood when Belle did. "*I* will escort Miss Flambeau home."

The coach ride to Soho Square was completed in silence. Belle stared out the window without seeing anything. She had expected the baroness to oppose the match but refused to be intimidated. The baron's behavior was an entirely different matter. His failure to defend her had been a surprise, and she should reconsider their relationship. His mother would never accept her, and a less than loyal husband was unacceptable.

"Darling, we have arrived." Charles walked her to the front door and raised her hand to his lips. "I apologize for Mother. You should not have argued with her, though. Now we will need to placate her before moving forward with our betrothal."

Belle managed a smile but refused to apologize for her behavior. The baron would need to choose—her or his mother.

"May I come inside?" Charles asked.

"That would be too tempting," Belle said in refusal. "My sisters are gone for the day."

"I did mention to Mother that Prince Stepan was picnicking with your sisters." Charles gave her a wry smile. "I hoped that would impress her."

Belle unlocked the door. "Good day, Charles."

He grabbed her hand again. "I promise to speak to Mother."

Belle stepped into the foyer. Turning around, she smiled at the baron once more before closing the door.

Someone grabbed her from behind. When she tried to scream, a hand covered her mouth, and only muffled squawks came out. Her attacker yanked her against his muscular frame, and she kicked out wildly.

Something sharp stung her cheek, and she bit the massive hand covering her mouth. With a masculine yelp, the man pushed her away, and she landed facedown on the floor, the breath knocked from her body.

Unable to move, Belle turned her face in time to see

her assailant hurrying down the hallway toward the rear of the house. When she tried to stand, Belle saw the droplets of blood where her face had hit the floor. She touched her right cheek and stared in a daze at her bloody fingers.

The bastard had sliced her cheek.

About the Author

Patricia Grasso lives in Massachusetts. She is the author of fifteen historical romances and is currently working on her sixteenth, which will be published by Zebra Books in 2007. Pat loves hearing from readers and you may write to her c/o Zebra Books. Please include a self-addressed stamped envelope if you wish a response. Or you can visit her website at *www.patriciagrasso.com*